CORYDON

& THE FALL OF ATLANTIS

CORYDON

& THE FALL OF ATLANTIS

TOBIAS DRUITT

ALFRED A. KNOPF NEW YORK

THIS IS A BORZOI BOOK PUBLISHED BY ALFRED A. KNOPF

This is a work of fiction. Names, characters, places, and incidents either
are the product of the author's imagination or are used fictitiously. Any
resemblance to actual persons, living or dead, events,
or locales is entirely coincidental.

Copyright © 2007 by Tobias Druitt
All rights reserved.
Published in the United States by Alfred A. Knopf, an imprint of Random House
Children's Books, a division of Random House, Inc., New York.

KNOPF, BORZOI BOOKS, and the colophon are registered trademarks of
Random House, Inc.

www.randomhouse.com/kids

Educators and librarians, for a variety of teaching tools, visit us at
www.randomhouse.com/teachers

Library of Congress Cataloging-in-Publication Data
Druitt, Tobias.
Corydon and the fall of Atlantis / Tobias Druitt.—1st ed.
p.   cm.
SUMMARY: Corydon, an outcast Greek boy with the leg of a goat,
reluctantly sets off on another adventure with the "monsters" of Greek mythology
when the Minotaur is apparently kidnapped by the people of Atlantis.
ISBN: 978-0-375-83383-0 (trade) — 978-0-375-93383-7 (lib. bdg.)
[1. Mythology, Greek—Juvenile fiction. 2. Minotaur (Greek mythology)—
Juvenile fiction. 3. Monsters—Fiction. 4. Adventure and
adventurers—Fiction. 5. Atlantis—Fiction.] I. Title.
PZ7.D8245Cop 2007
[Fic]—dc22   2006031500
Printed in the United States of America

February 2007

10 9 8 7 6 5 4 3 2 1
First Edition

Dedicated to the cities of New York and Venice

CORYDON

& THE FALL OF ATLANTIS

ONE

CORYDON RAN TOWARD THE CLIFF. HE COULD HEAR the goat's plaintive bleating. As he ran, he called hastily, "Gorgos! Gorgos, where are you? I need your help and I need it now!"

There was no answer. Corydon was not surprised, but he still felt a chill.

He had reached the edge of the cliff. He lay flat on his stomach and peered over the edge, the blue glitter of the sea below burning his eyes. There, halfway down the cliff, was a narrow ledge, and on it was a goat, lying on her side, bleating faintly. She did not have the energy to rise.

"Eripha," Corydon crooned, hoping the beast could hear her own name, the tender name he had given her when she was a tiny dancing kid. But she made no response.

"Gorgos!" Corydon shouted once more. Again there was no reply from Medusa's half-divine son. Furious, Corydon began lowering himself over the edge of the cliff, his feet feeling for footholds. There were small crannies in the straight rock wall, and his eager toes and then fingers found them, though as the cliff crumbled, he had to hurry from one hold to another before they broke to powder in his urgent grasp. His sturdy goat hoof helped him keep his footing.

He had no idea how he would get back up the cliff, but he couldn't leave Eripha on the ledge; the animal might take fright and slide over.

A handhold gave way, and for one very long moment, Corydon was dangling by one hand from a stiff thyme bush jutting from the cliff edge.

Then, to his relief, his foot felt the dust of the ledge where Eripha waited, her yellow eyes glazed and dull.

He took off his short rope belt and, bending down, tied the animal's near foreleg to his wrist. She bleated.

Then he sat down and gazed angrily at the sea.

Where was Gorgos? And where had he been when Eripha had stumbled over the edge in the first place? He was supposed to be looking after the goats.

After a few more minutes of fury, Corydon's thoughts stopped whirling and began to slow.

He had been too angry to think before.

He was thinking now, and it was painful.

Why hadn't he asked the immortal Gorgons, Sthenno and Euryale, to help him? They often did when sheep were trapped. Why hadn't he brought some rope? Why had he left his flock with Gorgos in the first place?

Corydon should have known what Gorgos was like. After all, they'd spent six months together. A winter of storytelling and songs by a warm hearth, listening to the riddles of the Sphinx,

Euryale's hunting tales, Sthenno's excitement over new prophecies. A winter of drying herbs and eating cheese. A winter in which he, Corydon, had turned their own adventure in fighting the seething army of heroes bent on destroying them into a memory, and then into an epic song.

Then with the lengthening days came lambs, lambs, lambs, born into the heavy snow of the mountains. Some of them born in terrible, bitter agony that reminded him of the birth of Gorgoliskos. He could hardly bear to think of that day.

And he had to care for the ewes and the lambs they bore. The weakly little lambs, especially. The mothers sometimes rejected them, and Corydon became their mother, feeding them and sleeping by them to keep their shivering little bodies warm.

Oddly, his favorite ewe had rejected her lamb this year.

It made Corydon wonder about his own mother. And about Gorgos.

Corydon had tried his utmost to teach Gorgos the art of shepherding. But Gorgos never seemed to understand.

When Corydon told him that it was important for pregnant ewes to get special grass, hand-pulled from the lush slopes lower down on the mountains, Gorgos laughed and said it was too much work. Corydon had found Gorgos keeping one great-bellied ewe on a snowy mountaintop with no green food for miles. She was gaunt and wild-eyed, and Corydon had nursed her by hand for two weeks to bring her back up to strength.

Gorgos couldn't sit and watch sheep or goats and do a little piping. He was only happy when running feverishly on the hillside, playing wild games that only he seemed to understand, acting out strange, half-remembered hero tales of the deaths of kings and the burning of cities. The only animal Corydon had ever seen him care for, or even watch, was a wolf that had once ventured among the sheep in winter. Gorgos had stalked the wolf, imitating its movements, and then stared at it, like a wolf himself. To Corydon's surprise, the wolf had retreated before the snarling boy, bowing his head in submission. Gorgos had one deep scratch from this encounter but had hardly noticed it. He never noticed bruises or wounds that would have made other boys limp or cry.

The only other creature Gorgos found interesting was the nightingale that sang every night in the hazel tree. As she tuned up for spring, daily improving her song, Gorgos would stop running around the mountainside to listen, in a stillness so complete that it reminded Corydon of the way a wild animal sits looking at the moon. Corydon liked her song, too, but Gorgos seemed to hear in it something that no one else could detect.

As he sat on the ledge, thinking slowly of these things in the careful shepherd's way, Corydon couldn't help feeling angry all over again. Where *was* Gorgos?

His rage made him feel lonely. He had hoped that Gorgos would be his friend, as Gorgos's mother, Medusa, had been. He had begun to see that Gorgos was not the same as his mother but entirely different. It was like losing her a second time.

It hurt because it meant he was alone.

Well, not really alone, he told himself quickly. There were the other monsters, after all, and they were his friends. It was too long since he had seen the Minotaur or the Snake-Girl, though. After the Battle of Smoke and Flame, after the heroes had departed, the monsters had gone their separate ways, each drifting back to his or her own solitary life. They had met only twice in the last, long, working year: once at grape-harvest time and once in the first bright days of spring, when the hills were mantled with flowers. Corydon loved those festival days. Even the villagers were less wary of him now, not eager to have him among them still, but willing to buy his cheeses.

So perhaps he didn't need Gorgos. . . .

As he thought this, Corydon shifted his position a little on the hard stone of the ledge. Disturbed, the goat gave a faint bleat. Then, abruptly, there was a heavy rumbling noise, like a cart being driven along by swift horses. Yet no cart could be near a cliff. . . . As his mind shaped this thought, the heavy stone of the ledge lurched under him, like the deck of a ship tossed by a wave. It almost threw him over the edge of the cliff. Desperately clutching Eripha, he tried to grip the shifting ledge in his hands as it swayed. Then he was hit by a flood of small stones from the cliff face, and the ledge jolted again, so that he almost plunged over the edge.

Looking out to sea, Corydon saw that whatever had disturbed the earth had affected the waves, too. One huge wave raced toward the cliff, hitting it with a hard slap. The cliff shook with the impact, but only the spray reached Corydon. Other waves followed, smaller but still ferocious in their energy.

What was happening to the world? At once, Corydon began to guess that this was the anger of a god, for surely only a god could shake the earth and beat it like a housewife shaking dust from a rug. He knew at once which god it must be, but he did not speak the name. Not now. Instead, his mind shaped the word "earthquake," a word he had heard but a reality he had never experienced before. As his mind cleared, there was a cry from above him.

"Corydon!"

It was Gorgos at last.

He looked up and saw Gorgos's pointed, dark face above him.

"Well, don't just stand there!" Corydon felt all the anger of the afternoon in a long, heady rush. "Get a rope or something."

Gorgos nodded. Then, without apology or explanation, he disappeared again. Corydon was left to listen to his growling stomach, and to wonder if the earth would shake again anytime soon, and to stroke Eripha. He did all these several times before he saw Gorgos peering over once more. A rope slapped the cliff face above him. Gorgos was holding it.

"Tie it to a tree!" shouted Corydon.

"I've got it!" Gorgos shouted back. "I won't let you fall! Anyway, there isn't a tree!"

Knowing Gorgos, Corydon decided to send the goat up first. He untied his belt from the creature. She bleated miserably. He looped the rope around the goat's belly, trying to ensure that it was wound around the goat's legs so it couldn't slip and strangle the beast.

"Okay!" he yelled. Gorgos began hauling on the rope. Slowly, bleating frantically, the goat rose into the air. She kicked showers of small stones off the cliff face and onto Corydon. Watching her struggles, Corydon began to laugh, the long tension and rage somehow escaping in gales of insane mirth. The goat was curious; she stopped struggling and listened to the odd noises he was making. Corydon laughed so much he had to lie down on the narrow ledge.

The ledge, weakened by the earthquake, suddenly gave way, and Corydon found himself clinging desperately to the cliff face, his feet braced on the few sharp shards of rock that were all that was left of the ledge. He hung between sky and sea.

Gorgos peered over; Corydon could see the strangely calm face. "Help!" he cried.

"What are you doing, Corydon? Stop messing around. I don't know what to do with this goat."

"I'm not messing around!" Corydon yelled. "I'm about to plunge down this cliff face and into the sea! Now, would you mind very much helping me by letting down the rope?"

"Oh . . . the rope? Okay. Just wait . . . er . . . hang on . . . while I get it off the goat. Bother—these knots are tight. You wouldn't have a knife, would you?"

Corydon didn't kill Gorgos, but only because he couldn't think of a way to do it from his present precarious position.

"GET THE ROPE! Before I fall and drown. Okay?"

"It's all frayed now. Don't worry, though—I have an idea."

Corydon felt an immediate premonition of disaster. Rarely had he heard such ill-omened words.

His worst fears were realized almost at once.

Above him, there was a scrabbling sound. Gorgos had lowered himself over the edge. His bare feet hung about eighteen inches above Corydon's head.

"Grab my feet!" Gorgos shouted. "Then I can climb back up with you hanging on!"

"No, Gorgos!" Corydon shouted hastily. "I'll be too heavy for you to hold—it'll pull us both off the cliff! Climb back up and go and fetch Sthenno or Euryale or anyone who can fly!"

"It'll be fine! Just grab my feet!"

One of the pieces of rock on which Corydon was balancing suddenly gave way.

He had to try Gorgos's stupid plan or fall.

He grabbed Gorgos's feet and hung on firmly.

"Ow—you're so heavy," groaned Gorgos. "I'm not sure I can climb up—hang on—"

Corydon hung on. But his hands were already aching, and they were damp with sweat.

"I can't hang on for long," he said. He remembered that on another cliff, the one in Hades' realm, the great winged horse Pegasos had saved them. Was there anything, anyone to help them now?

He had to trust Gorgos's strength.

And Gorgos gave a great heave almost at once. Corydon's torso was now over the top, so that he was half lying on the cliff edge. Corydon scrabbled desperately with his feet, but he could get no purchase at all. Gorgos gave another great heave; even in his fear, Corydon was amazed at the boy's strength, the sheer might of his hands, his arms. Now he was suddenly up, safe, lying on his face in the grass, smelling the hot wool of the goat, breathing in dust. Alive. He felt like shouting for joy. But he had no breath. All the air had been forced from his burning lungs.

He sat up, winded. He drew in his breath.

Awkwardly he said, "Thanks, Gorgos."

Gorgos was already on his feet. Another thing Corydon found hard about him was that he was never still.

Then he cocked his head to one side, as if he were listening to some sound only he could hear. His face closed up, became smooth and unreadable.

"It's fine!" he yelled as he began to run off toward the hills again, long, easy, loping strides kicking up little puffs of dust around hard bare feet.

"Where are you going?" Corydon bawled. "We have to get the goat home! She's hurt!"

"You can do that," came Gorgos's voice faintly. It was as if he were listening to something else. As if Corydon's shouts and calls were only an annoying reminder of a reality that didn't matter to him.

Corydon sighed and gave up. He still felt winded, and his fear had drained him. Gorgos apparently felt nothing of that kind. He was almost out of sight now, lost in the heat haze, among the furze, as sure-footed and as hard to pick out as a goat.

Corydon was left with the prickle of uncomfortable thoughts: Gorgos had saved his life, but could they ever be friends? Slowly he began to heave the injured goat onto his shoulder. Now his body was as heavily burdened as his heart, but the warmth of the goat was comforting. It was the only comfort in a world suddenly and unbearably bare.

TWO

Euryale was eating a particularly juicy duck's head. She sank her teeth into flesh, ignoring the feathers still clinging to it. Dark blood filled her mouth, and she gurgled happily, like a satisfied baby.

As always, Euryale was only really happy while eating. But she had come again to dread the end of a meal, the moment when even her monster-belly couldn't hold another mouthful. The moment when the meal was over and life began again, a life that now seemed more achingly hollow than before the recent war.

She pushed the thought away. As her teeth met in vibrant raw duck, she felt contentment rush back.

The only flaw in her contentment was the racket Sthenno was making. She was rustling, rummaging, clawing her way through a vast pile of parchments and fragments, evidently searching frantically for something.

Euryale heard her muttering, "Where is it? Where is it? It's important, important—I can't have lost it—where is it?"

There would be no peace until Sthenno found it. "What's wrong, Sthenno?" asked Euryale, a trifle irritably. "Have you lost another earthshaking prophecy?" Sthenno did not reply, but the desperate clawing and rustling sounds grew faster and louder. Then, to Euryale's surprise, the rustling stopped. Euryale took another bite of duck's head. As she was chewing, Sthenno rushed into the room, a torn parchment fragment clasped in her talons. "I've found it! I've found it!" she cried, and brandished it in triumph.

"What is it?" asked Euryale, concerned. "Are the heroes coming back? Is the mormoluke in danger? Is it about the Kingdom of the Many? Or the Olympians?"

Sthenno was scanning the parchment. "No," she said absently, "nothing like that. I've found the recipe for barley bread."

Euryale's mouth opened and a fragment of duck dropped out.

She struggled with herself and decided not to say what she was thinking.

Euryale valued her sister more since they had lost Medusa. And she knew that Sthenno wanted to make barley bread because it was Medusa's recipe. It wasn't like being with her, but it was Sthenno's way of showing that she had not forgotten.

Euryale gave a rattling, brazen sigh. If you are an immortal, your grief, too, can live forever.

Sthenno took no notice of her sigh. She was scurrying around the cave, tipping flour into a bowl, finding the sourdough starter, which she had been feeding with decaying mushrooms and old milk to make it stronger.

The scent of sour, rich dough began to fill the cave. It made Euryale feel hungrier than ever, and she began on a slab of liver.

Sthenno, kneading the dough expertly with swift claws, suddenly paused. "Euryale," she said, "what this bread needs is honey to put on top of it." They both knew this meant a visit to the Minotaur.

Since the battle with the heroes, the monsters had left one another alone, but the Gorgons knew that the Minotaur was still a beekeeper. With his thick fur, he didn't feel stings, and his bees were company for him. They grazed on the thyme and pine that surrounded his tiny hut and made lavish rivers of golden honey. The Minotaur had learned to make stone jars to contain it. It was so good that even the villagers sometimes came to buy it.

Euryale said, "Shall I go?" She knew that Sthenno might want to stay and finish the bread.

"Let's go together," said Sthenno reluctantly. She gave her dough a final pat and left it to rise in a part of the cave where the sun warmed a nearby wall.

The sisters opened their huge metal wings and sprang up into the blue day. Sthenno, looking down, saw the stream, no more than a thin blue line. She liked seeing the earth and everything on it made tiny, trees reduced to the landscape's fur, animals smaller than insects. Even Euryale could seem no bigger than a fly when seen from a distance. It calmed Sthenno, made problems seem manageable.

The sea crept beneath her, like wrinkled blue silk.

They could see the Minotaur's hut now, on the coast.

And almost at once, Euryale felt that something wasn't right. It took her a moment to work out what it was. Then she knew. There was no smoke coming from the chimney.

She tried to reassure herself. Perhaps he had gone to pay a visit to other monsters, just as *they* were visiting *him*.

But it felt unlikely; the Minotaur was even more solitary than she and Sthenno, even more unwilling to go beyond the boundaries of the small and ordered world he had made for himself.

"Sthenno," she shouted, "he's not there."

"I know," Sthenno called back in her high bird-voice. "There's something wrong."

Euryale landed, claws outstretched to steady herself, panting from the flight. "Could he just be away? On a visit?"

Sthenno was beside her. "No," she said, her voice stern. "Look."

The Minotaur's tiny garden had been trampled by many feet, the crushed plants turning brown and dead in the harsh island sun. Two of the beehives had been knocked over and were lying on their sides like abandoned hats. The door of the hut stood open. Inside, Sthenno and Euryale could see that the Minotaur's simple wooden table was broken in two, his hearth ashes scattered across the room, his plain benches smashed as if by a giant hand. Sthenno pricked herself on a shard of pottery.

"This happened days ago," she said grimly. "Look at the plants. Five, maybe six days. And the bees have fled, too. Maybe as long as a week ago."

Euryale was studying the marks on the ground, in the soft earth of the vegetable patch. She lifted her head. "Men!" she almost spat. "Not villagers either. The heroes! Could they have returned? And yet these marks aren't quite the same—a narrower heel, see, and more pointed toes . . . and the men not quite so heavy. . . ." A picture of them began to form in her hunter's mind.

Sthenno was looking around, too. "Which way did they go?" she asked. "To the sea?" She pointed to one boot print. "This one might have been carrying something heavy. . . ."

Euryale took a quick glance, agreed. "We need to get after them immediately." Both sisters were about to spring into the air again when they felt the ground judder like a ship turned too fast into the wind. There was a rumble, like thunder in the rocks.

"What was that?" said Euryale, startled. "The earth—"

Sthenno shouted, "Look out!" and Euryale sprang into the air. A huge pine tree crashed to the ground where Euryale had been standing a moment ago. Twenty feet up in the air, Euryale was safe.

"Hurry up, Sthenno," she shouted. "We have to hunt!"

Not a word of thanks. Sthenno grunted irritably and leapt for the sky. No time to quarrel. The Minotaur needed them.

They searched all day and found no sign.

They divided, to make their search more efficient. Sthenno went north and flew far and wide, close to the ground, darting like a swallow. As she swooped low over the mountain, she saw Lady Nagaina, basking outside her stronghold like a lizard on a rock. Her hydra heads were spread out like flowers, and her many eyes were closed. Sthenno thought Lady Nagaina was asleep until her sweet hissing voice suddenly spoke. "Sthenno. How nice. A fresh crisis, perhaps?" She opened one eye; it was lilac-colored. Some of her eyes were green, Sthenno remembered. She felt nervous. Lady Nagaina always made her feel shy, as if she were a villager talking to a great lady. She spoke quickly.

"Have you seen the Minotaur?"

"No," said Lady Nagaina, already bored. Her eye closed.

Sthenno tried again. "He's missing. And men have been at his hut. There are marks, things broken."

Lady Nagaina hummed a little, loudly. "The heroes? Oh dear. Does that mean you're all coming to live with me again?" She opened all her eyes wide in horror, then closed them all again tightly.

"Not if we can help it," snapped Sthenno. "And we don't know it's the heroes. Only that it's somebody."

"Of courssssse," said Lady Nagaina, with a sibilant hiss of disapproval, "you could always ask that *very* intelligent lion over yonder. I don't know anything, I'm afraid." Pointedly, she settled her heads back on the rock.

Annoyed, and increasingly worried, Sthenno flew on toward the Nemean Lion's desert place. When she reached it, she found the lion trotting around his rock. He heard her wingbeats and looked up in surprise. A low, rumbling growl rose from his throat. It grew into a howl.

In his bemused mind, the lion knew that in the battle against the heroes, he and Sthenno had somehow failed together. Whenever he saw her, he sat on his haunches and howled.

Sthenno wished she'd remembered this earlier. As his earsplitting lament cracked her eardrums, she tried to get him to listen.

"Lion!" He was deaf to everything. "LION!" she roared, high and piercing. Sthenno put her mouth right to his ear. "LION!" she screeched.

"Don't try to comfort me!" he growled. "I know what I am!" He began to howl again.

"I'm NOT trying to comfort you, you stupid creature!" snapped Sthenno impatiently. "I'm trying to ask you something!"

He turned great, vacant tawny eyes upon her. "What?"

"We're looking for the Minotaur," she said slowly, carefully, emphasizing every word. "Have you seen him?"

The lion sighed, a small puff of smoke. "He lives in a hut. Have you knocked on the door? He might be inside the hut."

"We've BEEN to the hut," said Sthenno, trying hard not to sound as impatient as she felt.

"Oh." The lion blew out a small jet of flame. "Then I do not know where he may be found," he said finally.

"You understand, Lion? He's missing, and there were signs that men had come for him—booted feet left marks in his garden, there were signs of a fight. His furniture was all broken."

"He might have fallen down," said the lion, chewing his paw. "I sometimes break things when I fall down. Rocks, for instance. Do you like my rock, Sthenno?"

"It's lovely," said Sthenno hastily, trying to keep him in a good humor. "But the Minotaur, Lion—have you seen any men?"

The lion brightened. "I saw the heroes," he remembered. "But it was a very long time ago. Do you remember, Sthenno? We fought them." Suddenly he remembered. "I was stupid," he said, and began to draw in his breath for another howl. "I did wrong," he added. Tears ran down his face.

"I remember it perfectly," said Sthenno a little coldly. She wondered if the lion had seen the heroes since the battle. Could that have triggered a rush of remembrance in his poor, slow brain? There seemed no way of finding out from him. She decided to seek more intelligent company. Telling the lion that he must find her or Euryale if he saw any signs of men in boots, and trying to make sure he understood that she didn't mean villagers—all that took an age, and the sun was setting in brilliant swaths of pink cloud by the time she leapt tiredly into the air again, weaving her way across the sky like a spider weaving a web.

*　*　*

Euryale was having more luck.

She had flown to the Snake-Girl's home on her rocky promontory, knowing that the Minotaur had always valued the Snake-Girl's wisdom. Perhaps he had told her something. When Euryale reached the narrow spit of land, the Snake-Girl was holding a bird in her hands.

"Careful," she said over her shoulder. "You'll frighten him." As Euryale watched, the bird looked trustingly into the Snake-Girl's gentle face with its bright dark eyes. It whistled a small note of song.

The Snake-Girl smiled. She whistled very softly back. The bird cocked its head to one side.

Opening her pink mouth wide, the Snake-Girl popped the bird in. Euryale heard a crunching noise as she chewed the delicate bones to shards. She was engrossed, fascinated, like the bird itself. The bird in Euryale was spell-held for a second; she almost wanted the Snake-Girl to devour her, too.

The Snake-Girl spat the snapped bird bones delicately, accurately, into a little wooden box she had ready. Two tears rolled down her cheeks.

Hypnotized, Euryale watched her as she carried the tiny box and its fragile burden to a place where hundreds of tiny mounds of earth marked the resting places of the Snake-Girl's other victims. Each small grave bore a wreath of tiny flowers, a fresh one. The Snake-Girl tended the graves every day. Some special graves had sticks with carefully marked letters. But the sticks were all alike. They all said simply BIRD.

17

The Snake-Girl put the newest coffin into the tiny grave she had dug, and with small movements, she filled in the earth and firmed it down. She placed a small wreath on the new grave.

Euryale shook her head, hard, and spoke. "The Minotaur?" she finally managed to say. At the sound of her own voice, sweet and high, the glamour faded.

The Snake-Girl was careful not to meet Euryale's eyes. "Sorry," she said, blushing. "I can't help it, you know. What about the Minotaur?"

"He's gone." Euryale's voice took on a harshness that came from memories.

"Where?"

"We don't know. But there's something wrong. His hut. There's been a struggle. And men in boots have been there."

The Snake-Girl pondered.

"I have seen no men," she said at last. "But last week, I found a strange token. Maybe it has nothing to do with the Minotaur, but maybe it does. Come and see." She led the way to a curious little recess in the rock. From it, she drew what looked like a small gold disc, intricately worked. The disc had a tiny raised picture of three towers. One of the towers was set with a jewel; it was small, but it glowed green-blue like the sea itself. Rays of light were shown coming from the jewel.

Euryale was gripped by the exquisite fineness of the picture, infinitely more delicate than her own sketches of hunting. She could even see tiny windows in the towers. Was that a person's face looking out? She brought the radiant disc closer to her eye; yes, she could see a small, pale face, inlaid somehow to look white. And tendrils of hair.

Who could have made such a thing? No one from the village.

Euryale was sure of that. And it wasn't like the heroes' jewels either. They had worn plenty of brooches and chains around their necks, but they had been crude, flashy. This was made by someone who loved their work.

Euryale felt shamed, silenced, by an art so far beyond her own. She sighed. The Snake-Girl understood and put her small, scaled tail softly on the Gorgon's claw.

"Your pictures have different strengths," she whispered. "And anyway, perhaps you could learn how to do this—if you wanted to."

A breathtaking idea crossed Euryale's mind. If only she could! It had never occurred to her before that her pictures might change, that there might be new pictures, new ways of doing things. Perhaps she might carve something . . . wood would be best . . . and claws would be useful. . . . Then why not try painting it with ocher or one of the vegetable dyes? She must ask Corydon what would take on wood. Murex shell dye? Oyster's blood? She let herself plan for a moment. Then she wrenched herself back to the present, pushed the enticing thoughts aside. She must find out what the tiny disc meant, for the Minotaur's sake.

"I shall take this to the Sphinx," she announced.

The Snake-Girl smiled and handed it over. "Yes, she might know. She knows so much that we do not."

As the stars came out, Euryale flew off, holding the tiny, bright disc in her claw so tightly that it almost left a mark on the bronze.

The Sphinx was sleeping, as she always did after dark. The spring night had been utterly silent, so the sound of wings, brazen and heavy, woke her long before Euryale's arrival. When Euryale finally dropped down in front of the pillared gateway to the Sphinx's home, the Sphinx was there to meet her.

"Welcome," she said, her voice like falling blossom petals, a mere breath in stillness. "It has been a long time, my friend. You have come to ask me about something that the Snake-Girl has found. Is it not so?"

"It is," admitted Euryale. "The Minotaur is missing. Perhaps this is a clue."

"Show me," said the great white still monster, holding out her clawed foot to Euryale's bronze claw. Her golden eyes flashed. Euryale avoided looking directly into them—the Sphinx's eyes could burn.

"It is this," Euryale said, dropping the precious disc on the ground. The Sphinx examined it carefully.

"Three towers . . . ," she murmured. "A sea stone, an aquamarine. And this is made of orichalc. Euryale, your token is from the greatest city in the world. . . ." Her voice became singsong. "A city of many bright towers, many chariots, pyramids, gardens. Many, many men. Thousands of men. And lamps to break the night. And fires to cheat the cold. And everything men long for is there, and much that they fear. A monument of unaging intellect."

Euryale was getting bored with this. She was never happy with words, and the Sphinx's icy singing filled her with a kind of fear; it made her feel emptier than ever.

"What do you mean?" she asked. "Where does it come from?"

The Sphinx smiled enigmatically.

"Look," said Euryale desperately. "I can't do poetry and things like you and Corydon. Just tell me."

"And yet . . . ," the Sphinx mused, her breath coming softly, "you are an artist, are you not? And . . . yes!" She cocked her head, as if listening to Euryale's heart. "You are finding yourself more of an artist than you thought. Indeed, you are finding the singing masters of your soul in this gem you bring me. That is why you so badly want me to tell you of it. Not for the Minotaur."

Euryale hung her head. It was true. She who hated dishonesty had been guilty of it.

She raised her eyes and looked straight into the Sphinx's golden, glazed gaze.

She knew the risk she took. But the Sphinx withheld her powers.

"Yes. You are right. I did not know myself. Now I do. But I do care about the Minotaur, too."

"I know." The voice was soft again, creamy and soothing. "It is your time to find yourself more. The disc is from Atlantis. And the oracle is over. Go."

Euryale went. She wanted to find Sthenno and to tell her the news. She also wanted breakfast. Badly.

THREE

As she and Sthenno sat by the fire, Euryale stared into the wavering flames. She was silent, gnawing on a boar bone. Sthenno stared even more intently at the disc.

"I don't understand," she said finally. "What is the link between this disc and the Minotaur's disappearance?"

"I think the Sphinx was telling me that those who took him were from Atlantis." Euryale wasn't sure of what she said, though. Would people who made things of such beauty really take a monster by force? Could beauty go hand in hand with such cruelty?

"But . . . Atlantis is the most powerful city in the entire world!" exclaimed Sthenno. "Why would they wish to steal a humble monster? Surely the Atlanteans are not like the pirates who came here, before the heroes. . . ."

"You have never been there," said Euryale. Flatly. Sthenno bristled; her feathers ruffled with harsh grating sounds.

"Of course I haven't. Neither have you. But I still know of it, and of its might. I have a parchment, a star chart I think came from there." She began to rise. Euryale gripped her arm. "Don't start rustling about like a mad vulture, Sthenno."

Sthenno sat down again. "You are right," she admitted. "What we need to decide is how to help the Minotaur, if the Atlanteans *do* have him."

"Could he have been taken by pirates who had stolen an Atlantean medallion?" whispered Euryale.

"I suppose so, but, Euryale, remember the booted feet: his kidnappers did not wear heroes' shoes or even Hellenic shoes."

Reluctantly Euryale bowed her head, poking the fire with a burned stick and then beginning to make a little sketch on the rocky floor.

"There was a scent, too, something even I have never smelled before. The Atlanteans have him."

"We must talk to Corydon." The idea made Sthenno feel happy. Corydon had never failed them. And she would see Gorgos, perhaps. Secretly Sthenno longed to look after Gorgos as his mother had done, crooning tender songs about entrails and pus, helping him do mischief with many hugs. Yet Gorgos never seemed to want her. Her heart sank. Patiently she pushed the feeling away, like a parchment she didn't want to read.

Euryale thought for a minute. Then she said, with real firmness, "Sthenno, could we not solve this ourselves? Has he not done enough for us?" She hated the thought of asking more of Corydon. More than Sthenno, she understood that all he wanted was the quiet simplicity of his shepherd life.

Sthenno's eyes were huge in their purple hollows. She did not hear Euryale's words. A smile spread across her face, and she seemed to be looking at something that wasn't there.

"Euryale!" Her voice was an exultant scream. "We must find him! Corydon! Now!" She ran out of the cave and took to the skies without waiting for Euryale, who followed, slow and reluctant.

Corydon had moved to a shepherd's hut on the mountainside to be closer to his new lambs and kids and their mothers. He shared the hut with Gorgos. After only a few minutes' flying, Sthenno could see its lumpy straw roof below her. She dropped to the ground. Suddenly she wondered whether it had been a good idea to come here before dawn. Were they sleeping? But almost at once, Corydon poked his head out of the door.

"Sthenno!" he said, then looked around wildly. "Where's Gorgos?" he demanded. "Isn't he with you?"

"No," said Euryale, landing heavily by Sthenno. Sthenno felt a sharp stab of dismay. Could the Atlanteans have him, too?

Both sisters began talking at once, each telling in her own words of the Minotaur's disappearance and their search for him. Corydon could hardly make out what they were saying at first, but as they interrupted each other over and over, he began to piece together the story.

The Atlanteans had taken the Minotaur? But why would so mighty a city need a monster like him? And where *was* Gorgos?

"Have you seen the Minotaur?" Sthenno asked just as Euryale exploded with her own question: "Did you see the men?" They glared at each other.

"I have seen neither," said Corydon sensibly, trying to calm them before they could really begin a quarrel. "Because I was stuck on a cliff ledge with a fallen goat for the whole morning. The only unusual thing that happened was that the ground shook. And that Gorgos eventually heard me yelling."

Sthenno flinched. The ground shaking reminded her of Talos. "It wasn't . . . like a metal giant?" she asked nervously.

Euryale snorted. "Oh, Sthenno! We felt it ourselves when we were at the Minotaur's hut. Remember? And it was nothing like the footsteps of Talos. No, the Atlanteans can't possibly have Gorgos if Corydon saw him this morning. The tracks I saw were older than that."

Sthenno felt relieved. She made a birdlike dart at Corydon and hugged him, bronze feathers rasping him. "Mormoluke," she said, using the old, sacred name, "there is a prophecy about you."

Corydon felt tired already. "Is this the same prophecy," he asked, "or is this a new one?"

"Well, that is something people might debate, but it could be seen as a gigantic whole, with your entire life lying before you in every detail. . . ."

Corydon felt trapped. He looked around at the silent, starlit hillside.

"I just want to be a shepherd," he blurted. "I thought I'd already done the things in the prophecy. What more am I supposed to do?"

He hoped no one would tell him. But Sthenno began at once.

"Well," she said, "it says that after the mormoluke has cleansed the Realm of the Many, then he will follow the furrow for a year and a day."

"What is the furrow?" asked Euryale.

Sthenno frowned at the interruption. "The furrow is the cleft in the earth made by a PLOW," she said.

Corydon held his head in both hands. So now he was to be a farmer.

"He's a farmer?" said Euryale, puzzled.

"NO!" cried Sthenno crossly and desperately. "He is to follow the foam furrow!" Seeing that Corydon and Euryale still looked blank, she added, "The furrow in the waves. Made by a ship's prow. Which is pointy. See? Like a plow. See? The words even sound alike!"

"But . . . I don't know anything about sailing!" Corydon wailed. He had spent the whole morning looking at the sea. He didn't want to look at it for a year and a day. He wanted to stay right here, on his own mountain.

Deliberately, firmly, he turned his back on Sthenno.

"No," he said. "Not this time."

Sthenno skittered around in front of him so that she could look at him. He bent his head low to avoid her gaze.

"Corydon," she trilled. "Corydon, no one can escape destiny."

"I can," said Corydon fiercely. "I just want to tend my sheep and goats. And that's what I'm going to do. See?"

Euryale spoke reluctantly. But she could see that Sthenno was getting nowhere.

"What about the Minotaur? Would you abandon him?"

Corydon felt his stomach lurch guiltily. He remembered how the Minotaur had saved him from the shrieking shades in the Land of the Many, how the great beast-man had guided him tirelessly, carrying Corydon when he was too exhausted to walk another step. For the first time, he really began to think about what might have befallen his friend. Like the other monsters, Corydon had never been able to forget his time in the pirates' sideshow. What if the Atlanteans wanted to put the Minotaur in a show in the same way? What if they had hurt him? He was suddenly filled with rage at the idea of the gentlest of the monsters being made to suffer.

"Couldn't it be . . . someone else . . . for once?" It was his last, desperate plea. Already he could see he would have to go.

"Who?" asked Sthenno in surprise.

"Well, us, actually." Euryale spoke firmly, from that new well of hope she'd found in her heart at the thought that she might, just might, learn to make things like the Atlantean medal. "After all, we might be able to fly to Atlantis."

"Euryale"—Sthenno chose her words with unusual care—"it is thousands of miles away, and the last thousand miles are over open sea. Not even an immortal could get there without a ship."

Corydon saw Euryale's shoulders slump and saw—could it be?—a molten bronze tear trickling down her cheek. Was she weeping for the Minotaur? He thought not. Something was happening to Euryale. She was changing.

But that's not fair! he thought. Immortals shouldn't change! She's been alive for thousands of years! Why are things so different now? Then he caught himself. He gave a surprised laugh. Actually, the monsters did change; he himself had changed, and so had his father, and even the other gods—

The gods! The word was an ominous drumbeat in his head. Could the Minotaur's disappearance have something to do with the Olympians? Reaching out to the Island of Monsters once more? He knew better than to think that All-Thundering Zeus would take defeat lightly. They might use mortals, like last time—or would they summon forces more dark and deadly? And Euryale . . . it was as if she were enspelled by the idea of Atlantis, as if something were pulling her there by the heart. With a sensation like snowflakes settling on the back of his neck, Corydon suddenly realized that the disappearance of the Minotaur could be a trap. What if the Olympians were leading them to Atlantis in order to destroy them?

He had to tell Sthenno. To warn her.

But when he did so Sthenno was reassuring. "Mormoliskos," she said tenderly, "Atlantis lies outside the realm of the Olympians. The Atlanteans worship only Poseidon—and the Gray-Eyed Goddess."

Corydon kept to himself the thought that Poseidon and Athene *were* Olympians. Instead, he said thoughtfully, "Perhaps that's why they took the Minotaur, then. For he is Poseidon's grandson."

"I hadn't thought—oh gods!" Sthenno began to spread her wings, with a sharp metallic rattle. "Gorgos! He's Poseidon's *son*. What if he—"

"—creeps up behind you and pulls your feathers?" shouted Gorgos. Sthenno jumped so far she was almost airborne. Euryale began to laugh. Corydon frowned at Gorgos, who didn't even notice. He was running round and round Sthenno, pinching and tickling her. Sthenno's high bird-voice squeaked happily.

"Gorgos!" Corydon had to shout to be heard above the din. "Gorgos! Where have you been?"

"On the mountainside," Gorgos said, crawling on the ground in order to nip Sthenno's bronzy claws, evading her attempts to smack his head with laughing ease. Suddenly she put both arms around him and they hugged, tight and hard. Euryale joined in the hug, but Corydon couldn't bring himself to do the same. He still felt too prickly. He knew he was the one being silly, but he was flustered. Disturbed. But as he watched the three Gorgons, his heart melted, and he ran over and flung his arms awkwardly around them all. They all hugged, getting bronze feathers jammed into necks and elbow bends.

"All right," said Corydon at last. "I'll need a ship."

"What do you mean, *you* need a ship?" Gorgos demanded. "Don't you mean that *we'll* need a ship?"

"No, Gorgos. You'll stay here and look after the sheep and the goats."

Gorgos broke from the hug. He looked Corydon up and down, and then he began to laugh again. "Look, my friend," he managed to gasp, between bellows of laughter, "if there's a choice between looking after a few dumb animals and going on the adventure of a lifetime, leading to the most magical city on earth . . . which would you choose?"

Corydon was silent. Actually, he would have chosen the sheep. But it did seem a bit of a dull choice when Gorgos described it in this way. And it would be good to have Gorgos's company. Well, it *might* be good.

Euryale had been listening. Now she spoke abruptly. "I'm coming, too," she said.

Corydon was amazed. He had never imagined her leaving the island; she seemed so much a part of it, like the very rocks on which they stood.

After a stunned, hurt pause, Sthenno cried, "Why?" Her tone was almost pleading. "Why?" She didn't say that she would miss Euryale unbearably. She couldn't imagine the island without her. But neither could she imagine a long sea voyage.

"I have to," said Euryale miserably. She knew she had hurt Sthenno. "I have to find the one who made that image and learn how to do it, too. I have to. I have to, Sthenno."

Sthenno bowed her head. Suddenly looking very old, brittle like a frost-rimed leaf, she put her clawlike hand on Euryale's arm. "Go," she said, very gently. "Indeed, you must."

"Come with us!" Corydon and Gorgos both begged.

"I cannot," said Sthenno. "No." And she would not say more. She spread her wings. "There is a star chart I need . . . ," she said vaguely. And she flew away, leaving the others gazing blankly after her.

F O U R

For the next few hours, Corydon simply sat by his own fire and worried.

How was he to get a ship? He knew nothing about ships. When the heroes had been on the island, he had seen their ships—like low-flying waterbirds, topped by great wings of sail. He had an idea that they had been made of wood, but that was all he knew.

The irony was that the Minotaur would probably have known more about ships than any of the other monsters. He might have had tools to help, too. Now Corydon was afraid they couldn't rescue him without the knowledge that he had taken with him.

When at last he lay down to sleep, he tossed and turned. Gorgos was out again, running wild on the mountainside. Haunted by dreams, Corydon woke instantly when Gorgos crept light-footed back to the hut.

He began to say, "Where were you?" and then decided not to. He was now saying it so often that even he felt bored.

Instead he sat up and did his best to smile. "It's all right," he said awkwardly. "I know you won't tell me where you were. And I don't mind. It's only that I keep thinking I have to look after you, because your mother said I had to love you. But love isn't the same as looking after."

Gorgos was silent for a minute. Then he said seriously, "I do need your help. I don't know what to do anymore."

Corydon was amazed. Could Gorgos really be asking him . . . ? He waited, almost holding his breath. Gorgos spoke, his words tumbling out, like streams breaking out of the winter dams and pouring headlong down the rocky slopes.

"It's the wolf. Well, she's been my friend for so long, I've always looked out for her, and she used to teach me things, like how to use scent to hunt and stuff, and when the pups were born, we all played together, but lately game's not so plentiful, the rabbits all seem sick, Corydon, with some kind of disease in their eyes, and she won't let the pups eat them, so she's started taking kids from the villagers and then the odd sheep. I made her promise not to touch yours."

Corydon noticed in passing that he said "yours," not "ours." Gorgos had never belonged with the sheep. It made perfect sense for him to belong with the wolves instead. He tried to conceal his revulsion. To him, as to all shepherds, wolves were the enemy. The ultimate enemy.

"But now the villagers are angry. Oh, Corydon, I heard them. They said they would hunt her tomorrow, at dawn. The spearmen are assembling. They'll find her and kill her, and she was only trying to feed her pups."

Corydon frowned. As a shepherd, his instincts told him to side with the villagers. After all, the villagers were doing the same thing as the wolf: trying to make sure their families had enough to see them through the winter. But Gorgos had asked him for help. He must hold on to that.

"The mother wolf mustn't take the villagers' sheep," he said. "If she does, we can't protect her. Perhaps we could talk to the shepherds."

"What good is talk?"

"What's the alternative? We can't fight them."

"I think I could."

"Maybe, but you don't want to. Why don't we at least try talking? If the wolf could agree to leave the villagers' flocks alone, we might give her something to keep her from starving." He felt a pang but went on resolutely. "Some of my sheep, for example." Even as he spoke, he was wondering which one he could bear to give up.

Gorgos was silent. Then he said, astonishment clear in his voice, "Would you really do that?"

"If I must," Corydon said firmly. "Why don't you ask the village headman if they can contribute a sheep twice a year, and I'll do the same?"

Gorgos smiled. "You ask them," he said shyly, ducking his head.

"They'll listen more to you," Corydon reminded him. "They still don't like having a mormoluke near them, but they feel as if you're one of them." Thinking of this, he paused, then asked slowly, "Gorgos, how did you get to know a wolf?" Again, he fought to keep horror from his voice.

He must have succeeded, because Gorgos looked at him with renewed trust.

"I didn't want to tell you," he said, still hesitant. "But . . . I can hear them. Wild things. I hear them all the time."

Corydon felt much as he had on the cliff ledge, precariously poised above a drop where a false step meant death. "Which wild things?" he said, making his voice the gentle one he used with hurt animals.

"All of them," said Gorgos, embracing the starry hillside with a wide-flung arm. "That bird behind you, the nightjar—she's saying, 'Go to sleep, little ones; go to sleep, little ones.' And from far off, I can hear a hunting fox, and he's not saying anything now, but a minute ago, he gave the hunter's cry, 'Leave me to follow my scent!' And I heard a frog just now calling to a beloved he's never met, calling, 'O my love, my fair one!' " He paused. "There's a snake asleep over there in a hollow in the rock. I can hear her dreams. She's listening in her dream, and she's just felt a mouse's warm heart beating fast in terror."

"Are all of them your friends?"

"Oh no." Gorgos was shocked. "Only Mother Wolf and her family, the lammergeiers, and of course the family of lizards who live in the rocks above the summer sheep pen."

Corydon thought he should stop asking questions, but he was consumed with curiosity. He was also anxious; it seemed Gorgos had chosen to befriend not one but two lamb stealers. If he managed to help the wolves, he thought grimly, he would soon find himself making regular donations to the lammergeier family larder as well.

Gorgos was unaware of his tension, so he continued, expansive and relaxed. "The first ones I made friends with were the lizards. I was sitting on the hillside one day when I heard someone crying. I looked around everywhere, and finally I saw a tiny little lizard; he was just stretched out on the warm rock, the way you see lizards all the time, and but for the crying I'd never have realized anything was wrong. I asked him why he was crying, and he said that his whole family had been buried in an earthquake only a few hours before. I was mystified because I hadn't even felt the ground shake, but I asked him where they were, and he showed me a little pile of rocks and told me the rocks blocked what had once been the door to his home."

Gorgos paused, seeing the scene, feeling the heat from the rocks, the hot dazzle of the blue sky.

"It was my fault," he said with a gulp. "I'd knocked the rocks down myself. Just skipping along. I'd barely even noticed. But I'd almost stepped on his home. Corydon, I was the earthquake. I was Earthshaker."

Corydon felt cold awe. Did Gorgos know that his father, Blue-Haired Poseidon, was the source of all earthquakes? Poseidon Earthshaker? Then he shrugged. Maybe it was only a coincidence.

"So of course I cleared away the rocks. And his mother and father were fine, but his little brother—oh, Corydon!—he just lay there, very still. So terribly still. A small pebble—it'd be a pebble to us, but to him it was like a gigantic boulder—had hit him on the head. The mother and father just sat beside him, almost as still as he was.

"He was dead. And I'd killed him.

"It was the hardest thing I've ever done, but I told them. That it was me."

Corydon willed himself *not* to say, "By the powers of earth, it was just a lizard!" And when he thought of the tiny body, he didn't feel much like saying it anyway. Why should being big make for importance? He realized he'd never really thought at all. He was suddenly seeing the world through lizard eyes: full of cruel and careless giants who trod where they wished and crushed and maimed without even seeing the bodies of those they trod on. With a shudder, he realized that he had been as careless about lizards as the Olympians were about men.

"Go on," he said.

"They said that to atone, I should learn from them. Because they live in rock, they know all its secrets. I still don't understand the pure language of stone the way they do, but I do know that all stone contains story, the story of the volcano that birthed it, the river that shaped it, the animals whose forms are held in its memory. Every piece of stone has its own tale to tell. We never listen. We pretend it's just stuff we stand on. But the lizards say that stone sings, only the songs are so long and slow that only the trees and the other stones are around long enough to hear them."

A sudden idea flashed into Corydon's mind. What if the stone knew about the earth quaking as it had yesterday? He felt certain that it was somehow linked to the kidnap of the Minotaur. He said as much to Gorgos.

Gorgos looked thoughtful. "The stone would know," he said, "but it would take too long to answer. I'll ask the lizards, but first we have to help the wolves. I'll go now to the village. You come as far as the outskirts."

They set off, though Corydon had a sinking feeling in his belly. Sure enough, by the time they reached the village, the men had already formed a hunting party, with a few big wolfhounds straining at the leash. To Corydon, who had faced lines of warriors, the party didn't seem especially formidable, just a few bronze spears.

But to Gorgos, who could hardly remember the heroes and their army, it seemed like a huge, dark cloud of men, about to engulf his friends.

Corydon hung back, trying not to be noticed. Gorgos strode forward eagerly and greeted the headman formally, raising his fist in salute and then placing it over his heart. The headman responded in kind, but Corydon thought he looked grim and determined. He didn't look like the sort of man who liked to talk. And Gorgos wasn't good at it either. He blundered at once. "You mustn't hunt the wolf!" he began, waving his arms emphatically. "Really!" Then he stopped.

The village headman stared at Gorgos, waiting for him to say something that made sense. Then he said coldly, "Why not?"

"Because she's nice! And she's got pups to feed."

A murmur ran round the group. Pups! A further menace: get rid of them quickly. Corydon offered a prayer to the Muses, the holy goddesses of art and poetry.

Perhaps it worked. Gorgos added, "And she only takes sheep because she's hungry." Then he stood with his feet apart, arms folded tightly, blocking the hunting party's route out of the village.

The headman smiled. The boy was not lacking in courage anyway.

"We go," he said firmly. "She has taken so many of our sheep that we can no longer put food in our children's mouths."

"We'll restore your sheep!" Gorgos pleaded. "And if you just feed her sometimes, she won't—"

The headman interrupted. "Feed a wolf?" He laughed. "Come, boy. I know you're not truly one of us, but even you must know we cannot do that. Now go. Leave us be."

Not even Gorgos could fight them all there in the village

street. Miserably, his shoulders slumping with defeat, he stood aside. And then his whole body went tense again, and before Corydon could react, he had hurled himself out of the village, running full tilt up the mountainside, past the stronghold. Corydon followed as best he could. He had always been strong and sure-footed, his Pan-leg tireless, but Gorgos was far stronger and swifter. Gorgos ran, headlong, desperate, and Corydon soon saw that he was heading for a steep cliff face with a dark cleft below it. Without checking his pace, Gorgos ran straight for the cliff, as if he were going to slam into it; but when he reached it, he swung himself rapidly down into the cleft. A howl of greeting met him, and Corydon realized he'd been right to think that the wolves lived there. He plunged into the cleft himself, without stopping to think whether it was a good idea to burst in on a group of wolves.

He landed with a bruising thud. He found himself in a long, low cave, and as he straightened up, he bashed his forehead painfully on the low and rocky ceiling.

Straight ahead of him, a huge gray wolf was bent low to the ground, her long teeth bared in a snarl. She was growling continuously. Corydon wondered if she was going to leap at his throat before he could explain that he had come to help.

Gorgos may have shared his fear, for he flung himself between them, speaking to the she-wolf in a low and guttural language of growls and snarls. After a few minutes, she slowly lowered her hackles, but Corydon could see that she didn't really trust a shepherd. He smelled like an enemy to her. And she smelled like one to him.

Besides, now they were here, what could they do to help? Only lead the wolf from place to place, always pursued. They couldn't fight the whole village.

It was no good appealing to the powers of earth either. He ran over them in his mind, as a man might count the sheep in his flock by name. He thought of his own great father, Pan, but Pan was a shepherd and would feel just as he did. And the Moon Girl, Artemis, was a huntress; she would hunt a wolf with cool delight. Hades of the Land of the Dead wore wolfskin and was also a hunter. Perhaps his bright lady, Persephone. . . . And her mother, Demeter, who loved all things that grew. . . . This was a mother wolf. . . .

Afterward he wondered if he had somehow invoked them by simply thinking their names.

There was a noise—slithering rocks, voices. The village hunters were here. Corydon got up and managed to look out of the rocky cleft without being seen himself.

He saw the hunters, yes. But he also saw something else.

A gold man in gold armor. Six feet and two handspans. Towering above the tallest villagers.

In the pale light of dawn, he looked just like the heroes. No, he looked just like the heroes *wanted* to look.

His memory tugged at him. Then recollection flooded in.

This man was the one formed from the dying blood of Medusa. In a fashion, he was Gorgos's brother, something Gorgos might even become. Perhaps it had been Gorgos who had somehow summoned him.

With a strange yelping roar, the gold man charged toward the hunters. He did not draw his sword or point his spear, but without even making a stand, the hunting party simply turned tail and fled. And then the man of gold vanished—as quickly as he'd come.

Corydon looked back into the cleft.

Gorgos was lying, panting, beside the mother wolf, who was

suckling her pups. Her face looked genial now, and Corydon suddenly saw that she, too, had been afraid. Gorgos put a hand out and stroked her fur, a long, gentle caress. With that one gesture, he made it clear that it was from her that he had found the maternal love he had lost when his own mother was murdered.

He had found what he needed, but it had no name, no god. His life held a wildness beyond any gods, Olympian or earthly. He was untamable.

Corydon grinned at him, feeling that at last he understood.

"Gorgos," he said, "why don't you ever talk to the sheep?"

"I can't hear them," Gorgos said. "They aren't wild. I can only hear wild animals." The mother wolf said something to him then, and he laughed and answered her in her own speech. Courteously he translated for Corydon. "She says you are welcome, but that you think like a shepherd. Sheep have very boring speech."

Corydon thought it might seem boring to a wolf but might perhaps be interesting to him. It would be useful to know when a sheep was about to run off or step over a cliff. He sighed, then calmed himself. They'd saved Gorgos's friend. Now they had to help the Minotaur.

The she-wolf was surprisingly knowledgeable when Gorgos questioned her. She said she thought it was indeed the Atlanteans who had taken the Minotaur, that every wild thing on the island had heard them, and the tale had run through the rocks and leaves. "They loaded him on a ship, as if he were one of us," she said, with Gorgos translating. "He didn't want to go." Then she and Gorgos had several minutes of excited snarling, and Corydon couldn't follow a word of it.

Suddenly Gorgos hugged her and rushed out of the cave,

running down the hillside as if the hounds of Hades were at his heels. It was just after dawn, and the grass was slick with dew. Gorgos ran on, leaving Corydon to pursue as usual, until he reached the tiny bay at the end of the island, not far from the Snake-Girl's home. Rummaging behind a rock, Gorgos pulled out a huge shell, the biggest Corydon had ever seen; it was gold and pink and whorled, and Gorgos put it to his lips as if it were a cup. But he did not drink; he blew, a single note, louder and harsher than the horns of Hades, deeper and heavier than the horns of Artemis.

And he was answered.

The sea in the bay erupted as six sleek dolphins burst out of it, leaping for the sky, squeaking and singing, their tails and fins slapping the water. Without a pause, Gorgos flung himself into the water and began swimming toward them, using a fast and powerful stroke. Then there was more squealing.

"Come on," shouted Gorgos.

Corydon hesitated.

"Gorgos," he yelled. "I can't! I can't swim!"

"It's okay," cried Gorgos. "You'll be fine! Just kick with your legs! You can do it!"

Corydon had absolutely no intention of trying. Besides, how would it help? They couldn't swim to Atlantis. He said as much to Gorgos.

"You won't have to," Gorgos shouted. "Arion and Apollo and their pod are going to take us as far as Korkyra."

"Why are we going to Korkyra?" Corydon asked hopelessly.

"To get a ship, of course!" Gorgos yelled. "It's near, and it's a big port. All we'll have to do is find a ship, sneak onto her one dark night, and then sail it away."

To Atlantis? Corydon stood still. It wasn't that bad a plan, though he couldn't help imagining what might go wrong: angry sailors, other ships giving chase . . . and did Gorgos know how to sail? Corydon had no idea. However, he could see that if they tried to build a ship on the island, they might be at it for months while the Minotaur suffered at the hands of the Atlanteans. Like Gorgos, he felt on fire with impatience to start the rescue. He felt in his waist pouch; he had his pipes, his slingshot. And he could see Gorgos's waist pouch bulging with his usual possessions.

"All right, Gorgos, I'll try!" he shouted. He splashed forward into the water.

As he did so, he became aware of two things. One was that one of the dolphins was beside him, encouraging him to climb onto its back by rolling to and fro. This had the effect of rolling plenty of waves at him so that he kept getting mouthfuls of water. He spluttered. Then he noticed something else. He was not alone in the shallows. Beside him was a slender figure, also moving tentatively into the water.

Suddenly, guiltily, he remembered that Euryale was supposed to accompany them. But this couldn't possibly be her. It was the Snake-Girl.

Before he could open his mouth, she spoke with quiet firmness. "I'm coming with you," she said. "I heard everything you said. Sound carries across water. I can be useful. Really. And I want to help. But I can't swim either."

Another of the dolphins, prompted by a long, singing cry from Gorgos, whooshed in front of her. Carefully, spluttering like Corydon, she managed to pull herself onto its broad back and grasp the dorsal fin. Because of her long tail, she had to sit sidesaddle.

Corydon at last managed to throw his leg over his own dolphin mount. Gorgos gave another strange cry; you didn't need to speak dolphin language to know that it was an order for the creatures to go.

Perhaps Euryale would be better off staying with Sthenno, Corydon told himself. Anyway, it was too late now.

Dawn was breaking in fragments of pink cloud, lighting up the green calm of the sea. Corydon's dolphin swam smoothly, quickly, cutting through the small waves, whisking up froths and foams of brilliant, light water all around. As the sun rose higher and the sea became almost too bright with light to look at, Corydon began to enjoy himself. He could feel the water cool against his legs, the dolphin warm between them. The speed was thrilling. Now Gorgos's dolphin drew near. "Let's race!" yelled Gorgos, and the two shot off at twice their previous speed. Gorgos's dolphin narrowly streaked ahead and celebrated with a long, high leap into the dazzling blue sky. Then all three rushed on together.

When they passed a very small, rocky atoll, Gorgos suggested stopping there to give the sea beasts a rest. They had brought no food, but they found a fresh spring and a date palm on the island, and they all ate a few succulent dates and lazed on the beach in the hot embrace of the sun. Then the dolphins were ready, and they set off again, with the sun on their left, heading north. Now they were coming close to the great sea highways, unmarked except in men's minds, the roads where men traded and robbed and made war. They passed a small trading ship, sail up, running free before the wind, and they passed a laden cargo boat bringing spices from Egypt to the lands of the Hellenes. A great ship of war went by, a fast pentekonter, its huge banks of oars falling and rising, creaking, its sail out, too, at full stretch. One of the rowers glimpsed the three, mounted on their sea steeds, and gave a hoarse cry that he had seen King Triton. Another time the Snake-Girl was mistaken for a mergirl by a little girl aboard her merchant-father's trader. But they managed to dodge and dive, and they were soon safe in empty seas again. The sun began setting on their left, painting the water crimson. As the first stars pricked the sky with light, the tired dolphins made their way past the turning for Korkyra harbor. A long man-made spit of rock, called a mole, kept the harbor safe and afforded men a place to tie their boats.

The dolphins swam up to it, as close as possible, to let off their riders; there was no danger that they might beach themselves here, for the waters around the breakwater were still deep. Landborne again on the hard rocks of the mole, Corydon stroked the strangely warm, firm skin of his sea mount. He was grateful. Somehow he felt incredibly happy and hopeful. He knew that it would be no light task stealing a ship from grown men, but he couldn't feel worried about it. Not now.

Euryale stared unhappily into the fire she'd made. She knew that she'd made Sthenno miserable. She could hear her sister now, scratching about, trying to pretend everything was normal. But that morning, Euryale had picked up a parchment in search of a quick snack and found it blotched with Sthenno's bronze tears, hardened into metal.

She'd tried asking Sthenno to go with her to Atlantis. But Sthenno would not even say no. She simply scuttled away. Euryale knew Sthenno was waiting for her to say, "All right, I won't go without you." Part of her wanted to say it. But somehow she couldn't, couldn't give up her vision of a place where she could learn to draw, to make, to create pictures unlike any she'd ever made before. Why couldn't Sthenno understand? Moodily she poked the fire, hoping to uncover a singed bone or two.

Just then, Euryale heard someone cough. A polite, impatient cough. She knew that cough all too well. But she was astonished. Lady Nagaina never normally left the stronghold.

"Why have you come?" she asked abruptly.

Lady Nagaina sounded surprised. "Come? Well, I was actually looking for the Snake-Girl. She's run off to Atlantis with Corydon and Gorgos. . . . Oh, you didn't know they'd gone? How funny."

Stricken, Euryale gazed at the five heads of Lady Nagaina.

"Corydon wouldn't go without me," she said finally.

"I'm afraid he has," Lady Nagaina said smoothly, looking around the cave with an expression of distaste. "I can see why he wanted to go, too," she added, sniffing the air.

Euryale suddenly felt enormous and heavy and useless, like a great bag of turnips. Not knowing what to do, she turned blindly, hoping that Lady Nagaina wouldn't notice the boiling tears welling up in her eyes.

Suddenly Sthenno burst in.

At a glance, she saw that Euryale was crying. Sthenno had been miserable and furious with Euryale all day, but that didn't mean she was going to let the Hydra make her sister cry. With one of her swift bird-movements, she put her thin arms around Euryale's waist. Both of them glared at Lady Nagaina, their enormous golden eagle eyes overwhelming.

But Lady Nagaina didn't flinch. She'd seen worse things in a long life. She only looked amused.

"Well, if you can't bear to hear the truth . . . Actually, I'm a trifle disappointed, too. You do know I come from Atlantis?" For just a fraction of a second, something that might have been real sadness disturbed the liquid calm of her voice. "They left this morning on dolphin backs. I think Gorgos must have arranged it; he seems to be always off talking to toads and other vermin. They've gone to Korkyra, I imagine, to steal a ship."

"Well," said Sthenno uncertainly, still holding Euryale tightly, "perhaps they'll come back when they find one."

"Why should they?" asked Lady Nagaina, all surprise.

Sthenno and Euryale didn't know. Sthenno wanted to say that Corydon loved them but remembered that Euryale had been willing to abandon her and that she had been willing to let her go.

"Anyway, to the point," continued Lady Nagaina. "I wish to revisit the city of my birth and to recover my property. I can't swim and I can't fly, but I suddenly thought that if you two were going that way, you might be willing to give me a lift. I've prepared a sling, a mat, made—well, out of myself, in fact. It's very strong. . . ." From some part of her, she produced a roll of what looked like spiderweb.

Sthenno and Euryale said nothing. Lady Nagaina unrolled the spidery mat and sat down on it. All of her heads were smiling sweet, false smiles.

"See?" she said. "Easy as pie. Each of you takes one side, and then, up and away." She yawned. "Goodness, it's tiring—and a bit boring—all this talk. You might want to try Korkyra first. That's where they went for the ship." With that, she closed her many eyes and lay down flat on the mat. The Gorgons looked at each other again.

Then suddenly they were both laughing. They laughed so much they were bent double with it. Euryale gasped and giggled, clawing the walls in paroxysms of mirth. Sthenno clutched her, roaring with gales of laughter. Still gasping and gurgling, each of them picked up one side of the mat.

"She's no light weight," said Euryale through gritted teeth.

"No—but she can be useful when she wants to be," said Sthenno with a grin. "Come on, then. Up and away!" And flying more slowly and heavily than usual, bearing the slumbering Hydra between them, they headed out east and north, leaving the island's coast behind them, setting their hard bronze faces toward the lands of men.

FIVE

IN KORKYRA, THE THREE MONSTERS SCRAMBLED AWK-wardly up the side of the mole. Its stones bit into Corydon's leg, and the Snake-Girl winced as she grazed herself. But they were at the top in a few minutes. They crept cautiously along, feeling hideously exposed. But the friendly darkness hid them from the many eyes of the little port town.

They crouched low and looked the ships over. Gorgos examined them carefully. After a minute or two, he pointed to a small sloop, a trader.

"That one," he said firmly.

Corydon would have preferred the tiny sailboat that lay conveniently at one end of the harbor, all ready to be taken to sea. "Why that one?" he asked.

"Because it has to be. It's the right one. It's the only one that's safe. I know it."

"How?" Corydon kept his voice low, but he was getting annoyed.

"Because I just do. Anyway, it's almost hidden by that big pentekonter if you're looking at it from the town. That should help us sneak on board."

Gorgos began to creep forward. Corydon and the Snake-Girl followed.

Close to, Gorgos's chosen ship looked fairly seaworthy, though even in the faint light, Corydon could see that the paint was cracked in places. On the bow, though, was an immense figurehead of King Poseidon himself, with flowing hair and a long beard, ready to beat against storm and wave. Corydon didn't like it; having that figure there seemed too close to the Olympians for comfort. The wooden eyes, painted bright blue, seemed to stare straight at them, watching every move.

Gorgos splashed out across the short stretch of water that separated the boat from the land and began climbing up the boat's wooden ladder. Hesitantly, trying to keep to the shadows, Corydon and the Snake-Girl floundered after him, desperately struggling to stay afloat. As Gorgos's feet touched the deck, something went wrong. Inexplicably, the boat gave a sudden sharp rock, a jolt as if a big wave had hit it. There was no wave, though, and Gorgos's weight wasn't enough to make it move like that. Corydon and the Snake-Girl clung to the ladder, fearful.

On deck, a hatchway opened, and the head of a man appeared. He held up a lamp . . . and saw Gorgos. His mouth opened to yell, but before he could make a sound, Gorgos sprang at him like a wolf. The man reeled back a pace or two under his onslaught. Gorgos held the man by the throat, but he managed to writhe free, his eyes bulging with fear.

Somehow Corydon's own feet found the wooden deck. The

Snake-Girl was right behind him, surprisingly quick, for she had had to use her arms to pull herself up. Before Corydon could act, she had slithered—one long slither—between the two fighters and was staring directly into the sailor's eyes. His expression fixed, almost the way people had gone rigid when Medusa turned them to stone. His body, too, was stiff and straight. A faint smile spread across his face. Then he tumbled to the deck.

Gorgos clapped the Snake-Girl on the shoulder. She winced.

"Well done!" he cried. He was already untying the boat from her mooring, bustling about raising the sail, then running to the rudder rope, ready to steer her. His light-footed energy was heartening. Corydon grabbed the maneuvering oar to row them out of harbor.

But as they began to pull slowly away, there was a noise behind them, confused shouts and cries. "Don't leave without us!" cried a voice. "Stop!"

There were running footsteps. Four or five men had burst suddenly out of the inn, realizing what was happening. "Hey! Someone's stealing our ship! Hey! Stop! Pirates! Stop!" More men came running out of shops and houses. One began blowing a sharp horn call: "Pirates! Fire! Thieves!" More and more men ran down to their own ships. Rowing hard, sweat pouring down his face, Corydon saw men running to the huge pentekonter that had lain beside them. They were throwing their oars out, hoisting sail, preparing to give chase.

They passed the harbor mouth, heading for the open sea. A great wave slapped against the side. Gorgos leapt to the rudder. "I have a trick in mind," he cried, and Corydon saw that he was grinning. Jerking the rudder abruptly, Gorgos steered the ship around, apparently heading back to land. The pentekonter checked momentarily, preparing to block their way. As the big ship turned, Gorgos reversed their own smaller, more maneuverable craft again and pressed for the open sea once more. "Row, by the gods!" yelled Gorgos. "Row! Row, if you want to live!"

Corydon strove to obey. A hand touched him on the shoulder. Corydon looked around in surprise to see the face of the man who he had thought was dead. "Let me help you." He said it stiffly, as if the words were hard pebbles being pushed out of his mouth. The man grabbed the oar and began rowing fiercely, with godlike strength. Corydon found another oar and began rowing on the other side of the boat. The sail caught the wind, filled, and the little boat shot forward. Gorgos leaned out from the port side, holding on to a wooden spar, his hair blown back by the wind. The Snake-Girl suddenly thought that he looked quite like the ship's figurehead. He looked much more confident than he did on land, much less clumsy and careless, more controlled.

"Come on!" he cried eagerly. "Crowd on more sail. Let's put up our tunics if we must. We're ahead of them now, and we'll stay ahead." His lips were parted in a grin of pure pleasure; he was drenched with foam. The Snake-Girl slithered over and began hoisting the small sail on the foremast. Then she wriggled up the mast to act as lookout.

Behind them, the pentekonter had crammed on sail, too. And all her oars were out. The silken shrouds billowed in the moonlight. She was about sixteen stades away, a couple of miles off, and gaining. The Snake-Girl saw the white furrow she plowed through the dark sea. Her heart sank.

"They're coming faster!" she shouted. Then she moved aft.

As he rowed desperately, Corydon tried hard to think of a plan. Suddenly he remembered the battle against the heroes. An image came into his mind of the flaming missiles Lady Nagaina's catapult had hurled. . . . Pity she wasn't with them. . . . But there might be a way. . . .

"Is there any oil on board?" he shouted. Gorgos looked baffled. "Oil?" he said. "Yes, I did see a big stone jar. . . . Corydon, keep rowing!" But Corydon had jumped up and had swung himself quickly into the ship's hold as Gorgos seized his oar and rowed frantically. Corydon saw a huge stone jar in the corner of the hold; hastily he lifted it, tiny green-gold splashes of oil spilling out and staining the boards as he hefted it awkwardly up the ladder. He managed to manhandle it to the stern and tipped the oil into the sea. Then he caught up the riding light, burning with a low flame, and hurled it onto the oil. To his delight, a wall of flame sprang up like a hearth fire that has been well fed. It was between the little trader and the pentekonter, and it forced the pentekonter to stop; Corydon could even hear the shouts. Meanwhile, they drove on.

But the fire burned itself out in just minutes. They had increased their lead, but the pentekonter was pursuing again. They would have to think of something else.

Gorgos had been watching Corydon. As soon as he saw the pentekonter begin to press swiftly forward again, he ran to the stern and dived into the foaming sea.

"What are you doing?" Corydon cried. He grabbed his oar once more and rowed, stealing frantic glances over his shoulder. The hypnotized sailor was rowing tirelessly; Corydon found it hard to match his strokes.

Gorgos ignored his cry; the smooth, cool water flowing over his skin seemed to fill him with power. He swam strongly toward the pentekonter. She bore no lights on her prow, and the men on board were far too busy chasing the little trader to notice a swimmer. He had to dodge about to avoid being run down by her, but he dived as she came on and ended up surfacing silently on her port side.

Now!

He knew he must be quick. He pulled a small dagger with a sharp point from his belt. He reached the side of the ship, clung to it like a limpet, and managed to find by touch one of the wooden pegs, the trunnels, that held the ship's hull together. He chose one near the waterline. Using his dagger, he swiftly prized it out and then loosened the board it had held in place. The trunnel fell into the water with a soft *plop*. As Gorgos clung desperately to the side, the wooden plank shifted, and the sea began to pour into the pentekonter's hold through the gap he had made; the very speed of her onward rush made the water pour in faster.

Looking up, Gorgos saw that the pentekonter was only a few stades from the stern of the little trader, almost within javelin range.

A man on the bow was poising his javelin for a throw, targeting the Snake-Girl in the stern. But suddenly the pentekonter lurched. Gorgos let go of it at once and dived back into the cool, friendly sea. The man put down his javelin as the pentekonter listed hard to port and water continued to pour into her hold. There was a lot of confused shouting and running about. Finally, one of the crew found the cause and yelled for bailers. The men raced below and began bailing frantically, but they could not bail the water out as fast as it poured in. At last, the captain's voice was heard, reluctantly ordering a halt while the ship's carpenter repaired the damage and the water was bailed out.

Gorgos was already swimming back toward the trader.

Corydon had slackened his rowing to wait for him. The Snake-Girl threw him a rope, and he swung himself aboard, soaking wet. "Go, go!" he ordered, taking the oar from Corydon. As usual, he was tireless.

Gorgos had hoped that his tactic would delay the pentekonter during the hours of darkness, which gave them their best chance to slip away. He set a new course, thinking a change of direction would confuse their pursuers.

But at first light, the pentekonter sighted them away to its starboard side, and by then Gorgos could see they were done for. Corydon was exhausted with rowing, even his monster-strength taxed to the limit. The crewman was still hypnotized, but his muscles would no longer obey the Snake-Girl's command; he, too, was simply beyond what human strength could do. To make matters worse, the wind was dropping, the sail no longer full-bellied but limp. This gave the pentekonter a huge advantage: she had far more rowers, though they, too, must be tired.

Gorgos had no fresh ideas. He turned to Corydon and saw his own blankness reflected in his friend's frightened eyes.

The predatory bronze beak of the pentekonter drew ever closer. Its eyes seemed to glare at them angrily. It was a monster, but not like them. Corydon and Gorgos could see the grim men on board. They knew what would happen if they were caught. "They'll kill us," Corydon whispered.

"I could try calling—" the Snake-Girl began, but as she spoke, Corydon became aware of a sound, an oddly familiar sound, so familiar that, at first, he almost didn't notice it amidst the shouts of the men on the pentekonter and the slap of waves.

It was the sound of clashing bronze wings.

"Euryale! Sthenno!" Corydon cried out. As he did so, something astonishing happened. They had been sailing forward in brightening dawn light, under a cloudless sky. Now, without warning, silently, suddenly, they were enveloped in a thick gray sea fog, so thick and so gray that they couldn't see half a stade in front of their faces. Mist beaded on the sails and ropes, hung heavy in the air. The pentekonter was barely visible. Next moment, she was utterly swallowed up in the thick walls of grayness. The sound of clashing bronze grew louder as the fog thickened. With it came a voice, though not the voice Corydon had been expecting. It was the thin, cool voice of Lady Nagaina.

"Faster, slaves. We've nearly reached the ship. And having saved you all *yet* again, I must say I'm feeling excessively tired."

Joyfully Corydon looked up. There, hovering above the deck, were Sthenno and Euryale, great wings beating hard, carrying Lady Nagaina in a kind of net. Both Gorgons looked tired, and Corydon realized that neither had answered because they had no breath to spare. They glided down and set Nagaina on the deck. "Ow! You bumped me, you stupid brutes!"

Corydon ignored the Hydra. Running to Sthenno, he flung his arms around her and hugged her hard. He could feel her heart beating heavily under her thick, bronzy plumage, her skinny ribs. He felt a silly desire to burst into tears. Gorgos was hugging Euryale, who stroked his curls with a heavy claw. Lady Nagaina interrupted again. "I suppose none of you will thank me, even though I was the one who whipped up this fog. . . . Oh well. Time for a nap." She moved slitheringly toward the companionway. She went down, then one of her heads popped up through the trapdoor.

"I can't possibly rest down here. It's quite unsuitable. There are oil jars. They smell."

Euryale looked at her over the top of Gorgos's head. They were still hugging. Her heart was singing, and she was so happy that she didn't even want to snap at Nagaina—who had, it was true, saved the day.

"There isn't anywhere else," she said. "And none of us are much good at cleaning. Let's just make it as orderly as we can. We'll all be cooped up on this little boat for quite a while."

"Why didn't you steal a lovely big ship?" Lady Nagaina asked grumpily. Gorgos suppressed his grin.

"We didn't have enough people to row the lovely big ship," said Corydon.

"Well, at least I'll see the home of my childhood. . . . I just hope it won't be too crowded and uncomfortable on the voyage! You know, I'm so tired I'm going to turn in, even in that rather . . . rustic . . . little cabin." With that, she vanished down the ladder.

Euryale was calm. "I'm going to fly out of this magical fog and find some fish and bring back some supplies. I'm hungry, even if no one else is."

"Can we cook fish, though?" the Snake-Girl wondered.

"No, but we can eat it raw if it's fresh," Gorgos said with a grin. "I like it raw. And there's lots of olive oil to have with it." He went on dreamily, "Sometimes I can hear their last thoughts."

Sthenno descended to search the hold for other foodstuffs as Euryale flew off, her strength restored by hope. Everyone stopped rowing; the Snake-Girl released the sailor from his duties, though she renewed her spell to keep him under her control. Corydon decided that he wanted sleep even more than food, especially if food was going to be raw fish. He followed the Hydra down the hatch into the hold. Lady Nagaina was taking up quite a lot of space, but it was also warm next to her smooth flanks. Exhausted, Corydon pulled an old fragment of sail over himself and fell into a heavy sleep beside her.

The Minotaur awoke in a space that was all white, as if thick snow had fallen. It reminded him of the Realm of the Dead before Panfoot redeemed it.

He lay, tightly bound, in the center of a circle of priests. The priests wore white; their skin, too, was white, their hair and beards white. They carried plain white staffs in their hands.

Somewhere music began. It was sweet and heavy, like lime blossom in springtime.

One of the priests raised his white staff and began chanting in a strange language. All the others followed his example.

From somewhere behind the Minotaur, a white flame leapt up, its light reflected in the white ceiling. Almost at once, there was a warm smell—like honey, like amber. As the smell twined itself about him, blending with the music, the Minotaur began to long for sleep. His head grew heavy, heavy. . . .

He was dreaming. He was back in the labyrinth being chased by Theseus, and this time there was no friendly, familiar tunnel out through the south wall. Finally he was cornered in the center, a big pentagon, and as Theseus advanced on him, the man changed. Theseus changed into one of the captains who had kidnapped him. But instead of charging him as he expected, the man beckoned to him. Suspiciously he followed his captor out onto a big wall.

Below the great rampart on which he stood, the Minotaur could see the prickling black shapes of an attacking army. Wherever he was, it was under siege by a vast force. The captain turned to him.

"Help us. Help us as you helped your own people at the Battle of Smoke and Flame."

The Minotaur stood silent. He hated fighting.

Suddenly Medusa stood behind the Atlantean captain.

The Minotaur's heart lurched. He loved her still. He thought of her every day. He knew all through him that one day he would see her again.

And *because* he loved her so much, he knew at once that this wasn't really her. This was his dream. This figure was made of his longing, his memory. There was nothing of her in it.

She spoke. "You have to help them," she said urgently.

Oh, he remembered her voice well, like a high-pitched bird's cry.

"No," he said. "This isn't you. I loved you because you were so truly monstrous. I never controlled you, managed you. No one did. And you never managed me. This is your image. It isn't you, and I can't love it."

Medusa vanished. Now a slender, dark woman stood in her place. Her face was thin and pretty and loving and angry, all at once. The Minotaur knew her. It was his mother.

"My son," she said, sounding just as she always had, stern, a little angry with him for existing, for not being a hero-prince. The Minotaur ducked his head. He knew this, too, was fantasy, but even in dreams, he did not like to see his mother. He could always read the rejection in her eyes.

"My son, you must help these good people. Yes, you are a monster, but you have a fine mind. You can redeem yourself. You may look wrong, but you can at least do right."

The Minotaur knew he could never redeem himself, as his mother put it. His heart knew that this was what she wanted—some way for him to be other than who and what he was.

Again, he refused.

He sat down on the wall.

Others came: crying children; seductively beautiful girls; beautiful boys, too; old men and women; and finally his god-grandfather, Poseidon himself. But the Minotaur knew. None of it was real. He could only refuse and refuse and refuse. That was his sole weapon. When he had rejected a god waving a trident, his captors themselves apparently gave up the struggle.

The Minotaur was dragged from the white marble Hall of Illusions into a dark stone cell. It contained a lump of straw and a bowl of water fit for an animal.

He was thrown in. He sat, bruised and stubborn. He knew in his heart that he would rather die than help to fight another war. He still thought of the crushed limbs of the men he had killed.

The Atlanteans did not speak to him. He did not speak to them either.

Silence enveloped him.

He began to work on a mathematics problem in his head. And he did not mind how long he sat there. It was like his hut.

Only . . . he worried about his bees.

SIX

THE SHIP ROCKED, AND CORYDON, DISTURBED BY THE untrimmed motion, opened a sleepy eye. He got up, his legs and arms still aching from all that rowing, and stumbled forward. Grabbing a piece of the hard ship biscuit the others had uncovered the night before, he clambered up the ladder to the deck.

The world had changed in the night.

When he'd gone to bed, they'd been sailing on an endless sea swathed in fog. But now, away to starboard, he could hear the roar of heavy surf breaking on rocks. The water there was as green as the grass his sheep grazed on, with foam as white as their fleece. Gorgos suddenly appeared beside him, his face tense.

"Shoalwater," he said tersely, pointing. Corydon wondered once more how he knew so much about sailing. The knowledge seemed to float on his blood.

"What's shoalwater?" he asked.

Gorgos ran astern and took the tiller before he answered. Corydon saw that he was piloting the ship, which tacked suddenly to port. "Rocks," he explained. "Water between rocks. If we hit those rocks," Gorgos panted, "they'll drive holes in the bottom of the boat, and she'll fill up with water and sink."

"Can I help?"

"Take an oar," Gorgos shouted.

Corydon tried not to groan aloud. He took the oar, and yesterday's knotted muscles protested silently as he began rowing slowly.

"Faster!" shouted Gorgos. "We must keep well to port of those big shoals—see?"

Corydon could indeed see the dark shapes in the water.

"Where is everyone?" he yelled into the freshening wind.

"The Gorgons went hunting. The others are still below." As he spoke, however, Corydon noticed the Snake-Girl's delicately boned head appear in the hatchway. Not for the first time, he thought how pretty her face was, glistening, bright, like some expensively laminated jewel for a princess.

"Can I help?" she asked politely.

"Take the tiller," Gorgos shouted. He rushed forward to reef the sail and slow their rush toward the shoals. The sail shrank to a fold, and their speed dropped. Corydon still rowed, to keep them on course, and out of the currents that swirled around the rocks that menaced their frail craft.

Corydon looked ahead and drew in his breath sharply. All around the boat were shoals, forming themselves into a maze with narrowing lanes of stormy green water. Waves shot skyward in thick plumes of foam where they hit submerged rocks. Their way was almost impassable. Was the sea here even deep enough for their little craft? Corydon had a strange feeling that he was being herded, like a sheep, toward the gateway where the butcher waited, knife in hand.

But by whom?

Only the gods could have built this maze of rock. Corydon felt colder, drenched in sea spray.

Then something strange happened.

He thought he heard someone singing, very faint and far away, the voice mingling with the sound of the waves breaking on the rocks.

It was a high voice, like the voice of a child—a lonely child, full of longing.

It was calling him.

He began to hear more voices, three more.

They were making a poem, he now realized. A calling-poem. It was about their loneliness. They had never had any friends. Corydon sympathized with this. Like all monsters, he knew what it was to be alone and to exult in the piercing pain of solitude. The voices promised that they knew his pain. And they understood how only the silence of solitude brings forth song. Since this new adventure had begun, Corydon had not had a chance to sing, to make up songs. The voices promised to share their solitude with him, to release him from his overcrowded ship. They promised to teach him their songs and to listen to his.

No one had really listened to his songs except Medusa.

As the eerie song invaded his ears, his heart, Corydon's hands slackened on the oar. Song . . . he had to go, to become a singer.

The oar slid to the deck with a clatter. The boat began losing her way, bobbing helplessly in the vehement currents among the shoals. But Corydon, enveloped in cold silver song, did not see. He did not hear. He did not notice Gorgos stumbling toward him, his eyes glazed.

What he did see was the huge rock dead ahead of the ship's prow.

On it sat four shapes.

They were not women, though they had long green hair that blew in the strong breeze. They had fingers like twisted trees, also green-blue. They had huge eyes, lidless like the eyes of serpents. And their teeth were sharper than the teeth of sharks. And yet they were beautiful, slender and odd like winter saplings, with the strange beauty of creatures who make their home in water. Their skin looked thick and soft, like the dolphins' skin; Corydon wondered dazedly if they might even be part dolphin.

The song grew louder, bolder, more confident. Gorgos was poised to dive into the water and swim to the island. As he noticed this, Corydon was hazily aware of what seemed to him a magnificent work of art—an arrangement of delicate white sculptures all around the island. Some were round, others long, and all were polished by wind and wave.

The song seemed to be pulling the ship closer to the island.

Dimly Corydon heard a clatter behind him. The hatch opened.

Lady Nagaina's five heads burst furiously out.

"Oh gods! Sirens!" she muttered furiously. "Of all the—here, you!" She addressed the gleaming green girls as if they were a flock of chickens. "Be off with you! Really! Just stop it."

The sirens grinned. They went on singing.

"Oh dear," said Lady Nagaina. "I do deplore violence, but what can I do? That water looks very cold." Gently, exquisitely, she blew a bubble of flame from her mouth and sent it toward the sirens. They flinched backward, squawking loudly, like flustered seabirds. The singing broke off on a harsh discord. Gorgos, who was still poised to jump, looked up, confused. Corydon looked up, too, straight at the white sculptures.

What he had taken for sculptures were piles of bones, skulls and long leg bones that once strode the decks of barques and pentekonters.

"You're giving me a headache," Lady Nagaina complained.

The sirens wailed. They leapt into the shallow water and waded toward the ship. They clung to the sides, resuming their song, pleading, stretching out their hands. Casually Lady Nagaina pried them off; they sank suddenly from sight. Corydon saw them surface and sit crying with rage on a nearby rock.

The ship was suddenly afloat in clear water once more.

Corydon felt like crying, too. He couldn't say what he had lost, but he knew he had left something precious behind with the green nymphs and their inviting, deadly song.

Timidly the Snake-Girl approached him and put a gentle hand on his shoulder.

"They meant what they said to you," she said. "And they *are* artists. But they always forget art when they are hungry." Corydon gave her a watery smile. Gorgos still seemed dazed. Corydon wondered what the sirens had offered him.

A tired-looking Sthenno and Euryale thudded onto the deck, carrying gigantic fish, long and silver.

"Sirens?" Sthenno asked. "Quite common around here. Daughters of the Earthshaker. He hates the way they act, so he shuts them up in vast mazes of shoals. But they eat many of his sailors, his favorites. Against his orders. He can't control them."

"They promised me—" Gorgos stopped short. "They promised—" Suddenly his eyes were full of hot and angry tears. He dashed his hands over his eyes.

"Poetry?" asked Corydon gently.

"No! To be a dolphin, to live in the sea. . . ." His voice trailed off. Timidly the Snake-Girl put her hand on his arm. He shook her off, then looked at her, his eyes apologetic.

The hypnotized sailor staggered onto the deck, rubbing his aching arms. "Where am I?" he asked. Plainly, the Snake-Girl's spell had worn off.

"Hadn't you better have another go at him?" asked Euryale.

"I can't keep on doing it," the Snake-Girl replied. "If I do, he'll lose the power to think and feel for himself. I have to let him go now."

"Where exactly do you think he's going?" Sthenno asked. She looked pointedly around at the vast blue sea. So did the sailor. With a cry of horror, he seemed to realize that he was sharing the deck with two ten-foot-tall monsters, a girl who was part snake, and a five-headed Hydra. He ran to Corydon and hurled himself at Corydon's knees, but as he did so, he noticed that one knee was not like the other and recoiled with a shriek. Flinging himself at Gorgos instead, he seized his knees and began babbling out a plea for protection. Gorgos gave him his hand, trying to reassure the terrified sailor, but the sailor saw he had six fingers. He threw himself backward and lay on the deck, screaming.

"Stop it!" Euryale shouted. "No one has hurt you, and no one will. In the name of all the powers of earth, calm yourself."

The man looked up. He had a round face, rather foolish, but probably a face more used to smiles and jokes than to frowns. But now his eyes were huge circles, omicrons of fear.

"Who—who are you?" he gasped.

Euryale bowed. "I am the Gorgon Euryale," she said, "and this is my sister, Sthenno."

Sthenno tried to make a friendly face. Unfortunately, it involved an attempt at a smile, one that bared her many sharp teeth. The sailor's face went completely white; he looked ready to faint away. Undeterred, Euryale went on clumsily, sociably.

"This is Gorgos and this is Corydon," she said. "Both monsters." Gorgos was dying to laugh but managed to suppress his grin. Corydon tried to look serious but friendly. The man stared at them both with horror. From behind him came a series of coughs. Five coughs. A plaintive and icy voice said, "What about me? I'm sure our friend is longing to meet me."

"And this is the Hydra, Lady Nagaina," Euryale said hastily. "And this is—the Snake-Girl—we don't use her name. . . ." The man looked around again.

Suddenly he started to laugh. He laughed and laughed and laughed. He sat up and looked at all the monsters, then fell back again, his legs waving feebly. Gasping, he cried, "Please—just eat me now. Just eat me. Eat me."

"No thank you," said Lady Nagaina. "We don't eat things like you. What a hateful idea. You're not even very clean." She glared pointedly at his dirty chiton.

"You"—the sailor burst into laughter again—"you look like the monsters Perseus and his band of heroes killed," he managed to gasp.

"WHAT?!!" Euryale screamed, clashing her wings in indignation. "You mean he said he'd *killed* us?"

"Of course!" cried the sailor. "He told everyone. We all saw

66

Zeuxis's magnificent painting. Perseus slaying the monsters. You must have—" Suddenly he seemed aware that he was being tactless and fell silent.

"Indeed?" Sthenno asked, tapping her bronze-clawed foot on the deck. "Indeed?"

Corydon felt sick with fury. "I bet he described one of them," he said, his voice shaking with rage. "Because no one can look at her."

"That's the one whose head he cut off." The sailor nodded knowledgeably. "He's got her head in a big casket surrounded by mirrors. Anyone can look if they pay a drachma."

Corydon could hardly see: tears of rage blinded him. He heard thudding feet, then saw Gorgos spring at the sailor and pin him to the deck, his hands on the man's throat. Between his teeth, he hissed, "You mind your tongue! You speak of my mother!" He shoved the man backward, so his head hung over the edge of the deck.

"Stop!" Corydon shouted. He took Gorgos by the shoulder. "I know," he said. "I'd like to kill him, too. But it's not really him at all. It's Perseus." Gorgos, however, did not relax his grip on the sailor. He ignored Corydon, staring into the sailor's eyes, hard, relentless.

"Did you," he said through gritted teeth, "did you—ever—by any chance—pay a drachma to go and look?"

The man could tell his life depended on saying no. He was delighted to be able to say it. "Never, my friend!" He raised his hand and swore. "By Zeus Herkodon, I swear—"

Corydon cut him short. "If you want to swear," he said, "swear by Pan or one of the other powers of earth. We do not take or hear oaths sworn in the name of the Olympians."

The man looked taken aback but said, willingly enough, even

a little too willingly, in a fast gabble of names, "By Pan, then, by Hades, by Persephone, by the Lady of the Dark Moon, by she who brings the harvest, I have never seen the head of the Gorgon. I know of it only because they sell medals with its image, and my brother bore one as a good-luck charm."

Slowly Gorgos relaxed his grip. "Just as well," he said. "Just as well for you. Don't speak of my mother again!" He got up and stalked to the other end of the deck.

Sthenno and Euryale watched him, their mouths open. They had never known Gorgos to act like this. Corydon was surprised, too, but reflected that it seemed part of Gorgos's new seaborne personality, confident, heroic, fearless. The sailor got up, rubbing his throat.

"You really have no choice but to serve with us," Corydon said politely. "But we will pay you for your labors when we reach our destination."

"Where's that?" the sailor asked.

Corydon looked hard at him. "Atlantis," he said. Then he paused. "You don't by any chance know the way?" he asked.

The sailor shook his head, dumb with dread.

Corydon had been worrying about this for some time. Sthenno and Euryale's powers of flight meant that the little barque could sweep bravely into the deeps, that it didn't have to keep hugging the coast like most small craft. With the Gorgons to spy out the way ahead, they could never be lost at sea. But Corydon knew only that they must follow the prow toward the setting sun if they wished to reach Atlantis. Beyond that, he had no idea where to go or what to do.

"Don't worry!" Gorgos cried. "The figurehead will find it. He knows where it is!"

Corydon stared. Was this another of Gorgos's mad plans?

"Gorgos," he said, "the figurehead is made of wood. Wood doesn't have any mind. The figurehead can't know anything. And if it did know something, it couldn't tell us."

"No, Corydon, it can, really. Tell us things. Well, tell me things, at least. You'll see. Not now. Soon." And he was off up into the rigging, hand over hand, swift as the flap of a partridge's whirring wings.

The day stretched ahead, calm and boring. Corydon began to see that sailing was a bit like shepherding: either everything happened in a frantic rush, or nothing happened at all for long, long stretches.

With that thought came a startled recollection. His sheep! He'd assumed Sthenno would keep an eye on them . . . and now—"My sheep!" he cried suddenly.

Gorgos clapped him on the shoulder. "Don't worry. I thought of that. A bee is taking a message to Mother Wolf. She'll look after them for you!"

Corydon wanted to say many things; an awkward thank-you and an angry outburst fought each other for utterance. He contented himself with thinking, I bet she will. Her way of looking after them will be to transform them into lunch for her cubs. But there was nothing to be done. There was something numbing about voyaging, he thought—something that kept what had once been life at a safe distance. He began to feel the rhythm of his turns at the oars as the beginnings of a song. He helped Sthenno dry the fish on the deck so it would keep. They still had plenty of ship biscuit and enough freshwater for several days; none of the monsters drank much water anyway. The sun shone. Lady Nagaina slept, her heads arranged neatly like a young girl's plaits. Corydon began to feel sleepy and lazy, too. The Snake-Girl took over at the oar, and Corydon heard her singing one of her soft little birdsongs. A gray gull landed on the railing by her hand, and she imitated its wailing cry. It flew off before she could tame it or eat it. She looked regretful.

Suddenly Sthenno and Euryale both went stiff all over. Their bronze feathers stood up like dog hackles.

The Snake-Girl was different, too. The scales on her tail seemed suddenly brighter green, deeper green than the sea, and sparkling with gold. Her hair flew green in the strong wind. Her eyes grew wild.

The Gorgons gave happy little cries, little shrill cries of pleasure, like joyful babies.

Then Lady Nagaina's heads shot suddenly up, like flowers bursting from the ground in spring. Her colors burned brighter, too, and her tail turned iridescent blue, glossy and glowing, like Egyptian lapis. Her heads swayed slightly.

What was happening? Corydon tried to clear his fuzzy brain.

Then he saw the green figure sitting on a rock.

It was a male siren this time, with thick green dolphin skin. He was holding some kind of lyre made from a turtle shell, with seaweed strings. He swept his hand across it, playing a chord of such aching tenderness that Corydon felt his own heart stir.

Sthenno ran forward and poised herself for flight. Without thinking, Gorgos stood imperiously in her way. "No, Sthenno!" he cried. "No! It's a siren, I tell you. No." Sthenno dodged from side to side in the bow. Euryale and the Snake-Girl pressed forward, too. Lady Nagaina was coiling and preening herself. Corydon ran forward and tried to help Gorgos, shouting loudly, too, to block off the siren's hauntingly beautiful song.

But it was too late.

Sthenno took off, her flight wobbly and heavy, and landed beside the siren.

The siren looked up.

His song faltered, and he fell silent altogether as he saw her ten feet of sharp bronze feathers, her claws, her pointed teeth bared in a happy, eager smile.

His mouth fell open. No song came out.

As his song ceased, Sthenno came out of her dream.

The others who had been under his spell wailed at losing their visions.

Sthenno looked down at the green dolphin-man.

"Oh!" she said. "Oh." And suddenly she put her face in her hands and began to cry, softly and bitterly. The siren saw the molten bronze tears falling beside him, hardening instantly into metal discs, the currency of a terrible sadness.

The siren didn't pause to comfort Sthenno.

He didn't wait for a second.

He dived at once into the friendly sea and disappeared from view.

Sthenno gasped. For one moment, Corydon thought she, too, would plunge into the glittering blueness. But she shook her head sharply and made a single scrabbling movement with her claws, as if she were seeking something she'd almost held. Then she flew back to the ship, her wings slow with disappointment.

But on board, everyone was helpless with laughter. Gorgos kept gasping, "The look on his face!" and that would set them all off again. Sthenno looked hurt at first, but Euryale flung an arm around her, almost howling with mirth. Soon Sthenno, too, began to grin.

It wasn't till later, when the stars were sprinkling the sky and the ship was sailing serenely over the cool and glassy sea, that Corydon had a chance to ask Sthenno what the siren had offered her.

Sthenno smiled. "What he offered you, too, my little mormoluke. The ultimate truth. The solution to everything. The future rolled up like a scroll."

Corydon felt a pang. Just for once, he would have welcomed a vision of the future. As it was, all they could do was to sail on and on and on, driven by the winds of hope.

That night, his sleep was disturbed; he found it hard to get comfortable on his coil of ropes and sacking. He tossed restlessly, and as he did so, his discomfort merged with a dream. He felt he was back in the Land of the Many, not dimmed by winter as when he had first seen it, but fresh and green, redeemed. Before long, his wandering gaze found Medusa, sitting calm and quiet on an outcrop of rock. He rushed to her, but she put a finger to her lips and pointed to a small pool of clear water near her.

Obediently Corydon turned to look at it, and as he gazed, hazy pictures began to form. He saw a huge moving tower hurling flame at running men. One bolt caught a fleeing soldier, and Corydon saw with horror that he had barely time to scream before the flames swallowed him. Then the picture changed, and he saw the Minotaur, his brow furrowed, bending over a drawing of another tower, this one apparently armed with bristling arrows. The huge monster's face was alert, but somehow Corydon sensed his mixed feelings; there was sadness, too, and Corydon remembered how little the Minotaur loved war. Suddenly a new face appeared, behind the Minotaur's shoulder, high in the sky—a ferocious face, huge, murky green, with a flickering tongue. Who—or what—was it? Something about it made his blood into ice.

Then the pool went dim again, and this time no more visions came. Corydon turned, but Medusa, too, had gone, and only the level grass stretched far away.

He woke with a feeling of urgency. They must not delay. The Minotaur needed them.

And as if in answer to his thoughts, the very next morning, they sighted land. It was only a dim smudge at first, northward, but they turned for it eagerly. Corydon was ridiculously hopeful that this might be Atlantis at last, as if his own sense of urgency could make it true.

The dark smudge grew only slowly. The gentle breeze pushed the ship only softly. They moved as slowly as if drugged. As day dimmed into night, the land became visible as a faint red glow.

"A city?" Gorgos asked the sailor.

"Maybe," the sailor replied, "but I'd have said not. It might be a big fire, perhaps. I once saw a whole forest afire, and it glowed red like that, far into the night. . . ." He looked uneasy. It was plain that he was beginning to think the fire might have to do with something uncanny.

Or with a god, Gorgos thought. He did not share Corydon's dislike and dread of the Olympians. He thought about them much less than his friend did. When they did cross his mind, his chief feeling was a longing to get at them at once, have a straight fight, get it over with. The notion that an Olympian might be the source of the red light excited him; perhaps the time to fight would come soon.

When he was alone, in the ship's bow, Gorgos opened his tunic and carefully unrolled his hidden pouch. Inside was his greatest treasure, wrapped carefully in a piece of thick, soft cloth. It was the broken blade of his mother's sword and its shards and carved hilt. He had kept it in the hope that it might be reforged and that, with it, he might show the Olympians how it felt to die with a sword in the belly. That hope blazed brighter than fire; it was the light he followed.

S E V E N

The next day, Gorgos woke at dawn. The dark smudge was now an island. Frowning cliffs jutted into the sea.

And, astonishingly, the red glow was now visible by daylight. There was also a huge plume of thick smoke, full as a storm cloud and the color of gray rocks. It rolled slowly upward from a triangular peak at the center of the isle, and it was also from this peak that the red glow came.

Gorgos could see no large cities. This was not Atlantis.

"No," said Euryale. She had been on watch since midnight. "It's not Atlantis." Her voice was low with disappointment.

Gorgos smiled and patted her arm. "Don't worry," he said. "We're not far away now. I'm sure of it. Perhaps the people who live here might know how to get there."

Euryale didn't know what to say. Gorgos's optimism was that of a young child—of course he *had* only been alive for a year. He was emotionally still a baby, thinking the world was as yielding as his mother's warm arms had been. But it wasn't. Gorgos had the body of an incredibly strong boy of eleven, thanks to the goddess Hera's milk, but his heart was untried. By contrast, Euryale had lived for thousands of years, years beyond counting.

And yet, Euryale thought, have I really lived at all? Did Sthenno and I live, or did we just exist, in our cave on the island? She shivered. In her own heart, she knew that Medusa had crowded more life into a mortal span than she and Sthenno had into centuries. Now Gorgos, too, was eagerly facing out into the world, drinking it in with hope and ferocity.

Euryale suddenly felt old and tired.

Gorgos sensed her hesitation. "Don't worry," he said, clumsily patting her arm. "Don't worry."

Then he sprang down, apparently listening to a seabird that was following the ship, hoping for scraps.

"Island ahead," he shouted. "Everyone on deck. Quick."

Corydon burst up the ladder. Sthenno followed. They gathered eagerly on the starboard bow rail, peering ahead at the sinister glow, the smoke, the fire. "What is it? Oh, what is it?" The whisper came from them all.

Lady Nagaina slithered up from below, murmuring, "Such a noise!"

She took one look at the island. Yawned delicately. "It's a volcano," she said casually.

Corydon was just as annoyed as the others but far more curious. "What is a volcano?" he asked, puzzled.

"A mountain that is sometimes sick," said Lady Nagaina, smiling. Corydon felt he wasn't getting anywhere. She saw his bewilderment and explained kindly, patronizingly, as one might to a very little child: "It's a mountain that vomits out hot rock, melted rock, and sometimes huge rocks that are on fire, and sometimes'—her face became dreamy, rapturous—"huge clouds of deadly gas, and everything mortal that is touched falls dead instantly. . . ." Her voice trailed off. She was smiling like a contented baby on all five faces.

Her expression reminded Corydon of the battle, the weapons she had made. . . . Could a vulcorno—he felt he'd got the word wrong—do that kind of damage? He decided not to ask, only too certain that Lady Nagaina would enjoy answering. It was clear that the mountain was very dangerous anyway.

Gorgos stared at its flaming peak. "It might not hurt us," he observed, "because we're monsters. We don't get hurt by things that kill men."

"True," Euryale said. "And those of us who can fly could always get away. . . ."

This was enough for Gorgos. "Let's land!" he said, eager and curious. "But you'd better stay on board," he said to the sailor. "Don't try to steal the ship, though. Remember who will come after you if you do." The sailor tried to look as if he'd never thought of such a thing. He eyed Sthenno's sharp claws with dismay.

Gorgos was already lowering the ship's dinghy, and Lady Nagaina was already seated in it. The Snake-Girl crept in, too. Sthenno smiled. "Want a lift, Corydon?" she asked.

"No, I'll get in the boat, too," Corydon said. "Gorgos might need help with rowing." But Gorgos already had the oars, and as Corydon leapt in, nimble as a goat, he began rowing at a furious pace toward the smoking mountain. Sthenno and Euryale followed on brazen wings.

* * *

The shore was silent apart from a faint booming from the mountain itself. The monsters looked at one another, and all turned toward the mountain. They set off through the lush jungle that covered its slopes. After some hours of slow climbing, in which Euryale caught a strange little deerlike creature and roasted it carefully for them all for a hasty lunch, they reached the bare slope they had seen from the deck of the ship. It stank strangely, with a corrosive reek that reminded Corydon of the battle again. Here and there, patches of yellow rock smelled like eggs that had gone bad.

"Did someone drop a basket of eggs here?" the Snake-Girl asked, sounding almost indignant about the waste.

"No," Lady Nagaina explained. "It's an element called sulfur."

"Why is it here?"

"The mountain breathes it out," Lady Nagaina said. She had been surprisingly energetic about climbing this far, but now she stretched her scaly limbs as if they hurt. The Snake-Girl was tired, too; her belly had been scraped by bushes low down on the mountain, and now it was not liking the sharp rocks near the summit. She did not complain, but Corydon noticed her wincing.

"Why don't you fly over the top?" he suggested to Sthenno. Sthenno was more than willing, but Lady Nagaina said a sharp no. "If the volcano were truly to erupt while you were flying over the caldera," she said, "then even you could not withstand the heat. As it is, we take a risk. Better stay on the ground." Corydon didn't understand exactly what she meant, but he knew she was serious about the danger. He turned and plodded on.

They had walked for perhaps half an hour more when something began to happen.

The mountain started to shiver. It reminded Corydon of

his recent experience on the cliff. Here, too, the earth suddenly seemed alive. And as it shivered and shook, it roared.

Great cracks began to open in the rock. The monsters, alarmed, stood still. Smoke poured from the top of the mountain, so much smoke that it grew dark as night. With monster-sight, though, everyone could see that the ground under their feet was being ripped apart. One great crack tore right up to where Euryale and Gorgos stood. Steam poured from it in great gouts, as if the earth were boiling inside.

And amidst the steam, Corydon suddenly saw a small black figure, smaller than himself, no larger than a five-year-old child. The little figure shot swiftly out onto the mountainside through the vast aperture, and Corydon saw with something like horror that this was no child. The face was blackened with soot and smoke, slick with sweat, and it was not a child's face but a dwarf's, shrunken, wrinkled, with soot in every crease. The barrel chest was wrapped in a leather apron, the kind the village blacksmith had worn. In one hand, it held a hammer, a huge hammer half its own size.

The dwarf's mouth opened in a furious shout, and a deep voice came from the creature, a voice ten times too big for the wizened face and body, a deep, sonorous voice like a warning bell. "You are trespassers, invading my mountain. My forge. My volcano! Go back. Back!" He raised the hammer threateningly.

There was something comical about his fury, yet the deep voice was oddly menacing.

Gorgos stepped forward, evading Corydon's restraining hand.

"*Your* mountain?" he said. "*Your* volcano? How are these things yours? Who gave them to you?"

The little man almost danced with rage. "They are mine by

the gift of the king of the gods," he said, his deep voice ringing from every rock. "And more. They are mine by the right of my craft. I am a smith. I am *the* smith. And not long ago, the smith was always the king."

Gorgos threw back his head and laughed. "Fine king you make," he said. "Why, you're not even as tall as I am. And in my land, the smith is just another artisan. Soldiers are kings."

The smith stood absolutely still, as if Gorgos's words had speared his heart. Then, with a deliberation that contrasted with his earlier quick and birdlike movements, he lifted his hammer and brought it down, hard, on the rock before him. At once, a fountain of brilliant gold and red sprang up from the rock. It poured, roared out. It was the most beautiful thing Corydon had ever seen.

It was also hot. It was rock so hot it was liquid.

Corydon realized that they were all in danger. The smith was laughing. The molten red stream poured toward them, flowing like water. . . .

Like water. . . .

Corydon shouted above the smith's roars of laughter.

"Quick! Get to high ground!"

He scrambled hastily onto a spur of rock to his left, one that stood out well above the course taken by the thick, boiling stream of red. Lady Nagaina followed, and Corydon grabbed the Snake-Girl's arm and pulled her to safety just as a stream of lava bore down upon her. Sthenno and Euryale flew swiftly to an even higher point, watching anxiously in case Corydon's rock should be overwhelmed.

But Gorgos didn't move at all.

He stood in the path of the red river of rock, watching it, his face exultant.

The heat crisped his white robe. But he stood, smiling. Sthenno and Euryale gave great birdlike cries of warning and sprang into the darkened air, ready to snatch him to safety. But they were caught on a hot updraft. And before they could reach him, the lava engulfed him.

He stood knee-deep in molten rock, smiling. The hot lava sprayed his clothes and hair. He threw back his head and shouted with triumph, with joy.

The lava flowed around him and slowly began to thicken.

Like someone stepping delicately out of a trap, Gorgos stepped onto the flow as it hardened into blazingly hot rock. His bare feet were still on the blistered, blackened surface, and where he walked, he left the black surface cracked red. He walked slowly toward the smith, who had stood watching him through glittering, narrowed black eyes.

Then Gorgos smiled, open, friendly, and held out a hand.

After a moment, the smith took it in his callused one.

"Be welcome," he said in his heavy voice. "Be welcome. Now I know who you must be. And we are brothers, after a fashion. My mother nursed you, I think." Gorgos looked surprised but smiled again.

Waving a casual hand at the monsters, the smith said more loudly, "Your friends are welcome, too." He waved again, and somehow the lava flow became more solid, much cooler, cool enough to step on. The monsters climbed down and followed the smith and Gorgos into the cleft.

Corydon and the other monsters slid down the small passageway and into paradise.

Corydon looked around in awe. He was standing in the middle of a group of trees, trees unlike any he had ever seen before.

Their enormous roots stuck out from the ground, like thin walls of wood, and they were hung about with thick and woody vines. They had huge leaves, too, and from some hung banners of scented flowers, red and purple.

Or *were* they flowers? As Corydon looked at them more closely, he saw that they were not real growing things but had been formed marvelously of jewels, cut thin as petals, and gold worked into stamens, pistils, pollen. The leaves, too, were jewels—emerald, peridot, tourmaline—many lightly spangled with gilding. . . . And the trees, which had seemed so real, were glowing brown jasper and green chalcedony, worked and carved, too, like rime-riddled bark. . . .

How could anyone make this?

How could anyone do it?

In the trees' highest branches, scurrying movements caught Corydon's eye. Watching closely, he saw strange animals with long, fine golden fur running through the trees. They looked uncomfortably like human babies, but they had long tails and long, thick orange manes, like the Nemean Lion's mane. The smith noticed Corydon's interest and spoke again. "These animals are my servants. They come from far Afric. No, they are not monsters," he added. "They are animals. Their name is tamarin. Some sailors have seen them. They come from beyond—beyond the Pillars that close off the Inner Sea."

Corydon looked up in amazement. He noticed they were picking fruit and while eating were hanging upside down like bats. One hung by one foot; another, more astonishingly, by the tip of its tail, which was curled around the branch like a finger.

"Hurry up. We must get to the river." The smith ran on, scuttling as swiftly as one of his monkey-servants, and the monsters followed.

After passing more trees and more of the creatures called tamarins, the monsters came to the river.

But it was no ordinary river. For one thing, it was a deep blue, too deep a blue for a river.

"Liquid sapphire," the smith said casually. The heat from the river was so extreme that Corydon felt sweat breaking out all over him. The steam from the river warmed the forest, too, so that a mist hung over it.

In the river was a boat. Corydon noticed that it had no sail. The smith gave a piercing whistle, and out of the trees dropped a group of the strange tamarin animals. They settled down at the front of the boat in rows. The smith whistled again, this time a different note, and the creatures took up oars. The smith smiled, his blackened face split by his fierce grin of pride. He climbed into the boat and beckoned the others to follow. As soon as Corydon and the other monsters were on board, the tamarins began to row, and the boat began to move swiftly downriver.

Corydon looked at the tamarin in front of him; he had never seen an animal like it. "Can you hear them?" he asked Gorgos in a very low voice.

"Of course not," Gorgos said. "They're tame, and I'm not sure they're really alive."

Corydon looked at the creature in front of him, rowing with strange, perfectly even strokes. Any normal animal would have tired by now, varied its stroke a little. But the tamarins rowed on. . . . There was something hypnotic about the rhythm. As he watched, he noticed that one tamarin's fur had parted a little, and he felt sure he caught a gleam of metal. . . . Was it a small bolt? Suddenly, startlingly, he was reminded of Talos, the metal giant who had killed the Harpy and been killed himself by the numberless dead.

The smith smiled fiercely, his teeth a flash of white in his blackened face. He had noticed Corydon's attentive stare.

Corydon lowered his voice to a whisper. "They're not real, are they?" he asked.

The smith scowled. He looked away at the deep blue waters. Corydon sensed that he was unwise, but he persevered; he didn't like the tamarins now that he realized they were like tiny versions of Talos. He even felt afraid of them, of their relentlessness, so like the unstoppable metal giant who had killed one of his friends. In a sudden blinding insight, he realized that the god before him must have made Talos, too.

The smith suddenly turned furiously around, his black hair almost on end with rage.

"What do you mean, not real? They are just as real as you are, just as real as I am. Not real! They are my friends. Mine. My friends. They belong to me. Me, you understand? I made them. They are all mine." He was hoarse, shouting, but he was also— surprisingly—on the verge of tears.

"You can't *make* friends like that," Gorgos said firmly.

"Why not?" Now the smith was almost pleading. "I heard people say it all the time. 'Why don't you make more friends, Hephaistos?' My mother used to say it to me every morning. So I did. I made friends. These are my friends."

Corydon felt horribly embarrassed. He hardly liked to tell the smith that his mother probably hadn't meant him to manufacture friends. But Gorgos had no qualms at all. He burst out laughing and clapped Hephaistos on the back.

"You silly!" he said. "That's not what she meant. You can't *own* your friends. Friends aren't toys. They have to be able to choose to leave you. If they can't, they can't truly love you."

The smith stared at Gorgos.

Two enormous, lava-hot tears welled up in his eyes. They streaked his black cheeks with silver.

He made a gasping sound, like a fish that's been caught on a sharp hook and hauled on deck. Then he turned and bent forward, about to hurl himself into the sapphire river. Even a god would have been scorched to death by that stream.

Everyone lunged forward to try to stop him.

But the first to reach him was one of the tamarins. The tiny creature grabbed the smith's lame foot in its slender golden arms. It hung on desperately. Soon it was joined by the others; a tide of tiny tamarins flooded toward the smith, a small golden river of devotion. All cheeped, and all clung to him, forcing him back from the side of the boat.

"Trim the boat!" shouted Euryale desperately as the craft tipped dangerously, nearly plunging them all into the river. The tamarins would not let go of their master, though; he was almost invisible under them. They were around his neck, too, hugging him. One hurled himself at Gorgos and bit him sharply on the leg. "OW! Why did you do that?" Gorgos asked.

"Because," said the little creature, "you call us toys. We are not toys. He made us. But we are free."

Hephaistos was crying again and hugging his—pets? The

tamarins went back to rowing, and the smith, casting one triumphant look at Gorgos, went back to directing the boat.

After what seemed like hours—long, dreamy hours of heat and scents—the Snake-Girl gave a cry.

"Look! It's—"

Hephaistos interrupted, impatient as ever. "It's my home. My home. And my forge. Where I make things. And friends." His grin was triumphant and teasing.

EIGHT

Looking ahead, Corydon saw a building, vast, domed, golden. No, brazen. Studded with bright jewels, red and green and blue. It dazzled, but—Corydon hesitated—somehow it was clumsy, like the houses the village headmen sometimes built for themselves. A long, long staircase climbed to a vast portal from the landing stage. It was a tiring, sweaty climb in the heat. Inside, it was hotter, so hot that even Gorgos at last began to feel discomfort; he wiped his forehead and sank into one of the vast chairs. The chair was covered in some strange, striped skin, black and white, irregular.

"Zebra hide," said the smith proudly.

"Now," he said as the tiny tamarins brought them golden drinks, "why are you here? What do you wish me to make for you?"

Corydon was nonplussed. Euryale opened her mouth to say that they didn't want anything made, only directions to Atlantis, but she was prevented from speaking when Gorgos stood up and strode forward.

Opening his singed bundle, Gorgos drew out some battered pieces of metal—fragments, shards.

"I have come," he said ringingly, looking straight at the smith, "to beg you to reforge my mother's sword. She died wielding it. Now it is mine by right."

The smith was silent, his dark eyes gleaming. He stroked his chin softly. Then he looked sharply up at Gorgos, standing tall and straight.

"Reforge your mother's sword," he said. "And why do you need such a sword?"

Gorgos did not even pause.

"I want the Olympians to know what it feels like to have a sword in the belly!"

Corydon started forward but then paused. The smith did not react angrily. He looked down, his head tilted. Then he looked up; his glance was full of cunning.

"You wish to destroy *all* the Olympians?" he asked, his voice shrill and harsh.

Gorgos! NO! Don't be an idiot! Everyone tried to convey their urgent worries to Gorgos. As usual, he didn't notice. Corydon put his hand over his mouth, miming silence. But Gorgos didn't spare him a glance; his eyes fearlessly met the smith's.

"Yes, I know you are one," he said. "I may spare you if you help me."

The smith grinned. "May?" he said. "May?"

"Yes, may," added Gorgos firmly.

The smith stroked his chin again. "Have you noticed, my fine little cockerel, that you are in the heart of my realm and that I have a thousand *friends* within call, friends who will defend me to the death?"

"Yes, I have," Gorgos agreed simply. "Nevertheless, you will reforge my sword as I ask. I know you will. I have seen it. In dreams."

The smith began to show signs of rising rage. "And why, exactly," he snarled, "why for the love of the stars and skies, why on earth or under it should I do any such thing?"

"Because I ask it," said Gorgos. "And because you know I ask it in justice. They say you are crooked, but I know you are just. Only a just man would give freedom to those he could enslave. Love means more to you than power. So you will not kill me for loving the memory of my mother."

"You were testing me? With the tamarins?"

"No. I do not test. But I can see what is written plainly. You love your mother, and it is only for her and for yourself that you fear. I will make a bargain with you, smith. You reforge my sword, and I will not harm either of you."

The smith gave a gasp that was half a laugh. Corydon held his breath. He waited for the smith to summon a mechanical avalanche that would crush them all. But the smith shook his head and glanced up—that swift, fiery glance—at Gorgos.

"All right, little king," he said at last. "All right. I admit I have no great love for all my family. But you must not harm my mother."

"I shall not," Gorgos agreed. "After all, Hera is, as you said, my mother, too, in a way."

"We are indeed alike," Hephaistos said. Again, the words seemed to carry a dark meaning; he smiled to himself "We have both been fed to greatness by her. And she does not love either of us."

His voice was suddenly as sad as the wind on a cold day at sea. "You," he said. "Your mother loved you."

"Yes, but I lost her," Gorgos said. "And I do not forget who took her from me. The Minotaur's mother did not love him either. My first task is to find and rescue him." Now he was like a child again, confiding in a helpful adult.

Corydon knew he should feel pleased. It seemed that Gorgos had made a good bargain with the smith. But he couldn't quite rid himself of a feeling of apprehension. He saw the smith looking at Gorgos, and the odd glitter in the god's fathomless black eyes did nothing to reassure him.

He was planning something. Corydon felt sure of it. But what could they do? They were trapped in his kingdom.

Dazzling white and golden light. Heat so fierce it made Corydon feel as if the hairs on his head were crisping.

And the noise! As if a thousand thousand bronze-beaked ships were ramming one another. As if a giant were pounding his fist on a gaming table in frustration. *Slam! Bam!* The noise annihilated words and thoughts. Corydon was back against the edge of the cave, sweat pouring from him, longing to be somewhere else.

But Gorgos seemed to enjoy the racket. It was he who held the hilt of Medusa's sword while the smith worked to reforge the blade. In the dazzle of the smith's fires, Corydon could barely see, but he thought the smith had glanced up, just once, and met Gorgos's eyes with a look that seemed almost approving.

At last, it was done. Corydon had not seen the moment when the blade came together, but suddenly Gorgos held it above his head, two-handed, brandishing it like a victor's trophy. Red and gold sparks flew from it. Gorgos turned and plunged it into water nearby. The sword hissed as vehemently as Medusa's snakes. Clouds of steam rose.

Gorgos turned and brought the sword down with a fierce and sudden stroke on an anvil.

The cold iron broke in two under the sword's edge. Gorgos grinned.

"Sorry about that," he said, smiling. "But I had to test it, of course."

He held it out to Corydon.

Corydon gingerly took the hilt. It was so hot he nearly dropped it. He saw at once that the sword had changed. The hilt was the same, a fierce dragon with green jewels for eyes, its jaws agape, its teeth made of some milky-white substance. But the blade was now straighter and more sharply beveled; it was decorated— "chased," said Hephaistos—with two golden serpents, intertwined, twisting up the sword as if around a tree. At the widest point, just below the hilt, was the fierce, never-to-be-forgotten head of Medusa herself, from which the snakes flowed.

Euryale was the only other monster who had decided to watch the forging. She had come to ask questions, at first shyly, but then more boldly, and they began to pour out more and more eagerly. How do you get the pieces of metal to come together? Does iron differ from bronze? From gold? What was the fire made with? How hot is it? How hard do you have to hit hot metal to make it bind with hot metal? How do you make patterns on it? The smith god answered her questions patiently, explaining the mystery and magic of making things with metal. At last, he let her try to work the bellows herself. Euryale managed, with his help, to pour some molten gold into a small mold and then to harden it.

Gorgos swung his sword to and fro. He was bored, but somehow he didn't quite like to leave. Nor did Corydon. He was still not sure the smith could be trusted. Watching Euryale's eager, hopeful face, he looked at the smith and noticed that he seemed reluctant, almost—regretful?

"You'd make a fair apprentice," Hephaistos said slowly, as if it pained him to say it.

Euryale beamed. Shyly she said, "I suppose . . . you wouldn't . . ."

"Never had an apprentice," the smith said abruptly. "But there are plenty who've learned from me in Atlantis." He smiled, and again Corydon mistrusted the smile.

The evening should have been pleasant. They were served a curious, intricate banquet by the tamarins, delicious towers of food borne in on odd little wagons that moved by themselves. A pie the size of Euryale was drawn by a team of tiny birds pulling ribbons; it burst open, and more birds flew out, sugar birds who perched on the diners' hands and then kissed their lips with sugar beaks. Sugar-and-honey flowers suddenly sprang up from the center of the table and twined themselves, luxuriant and menacing, around the diners' chests. Loaves of bread floated on an olive oil ocean, their shape an exact replica of a Greek warship. Golden and green food was accompanied by huge wreaths of golden and green flowers, which turned out to be made of precious stones—emeralds and chalcedony and chrysoprase. A fat little boy flung a huge load of grapes into a golden basin, danced on them, and dipped goblets into the rich wine that he had made. A smiling golden young man took more grapes, crushed them in his hands, and gave everyone a drink from his cupped fingers.

You could eat this food. It was even refreshing after days of rough oil and parched biscuit. But there was something about it that made Corydon more and more uncomfortable. Something about it made him long for a plain and honest cheese made from the milk of his sheep. It was fake—not, perhaps, like the Waters of Lethe, but still a lie. And the smith, genially presiding, welcoming all the diners with cheery cries, ushering in one astounding display after another, was the least believable of all.

The tamarins did a complex dance that ended in gold dust being showered on everyone. The Snake-Girl looked quite pretty with gold in her hair, and it suited Gorgos well enough. But Sthenno and Euryale looked silly, and they felt as if they did. Corydon hated to think about how he must look himself. As for Lady Nagaina, she brushed the gold off her heads hastily. Then she sneezed loudly.

"Please," she said faintly. "Such . . . excess. . . . Still, it's been quite stylish by provincial standards. . . ." As she spoke, a ruby-encrusted dragon broke through the ceiling, bearing melting red fruits in his mouth, which he extended to the guests on his long red tongue.

"No thanks," said Euryale bluntly. Corydon turned, astonished. Surely Euryale couldn't be refusing food?

As he thought this, he noticed that the Snake-Girl was telling the story of their voyage to the smith with increasing animation and vivacity. She was laughing, flirting even, pinching Hephaistos's dark cheek.

What was going on?

Gorgos, however, was sniffling and murmuring a few broken lines of sad poetry to himself as he drained the golden wine from his cup. His new white tunic was spotted with tears.

Sthenno barely drank because she was so busy stuffing herself

with food, grabbing at each new delicacy with outstretched claws. . . .
When had Sthenno eaten like that?

A burst of song broke into his thoughts, a sea chantey sung by
the roughest sailors, with a lot of "yo-ho-ho's" and "heave-ho's." It
sounded as if a full choir of sailors were singing, but really it was
only all five of Lady Nagaina's heads, bobbing merrily as they
roared out the chorus. With her tail, she slapped the wooden table
in time with her own singing. She, too, was drinking the wine in
thirsty gulps and then spraying it on the table and laughing.

There was something wrong. . . . Suddenly Corydon himself
felt an overwhelming urge to play some riotous game. He wanted
to run and shout and kick. Hardly knowing what he was doing, he
leapt up and began bowling one of the cups around the room,
kicking it between two chairs and yelling with triumph when he
succeeded. Now again!

The smith alone remained still, watching his guests. But when
he was satisfied that they were all absorbed in their strange pas-
times, he slipped quietly from the room.

The monsters were so preoccupied with the new, inside-out
selves that the smith had somehow conjured into being that they
didn't even think about his departure. They went on, exploring
strange worlds of sport and extroversion, until they all fell into an
exhausted tumble and slept, heavy with food and wine.

Maybe it was the unaccustomed meal that brought Corydon
to nightmares again. In his sleep, he stood again in the Land of the
Many. This time, it was not Medusa who stood beside him but
the Lady of Flowers herself, Persephone—or was it her mother,
Demeter? He saw again the goddess's tapestry, its glowing colors
brilliant against the gray stone of the chamber that housed it. The

tapestry seemed to rush toward him, eager to show him what he needed to see. And now he saw the Minotaur arguing over something. He was pointing at a jewel, a ruby—or was it a garnet?—and a man in green robes was holding the gem and shaking his head, scowling at the Minotaur. The Minotaur gave what Corydon thought was a roar of anger and frustration. The man in green clapped his hands, and soldiers wearing the same green livery appeared. They laid hands on the Minotaur, threw a heavy metal net around him, and dragged him away. The Minotaur struggled, but the net held him fast, and he sagged, his head drooping, defeated. Corydon saw the man in green pick up a knife and try the edge of it on his finger. He was smiling

Above him in the sky, immense green clouds gathered into a frightful face. The same face he had seen in his dream before. As he watched the tapestry change, a lizard tongue swept out of the face, and Corydon could *feel* it searching for prey. Then he heard screams. People were running from this face, and they were crying out a name, the name Vreckan. Vreckan. The name made no sense to Corydon—vaguely he thought that he must ask Sthenno—but the panic of the people in the tapestry's scene was overwhelming.

His fear seemed to catapult him out of the dream and into a thick, mercifully dreamless, slumber.

It was hours later when Corydon opened his eyes. His whole body felt stiff from sleeping on the ground. Blurrily he sat up. Why were they still in the dining hall? There was the banquet table; no one had cleared away the remnants of the feast. How odd. There were all the monsters. One of Lady Nagaina's heads was snoring softly.

There were cups and platters scattered around. He got to his feet, feeling oddly unsteady and queasy. Some water would be good, but there had been none on the table. He clapped his hands softly for a servant, but nothing happened, and he didn't like to clap louder for fear of waking the others.

He went to the big, heavy brass doors of the dining room and pulled on one. It didn't move. He tried again. Then he knocked quietly, anxiously, on the door. Nothing.

He looked around. There were no other doors. And no windows either.

Now he banged sharply on the door.

Nothing.

He was becoming more and more uneasy. He pulled on the door with all his strength. The rattle woke Sthenno and Euryale.

"What's wrong?" Sthenno asked.

"We're shut in," Corydon said, still quiet. "Unless you can get this door open."

Sthenno and Euryale heaved at it. It was immovable.

Now Gorgos woke and, as always, woke alert. "I'll do it," he said casually. "Here, step aside." His hand went to his sword belt. But his fingers found nothing.

The sword was gone. Gorgos gave a cry of rage.

Now all of them felt the weight of danger.

"Try the walls," said Sthenno. "They may be weaker." She and Euryale went around the room, testing for weaknesses, Euryale also finding some welcome banquet leftovers to snack on. Sthenno eyed her, exasperated. It was obvious that the walls were firm green malachite. Not even Gorgon-strength could break them. By now, the Snake-Girl was awake, too, her eyes round with terror; she hated being shut in. Only Lady Nagaina slept on, blissfully snoring.

The Gorgons tested the floor. Same result.

Then Sthenno, Euryale, and Gorgos tried to use the banquet table as a battering ram to open the doors. Nothing, though they managed to smash the table, which was some satisfaction.

"He can't be planning to keep us here forever," the Snake-Girl said nervously.

"Only till Zeus and the other Olympians arrive," Gorgos said grimly.

"Surely they won't bother with us?"

Gorgos looked contemptuously at the Snake-Girl. "Yes, they will. And we are . . . finished." He sat down and put his head in his hands in an unexpected gesture of despair. Euryale patted him on the shoulder, claw awkwardly curved.

Sthenno was looking up at the starry ceiling. It came naturally to her to look up at stars. Suddenly she drew in a breath.

She had noticed the point in the ceiling where the ruby dragon had come through with his banquet platter. It was a small trapdoor.

"Come on," she said brusquely. She flew up to examine the aperture; it was a tiny doorway, its outlines so faint that only an immortal could have seen them. Euryale joined her. They pushed on the door, but it wouldn't budge. However, Sthenno managed to wedge a curling claw in the cracks around the trapdoor. Pulling carefully, delicately, she managed to remove a small chip of what looked like painted marble. Now both the Gorgons worked together with their claws, chipping more marble away. At last, a small hole lay open to them.

"Now what?" panted Euryale. The hole was much too small for the Gorgons themselves to enter.

They looked down at the others.

Only the Snake-Girl or possibly Corydon or Gorgos could fit through the hole.

"Which one?" Sthenno asked in a whisper.

"Corydon," said Euryale. "This will take brains, not brawn."

So they flew with Corydon up to the painted, jeweled ceiling and pushed him carefully through the trapdoor. Still holding him, they shouted, "What do you see?"

"Shhhh!" said Corydon. "There's a kind of room up here . . . with beams and—there's the ruby dragon." Its gleaming eyes had given him a shock in the dim light.

"Does it lead anywhere?"

"I don't know. It's dark. Boost me in, and I'll go and explore. If I don't come back, you'll have to try something else." And he sprang off their hands and into the dusty dark. The Gorgons could hear his uneven footsteps going away.

Corydon pattered along the attic room. It was really a kind of upper cave, the kind of space he was used to, and it was full of junk—bits of what looked almost like toys, like the dragon. There was a rusty old suit of armor, a horse made out of wood and on wheels, and a toy ship. He was looking for a way out, though.

He explored the entire room. There was no simple door. But there were several other trapdoors.

He opened one and found himself looking down into a vast kitchen, a kitchen bigger than the Gorgons' cave. It was almost deserted, but Corydon could see a tamarin slowly beginning to work on a pile of shellfish that were heaped up on a table. As it worked, the golden creature was singing a little jigging song to itself: "The gods are a-coming, oh-ho, oh-ho, the gods are a-coming oh-ho oh-ho."

Oh no, oh no, thought Corydon grimly. It was obvious that the shellfish were going to be part of a banquet for the Olympians. And the monsters were probably on the menu, too.

Corydon closed the trapdoor gently and opened another one. There he could see a long corridor. It looked more hopeful, but as he thought this, a whole troop of tamarins came past. Corydon wasn't sure he wanted to tackle an army of mechanical monkeys that would probably be tireless and would certainly be determined.

He decided to try the kitchen. At any moment, Hephaistos might check on his guests and find out where he was. He couldn't afford to sit up here all day trying different exits.

He opened the trapdoor and swung himself slowly through it, holding on with his hands. He let himself drop the seven or eight feet to a nearby table.

The tamarin looked around. His eyes and Corydon's met.

The jeweled eyes were flat, lifeless. So was the voice. "You're a monster. You shouldn't be here."

Corydon spoke softly, gently. "I know. But he's keeping us locked up. We have to get away before the gods come."

"He keeps us prisoner, too," said the tamarin unexpectedly. "Last time the gods came, some of us died. Ares got angry. He always does here."

Corydon tried not to show his surprise. "Why don't you run away, then?" he asked.

"Well, he is our master. And we would die without him to fix us. Every year we need a new jewel in our heads. If we don't get it, we can't move or work. Or think."

The creature kept on shucking oysters as it talked. Suddenly it looked up, and this time Corydon could almost detect a spark of anger in its eyes. "I will not help you, but I will not stop you," it said. "Go and free your friends."

Corydon swallowed. It was a generous offer, but he could not accept it.

"The sword," he said. "Do you know—"

The creature became alarmed. "No," it said. "Leave it. Take your lives. They are worth more than a sword. Hurry. Go out of this door and turn left, then right. You will see the hall doors. Go. Go."

Corydon had no choice. As softly as he could, he ran—down the hall, across another corridor—till he saw the great bronze doors before him.

From the outside, they opened at a touch. All the monsters poured out, except Lady Nagaina. "Quick, wake her, somebody," shouted Corydon impatiently. "We must run for the ship."

"I have to get my sword," said Gorgos stubbornly.

"I shall come with you," said the Snake-Girl, surprising everyone. "I think I can help with Hephaistos."

Corydon looked at them despairingly. It was like the wolf all over again. "Just hurry," he said as Lady Nagaina emerged with an irritated expression. "We'll meet you on the ship."

Gorgos and the Snake-Girl set off down the long hall. They had expected it to be deserted, but they were almost falling over troops of tamarins. The little creatures made no attempt to stop them, apparently preoccupied. "Do you know where to go?" the Snake-Girl hissed. Her eyes were shining oddly.

"No idea," said Gorgos.

"We could wander here for days," said the Snake-Girl. "Look, catch one of the little servants." The tamarins were running to and fro, frantic, some still trying to prepare for the gods, carrying vases and tableware, others panicking at the sight of the monsters.

Gorgos grabbed a tamarin and held it firmly. "Where's my sword?" he asked it. The little creature shook its head, with a whirring noise. "It's mine," said Gorgos. "I want it back." Still the creature shook its head.

"Perhaps it doesn't know," the Snake-Girl suggested. She grabbed another from the seething mass. "Where's his sword?" she asked. "Take us to it. Now."

To her amazement, both her tamarin and Gorgos's bowed their heads, wriggled to the floor, and set off in the same direction. Gorgos and the Snake-Girl followed.

"I know!" the Snake-Girl whispered. "You have to give them a direct command. Not ask—tell. Asking just confuses them." The tamarins scuttled forward in an arrow-straight line. Then they turned suddenly up a flight of stairs. They went up and up and up a long, straight stairway, then down a fresh corridor, then up another stairway, at last coming to a small door, so small the monsters would have overlooked it if it had not been at the very top of the stairs they had just climbed. The part of Hephaistos's palace they were in now lacked the magnificence of the lower rooms. No marble or malachite or gold, but a plain wooden door, studded with iron.

The tamarins stood still.

"Open the door!" ordered Gorgos, trying to sound commanding.

Again, he was surprised to find that the tamarins obeyed his command. They pushed the door open.

It was Hephaistos's bedroom. And there lay the god himself,

in a simple wooden bed on a plain wooden floor. There was nothing else in the room except Gorgos's sword, standing against the wall.

Gorgos looked at the smith. Was he really asleep?

The Snake-Girl glided to the head of the bed. She put her hand on the smith's forehead.

She looked down at his closed eyes and began to sing softly.

Gorgos wasted no more time. He grabbed the sword and slung it on. The smith began to stir and opened his eyes. Even the Snake-Girl's enchantment could not hold him firmly. His longing to stop Gorgos shone from his eyes. Finally, thickly, he murmured, "Gorgos . . . hero . . . do not hurt . . . you swore. . . ."

"I remember," said Gorgos curtly. "And, unlike you, I will keep my word. You are lucky. For, otherwise, I would kill you where you lie, deceiver."

"Gorgos," the smith's voice came, "remember. Beware. If you are forsworn, you will die by the sword I made for you. Remember."

"Hurry," said the Snake-Girl. And taking Gorgos's hand, she fled with him down the stairs.

Before they reached the bottom, she felt her spell give like a cobweb when it catches a bird.

There was a bellow of rage.

"Run!" she shouted again.

Tripping over the hordes of tamarins, Gorgos caught one up. "Show us the way to the beach!" he ordered. The little creature shot ahead.

By now, the whole palace was shaking with the smith god's fury. Gorgos and the Snake-Girl felt the floor grow hot beneath them. The air, too, grew thick. Chips of marble began to shake from cracks in the ceiling. There were rumbling sounds.

"It's falling in!" cried Gorgos. He picked up the Snake-Girl hastily and ran at full speed for the bronze door at the end of the corridor. Chunks of ceiling fell around him, and the floor was so hot that his sandals began to smoke.

Thick black smoke was coming from elsewhere, too, almost blinding him. He burst out onto the beach.

It seemed to be nighttime. The sky was pitch-black, lit only by flashes of gold and red from the mountain. Now the mountain itself gave a ferocious rumble and shot a gigantic cloud of red fire into the black sky.

Gorgos paused for a second, then ran to the shoreline. Still clutching the Snake-Girl in a lifesaving hold, he began to swim for the ship, which had started out from the bay. As he swam, lumps of burning rock fell around him. But a wooden ship offered no protection against lava bombs. Gorgos could see that the ship, too, was in danger. Boosting the Snake-Girl on board, he plunged into the water again and managed to tow the ship away faster than it could have sailed. As he looked back, he saw a plume of red and gold lighting up the dark shape of the god's mountain.

But the monsters were free. Gorgos climbed on board.

NINE

Aᴛᴇʀ ᴛʜʀᴇᴇ ᴅᴀʏꜱ ᴏꜰ ʀᴜɴɴɪɴɢ ꜱᴡɪꜰᴛʟʏ ʙᴇꜰᴏʀᴇ ᴀ fresh wind, Corydon had begun to relax. At first, he had feared the immediate anger and vengeance of the gods. And he could not forget the immense green face from his dream. . . . Vreckan. The idea of him was so horrible that he hadn't even asked Sthenno about it. He had hardly slept, watching the skies for signs but seeing nothing except wheeling stars at night, blue and purple sea by day. Gorgos, too, was calm, with his sword slung by his side. Every now and then, he would go and sit in the bow and lovingly stroke the blade, dreaming of using it. But no god presented himself and challenged his right to it. Then, late in the afternoon of the fourth day, they sighted another island.

It was a green land, rolling and rich and fertile. A scent came from it, a powerful scent like sweet red wine. The monsters made harbor in a wide, shallow bay that was cradled between low hills. They went ashore as the light of sunset turned the green grass to rich emerald. The shoreline was unmarked, and there were no other boats; only a scarecrow, its eyes bright with paint, stood sentinel. As the monsters landed, they could see that every hillside was hung with the spreading leaves of grapevines.

Once they were on the beach, the soft ripple of waves mingled with another sound. The monsters could hear the shouts of girls. As they approached, they could see that the girls were dancing in tubs full of ripe grapes, plashing the grapes under hard brown feet, dancing on them until the grapes burst into thick purple juice that gathered between their toes. As they danced, their skirts pinned high, revealing their legs, they sang a strange, wild song, a song of pulsing rhythm. The monsters watched, captivated, as the girls danced faster and faster. There were three inside one of the tubs: one with golden hair, one with honey-dark skin and black hair like a waterfall, one tiny and birdlike. Others came down the hillside bearing fresh baskets of the heavy purple grapes, flinging them into the tubs. Somewhere someone was playing a drum.

No one seemed to notice the monsters, though usually Sthenno and Euryale at least were hard to ignore. The monsters felt oddly awkward. They were just about to turn and go back to make camp on the shore when someone hailed them. It was a very young man, dressed as a harvester. He carried a pruning hook for pulling down the vines. His thick golden curls were somehow familiar; they tugged at Corydon's memory, but before he could pin down his recollection, the young man called to them cheerfully.

"As you see, we are busy with the harvest, but we welcome strangers to the land. Join our feast!"

Corydon looked at the face of the youth. It was smooth, like polished wood, and the voice was sweet and high, the smile warm as sunshine. But behind all that, the monsters could sense something feline, something feral, ready to spring. . . . This was a hunter of some kind. Euryale gave an involuntary shiver. She wanted to be closer to this man, but she also wanted to get away at once. The girls went on singing and dancing, ignoring the conversation. The plash of grapes and the song made the monsters feel muzzy. The setting sun made it hard to see; the light was reddening, as if the sun were bleeding.

Finally Corydon managed to respond.

"Thank you. But as we are not part of your household, we do not want to intrude."

The young man threw back his head and shook his golden hair. Again, Corydon was reminded of a cat in the sun. The golden eyes narrowed slightly.

"But the stranger is sacred to Zeus," he said. "You are welcome. There is no place for shyness here." He smiled and extended his hand. "Come."

Corydon badly wanted to put out his own hand. A part of him was delighted that he and his friends were being invited to join a party, the sort of party his villagers would have fled from if the monsters had appeared at it.

But something held him back, that faint, nagging memory he couldn't quite identify.

"Thank you," he said again with an effort. "We are truly grateful. But we must repair our ship—there is much to do. . . ."

"Won't it wait?" Now the young man sounded, very faintly, cross and disappointed. Perhaps he wasn't used to people refusing his invitations; he was so beautiful and lived in such an enchanted land. "What about you others?" he asked suddenly. His bright golden glance flicked over them. In the glowing red light, his face was still and smooth.

Sthenno shrank back. Something about the smiling youth

aroused her worst fears. Euryale planted her feet firmly and looked down at him, her face stern. Gorgos sat down and began some kind of conversation with an ant he had seen. But Lady Nagaina smiled, all five heads at once. "Yes," she said loudly. "I, for one, will join you." And to Corydon's amazement, the Snake-Girl almost pushed past the affronted Hydra to agree eagerly to attend. The youth smiled warmly into her eyes.

"Yes," he murmured. "Yes. You are indeed my guests." His smile widened to embrace the others. "And you are all welcome." But the more his smile enlarged, the more unhappy Corydon and the Gorgons felt. Only Gorgos seemed relaxed, though he showed no signs of wanting to join in with the festivities. Head bent, he was still talking earnestly with the ant. "We'll turn in early," said Euryale, scraping the sandy ground with one clawed talon. They crept away. Gorgos followed, the ant running up his arm.

As they reached the shore, they all felt as if the scarecrow were watching. None of them, not even Gorgos, liked going past its bright, empty eyes. Without speaking anymore, they scattered to gather firewood and began heaping it on the beach.

Corydon was carrying a dry piece of driftwood when it suddenly began to twist in his hands. As he dropped it in surprise, he realized it had planted itself in the sand. Small red buds appeared all over it, as if it had caught the measles. With frightening speed, leaves forced themselves from the buds. They unfurled, and new ones began to appear. Corydon was so fascinated that it took a cry from Sthenno to make him glance at what had been their firewood pile. Every branch in it was alive. A small forest of vines and saplings was already springing up on the beach. Suddenly a huge stag sprang out of it, antlers thrust menacingly at the monsters. He ran straight at Corydon, who crouched, then leapt out of the furious beast's path.

Gorgos cried out something, but the stag didn't seem to hear him or to care. He charged ferociously on, aiming for Gorgos himself.

Gorgos sprang, not aside but toward the beast. He grabbed his head by the antlers and flung the stag onto the sand, lying on top of him, wrestling him down. The stag struggled to rise. Gorgos held the beast firmly, whispering to him. Gradually his eyes calmed, and his struggles slowed. They lay together for a moment longer. Then both rose slowly to their feet. Gorgos smiled and said something to the stag that sounded wuffly. Then he tore off along the beach, running full tilt, and the stag tore after him. They were obviously playing a game.

Corydon was so absorbed in watching that he didn't notice at first that a new creature was coming out of the enchanted forest. It was long and low and golden and dappled, and it walked with the easy flow of a river. At the same time, its long body held the tension of a plucked lyre. As Corydon watched, the creature opened its mouth and made a soft cooing sound, like a strange bird.

"It's a leopard," breathed Euryale. She was calm, for she had sometimes met leopards on her hunts, hundreds of years ago. She had killed those she saw, lest they take her deer. As a result, there were none left on the monsters' island, and Corydon had never seen one.

The leopard looked around, then climbed a tree at the edge of the forest. Corydon could feel it waiting for someone to enter so that it could fall as swiftly as a stone and crush that person.

They did not think it wise to gather more wood, so they did without a fire. The moon rose slowly, as golden as the leopard.

Then Corydon heard the singing of girls, now using a far wilder melody. Feeling restless as the beat of their dancing sounded in his ears, he wandered around, drawn to the forest, into which Gorgos and his new friend the stag had disappeared. The leopard's bright eyes forbade him to enter, but he came as close as he dared. Then he smelled something alien: among all the leaf smells and wood smells, among the sea smells, a rich odor of wine. At his feet splashed a great crimson stream of it, emptying itself into the sea. It had made a channel for itself in the sand and was turning the clear waves dark. It was running out of the forest.

As if compelled, Corydon bent to drink. The smell filled his head. He cupped the crimson liquid in his hands; it felt warm, as if from the impress of the girls' feet. The drumbeats sounded, louder and louder.

"No," said a stern voice, and to his amazement, Corydon was knocked flat on his back in the sand. His hands opened and the wine spilled. Where else had he drunk such wine, also from cupped hands? The memory escaped him, running away like the wine. He wanted to weep when he realized the wine was gone and bent to try to lick it up, but it had vanished into the sand.

He looked up, feeling furious.

Standing over him was the stag, with Gorgos sitting on his back.

"No," said Gorgos again.

Corydon scowled. "Why not?" he asked, and was surprised that he sounded so petulant.

"It is poison," said Gorgos clearly.

"Wine?"

"This wine is," said Gorgos. The stag snorted.

Corydon stood still. He had a ridiculous urge to cry. The smell of the wine curled into his nostrils.

"Come into the forest," said Gorgos. "It's safe, really."

Corydon looked at the wild vines, the tangled trees.

"You'll be safer in there," Gorgos said. Now his voice sounded almost urgent. "He told me they'll be coming soon," he added anxiously, slipping from the stag's back. Corydon had never heard him sound quite like that before.

Gorgos held out his hand in a friendly gesture. Corydon took it, surprised to see that Gorgos had been growing again. He now towered over Corydon, and his hands were large and very strong-looking. But when he took your hand, it was still like being held by a baby who trusts you to lead him.

Corydon stepped into the wood. Immediately all the smells and sounds of wine and revelry were gone, erased. All he could hear was the murmur of leaves. Sometimes small animals or birds scuffled in the undergrowth. It was quiet, though, and very warm.

They walked a little distance and reached a small glade. Corydon could see the stars overhead.

"Sleep here," said Gorgos, and lay down immediately, closing his eyes and falling asleep before Corydon could say a word. But somehow Corydon did want to sleep now, and he lay next to Gorgos, without protest, and fell asleep, too.

In his dreams that night, he heard two things: the drumming of the girls' feet as they danced and the bellowing of some great beast in pain.

It was the girls he saw. They were wild now. Shoeless, they trod the snow-clad slopes of a great mountain, singing as the thick white ice bit into their soles. Then they ran down the grassy lower slopes, laughing. Somehow, the leopard was there, too, its tail raised high over its body. All of them—the leopard, the girls—were shouting a single word: "Tragoidos!" Even in his dream, Corydon felt a shiver. It reminded him too much of the cries of "pharmakos" that had once driven him from his village. And tragoidos did sound like goat. . . . He had no idea what the word meant, but it seemed limned in blood.

In a panic, his eyes swam. Was that the leopard or the smiling young man? He thought he saw Lady Nagaina. He saw the Snake-Girl, her mouth open to pant, hair streaked across her face as she raced on.

Running before them was indeed a goat, bleating in terror.

They drove the sweating beast step by step to the edge of a cliff.

And then they grabbed him with hot, eager hands.

In seconds, they had ripped him to pieces. The air was filled with fragments of rended goat, a goat explosion. In his dream, Corydon wanted to laugh, even though he also felt terrified. Corydon saw Lady Nagaina in his dream: her mouths were scarlet with blood . . . or was it wine? His thirst reawakened, Corydon longed to drink again. As he fought against it, he saw the revelers sinking abruptly into sleep, lying heedlessly, half naked, on cold rock and damp grass.

And somehow Corydon knew that the smiling young man, or leopard, had meant *him* to be the sacrifice. He was the goat. His sacrifice would have brought something other than sleep: an ecstasy that might have redeemed, made future sacrifice needless. In his dream, he wept for the goat.

And it was through the half tears of dreams that he saw the

Minotaur. He lay recumbent, his head heavy. In his hand was a clay pitcher. Wine trickled from its wide neck. He lay like a tame animal, all man in him blotted out by wine. He had lost his monstrousness, his unsteady blend of man and bull, and was merely a pile of flesh, snoring softly.

As Corydon watched him in horror, the smiling face of the leopard-man formed before him. Corydon knew he was in the presence of one of the Olympians. The smile widened.

"I would have enjoyed eating you raw," said the smiling mouth. "It would have made us all stronger. My madness can heal, Panfoot. It could heal you. You seek it, and it seeks you. The sacrifice is redeemed also."

"The sacrifice is dead!" Corydon shouted.

"But freed from itself," the young man corrected, very gently. "That is why men and monsters seek me. They seek release from the terrible daily burden of being themselves. Their lumpish bodies and their endless desires. . . . Panfoot, do you not tire of being Corydon? Always the one to worry, the one to plan, the one charged with the most difficult tasks. . . . You see that those of your company who find themselves a heavy burden joined my maenads, my wild followers."

Lady Nagaina . . . the Snake-Girl . . . the Minotaur. Corydon knew the Snake-Girl's pain: she loved the birds her snake nature compelled her to eat. He did not know Lady Nagaina's; he was faintly startled to hear that she suffered at all. But the Minotaur had always hated himself, though he had come to a troubled peace by living alone, seeing no one.

"You have always been able to escape," said a deep voice he knew. "You can escape from yourself in song. You do not need the springs of Dionysos, for you have drunk the springs of poetry."

It was Pan's voice. Corydon turned hastily. His father stood there, solid, gnarled as an oak. His furry roughness was comforting against the slippery smoothness of Dionysos.

"That is true," said the younger god. "He does not need to escape anything now. But there may come a time when he must face true guilt, when the Furies fly after him in full cry, breathing their stink in his face. Then he will be glad to fall into the embrace of my wild girls."

Having passed the test of the Waters of Lethe, Corydon had thought himself armored against the urge to pretend that life did not exist. But now he yearned for the wine as if it were his mother's milk.

"Do we have to learn the same lessons over and over?" he asked his father unhappily.

"Sometimes," said Pan with a smile. "If they are hard lessons. And the hardest lesson is the simplest. Know yourself. Know what you are. And can any know himself without despair?"

There was a silence.

"Do you—" Corydon had been about to ask his father if gods, too, must learn. But awe held him back. His father, as often before, answered the question he had not dared to ask. "Yes, my little Panfoot," he said. "Oh yes. The gods, too, must learn. Like men. And like men, they can refuse to learn."

The golden laughter of Dionysos answered him. Behind it, Corydon could hear a kind of snarl, like a wild beast balked of prey.

"Ask him," said the golden voice. "Ask how he came to learn to sing." There was a catlike hiss.

Corydon ignored the advice, given with such obvious malice. But Pan responded. His voice was tinged with terrible sadness as he said, "Yes, Corydon, he is right. I did learn to sing at the cost of my only love. . . ."

"Do not tell me," said Corydon fiercely. He did not want to hear that Pan had not loved his mother—nor that he had somehow killed her. "There are some things it is better not to know."

"My point exactly," purred the leopard god. There was a silence.

"Enough," said Pan's deep voice. "My son, you are free." And Corydon found himself standing on the beach once more.

It was gray dawn. The wood had vanished. He was alone but for Gorgos asleep beside him. Toward the edge of the water, Sthenno was sitting with her arms around her knees, wings furled, watching the stars fading. Corydon crept close to her and put his hand briefly on her shoulder.

"Mormo," she said, "we must put to sea again. This island is no place for us."

Corydon nodded. He felt sure she was right. As the other monsters appeared, yawning, he wondered about the Minotaur. Where was he? Had he really been here? He shook his head; the dream was fading now into the simplicity of daylight, and he was no longer sure of what he had seen.

TEN

It was about noon on the fourth day from Diony-sos's island. Corydon was leaning over the ship's rail, keeping Gorgos a kind of silent company, when he noticed that the distant shoreline to his right was coming closer; the seas were narrowing. To his left, too—to the ship's port side—there was land.

They were coming to the narrows that led to the greater sea. By now, it was obvious that Atlantis lay beyond the Middle Sea.

Corydon felt a tremor of excitement. It was not journey's end, but it was the end of the known world, the end of Middle Earth and Sea. "Corydon!" Gorgos's shout was carried on the strong wind. "Better look. There's something strange ahead."

Corydon looked and at once saw that the land went on narrowing, forming a thin strait, a kind of sea valley with sheer cliff walls ahead. It looked like a nightmare to navigate; even at this distance, he could see clouds of spray flung upward when waves crashed against the cliff bases. "The Pillars!" he breathed, astonished.

But Gorgos was right. There *was* something odd. . . . As

Corydon leaned forward to see better, his chest pressed painfully against the wooden rail, he caught a sudden movement, a huge swirl of white; every seabird on the cliffs had taken to the air in a thick mass of feathers. Why? He hardly had time to frame the thought when he saw. The cliffs moved. With the swiftness of pouncing leopards, they rushed toward each other, sending up a plume of seawater.

Then they met.

Even over a mile away, Corydon heard the dull boom of the crash.

The cliffs sprang apart, like two angry animals. Then they clashed again. Then they parted, and this time, they seemed to settle into stillness, drowsing.

The sailor had seen, too, and he was a gibbering, panicking wreck. "You can't do it," he cried. "The rocks—they'll smash us. Throw us in the air."

He knelt in front of Gorgos, whom he seemed to recognize as leader. Seizing his knees, wailing, he begged, "Don't go this way! Please! Turn back while you still can!"

But there came another, fiercer shriek, from the stern this time.

It was Sthenno. She was pointing at the water behind them.

Out of it came a long, slender blue tentacle, covered in suckers. It was groping, reaching. . . . The water heaved. Two more enormous tentacles emerged and swung over the waves with terrifying speed.

Corydon saw that he had decided too soon that the gods did not want vengeance.

The sailor turned.

"Row!" he bellowed. "It's the Kraken! Row for the Pillars!"

Corydon didn't waste any time asking why the sailor had

changed his mind. Like him, he and Gorgos tumbled into the hold and took up oars.

Sthenno had not been idle. Her bird-screams had summoned Euryale and even Lady Nagaina. The two Gorgons flew out over the boiling sea and stabbed at the Kraken's tentacles, fiercely, with their claws. They succeeded only in maddening the creature; its thick black blood flowed, darkening the bright waves. But they did not stop it. It continued to search for the ship, and the end of one tentacle at last clipped the stern. It fastened on, its suckers expanding horribly. Sthenno tried to prize off the terrible tentacle, but its grip was too strong even for her metal claws.

The rowers below felt the ship lose way.

"It's got us!" yelled Gorgos, and dropping his oar, he ran for the deck, sword in hand.

"Can't you help?" shouted Euryale to Lady Nagaina.

"Can't, I'm afraid," she said. "Krakens are immune to most poisons."

Wildly Corydon looked at the Snake-Girl. She turned her head away in despair. They were helpless.

And then Gorgos burst onto the stern, his golden-and-green sword spilling light onto the deck. Corydon and the sailor followed him aft. The others tumbled back down to row. Corydon looked up at the cliffs; the ship was almost alongside the terrible Pillars now.

"You watch the cliffs!" Gorgos yelled. "I'll manage this thing!" He gestured at the Kraken. Then, lifting his sword high, he plunged it into the creature's livid blue arm. Black blood spilled over the deck in a thick flood. There was a howl. The Kraken let go of the ship. But behind them, it began slowly to rear up, an immense height of jelly and tentacle, beak mouth gaping, eyes glinting fury and death.

Corydon saw the seabirds on the cliffs begin to move restlessly.

"Gorgos!" he shouted. "They're about to close!" He had suddenly seen the only thing that could save them.

Now everyone flung themselves below, at the oars. The sailor hurled on more sails, then flung himself below to row, too. The ship shot forward.

The seabirds began to take off.

Corydon heard a terrible grinding noise, like the heavy rumble of Hephaistos's mountain, like a great churning water mill.

He rowed desperately.

And the ship ran forward and just cleared the cliffs as they crashed shut, slamming into the Kraken's soft squid body, sending its black blood and a great mass of blue flesh skyward. The deck of the ship was drenched with it.

But they were alive. And safe. And outside the Pillars, in the wide ocean. The ocean that men called the Atlantic, after Atlantis.

They burst over a slapping wave and Sthenno gave a hiss of apprehension as she looked at the water all around, dirty green and heaving. It was strange to think there were no islands, no friendly shores. The sea and sky stretched on and on. Something about their greenish sick color reminded Corydon of his nightmares . . . that face. As he thought this, Sthenno spoke.

"We enter the domain of Vreckan," she said. Her voice was bleaker than the chilly sky. The very name clanged on her tongue like a ship's warning bell.

Corydon gasped. His own tongue seemed to stick to the roof of his mouth. His dreams flashed before him. "What do you know of him?"

Sthenno scanned the restless sea. "The greatest and last of the Titans," she said finally.

Euryale patted her shoulder. "He has been imprisoned for millennia," she said. "By the Olympians. By Poseidon himself."

Corydon was surprised. Was this Vreckan another monster, then? One victimized by the gods? Before he could ask any more, Euryale changed the subject. "Has anyone," she inquired, "any idea what course to set?"

Everyone looked about anxiously and began to argue.

"North—"

"What about the polestar?"

As always, Gorgos was unruffled. He had a plan, but he didn't bother to discuss it with the other monsters. Wolfing down a hunk of ship biscuit, listening to all the monsters chattering about how they would be lost in a trackless ocean in another minute, Gorgos simply grinned at them all. He took off his tunic and ran to the rail. For a second, he stood poised, arms over his head, then, as the ship dipped low in the trough of a wave, he plunged into the sea.

It was several long, anxious minutes before Gorgos surfaced. As always, he came up with no sign of distress, no gasping, no spluttering. He intercepted the ship with a few effortless strokes, caught the end of the spar Corydon was holding out, and hauled himself aboard, hand over hand, as agile as one of Hephaistos's tamarins. Corydon felt a hard twinge of envy. He wished he could be like that, so graceful and easy in the sea. Away from his island, his rocks, he felt clumsy, useless. But Gorgos was in his element, shaking off the seawater like a wet dog.

"I have met a new creature!' he announced, his eyes bright with excitement. 'It is like a dolphin, but far, far bigger, many times bigger. And it has shown me the way to go. We must steer by the stars. It sent me a picture of which stars will lead us to Atlantis."

Now Sthenno was very interested. She scuttled forward,

sideways, crablike. "Here," she said. "Gorgos. Parchment. Draw it. So I can see, too." They bent together over the parchment, drawing with a burned stick, rubbing out, exclaiming, explaining. Sthenno raised her head. "I understand now," she said. "If this creature does not lie, I can get us there."

Now it was Euryale's turn to look excited, interested. Softly one claw caressed the small disc. Even the wonders she had seen with Hephaistos had not dimmed its magic for her. But being Euryale, she was thinking of things beyond art, too. "Gorgos," she said, "this creature. Did it have a name?"

Gorgos was still studying the chart he and Sthenno had made. He answered absently. "I cannot turn his name into your speech," he said casually.

"Might it be good to hunt?" Euryale asked wistfully.

Now Gorgos stood straight. "It is my friend," he said simply. "You will not hunt it."

Euryale put away the picture she had been forming in her mind, a picture of hunting a giant sea creature in a small boat, tossed by waves, with—how odd, but what a wonderful idea!—with spears on long ropes, so they could be drawn back. . . . She knew Gorgos would never let her do it, though. Still, she sounded a little sulky. "What exactly are we going to eat out here? Please, Gorgos, don't make friends with every passing fish or we're all going to get very hungry."

Gorgos grinned again. "All right," he said.

The Snake-Girl looked up at him timidly. How long was it since anyone except the Gorgons had been taller than Gorgos? Corydon wondered. Now he was among the tallest on the ship, even taller than the full-grown sailor. She asked softly, "Gorgos, how far away is Atlantis?"

"Many days, I think," Gorgos said dreamily. "Many days. And my friend said the waves could be as high as mountains and cliffs out here. And that a boat as small as ours could easily be swamped. But he said, too, that the worst storms come only in winter."

Everyone looked up at the vivid blue sky. All the monsters suddenly felt nervous, exposed. Corydon thought briefly of Zeus. He knew only too well that Zeus had not given up, and how better to hunt them than with a storm that could destroy their ship with waves like mountains? His heart sank a little. But Gorgos was still speaking.

"Don't worry," he said cheerfully. "It will be all right. Remember I am with you and will care for you." To Corydon's surprise, the others looked quite reassured by this statement. He wished he felt the same.

For the first two days, the weather remained clear and cold, though as they followed the sea beast's course, Corydon couldn't help noticing that the wind grew keener and every day blew a little colder. He began to feel shivery on deck, and hauling the sail up and down or taking reefs got to be hard work.

Then the rain began on the fourth day. And it went on. On the fifth day, it got heavier, and the wind blew stronger, sending the damp sail full and heavy. The ropes suddenly weighed a ton. It made the deck slippery.

And the waves were truly getting bigger.

The wind rose to a high-pitched keening. The only other sound was the steady complaining of Lady Nagaina.

"Putting out into the Atlantic in a *pathetic* little tub like this. . . . Quite impossible. . . . Really, I don't feel at all well . . . no stabilizers. . . . Ow! Feel that smack! That wave was quite uncivilized. Really . . . such manners. Gorgos, if you *want* to be useful, why not get your wretched father to help us? . . . Honestly . . . no one could go on like this. . . ."

As she went on and on, Sthenno and Euryale met each other's eyes. Had they been less frightened, they might have smiled. Had they been less frightened, they might have united to silence her. But in the end, they didn't need to. Another huge gray wave hit the ship, side-on, and poured a whoosh of freezing gray water down the hatchway into the hold. It caught Lady Nagaina full in all her mouths at once. She spent so long after that spluttering and clearing her throats that she had no breath for further complaint for a long time.

"Poseidon doesn't like criticism," hissed Corydon to the Snake-Girl. She was suffering more than any of them from the cold; her snake part made it impossible for her to get really warm without the heat of the sun to help her. She felt sleepy and dopey. Corydon finally took off his cloak and put it round her cold shoulders. She thanked him with a small, nervous smile.

The waves grew higher and higher and became like great gray beasts, like giants. They were coated in soft white foam—spume, said the sailor, his eyes showing the whites all around with sheer terror. The little ship was hurled up vast clifflike crests, then flung down into deep valleys of heavy gray sea. Rain and wind lashed her.

"Can we—could we fly?" Corydon asked Sthenno and Euryale. Sthenno smiled, a twisted smile. "We could carry you, little mormoluke, you and perhaps one other. Though even that is doubtful, for we cannot fly forever. But we cannot carry you all. Who, then, shall we take and who leave behind?"

Corydon gulped. Then he made himself say it. "T-take Gorgos," he said. "And the Snake-Girl. We cannot all die here." As he spoke, the ship twirled around in the grip of another vast sea. He was surprised to find he minded less as he said it. Somehow there was a calmness at the heart of this terrible storm, the calmness of an accepted destiny. He knew these great gray waves with their long trails of foam. In their way, they were like his mountains. At the same time, his heart ached for the feel of his mountains beneath his feet. And yet . . . he knew what it was to be one of Persephone's subjects. At least he would see Medusa soon. . . .

But Sthenno was shaking her head. "Not yet, little mormoluke," she said softly. "When the ship can take no more, then we will do all that we must. But not until then."

"Then let us all get up on deck," Corydon exclaimed, with a gasp of what he admitted was relief, "for that gives us some chance of swimming when—" As he spoke, another huge wave poured down the companionway, soaking them. It was obvious that even with their frantic bailing, the ship was taking in more water than she could manage. Their bailing was only delaying the inevitable by a few short minutes.

And yet on deck, the ferocity of the storm was far far worse. Corydon felt it was personal, as if the sea and sky were hurling themselves deliberately against the little ship, against all who sailed in her. Gorgos stood in the bow, erect, proud, barely swaying as the ship tossed and swung, heeled and lifted. He raised his arm to heaven and shook his fist.

"We will outlive you!" he shouted. And his voice did not sound frail but strong, despite the winds and their roaring.

As if summoned by his words, there was a moment of eerie calm. The ship wallowed in a pause between giant seas.

And for a magical, splendid second, the sun broke through the clouds. It lit the ship, the sea, with golden fire. If Corydon had been capable of it, he would have offered a prayer to Apollo Helios, not for saving them but simply for the sight of his face.

He stood, the words trembling on his lips as the sunlight shook across the water.

But he remained dumb.

And the sky sealed itself over with darkness once more. The sun was blotted out as if it had never been.

Immediately the waves mounted to new heights.

As the ship labored up a great gray hill of water, Corydon saw the wave. Nine times the height of the others, it was not a hill but a surging mountain of gray-green power. And as he watched, it grew. It drew more and more of the sea into itself. Looking at the gray wall that now loomed over the frail ship, Corydon, mouth open, thought that it was the very face of the gods set against the fragility of mortal men.

Gorgos gave a cry. "Abandon ship!" he yelled. Grabbing the Snake-Girl by the wrist, Corydon leapt to obey. But it was too late. Already the ship had been caught by the great sea giant's rolling edge. As the wave lifted the ship into the air, it was turned round and round, like a flake of grain in a mill, over and over.

Its passengers were scattered on the sea, insignificant as foam.

Then the great gray cliff of water crashed onto them.

No mortal man could live through the fury of the sea. But the monsters had more than mortal strength. There was a moment when Corydon was under the water, choking, mouth full of foam. Eternities of sea roared in his ears. But he managed to keep hold of the Snake-Girl, and slowly they rose to a tumbling surface, still gray, still furious. The air was so full of foam droplets that it felt as if they were still underwater. They rode gigantic waves. Then at last they came across a few boards, pieces of the ship's hull. They managed to pull themselves onto one each and to keep their hands clasped. On this primitive raft, they rocked up and down, uphill and down, up and down. As the waves grew smaller, they slept.

Sthenno and Euryale had leapt into the skies, dragging the complaining Hydra with them. They had flown for wing-aching hours into the storm winds. Lady Nagaina was supposed to be watching the surface of the sea, looking for other survivors, but as Sthenno said later, both she and Euryale were fairly sure she'd shut her eyes to keep the sea spray from stinging them. Carrying Lady Nagaina without a net was exhausting, and the slighter Sthenno had almost reached the end of even her great immortal strength when Euryale gave a hoarse cry. She looked down and saw the dim outline of an island's coast below them. It was night, but the huge waves breaking on the shoreline were visible in their foamy whiteness. Both Gorgons sped downward, landed on the smooth black beach, and dragged Lady Nagaina into the dunes. All three slept like the dead.

ELEVEN

Corydon and the Snake-Girl awakened to a calm dawn. The sea around them bore only the gentlest ripples. The sky was a soft pink and gold. The world itself seemed washed clean.

And ahead, Corydon saw the dim purplish shape of what must be land. He roused the Snake-Girl, and she began to paddle awkwardly toward it. By mutual consent, they abandoned the clumsy pieces of the ship and simply swam. Corydon was surprised to find that the Snake-Girl was a much-faster swimmer than he was. He was so tired that he could barely struggle up the black beach when they reached it. He fell forward on the cool sand.

He looked up. One of Lady Nagaina's five heads was poking toward him. Dazedly he wondered if her splendid blue glitter was a dream. But she spoke.

"Oh good," she said. "You're here at last. I've been awake for hours. Do you think you might rustle up something to eat?"

Corydon was so pleased that someone else had survived that

he would have hugged her if he had been able to get up to do it. It gave him hope, too, that—

"Have you seen the others?" the Snake-Girl said, her face flushed, eager.

Lady Nagaina pointed behind her. "Sthenno and Euryale," she said. "Back there. We flew here. They seem a bit tired now." The Snake-Girl hurried to see if the Gorgons were actually all right. Corydon gulped.

"What about the sailor?" he asked. "And Gorgos?"

"No idea," the Hydra replied. "But nothing will happen to Gorgos. He's that kind. Rather like me, in fact."

Corydon felt a sinking. He knew in his heart that no mortal man could have survived the storm. But Gorgos . . . Corydon could not quite think of Gorgos as strong and capable. He still saw Gorgos as little brother Gorgoliskos, the baby Medusa had entrusted to him. The one he was supposed to look after. Now he imagined having to go to the Realm of the Many to tell Medusa that her son had not lived out his span of years . . . that he had let the gods win. . . .

Lady Nagaina looked at him, not unkindly.

"You are usually wise, Corydon Panfoot," she said at last. "But your grief makes you lose hold of your monster-wisdoms. You are tangled in mortal thoughts, like a fish in a net. So you misread. Gorgos does not need anyone to care for him. It is his destiny to be the one who cares for us all. And now," she finished, "in the name of all gods and monsters, can you not get me something to eat before I waste away to an earthworm?"

He knew she was right. But her words were unwelcome. If Gorgos was truly grown, then . . . Medusa was truly gone. But that was Lady Nagaina's way: she spoke sharply, saw without sentiment.

He grinned at her with sudden real liking. "I don't know where you think I might find food. There don't seem to be many inns hereabouts," he observed, "nor any flocks I might milk."

"That's where you are wrong," commented Euryale, appearing over the dunes, landing beside them. "There are plenty of milking beasts here. But I think it would be unwise to milk them. I saw the brand."

"Brand?"

Euryale nodded, her face grim. "They belong to Geryon," she said.

Corydon was surprised that she looked so grim. The legendary Geryon was a monster, one of themselves, perhaps the strongest monster of all. His own heart lifted at the name. He hoped for help, though he knew better than anyone that monsters were not usually sociable or cooperative. "What's wrong with that?" he asked, puzzled.

"Only that they say he was driven almost mad by an attack from Herakles," Euryale reported. "About the time the heroes came for us, Herakles drove off some of his cattle. They say he loves his beasts, the way the Minotaur . . ." She paused, and in the uncomfortable silence, Corydon realized guiltily that in the battle to survive, none of them had thought about the Minotaur for many days.

Now Sthenno took up the tale. "He missed them so badly that he cried, even in his sleep. While he was weeping, he realized he hadn't seen his scarlet dog for days. The dog was a monster, too, two-headed." Lady Nagaina looked piercingly at Sthenno. She seemed about to ask what was wrong with having many heads. Hastily Sthenno added, "Came in useful for herding the cattle. A few days later, he found the body washed up on the seashore. Herakles had clubbed it to death. He doped it first with some kind of poison the gods sent."

The monsters were shocked.

"Oh, how dreadful," said the Snake-Girl softly. Corydon had not really noticed her before, but she, too, was joining in. She was holding a small bird in her hand, and she began absentmindedly plucking it. Its nearly naked wings fluttered desperately.

Now Euryale spoke again. "They say he went quite mad, then." As she said the words, Corydon heard a loud roaring noise over by the dunes.

"It's him," said Sthenno. She opened her wings. All the monsters bunched together, except Corydon, who advanced slowly. Then he stopped dead at the sight of the monster. Geryon looked like a giant who had been broken, then reassembled badly, using pieces of other giants where the original giant had been smashed beyond repair. The result was physical chaos on a scale even Corydon paused at. Heads at all angles. Enormous humped shoulders. Mighty arms set askew. And all of it seething with rage.

Corydon tentatively held his hand forward and cleared his throat.

But the monster, still roaring, ignored the gesture. Instead, something about Corydon seemed to madden him.

"So!" he cried. "You've come here again! To thieve! Yes, to thieve! I know a thief when I smell one!"

Corydon was startled. It was true, of course; like all shepherds, he was a thief, a kleptis. He couldn't deny it.

The clumsy, powerful monster was still advancing angrily on

him. Corydon began to make sense of what he saw. Geryon had three bodies rising from two legs; he had six arms, three rough block-shaped heads. His skin had the sheen of scales; Corydon saw the long, lizard-like tail hanging down behind.

"Yes," Corydon said, instinctively using the voice he used to calm frightened animals. "Yes, you're right. I am a thief. But I have never robbed you. Never."

The enormous monster still came on. He squinted at Corydon, then suddenly the lizard tail lashed. It missed Corydon completely, because he had seen it coming in time to dodge. But he noticed that at its tip was a long, dull-colored claw, a kind of hook. . . . Black venom dripped from it.

"Liar!" The monster's voice was ragged. "Where are the animals you took from me? Where's your bloody club?"

Corydon eyed him warily. "I used a club?" he asked.

"You know you did!" Geryon almost wept, and lashed his tail frenziedly again. Corydon leapt out of the way, but the huge, maddened creature came on.

Still trying to sound calm, he looked over his shoulder. "He thinks I'm Herakles," he told Sthenno, who was hovering nearby, ready to swoop in and lift him if the monster began to fight.

Sthenno gave a startled, birdlike laugh. Euryale, too, grinned. "Dear mormo," she said, "anything less like Herakles . . . The poor creature has hurt his eyes."

"I did not!" Geryon raged. "It was you—him—it was the one who took my red cattle! He made me sightless! You made me sightless. But I shall hunt you by smell. . . ."

To Corydon's surprise, Lady Nagaina was suddenly at his side.

"Stop making such a racket," she told Geryon sternly. "Really, my heads are simply splitting. If you can just be quiet, I may be able to help you see."

Geryon stood stock-still. "If you can do that," he said hoarsely, "I will worship you as my goddess for all eternity."

Lady Nagaina smiled. Everyone could see she thought this sounded pleasant.

"Come here," she said. "Kneel." The poor creature bumbled forward. Lady Nagaina took one of his heads between her hands and breathed into his eyes. A dark cloud formed around them, thick and gray and milky. Corydon wondered rather anxiously if she was really curing him or making him worse.

Suddenly Geryon gave a cry, not of pain but of triumph. Lifting his head suddenly, he grinned. And turned his head up and around and around.

In a whisper, he breathed, "I can see."

Lady Nagaina swiftly treated his other heads.

He knelt before her, kissing the ground. His hot tears smoked on the sand. Then he looked up at Corydon.

"I apologize most cravenly, votary of my goddess," he said. "I see now that you are not the one that harmed and robbed me. I took you for him, for Herakles. . . ."

Suddenly his faces changed. His mouths opened in great gaping grins. And he began to laugh soundlessly, sometimes slapping his legs. Finally he laughed so much that he lay down on the sand. He kept trying to speak, but laughter had conquered him completely. "You . . . you . . . Herakles. . . . Oh, by the gods. . . ."

Corydon grinned uneasily. He knew he was no Herakles. But somehow he didn't like the laughter. Especially when even the Snake-Girl gave a shy smile.

But she saw his discomfort. "Don't worry, Corydon," she said. "No one wants Herakles around."

Corydon felt a little better. Now the only worry was Gorgos. Where could he be? Should they rescue him?

He refused to think about the possibility that Gorgos was lost forever.

Sthenno and Euryale had been conferring about the same thing in their harsh birdlike voices, though Euryale had also been giving little gasps of laughter from time to time. Now they came forward. "We must find Gorgos," Sthenno said firmly. "This is an important time for him. I've seen it, in the stars. He will cross the gods again. Again and again. And it is so risky. We must help, we immortals. We will fly high and wide until we find him."

Corydon smiled. The Gorgons' loyalty was touching. For uncounted years, they had lived alone, solitary and eccentric. Now, suddenly, they were willing to go to any lengths for an impudent boy who had given them nothing but trouble. Neither Sthenno nor Euryale seemed to notice that they had changed, that the war with the gods had changed them. And in many ways, they hadn't: Sthenno still spouting prophecies, Euryale gnawing on a bone as she spoke. But they loved Gorgos. That made all the difference.

Geryon spoke in his hoarse, heavy voice. "Who is it that you have lost? I know what it is to lose. . . ." His voice trailed off. Tears began trickling down his cheeks again.

Corydon cleared his throat. "One of our company, Gorgos," he said. "The son of our friend Medusa, whom we all lost to the heroes."

"How old was he when his mother was slain?"

"He was only a baby, but through the miraculous power of Hera's milk, he has grown to manhood with godlike swiftness," Euryale explained.

132

"But," Sthenno added tartly, "his head has yet to catch up with his muscles."

Lady Nagaina yawned delicately. "You are wrong, you know," she said. "There is nothing wrong with Gorgos's head. He is not wise, but that does not make him stupid."

"He lacks experience," Sthenno said stubbornly. "He cannot think for himself."

"You mean he does not think like *you*," Lady Nagaina retorted. "Nor do I. It is not a defect. You all forget. Gorgos is a monster, like the rest of us. He finds his own way, so he needs no maps." As she spoke, she turned toward the endless blue sea. The sun had polished the waves to lapis lazuli and golden brightness. It made Lady Nagaina think of home. And so she started—they all started—when a deafening noise split the calm air. It came from out of the sea. At first, none of them could see what it was.

Then Corydon, straining his eyes, picked out something—two somethings—emerging from the sea. Two brown—what were they?

Two triton shells were making the trumpeting noise. They were joined by four others. The trumpet calls were earsplitting but joyful, triumphant.

Next the blowers of the shells emerged, small green aquatic men, their hair a tangle of dark purple-green, their bodies clad in seaweed. They were standing on the backs of dolphins, which were driving for the shore like arrows. Corydon saw that the dolphins were pulling something, something heavy that came slowly from the sea, as if the sea were reluctant to let it go. It was a mother-of-pearl chariot, which rose onto the waves and then skimmed over them like a skipped stone.

The top of the chariot sprang open. A head emerged.

"Greetings!" said Gorgos with an enormous grin.

In the tumult of joy that followed Gorgos's emergence from the sea, it took some time to work out what had actually happened to him. Corydon was just as glad and relieved as the others to see him. And yet somehow he couldn't quite stifle his qualms at the way he had appeared. Clad in the trappings of the gods! Dressed as—well, as . . .

As a hero.

Except that he was even brighter and more beautiful than any hero. Almost like a god.

What had happened to him?

Gradually, over a shared meal of grilled fish, and milk provided by Geryon, Gorgos poured out his tale. The monsters interrupted endlessly with questions. But the story was this, and Gorgos began it by saying that really it required a Homer to tell it well.

Corydon couldn't repress a shiver. Homer. The bard of heroes.

Gorgos had been on deck when the huge, malevolent wave overwhelmed the ship. As the ship pitched over, he and the hapless sailor were hurled into the sea. The sailor had immediately been swallowed up by another landslide of water, and though Gorgos searched, he had been unable to find the man. He was lost.

Corydon suddenly felt terribly cold. They had enchanted that man so casually, taking no thought for his life, his friends, his family. Now it was their fault he was dead. And none of them except Gorgos had even thought of rescuing him. They had just used their monster-strength to save themselves from the sea's fury.

He caught the Snake-Girl's eye and saw at once that she felt even worse about it. As always, when she felt miserable, she seemed to shrink, to coil up into herself.

While Gorgos was searching for the drowned sailor, he dived deeper and deeper into the raging seas. Being able to breathe in water, he had sought the relative calm of the depths rather than be tossed about on the surface. And as he went deeper and deeper, he began to see that the ocean in which he swam was utterly unlike the dear Middle Sea. The fishes spoke to him in strange accents. He asked them about the sailor and about the other monsters. But they did not reply, or not directly. "The king!" said one. "You must go."

"You must pay homage!" said another.

Gorgos had been indignant at first. "I do not pay homage," he had said. "Except to those who earn it. Who is your king?" But the fishes did not reply. So Gorgos asked one of them to lead him to the king.

Retelling the story, Gorgos grinned around at the monsters. "I thought the king would be a great shark who would tear me apart or with whom I could do deadly battle. That would have been great sport."

Corydon shook his head. Evidently, Gorgos's long dip in the sea had not cooled his head much. But Gorgos, unmoved by Corydon's disapproving glance, continued his story.

He had grasped the silvery tails of a pair of huge, great fish called cod, they said. Gorgos had never before seen fish to match them; they were like sea steeds. They swam fast, down and down, through green and ultramarine.

At last, Gorgos caught sight of what must be the palace of the sea king.

At first, he had thought it was all made of pearl. It gleamed livid white in the blue water. But as his fish guides drew him closer and closer, he saw that the palace was not *all* pearl but also shell and coral.

And the gleaming white walls were made from bones. The bones of drowned mariners.

The gateway was a row of skulls, their white jaws agape. The open door was encrusted with jewels taken from wrecked ships. The door itself was made from the timbers of wrecks.

It was a monument to the cruelty of the sea. Gorgos was repelled. But he was strangely excited, too; something about it drew him, almost against his will.

He swam up to the great gaping gate and passed through, unchallenged.

He found himself in a kind of castle courtyard, lined with neat rows of leg bones.

In front of him was a dais. And suddenly there was a man sitting on the throne on it. "Or at least," said Gorgos, "I *thought* it was a man."

"He looked amazing," he added, and then fell silent. Everyone waited for him to go on. But he seemed to have stopped for good. Finally, Euryale asked, "Who was he?"

Gorgos lifted his head and looked her straight in the eye. "He was my father," he said simply. "I have found him at last. My father."

Everyone gasped. Corydon felt a lurching sense of dismay. But the word "father" seemed to liberate Gorgos to go on with his story.

"Yes," he said. "My father is the sea. The sea god. Blue-Haired Poseidon, who rules the waves. And he is second in might only to Zeus among the Olympians."

The Snake-Girl asked shyly, wistfully, "What does he look like? Is his hair truly blue?"

"It has a bluish gleam," Gorgos said. "But his skin is black, black like ebony. And his lips are red, and his teeth are white, like the walls of his palace. He bears a trident made of gold, its haft jeweled with the blue gems of the sea. And he wears a crown of pearls, thick and heavy. None but he could bear it. He embraced me," he added, flushing with the memory, "and called me his true-born son. He said he had sent the storm to bring me to his realm."

Corydon's impatience had been growing. "And did he feel any concern for the mortal sailor who drowned in the storm?" he demanded. "Or for any of us caught in it?"

"No," said Gorgos simply, "he did not mention those things. He asked only that I accept my role as his son. And he said I could serve him in Atlantis. For it is he who rules it. Athene took violet-crowned Athens, he said, but Atlantis and all its cities are his. And he told me what I must do."

"And what is that?" Corydon asked, his mouth dry with apprehension.

"There is a war." Gorgos instinctively put his hand to his side to feel the hilt of his sword. "A civil war. The Atlanteans are fighting one another. I must find the side true to my father, and with my help, they will conquer. My father said that I am to be the greatest warrior Atlantis has ever seen."

"I see it!" Sthenno understood at last. "The Minotaur! He must be part of the war somehow. They must have taken him—"

"—because he can make war machines!" Euryale finished the sentence. "Perhaps they heard about those we used against the heroes."

Lady Nagaina spoke pettishly. "If that is so, why did they not take me?"

"I can think of many, many reasons . . . ," Corydon whispered to the Snake-Girl.

Gorgos shrugged. "I know only what he told me."

There was an awkward pause. Then the Snake-Girl spoke again. "But how are we supposed to get to Atlantis?" she asked. "We have no ship now."

"I can help you," said Geryon proudly. "There are trees. I have tools."

"That would take a very long time," said Gorgos. "My father said that he would provide. Fear not. He will. He is true."

Again, Corydon felt a prickle of unease. Such enthusiasm for an Olympian was terrible. Corydon felt his usual resources of tact and patience slipping away. Bluntly he asked, "Gorgos! How can you be so blind? Don't forget that it was the Olympians who were responsible for your mother's murder!" To his surprise, his words did not seem to make Gorgos angry. His friend moved toward him and patted him on the shoulder.

"I know," he said. "I know. That's what you always said and what you taught me. But it isn't true. My mother was killed by one man, one renegade hero. The Olympians regretted her death. My father most of all. He loved her."

"He had a funny way of showing it!" Euryale burst in. "He left her to be punished and to suffer, and not even once did he seek her out."

Gorgos looked uncertain. "Perhaps he was busy . . . ," he began, but caught Euryale's blazing bronze eyes. "In truth," he admitted, "I do not know. I know little of what drives a god. But he is my father. If my mother deserves my loyalty, does he not also have a claim?"

138

Sthenno spoke sternly, sharply, her head well forward. "Your mother carried you and bore you in pain and fed you and risked her life to save you and loved you. When has your father done even one of those things for you?"

Gorgos spoke angrily now. "He did not look after me as a mewling infant, for that is proper work for women! But he cares for me now. . . . You saw the gifts, the way he honored me!"

"I see that it is better not to talk of it," Euryale said. "However it is for you, I will not entrust myself to the goodwill of an Olympian. They have always sought our destruction. From time out of mind."

Gorgos rushed across the beach and took Euryale's claw in his hands. "I swear," he said, "that my father means no ill toward you. If you hate him for being a god, how does that differ from his hating you because you are a Gorgon?"

"I do not hate your father," said Euryale gently. "I do not trust him, though. We will find our own way to Atlantis. We will make a raft."

"But you must still cross his realm!" Gorgos cried angrily. "This is such folly. He can destroy us whenever he chooses."

"Maybe," Sthenno said softly. "Maybe he can. But we will not choose to trust him. We will instead choose to hope, and to trust in our own strength." Turning, she moved off, up the beach. Geryon and Euryale followed. The Snake-Girl extended a hand awkwardly, then flinched when Gorgos backed away. She, too, glided off, up the warm sands. Only Corydon was left.

"Gorgos." Corydon had been flooded with the memory of meeting his own father, Pan, for the first time. He recalled his passionate love, his longing to please this father he had never seen. . . . Had he, Corydon, asked, even once, "Where were you, Father, when my village was driving me out?" No, he, too, had been so delighted to be acknowledged that anger and prudence had evaporated. "I understand," he said at last. "It happened to me, too. It is not easy to be the son of a god. And the greater the god, the greater the burden, my friend." At last, Gorgos smiled at him. They embraced awkwardly, like brothers reunited after a long voyage. But Corydon couldn't still his fears. They couldn't trust Poseidon, of that he was certain. Could they trust his son?

As he was thinking this, Gorgos seized his hand. With a shock like being hit by a cold wave, Corydon saw that there was something different about Gorgos. His sixth finger was missing, the one that had always marked him as monstrous. Checking, Corydon looked at his other hand, the shield hand. Relief! It was still the same. All his instincts told him not to ask about the change. But it frightened him.

TWELVE

Again, Corydon's fears tipped him into night-mares. This time, he found himself beside the god of the Realm of the Many, Hades, the Black King. But Hades did not show him pictures as the others had. He spoke, and spoke very plainly.

"Panfoot," he said. His voice was still the coldest Corydon had ever heard, though it no longer ached with pain. "Panfoot. Beware. You may ask of me three questions. First I will tell you what is needful. Zeus intends to rule Atlantis. He wishes to give it to his daughter Athene as her dowry, to bring it fully into the Greek world. If he gains control of its wealth and power, he will use them to make a race of heroes that will destroy all that is different from them—all monsters, all beings unlike themselves." Suddenly Corydon remembered what one of the tamarins had said. "The gods kill us when they are angry. Ares is always angry." Zeus's ambition seemed equally impossible to explain.

"Why?" he asked. Hades smiled a thin smile like a waning moon.

"Because he wants to make all things like himself," he said. "Thus he is greater."

"How can I stop him?"

"You cannot stop him by joining his foes," said Hades, his complex smile appearing again. "Zeus is using them and their inventions. He hopes to absorb their power into his own. He fosters war in Atlantis. I am not entirely sure why. Perhaps because it makes heroes. It makes hatreds. He loves the games of blood, too, and they also make for heroes. Poseidon is but his tool, carving Atlantis to his design."

"How then? How can I stop him?"

"You must learn from Poseidon himself. And you must learn from the Morge and from the Selene. They are my people. Or they should be."

Corydon longed to ask who the Morge and the Selene were. But he knew Hades would vanish if he asked more than three questions. He waited. But Hades said just one thing more.

"Many things in Atlantis are deceits," he said. "You must hold to your own true self. That has always been your gift. Now it has been twice tested. Know yourself, Panfoot. Know yourself."

"But"—Corydon made himself say the word—"what of Vreckan?"

Hades was silent. But somehow the quality of his silence changed, became hard and bleak. It was abruptly the silence of death.

Corydon woke. He felt as if he knew less rather than more. And what was happening to the Minotaur? Now that he was sure the dreams he was having were true seeings, he was increasingly worried about the priest with the slender knife. He felt a desperate wish to hurry. But he knew the raft must come first.

*　*　*

Days of hard work followed as the raft was slowly hewn from the stubborn, hard wood of Geryon's forests. Geryon himself seemed eager to help, in a clumsy manner. He and Sthenno and Euryale were fast friends now. One night, as they were all sitting around Geryon's roaring fire, Corydon noticed the three heads close to the Gorgons' and thought he could trace a strange likeness between all five faces. He spoke of what he saw.

Sthenno was casual. "Yes," she said, "he is indeed our brother. Like us, he is sired by Typhon, and his mother was Echidna. Our mother had thousands of young, but we are all of us among them. So, too, was Orthrus, the dog that the hero slew."

It did not seem to make any difference to the Gorgons that now they had a brother. As Sthenno said, her mother had begotten so many young. But there was a calmness, a happy peace about the time on Geryon's island that reminded Corydon insidiously of his home. He missed his own land.

The Snake-Girl seemed to feel the same. Like him, she was not as strong as the larger monsters or Gorgos, so they spent time together, making needles out of the bones of fish, then making ropes and sails. Gorgos suggested once that they might acknowledge his father's bounty in providing the fish bones, but the Snake-Girl surprised him by spitting very deliberately into the sand. He went away angry. Corydon grinned.

One day, as they worked on the big square mainsail—it was nearly ready—Geryon ambled over to them. Gratefully, he plunged into the cool shade under their tree. "Ouf!" he said in his guttural voice. "It will be cooler for you in Atlantis, my friends."

To Corydon, it seemed cool here compared with home. "Is Atlantis very cold?" he asked apprehensively.

"So cold it snows even down by the sea," Geryon replied. "But only in winter. Summer is wonderful. The shade is cool, cool as the sea, though the sun shines."

"How can we know Atlantis?" Corydon asked. This had been on his mind.

"It is a City of towers and water," Geryon explained. "Towers as tall as mountains. The City is built on thick, hard rock. The towers are strong because they have their roots in that rock."

"How many towers are there?" Corydon asked.

"Beyond counting," Geryon replied.

The Snake-Girl stopped crooning to a small bird she had spied in a tree and looked up. Corydon, too, felt dismayed. "But how, then, will we find our friend?"

"You must ask the Selene. They will help you," Geryon said in a rumbling voice.

"Why will they?"

Geryon sighed. "In Atlantis, many serve Poseidon, but the Selene are allied to the goddesses."

"All right," Corydon said. "Where will we find them?"

"I do not know."

Now the Snake-Girl asked, "How far from here is Atlantis? How many days' sailing?"

"Let's see." The monster began drawing in the sand. The Snake-Girl and Corydon bent forward. "It is two weeks to Atlantis. You will see the lighthouse as you approach the Last Island. Like a red star, low on the sea. Sail for it. Then you cannot lose your way on the ocean's currents."

"How do we find the Last Island?" Corydon asked.

"The moon's path will lead you there," Geryon said. "Follow her track on the sea, keeping the shape of Callisto on your left."

The Snake-Girl began crooning to the bird again. Now it sat on her finger. Its bright dark eyes stared into hers. She stroked its warm red back, then broke its neck with a quick twist and began nibbling on one of the wings. Then she gave a cry of horror.

Corydon knew what to do: he put an arm clumsily round her shoulders while she cried and called softly, whispering, "Birdie" over and over again. Together, they dug it a small grave. By now, Geryon had begun crying, too. "Alas!" he cried, and beat his breasts. "Alas! My dog! Your birdie. . . . We are ill-fated, my friends. Finish, good lady; the bright day is done. And we are for the dark." Corydon tried to please the grieving monsters by making up a short song for the dead bird; he did in truth feel sad for it, and sadder for the Snake-Girl, who devoured what she most longed to keep. Part snake, part girl, she was as he was himself, neither one thing nor another, and sometimes a monster to herself as well as to others.

She liked his song and leaned against him softly. A snake slid down his arm, released from her eyes as she cried. He was reminded of Medusa and felt more cheerful. Anyway, he thought, Atlantis will be an adventure. And if it kills us, we shall die having seen a great wonder.

He held on to that thought as they said tearful farewells to Geryon, boarded the rocking, makeshift raft, and hoisted the sail. He held on to it through all Gorgos's complaints about their folly and about his father's wrath. He held it until, one morning, the wonder he had sought suddenly materialized ahead of them. Or if not the wonder, the bow that sped them to it.

He saw the light of the Last Island.

At first, it was only a pinprick of light, so tiny it was just a small,

145

angry star. But he knew it was made by men. As they drew nearer and nearer to it, carried by wind and wave as accurately as if they had charted a course, he saw that the light came from a tower, a tower taller than the giant Talos, lit by a fire at its tip as red as that giant's deadly eyes. The tower was tiered, and as they drew closer still, he could see many small windows in the surface of it; he almost felt it was watching him. It was so very tall that it frightened him. In front of the tower was a sheer cliff, but he could see a small artificial harbor to its right, and he began rowing awkwardly for it, helped reluctantly by Gorgos. The red glare of the tower lit the night. As Corydon looked up at it, even his monster-eyes dazzled and amazed by its hot glow, Gorgos gave a shout.

"Look!" he cried. "My father is watching us from that tower!"

Straining his eyes, Corydon could see that it was true. Above the light stood a bronze statue; it looked tiny from the ground but would be perhaps twenty feet tall if one were next to it. At once, he felt doubly spied upon.

Euryale was examining the tower eagerly, almost greedily, fascinated by its height, by the smoothness of the stone. It was she who noticed the carved frieze around its base, a frieze so lifelike that it appeared that its figures had been frozen by Medusa's stare and would return to life at any moment. The central figure was Poseidon again, painted blue and gold. In his hand, he held an immense trident, and that had been enameled in gold and gems so that it shone in the light of the fire.

"My father's trident," breathed Gorgos. His voice was full of love.

They dropped the raft's crude anchor and splashed through the shallows of the harbor.

As they came close to shore, they became aware that people

on the wharves were staring at them. Corydon suddenly saw how they must look. One honest fisherman's mouth fell open as Lady Nagaina unfurled all five of her heads and looked about her. Others began shouting and running toward the grubby little village port that clung to the shore. They were plainly going to fetch weapons.

"Oh dear," said the Snake-Girl. Without asking, Corydon knew she hated the thought of fighting these simple people just because they were simple.

Gorgos decided to resolve matters. He strode forward through the shallows. "Good people!" he shouted. The villagers waited, openmouthed. "I am the living son of the god Poseidon!" Gasps, then someone shouted, "Blasphemy!" Gorgos cut him off with a wide gesture. "And I can prove it!" he yelled. Without taking a breath, he sank under the water. Corydon saw him swimming toward the shore, then, without surfacing, he swam back to the monsters. The fishermen and their wives muttered among themselves. Gorgos shouted, under the water, "I can perform any swimming feat you care to ask for!"

After much muttering, the leading fisherman stepped forward. "Are these people your friends?" he asked. Corydon noticed that he didn't speak the same way as they did, nor the way the heroes had; it was still Greek, but the words sounded different, alien.

Gorgos raised his head above the water. He was not at all out of breath, and the villagers noticed; they began murmuring again. "Kouros!" shouted one. "He is indeed huios, kouros of Poseidon!"

At this, all the villagers flung themselves on their faces. Gorgos flushed and bowed graciously. Corydon muttered, "Gorgos, would you mind asking if we can come ashore? I'm getting sopped." Gorgos looked at him reproachfully but put the request in a lordly manner. They were welcomed with bowing and scraping and with gifts, necklaces of what looked horribly like teeth, a raw fish ("Yuck!" said the Snake-Girl rudely, and handed it hastily to the ever-hungry Euryale), and a piece of what looked like one of Sthenno's parchments. Corydon examined it closely, with Sthenno bending forward to see; neither of them could make head or tail of it, so Corydon folded it carefully inside his tunic.

The villagers ran about plying them with food and drink. All of it was both strange and poor-quality, and Lady Nagaina could be heard complaining loudly. "Don't you have any caviar?" she asked. "I thought this was supposed to be an Atlantean colony."

"No caviar," said the stocky village headman. "All ships gone in war. Big war, big fight. No caviar." He sounded apologetic, and he looked anxiously at Gorgos.

"War?" Corydon asked quickly. He hoped to learn more about this war by pretending a stranger's ignorance.

The headman looked surprised. "*The* war. Many years now war. Big ships come, oh, big ships come, all from over there"—he pointed to the harbor mouth—"like you."

"But who is doing the fighting?" Corydon and Gorgos asked together.

"There is the Dolphins, and there is the Shells," said the headman. Corydon blinked. What was he talking about?

"What are they?"

"Two sides. One in the city, one in the country. The Dolphins are moving; the Shells, they stay still. They do not like each other. Dolphins want Poseidon, Shells want Athene. Dolphins roam, Shells always stay still, see? They are all angry at each other. Many long years now fighting. But then Shells have new friends come.

Many new friends who help them. So Dolphins get new friends, too, and now they all fight more and more and more. Many are gone dead."

Corydon nodded. It made sense. "The Minotaur," he hissed. "It is as we thought. They are using him to make weapons for the war. But for which ..." Slowly, carefully, he began to ask, "Have you ever seen—" but before he could finish, Gorgos broke in.

"You are Dolphins, of course," he said. "I can tell from your loyalty to my father."

The villagers all shuffled their feet, and Corydon noticed an oddity. There had been women about earlier, but now only the men were left. A man who hadn't spoken so far cleared his throat.

"We love the God of the Sea," he said carefully, "but we are not Dolphins. We are not Shells. Our women love Athene. We try to keep the peace."

Gorgos frowned. "Do you not fear my father's wrath?" he said. They stood silent. His eyes narrowed. "Do you not fear my wrath?" he added in a new, softer tone. Corydon was suddenly and horribly reminded of Perseus.

The villagers flinched. "We do fear," they said. "But we also fear the Gray-Eyed Lady's wrath. We know what she can do when she is angry."

Gorgos thought briefly of his mother and was silenced.

In the pause, Corydon felt the full weight of what lay ahead. Civil war! Poseidon's message had been self-serving, might have been false, but these simple people were truth tellers. War, more war.

Falling back on his mission, he asked about the Minotaur again. "Have you ever seen a creature with a bull's head and a man's body?" he said.

He had thought they were silent before. Now he could have heard a mouse's footfall. They looked at him, one glitter of angry eyes.

One of them spoke. "You should not ask, stranger." His face closed like a door.

"But he is our friend," Euryale said. She stepped into the light, and the villagers drew back at once. As they looked up at her ten feet of bronze body, her long claws, their faces showed their dread. Euryale felt hot and ashamed.

"Oh, for the sake of all the gods!" Lady Nagaina stepped farther into the light in her turn. Idly, with one of her long, whiplike tails, she seized a villager, who at once began howling. She brought the young man around to face her and stared at him with all of her eyes. "Now," she said, "tell us. Tell us about our friend."

The man's mouth made a little noise that sounded like a chicken clucking.

Lady Nagaina opened one of her mouths and extended a forked tongue. "Come along," she said. "I'm getting hungry."

The man babbled hastily, "Dolphins took him, that big creature with bull head. Yes, Dolphins took that one. Last week, maybe. Or next week."

"You'd better be telling the truth," said Lady Nagaina. Casually, she jounced the man up and down a few times. "And call me Your Ladyship," she added thoughtfully. The man looked as if he might faint but managed to gasp out, "It is truth, Lady Ship."

"Not 'Lady Ship,'" said the Hydra irritably. "'Ladyship.' One word."

"Enough," said Sthenno abruptly. "All we can do now is sail for Atlantis and hope." The villagers breathed a sigh of relief.

"We will need supplies," said Corydon sensibly. The villagers were so pleased to see them go that they began scurrying to and fro, bringing out food in barrels and crates. Corydon could see that most of it was preserved fish. He asked for some olive oil to be added.

The villagers did not understand. Corydon said it again, several times.

At last, Corydon understood. He looked around. There were no olive trees in sight. He felt a pang of fright. How could that be? And how could any of them live without olive oil?

He asked for wine instead. The villagers shrugged again. He tried drawing a picture of grapes. Haltingly, the villagers explained that these were only for rich men who could bring them in by ship. Instead, they gave him a crude pottery mug full of some other drink; it was brown and bubbly and, to Corydon, it tasted worse than a satyr's armpit. He spat it on the ground.

"Water," he said firmly.

The raft was soon laden with barrels and boxes, though after the thick brown drink, Corydon wondered if any of it would be of any use. It was clear that Atlantis was not only hostile but *different* from anywhere they had ever known. How could they manage?

THIRTEEN

As they embarked, one villager stepped forward to the end of the pier and began what was plainly a song of farewell. At first, Corydon listened because he was intrigued by the song: it was off-key, wailing, unlike an island lament. Then he realized abruptly that the song was more than just obscure poetry. It was asking Poseidon to bless their voyage in the name of his twelve sons, the twelve sons who had founded Atlantis and made up its tribes.

"Oh, that old tune," said Lady Nagaina. All of her mouths yawned, and she lay down in a scaly heap on the tilting deck.

Corydon felt sure the parchment the villagers had given them would help them to understand what was happening in Atlantis. He took it from his tunic and handed it to Sthenno.

Keeping her balance by spreading her wings, so that they acted as a kind of jib sail, Sthenno carefully stroked the parchment. Corydon had been unable to decipher it, but Sthenno could see that its language was very like that which had been inscribed on the Staff of Hades. She wished she had the Staff now. She began to try to work it out letter by letter, whistling words under her breath, going to and fro, correcting, checking. . . .

"Sthenno, can you see?" The Snake-Girl's soft, hissing voice punctured her reverie. Sthenno suddenly realized that the sun had set and the moon was up.

"I think I have most of it," she said, anxiously scanning the parchment again. "That spiral should be some kind of omicron, and that thing that looks like a palace dome may be some kind of early form of kappa. . . . Fascinating. . . ." Her voice trailed off, and she bent once more over the parchment.

"But, Sthenno," said Euryale impatiently, "what does it SAY?"

Sthenno looked up, surprised. "Um, I think it says 'and.' "

Corydon groaned. "You mean you've only just worked out the first word???"

Sthenno smiled brightly. "Yes, mormoluke. But that is half the battle. Now I shall go much faster."

"Let's hope so," muttered Euryale, picking at a seagull's wing with bronze claws. "Otherwise, we'll be in Atlantis before we find out what's going on there."

Corydon noticed that Euryale, too, thought the parchment was important. He was pleased. Now, if only Sthenno could make out what it said. . . .

As Sthenno murmured to herself, Lady Nagaina opened one blue eye. "Oh, give it to me," she said sleepily. "I can read it. It's easy."

Sthenno made a nervous, birdlike gesture, clutching the parchment tightly. The Hydra uncoiled, and all five of her heads reared up. "I can read it," they all said together.

"I'm sure I can read it, too," said Sthenno anxiously. "I just need a little longer. . . ."

Gently but firmly, Corydon took the parchment and handed it to Lady Nagaina. He wasn't sure the Hydra could decipher it, but she had often known surprising things about Atlantis. . . . He patted Sthenno's claw reassuringly. Lady Nagaina began examining the parchment.

"A casualties list . . . captures . . . report of a major battle between the Dolphins' western forces and a Shell party of auxiliaries. . . . Oh, look!" Her voice rose in a squeak of excitement. "Spring fashions! Taupe replaces caramel. . . ."

Corydon was bewildered, as were all the monsters. Taupe? Caramel? What was the Hydra talking about?

"I really must order some new things as soon as we land," said Lady Nagaina decisively. "I'm not fit to be seen. . . ."

Gorgos interrupted her reverie. "Excuse me," he said, "but did you say something about a war?"

"War, war, war! I'm so bored with the war I could scream," said Lady Nagaina simply. "But I suppose you boys are longing to know more. Sillies. Well, this *is* a newssheet." She tried to sweeten her tone, and everyone felt ruffled, as if they were children being lectured by a none-too-kindly teacher. They had no idea what she was talking about, which made it worse. Brandishing the parchment, Lady Nagaina continued, "And a newssheet tells you what is happening. All about important things. Restaurants. Theaters. Clothes, of course. Shoe sales. What celebrities are doing." Her voice was growing dreamier and dreamier. The monsters began to feel as if she were hypnotizing them. Corydon felt his head swimming. He didn't understand a single word she had said.

"Is a restaurant useful in war?" asked Sthenno, trying to make some sense of it all.

Lady Nagaina looked exasperated. "Of COURSE not," she snapped, shaking her heads in dismay. "A restaurant is a place where you eat."

Euryale brightened up. "What can you eat in it?"

"It depends on the chef," said Lady Nagaina in a superior tone. "I once went to one where you could have snail porridge, meringue cooked in dry ice, bacon-and-egg ice cream. . . ." Her tongues came out and licked her lips.

Euryale looked baffled. It sounded utterly horrible. "Any meat?" she asked.

"Oh yes," said Lady Nagaina. "Some." Euryale subsided.

Gorgos was fingering his sword impatiently. "But what does all this have to do with the WAR?"

"Nothing," said Lady Nagaina sulkily. Gorgos looked as if he might explode. "Then . . . why are you telling us so much about it?"

"Well, it's so much more interesting," the Hydra explained.

"Not to me!" And Gorgos sat down angrily with his back to the Hydra.

"Well, if you are going to be so very rude and difficult . . ." Lady Nagaina left the sentence unfinished. She began slowly lowering her heads, one by one, into the coils of her body, with an air of affronted dignity.

Suddenly Corydon saw that she really *was* hurt. She had probably been homesick for years, homesick for a life he barely understood, a life wildly different from her life on the Island of Monsters. He understood her because he himself missed the island so badly, and the lonely hillside, his sheep, his songs that came only in that deep silence. "Taupe," "caramel"—the words sounded soft, seductive, exotic. . . . He didn't know what they meant, but he could hear that just saying those words made Lady Nagaina feel as he felt when he called his sheep and goats by their names. In her own way, she was trying to share her wonder with them, and they were failing her.

"Don't go," he said softly. "I want to hear about the spring fashions. What is taupe?"

Slowly Lady Nagaina uncoiled again. Now Corydon could see that she was trying to mask her eagerness, fearing more rejection. "Well," she said patronizingly, but hopefully, too, "it's a very light, soft brown. Dull. Like sand. But caramel has a golden element. . . ."

Corydon only had to listen to Lady Nagaina reading about Atlantean fashions for another five hours before she finally exhausted that part of the parchment and was ready to read about the war.

"The Dolphins are winning," she said. Gorgos was delighted and immediately began a long, heartfelt series of fulsome thanksgivings to his father. Corydon tried not to let his rage rise. "This newssheet is a Dolphin sheet, though, so it may be exaggerating."

"Do you mean lying?" asked Sthenno.

"No," said Lady Nagaina, who was now feeling so happy that no one could annoy her. Five hours of fashion talk had burnished all her scales with brilliant golds and greens of joy. "Exaggerating. Like Perseus. Remember how he said we had lots of treasure? To make people fight? Like that."

"Where is the war?" asked Corydon.

"Mainly in the west," said Lady Nagaina. "Especially on the plains of Brauron." She was scanning the newssheet again, all of her heads bobbing. Suddenly one of them stiffened.

"No," she murmured, and Corydon saw her look almost afraid. "No. Not Vreckan. No. They mustn't." Vreckan! Again. Corydon opened his mouth to ask what was happening, but the Hydra silenced him by crying out anew. "Look! There's something about the Minotaur here," she said, and all of them craned forward to see. "Apparently, he's been making weapons for the Dolphins to help them. . . . That's the reason for their success. . . . But now he's refusing to do any more. . . ." Her many eyes scanned the thick, wiggly print. "Soooo . . . they've imprisoned him . . . on the Pharos Island. What a coincidence! That's the Last Island, where we just were!"

The other monsters were silent, horrified. So the villagers *had* seen him—and they had missed him! "Let's turn around," said Corydon at once. "Come on."

Euryale, Gorgos, and Lady Nagaina all felt pangs of utter despair—to turn back so close, so close to Atlantis!—but none of them voiced their feelings. Everyone could see that Corydon was right. The first, the main thing was to help the Minotaur. So all the monsters helped with oars, turning the clumsy raft. They had to proceed by tacking; the wind, which had served them well, was now against them.

As they sailed back eastward, the seas began to change. The waves grew stronger. The little raft dipped and swayed. Corydon held stubbornly to the course he had set. He was so busy with wind measurements and horizon lines that the great gray wave was towering above the raft before he looked up and saw it.

This wave was not ordinary. It was leagues high, and it had a face—the face of a giant. No, not a giant. A god. Poseidon himself.

Gorgos prostrated himself. Poseidon's lips moved, but Corydon couldn't hear his words. Gorgos could. In a low, submissive voice, he said, "Yes, Father." He sounded both reluctant and exultant.

He turned to the monsters. "We have to go back," he said. "He won't let us return to Pharos. We have to go to Atlantis."

"What about the Minotaur?" shouted Sthenno.

Gorgos turned to the terrible eminence of the sea. "He says he will make sure he is safe. He says the Minotaur, too, is his and that he has served him till now. He will not let anyone hurt him. But we must go on."

Corydon was furious, but he could also see that any attempt to reach the island was doomed. Poseidon would simply swamp the raft and pick those he wanted to save—probably only Gorgos—from the sea wrack. The rest he would crush beneath an avalanche of water.

"Find out what he wants of us," he yelled. A plan was forming in his mind; it seemed to come from the cunning of his old kleptis-self.

Gorgos spoke again, his face alight with pleasure. "To help the Dolphins win, of course!" he yelled back. "But—oh, Corydon—he says that his own powers are weakened. We must restore him, and then he can act. . . . And he says we must seek for the deepest place, Cittavecchia, where a . . . bull is held captive. . . . And that we must play and win at the greatest game, called katabathos. . . . And that we must also fight in the last great battle, for so it is written."

Corydon's head thrummed with all the unfamiliar names and words.

"Does he say *how* we must restore him?" Sthenno asked. She was staring up curiously at the tall wave, still and yet instilled with the might of the sea. "He looks in good shape, actually."

Gorgos spoke, and the wave answered. "He says it is his might on land that is diminished. He is as strong as ever in the sea, but he has lost almost all power out of it. He has lost his Bull-son, his link with the land. The Shells have him penned somewhere. The Bull is growing angry. They do not know how to harness his powers. If he becomes truly angry, there will be great woe for all."

"Oh!" Gorgos suddenly understood. "The Bull is another son of Poseidon and the father of the Minotaur. That is why the Minotaur has been helping: he hopes to free his own father."

Corydon saw that his moment had come. He could see, too, that the Sea God really did need them. All right.

"Tell him," he said, "that we will do all he asks. We will free his Bull, his son. But on one condition."

Gorgos began to argue that one did not give conditions to a god. Corydon simply repeated his statement, louder.

"When we have freed the Bull, then he must bring us the Minotaur. On Atlantis. If you will not make this bargain, then we shall set sail for the Pharos Island, free him, and then return to our own lands and serve him no more."

Looking up at the wave, Corydon saw that Poseidon had understood him perfectly. The expression on the sea's face did not change, but he saw the foamy lips move, saw the spume-white brows draw together. And the huge, sea-dark eyes, two holes in a wave, looked toward him.

Corydon had seen the gods before; he was himself the son of a god. But he was eye to eye with an Olympian, one who was very angry. He felt a cold chill run down his spine that had nothing to do with the clouds overhead. But he straightened his back. Suddenly he remembered confronting a farmer once, a man who was sure that he, Corydon, had stolen one of his lambs. He had managed to bluff then, managed to deflect the man's rage, by keeping his back straight and looking innocent. What were the gods but angry farmers of the whole earth, after all?

"Yes, Great One," he said, looking straight into the huge, dark holes of the god's eyes. "Give us our friend, and you will find we can be your friends."

Then the gray-white lips moved, and to his surprise, Corydon could hear Poseidon's voice, but not with his ears—the voice sounded inside his head.

"Son of Pan," said Poseidon, "I know you. I know what you did in the Realm of the Many. I know what you did for my brother Hades. You have a power. It comes from your destiny. You can save my realm, too. But you must act soon, before the moon has waned to dark twice more."

Corydon was hard-pressed not to feel warm waves of relief, not to feel flattered. But he clung to what he knew of himself.

"Great Lord," he said humbly, "I am but the companion of your son, who I am sure will win more renown for you."

"Not all has yet been spun upon the distaff of your fate, mormoluke," said Poseidon. The words sounded ominous rather than promising.

"I know," said Corydon firmly. Actually, he had no idea what the god meant. And just now, he had no wish to know. He just wanted to find the Minotaur and go home.

"You do not know quite as much as you pretend, little one," said the thunderous voice of the Wave God. "You are my favorite son's chosen companion, and you are of importance to him. He is my son, mormoluke. You cannot deny it. Nor can he. And, as my son, he will be a great hero. Perhaps the greatest. You can help or hinder. It matters little. In the end, it will be the same."

Corydon's voice was shrill. "If it makes no difference what I do," he shouted defiantly, "why are you bothering to talk to me at all?"

The god was suddenly silent. Even the roar of wind and wave seemed hushed. Corydon could see that he had scored. He pressed his advantage.

"Give us back our friend," he said, "and we will do all you ask."

The wave gave an angry roar. White foam appeared on its crest, as if it were about to break and swamp the raft. Corydon could see long spume fingers forming on that dreadful crest. The Wave God longed to clutch him and pull him under. The Snake-Girl drew back, horrified. But Corydon stood firm.

"Do we have a bargain?" he shouted.

And the wave replied, as if the words were torn from it. "We have a bargain, mormoluke." With these words, it began to subside, to collapse into long, foamy billows. The god had gone.

And so the monsters turned their raft again and headed at their best speed for Atlantis.

FOURTEEN

They had been sailing westward for three days after seeing Poseidon when the Snake-Girl gave a cry. She pointed to something on the horizon. It didn't look low and green, like land. Rather, in the early dawn, it was pinkish brown, bumpy and lumped, shining in the sun with silvery light. It looked rather as though something thick and heavy were floating some way off.

"What's that?" Corydon asked.

"That's Atlantis," said the Snake-Girl. Corydon looked at her in surprise. He turned her face toward his and saw for the first time the fear deep in her eyes.

"How do you know?" he asked gently.

"I, too, lived here in my youth," she said. Corydon smiled; she still seemed young, though, as monsters can be, she was far older than she appeared. "I was at the temple here," she added. "Oh, Corydon, I am so afraid. Of them. . . ."

"Who? Why?" he asked.

"They—people—didn't like me," she whispered. "They didn't

know I was—like this. But they didn't like me. The god never favored me. He never gifted me with his secret knowledges."

Corydon was puzzled again. What god? And who could dislike the Snake-Girl? She was the kindest and most inoffensive of them all.

"Why didn't they like you?" he asked.

"I was different from them," she whispered. "Not like Lady Nagaina. She wasn't called that then, Corydon. She wasn't yet a Hydra. Everyone wanted to be her friend. She made the others do things to me. Put things in my bed, in my clothes. Then I'd get angry and put snakes in their beds—that part was fun."

"You were here with Lady Nagaina?" Corydon was dumbfounded. Why had neither of them mentioned it before? The Snake-Girl read his thoughts.

"She didn't recognize me at first. I wasn't important enough for her to notice much. Then she did know me, when we all went to the stronghold, but she still wasn't very interested. She's like that. And she's Atlantean; I only went to the temple there. She's from the most powerful family in Atlantis, Corydon. One of her ancestors was the eldest of the twelve sons of Poseidon."

"Wait," said Corydon. "Are you saying that Lady Nagaina is descended from Poseidon, too?"

"Yes," said the Snake-Girl simply. "Her real name is Amphitryte Murax. She comes from the Murax family."

"How did she—"

"—come to be a Hydra? I don't know," said the Snake-Girl. "And I think it might be unwise to ask her."

Corydon agreed.

The pinkish lump that was Atlantis was getting larger as a

freshening breeze filled the sail. It looked unnatural, and as they drew nearer, he realized it was far bigger than he had supposed. For the first time, he wondered how the Atlanteans might react to a goat-footed boy, two ten-foot-tall Gorgons with bronze wings, a Snake-Girl, and a five-headed Hydra—and a many-fingered boy with greenish black skin. . . . Somehow, he felt that Gorgos demonstrating that Poseidon was his father would not be enough to protect them this time. His mind was suddenly filled with pictures of people throwing stones. Would it be possible to land unnoticed?

The Snake-Girl spoke urgently, as if reading his thoughts. "Corydon," she said, "we will have to use magic to disguise ourselves, to beglamour the people. They will not . . . warm . . . to Sthenno and Euryale as they are. Nor to Lady Nagaina. Nor to any of us."

"How?" Corydon asked. He felt an idiot for not thinking about this obvious problem sooner.

"I can do it," said the Snake-Girl confidently.

Corydon was surprised. Somehow he had come to think of her as weak, in need of protection. But the nearer they got to that pinkish lump of—why, it was a kind of . . . palace—the bolder she seemed. It was as if she drew strength from her former fears of the place, as if the thought of her dreadful past there perversely made the present seem manageable.

"Do you need any . . . ingredients?" he asked humbly. She smiled at him, guessing his thoughts.

"I took what I needed on Pharos," she said. "I always thought we might need disguises."

All the monsters gathered around as she began unpacking a small bag, lifting out a large and beautiful shell, into which she poured a range of rich and sweet-smelling liquors from tiny bottles. A thick vapor began to rise, and she crooned to it softly.

"Sthenno, you first," she called. Softly she sang again. "Now," she said, "bend forward. Put your face in the vapor.'

"Seem what you must seem," she sang, the many *s*'s hissing. "Seem what you must seem."

As the Snake-Girl sang, Sthenno began to change. She grew smaller all over. Her skin paled from bronze to human color, pinkish brown. Her hair flopped from crisp metal to straggling gray curls.

There on the deck of the raft stood a thin, demure old lady in a brown mottled coat, like an eagle shrunk to a wren. The elderly woman held a strange square bag as if wondering where it had come from.

"Sthenno?" Corydon put out a hand. He could still feel her bronze brightness through the sheath of the soft, wrinkled hand illusion the Snake-Girl had spun.

"Sthenno!" It was almost a wail from Euryale. "Sthenno. Where are you? Sthenno?"

The old lady spoke. And her voice was Sthenno's. "I'm here, you silly things. Where did this bag come from?"

"It's part of how you look," the Snake-Girl explained. "This is the way people dress here. And you want to be inconspicuous. Ignored. Looking like this, you will be. Now Euryale."

Reluctantly Euryale leaned into the steam and emerged from it a plump old woman in a sensible brown woolly dress and battered felt hat. "You don't care how you look," the Snake-Girl explained. Next Corydon went in and came out a small, thin boy with a mop of brown hair. He, too, looked almost boring. His arms were as thin as twigs. But his legs—his Pan-leg was replaced by a boy leg, a human stalk. His new body felt stiff, like new clothes. He groaned. Then, with a flash of malice, he said, "Now you, Lady Nagaina."

But Lady Nagaina was surprisingly willing, even eager; she elbowed her way past Gorgos and stuck her faces into the smoking haze as if she were thirsty for it.

Corydon held his breath. The Hydra's many heads seemed to flow downward into her body, like a fountain being shut off. From the steam emerged a girl so palely beautiful that Corydon blinked. She was as slender as a spring birch. Her eyes were green gems that sent flashing lights to every corner of the raft. Her hair rippled down her back to her small waist. And she was wearing a gown that was the color of a newly opened summer lily, a white that was heartbreakingly close to gold.

She stretched. "It's good to seem like Fee Murax again," she said, and offered a smile of tender, new-moon joy.

Gorgos hastily shut his gaping mouth and moved forward into the steam.

But nothing happened to him.

He looked exactly the same.

The Snake-Girl shrugged. "I can't explain it," she said. "The magic knows its own ends."

"What about you?" said Gorgos. He was not at all dismayed to find himself just the same. How else could he possibly look?

The Snake-Girl sighed, then put her face into the steam.

When she emerged, she was utterly different. Her hair was now straight and black, and there was a thick streak of purple over one eye. Her face, always pale, was dead white, with bright red lips.

And she was wearing a black dress, a black coat, black leather boots. . . . It made her look sinuously thin. A narrow green scarf twined like a serpent around her neck.

The woman who was still Lady Nagaina sighed loudly. "For goodness' sake, Lamia!" she said. "That look is soooo over. Can't you look a little more modish?"

"No," said Lamia, the Snake-Girl. "Just as you can't look more inconspicuous, can you? The magic works on who we would be had we all been born here, lived here all our lives. It is made, too, from our dreams of ourselves, our nightmares of ourselves. This is me. Just as you are Fee Murax again."

Lady Nagaina—no, this slim woman was not Lady Nagaina. Had never been. She was Fee. Fee shook her head and then looked from side to side, an oddly furtive glance, as if she were missing her other heads. "Well," she observed dryly, "we look an unlikely group of bull tamers, I must say. Except Gorgos, of course. He looks like a bull boy. Actually . . ." She paused. "Gorgos," she said with sudden urgency. "Look, Lamia. What he's wearing. I didn't notice at first. . . . Look."

Gorgos had been wearing a light loincloth; he had taken off the armor of Poseidon on the voyage, keeping it in a careful bundle. Preoccupied with the fact that his appearance had not changed, none of them had noticed that the loincloth had been subtly transformed. It was now dark green and made of some oddly shiny material, thin and clinging tightly to Gorgos's hips and legs.

"Fee," said the Snake-Girl breathlessly, "it's a katabathos suit. See? The Dolphin sign—on the hip."

Well, now at least they knew what Gorgos would be doing, Corydon reflected.

While the Snake-Girl had worked her magic, the raft had been sailing closer and closer to Atlantis. It was now clear that what Corydon had taken for mountains were in fact buildings. The whole City was vast beyond any imagining. It soared upward in myriad towers like a mighty forest. To the left and right it stretched, almost farther than the eye could see, and its towers were beyond counting, threatening to pierce the tender blue sky above them. They were many-formed: the monsters saw square towers, triangles, round towers, towers that reached up like swords or spears. As the raft moved closer, everyone saw that they glittered: they were limned with something bright, as if they were covered in jewels. Between the towers grew bushy trees, green against the gray, lemon, and pink of the towers. Euryale snatched out the disc she had been carrying and scanned the picture on it. Now that she saw Atlantis itself, it was plain that even that picture fell far short of the reality. Surely only the gods could have built such a place.

"Does everyone in Atlantis live in a palace?" asked Euryale in wonder.

Fee answered absently, her eyes devouring the landscape before her. "No, few people live in the tall towers. You will see the houses of the people. . . . They cannot be seen from the shoreline. . . ."

"You mean there's more of it? More than we can see?" said Corydon, aghast. Fee and Lamia both smiled. "Much more," Fee explained. "This is just the edge. There is much more of the city and also much more of the country beyond it, the western plains, where the war is being fought. . . ."

As they approached the harbor, the sea became alive with other craft: a big sailing ship with *many* sails, not just one, and all of them white and also many small craft—little traders of various shapes, a ship with a sail that appeared to be made of thin pieces of wood, a small ship with a dragon sail, many rowing boats laden with goods. Some of their crews stared curiously at the ramshackle raft with its oddly assorted crew. So much for landing unnoticed. . . . Corydon's heart sank. Finally a man on a big ship hailed them.

"Are you all right?" he asked. "Been in a wreck?"

"That's right!" shouted Corydon at once. "About ten days ago."

"Need any help?"

"No, we're doing fine now!" shouted Corydon.

"Okay!"

"People seem friendly here," said Corydon, pleased. Lamia looked troubled. "Corydon, everyone," she said, "don't trust these people too much. They're not really friendly. Unless you're careful, they will try to trick you. Above all, don't tell them anything about why we're here. Remember they are at war."

"But," said Gorgos, "if they are at war, why have we not been challenged yet?"

"We will be," said Lamia grimly. And as she spoke, Corydon and Gorgos both saw the likely challenger. A swift, snakelike trireme was sliding across the harbor toward them.

All the monsters felt chills run down their spines. Heroes! The Athenians were here! Would their disguises hold?

"Of course," Corydon said, "the newspaper said the Dolphins were mainly in the west. And this must be the easternmost tip of the island. So it must be—"

"—held by the Shells," the Snake-Girl finished gloomily.

"But our disguises should hold," said Gorgos cheerfully. "They won't know we're not just outsiders."

"Except that you, my dear Gorgos, are dressed as a Dolphin athlete," said Fee. It was evident that her transformation had had no effect on her sharp tongue or her temper. Or, Corydon wondered, had she been that way before she was monstered?

"Oh. Yes," said Gorgos. "Perhaps I could put on my armor."

"Emblazoned with dolphins?" said Fee sweetly. "And with coral? Of course. Wearing that, no one will ever guess."

"Just put on a cloak, Gorgos," said Sthenno sensibly. "Here. Use one of the blankets." Euryale was still gazing at the towers, as if hypnotized. Sthenno reached for the blanket but had to make two grabs at it; she was ill at ease in her new, small body. She got it around Gorgos just as the trireme drew up beside them.

"Ahoy!" shouted a man on its deck. "Strangers, give your names and your errand to Atlantis."

Fee stepped forward. Eyeing the man imperiously, she spoke clearly and icily. "I am no stranger, little Greekling. I am Amphitryte Murax, a member of this island's most powerful family. Perhaps you may have heard of us?"

The man looked taken aback. He hesitated, then swallowed nervously. "Yes," he said. "I have indeed heard of your family, lady." Corydon had to repress a giggle; for a moment, he thought the man had been going to say Lady Nagaina. "But who are your companions?" he asked, looking doubtfully at the strangely assorted "monsters."

Fee waved her hand, embracing them all. "My servants, of course," she said. Corydon groaned inwardly. Lamia caught his eye and grinned. And Sthenno whispered, "Well, she's thought of us as her servants all along." But the man on the trireme remained grave. "And your . . . craft, lady? It is no vessel for a lady of the island."

"Indeed," Fee said, as haughtily as she could. "Had you the wit of an islander, you would realize that this craft was improvised after the ship carrying me on an exotic voyage was wrecked in a manner most untimely."

The man looked stern. "Then . . . you are on the side of the Shells, my lady? That blue-haired one would hardly wreck the ship of his own. . . ."

Fee hesitated. Then she spoke again, even more imperiously. "As you know, little sailor," she said, "my family have embraced both sides in this war. So, too, do I. I am a votary of the goddess, but I also give the Blue-Haired Sea God his due. Would that others do as I do!" She bent her head. Corydon held his breath. Would the sea captain fall for this equivocation?

He was frowning. "I did not know that there were any in the Great Families who yet strove to stay . . . uncommitted," he said. "But it does explain why some of your servants look like Dolphins. . . . That youth there . . ." He pointed to Gorgos. Everyone held their breath.

Fee didn't panic. She smiled up at him tremulously. "You have a most discerning eye, kind sir," she said in a soft voice.

The seaman's stern air began to melt a little. "Well," he said, "a lady so beautiful must have more pleasant ways to fill her hours than thoughts of war."

Corydon felt slightly sick. Evidently, Fee had charmed this susceptible seaman. He wished the man could see his dream girl in her true form. . . . Fee was smiling at him through her lashes. "It is true that I find the war a bore," she said gently. "But I am also very tired from my voyage on this strange craft. Do we have your permission to land, kind sir?"

"Of course," said the seaman. He shook his head, as if he were trying to clear it. Fee blew him a kiss. "Thank you!" she said, smiling exuberantly. "You must come and call at Murax House when you have leisure from your arduous duties," she called as his ship began to draw away.

As soon as he was out of earshot and they had tied the raft up at the huge gray wharf and clambered up the steps onto the pier, the other monsters all burst out at once.

"Fee!" "Lady Nagaina!" "We are not your servants!" "And asking him to *call*!" "What if he does? We may all be exposed."

Fee felt huffy. Secretly she thought she had handled the man with brilliant tact. "Don't all rush to thank me," she said sullenly, her charm falling aside for a moment to reveal a rather hydra-like scowl. Corydon wondered if he'd imagined a faint bluish sheen at her temple.

"Careful," said Lamia. "Your disguise is slipping."

Corydon asked anxiously, "I saw it, too! Why?"

Lamia frowned. "For a moment, she wanted to be Lady Nagaina again. The monster inside slipped its leash. Anger and grief can do it. Or sometimes happiness. Any really strong true feeling. The disguises are a kind of lie. They cannot bear much reality." Corydon understood. He remembered the Waters of Lethe, which had worked in the same kind of way.

"For all the gods' sake," said Euryale. "How can we bicker at a time like this? Have any of you looked around?" A strange assortment of Atlanteans had crowded about them. Corydon had expected all Atlanteans to look like Fee, but they were astoundingly different from one another. Some had hair thin and pale as flax; others had great masses of hair black like wood that has been

172

on the fire. Some had dark skin, dark as Gorgos's, others golden pink skin like Fee's. They were all talking at once, too, and although they were all speaking Greek, they were all speaking it very differently. Some had accents so thick that none of the monsters could make out what they were saying.

"Buy a bridge, sir?" said one. "Look, beautiful bridge. You can own him, see? Only seven drachmas." "Here, gold timepiece, lady? Very beautiful lady, very beautiful timepiece." "You come from a boat, sir? Need a place to stay? Come with me, sir, we have a very clean room just round the corner, only twenty drachmas." "You want a girl, sir?" "You looking for work, shipmates?"

"Shoo!" said Fee and Lamia together, interrupting Euryale, who was asking eagerly about the bridge. "You can't *really* buy it," Lamia said anxiously. "It's a scam. A kind of trick." Euryale looked crestfallen. Her shoulders slumped. To everyone's surprise, it was Fee who put her arm around the Gorgon's neck. "Don't worry," she murmured. "Everyone feels this way about Atlantis. That they want to own it, or at least a piece of it. But it doesn't really belong to these idiots," she said, brushing aside the salespeople, "and it *will* belong to you if you can succeed here. What you want is art lessons. My family will help."

Corydon almost fell over. This was *not* Lady Nagaina speaking. This was a new person. Someone he had never met before. He had always supposed that being a monster was a blessing, a chance to be a true self not available to the average person. But suddenly he saw that this was not the case for—Lady Nagaina, Fee? He didn't know which was her true name. But Lady Nagaina would never have said all that to Euryale, though she might have seen it. Maybe being Lady Nagaina had made her so unhappy that she had lashed out. And the more he pondered, the more sure he became. Fee might be a pretty girl who liked her own way, but when she was a Hydra, she was an *ugly* monster who liked her own way—with terrible weapons at her command. Nobody had benefited from the change.

He spoke to Lamia. "Can this spell ever be permanent?" he asked.

"I don't think so," she said. His heart rang with relief. She went on. "Not usually. Or not when I do it. When I do it, it weakens over time. Every time you have a strong feeling, it unravels a little, thins, and then it unweaves."

Despite his own relief, Corydon felt a pang of piercing pity for the Hydra-woman. "Does she know that?" he asked. Lamia looked at him, a long, dark look. "Yes," she said. "Yes, she does. All too well. She's tried it twice before."

Corydon felt he couldn't bear to know more. "Have *you* ever . . . ?" he began, almost despite himself. Lamia looked at him again. A level look. "Yes," she said.

They were walking away from the wide harbor, toward the thick forest of spires and towers that was the city.

Fee turned to them. "Welcome," she said. There was just a shade of irony in her voice that reminded Corydon of Lady Nagaina, of who she had been. Then, to Corydon's amazement, she put two fingers to her lips and whistled, short and clear. A single whistle.

And in answer, a small dragon dropped out of the sky with the speed of a diving falcon, front claws outstretched. He hit the ground in front of Fee, wings spread wide. He was a bright gold-yellow in color, but the yellow was somehow shabby-looking, as if the dragon tended to scratch at his scales. He looked slightly dilapidated.

"Well, if it ain't a lady I remember," he said, grinning at Fee. Fee inclined her head. "Where to, milady?" he asked.

"Murax House, please," said Fee, and invited the whole party to climb aboard. Corydon was uncertain; the dragon looked very small, only the size of himself, and he couldn't help wondering how the little creature could bear the weight of Sthenno and Euryale. But the dragon seemed to grow to be the right size as the monsters squeezed themselves onto his back. With a shriek of claws, he took off, soaring into the sky. Then Corydon realized that the bright yellow gleams he had taken for birds flying above the City were actually dragons like this one, each with a load of passengers or cargo. To his surprise, the dragons flew in single lines, as if there were roads marked in the sky. In fact, their dragon followed the course of the wide, tree-lined road below them.

"Are you sure about Murax House?" Corydon hissed to Fee. "I mean . . . how long have you been gone? What does your family think happened to you?"

"They think I'm ill. In a sanatorium. So infectious no one can come near me," said Fee.

"So what will they think when you suddenly reappear?" Sthenno asked pointedly. The ridge on the dragon's back was sticking into her, and she was uncomfortable still in her new body shape.

"They'll be pleased," said Fee briefly. "And I'll explain about all of you, say I promised to take you into my service—happens all the time to the Murax family."

Corydon noticed another dragon flying alongside theirs; this one was three times as big, with huge black wings and a fierce-looking muzzle. On his back were a group of heavily armed figures. All were carrying long, bright spears. He shuddered, reminded of the army of the heroes. It was plain that these were soldiers heading for the war. With this in mind, he asked Fee again about her family.

"What about the war?" he asked bluntly. "Your family—won't they mind all of us? Are they Dolphins or Shells?"

Fee ignored his question entirely. She was looking down at the city with lips parted in a happy smile. Corydon himself had noticed that they were swooping over astounding towers, some decorated meticulously. They swept along the side of a huge statue of the goddess Athene, and Corydon was distressed and furious when he noticed that she held the snaky head of Medusa firmly in one hand, while the other held a golden spear. A few yards away were the remains of what had plainly been a statue of Poseidon, now lying in broken pieces beside the plinth on which it had once stood. It was clear that the Shells dominated the city. Suddenly the dragon himself confirmed this.

"Yeah, there's that old statue. We all saw *him* off. A tyrant, that guy." The dragon spat a small ball of fire at the statue. "Waaay!" he shouted as the flameball licked at the broken remains of the god's face. "Hit him right on the nose. Yeah, bashed him right on the nut." Corydon could see Gorgos stiffening, his back expressive of his defiant anger. He only hoped Gorgos had enough sense to keep quiet. . . .

Before he could pinch Gorgos to silence him, the boy had spoken, impetuous as always.

"Look," he said, "you cannot speak of the god that way to me and live. My sword stands ready to fight for the greatness of the Lord of the Sea."

"Hoity-toity!" The dragon didn't seem offended. His voice was still calm and lazy. "It's illegal to carry a sword on dragonback, for one thing. And for another, I'm not much liking the way ya talk. So shut it, or I'll toss you off *my* back into that lake down there"—they were now flying over a green space studded with small pools and lakes—"whatever Miss Murax here might say about it."

"Gorgos," hissed Lamia and Sthenno together, "shut up! We don't want to fight the war just now."

Gorgos subsided into sulky silence. But now the dragon wouldn't let it drop. "Looks like one of yer servants might be a Dolphin, Lady Murax," he said, his tail twitching with annoyance. "I'd watch out for him in the city. I know your Murax family has some Dolphins in it, but there aren't many Dolphins in the city, and none south of the park. If you've been away, you won't realize that. So I'm warning yer. That little bloke'll get into all kinds of trouble if you don't call him off quick. Anyway," he added, "the big game is just around the corner, and that'll clear out any remaining Dolphins or other blubberrats who might make trouble." The dragon chuckled. Then he whizzed suddenly forward, swooped sideways, making everyone feel sick, and landed with claw-screeching speed in front of a large building, dismal brown in color, with a purple entrance. It looked impressive rather than beautiful.

"Murax House," said the dragon. "That'll be forty-seven drachmas."

Forty-seven drachmas! Corydon felt faint. He hoped Fee had a plan. "Just hang on," she whispered, then ran up the steps. Knocking loudly, she spoke firmly to the servant who opened the door. "I'm back. Pay the dragon, please," she said. The servant smiled, bowed, and obeyed instantly. The dragon gave a contented hiss as the coins clinked into his harness purse, then took off in search of more passengers.

"Come on," called Fee. The disguised monsters ran up the steps and trooped into a huge tiled atrium, filled with plants. The smiling servants assembled. Fee waved her arm happily, embracing them all.

"I'm back," she said simply. "These are my new attendants. Where is my brother?"

One of the servants bobbed a curtsy, then spoke in a deferential tone. "He's out practicing for the katabathos game, milady."

Fee sighed. "Is he still as keen as before?"

"Oh yes, milady," the maid answered, bobbing another curtsy.

"And . . . is he still a Shell?"

"Oh yes, milady," said the older man, the butler. "And we're all Shells here at Murax House. But of course . . ."

"Yes, what is it, Andronicus?"

"Well, there are still Dolphins in the family, too, but . . . you might need to know that your brother doesn't welcome them here, not anymore. He wouldn't be best pleased if he came in now and found you'd taken one of them into your service." He gestured at Gorgos. "When your lady mother brought a Dolphin friend for tea, your brother ordered her out of the house."

"Good lord," said Fee. "Is everyone becoming a fanatic?"

"That's not for me to say," said the old servant primly. "But if I were you, I'd get that young man of yours some new livery."

Fee turned to Gorgos. "What about it, Gorgos?" Her voice was sharp.

Gorgos shook his head and looked straight into her eyes. "No," he said. "You know I cannot do it."

"Well, you can't stay here with us if you don't," said Fee a little crossly.

Gorgos was calm. "All right," he said. "I'll leave." Before anyone could speak, he had turned on his heel and was marching toward the door.

Fee sped after him, took him by the shoulder, and pulled him back. "Gorgos," she said, "I know I can't stop you. But this city is a Shell stronghold now. You won't be safe anywhere. At least take some money. And if you get into trouble, you can call here and my family will get you out of it. I promise."

Now Corydon approached. "Gorgos, you can't go alone. Someone must go with you."

Gorgos shook off Corydon's hand. "I don't know if it's occurred to you," he said, with a grin that was pure anger, "but I've been alone for some time now. None of the rest of you share my feelings about the great God of the Ocean. Nor do any here. Very well. I can serve that god best by going to find those who care for him as I do, for that is what he bade me do. And I need no company from those too faint of heart to serve him as he should be served."

The two Gorgons and Lamia moved forward to reason with him in their turn. But he flung up his hand. "Enough!" he said. "I will take no money, use no influence. I know exactly where I need to go and what I must do. You are still my friends, and if I can serve you, too, I may. But I will choose the god first." With that, he reached the door, opened it, and vanished into the street before any of the monsters could stop him.

The servants were only too glad to see him go. Corydon was about to rush after him, but Sthenno, to his surprise, held him back. "Corydon," she said, "he's right. He's not really one of us anymore. And we all know it. You have to let him go. A child is not his mother."

Corydon swallowed. Lamia put a long white hand on his arm. "But *we're* not Shells," he burst out.

"No, nor Dolphins either. But Gorgos is."

Corydon suddenly bowed his head. Lamia's hand on his arm, warm and friendly, was all that kept him from sudden tears. It wasn't only the loss of Gorgos. It was that he saw how stupid he'd been about him.

"So," he said wearily, "now what? We must keep our end of the bargain we made, rescue our friend, and then get home." It sounded simple, but as he spoke the words, he looked around at the high ornate hallway, the complex-patterned tiles, the rich ornaments. Murax House alone was a deep well of strangeness, bottomless and frightening. As he turned round and round, disoriented, he wondered if anything in this city would be simple.

FIFTEEN

CORYDON HAD IMAGINED THAT THEY WOULD JUST embark on the tasks Poseidon had set, one after another, collect the Minotaur, and go home. But the terrible complexity of life in Atlantis defeated his simplicity. The first thing was to settle into Murax House as unobtrusively as possible. Even in a large household, they stood out. But Fee was ingenious in finding jobs that they could actually do.

Sthenno was set to cataloging the library and dusting it, which she did with great care, reverently handling the strangely lettered scrolls in their wrappings, which Fee called codices. Partly in hope of finding clues as to the Bull's whereabouts, she began trying to learn the language in which the Atlanteans wrote and made such quick progress that she was able to find out many things about the conflict now raging in Atlantis. After much difficulty, she had learned that the dragons were not only used as transports but were also used to attack settlements by raining fire down upon them; several villages had been destroyed this way.

The Shells, she found, excelled at the creation of new and exotic weapons. The Dolphins liked a straight fight, man to man or woman to woman. The Shells excelled, too, in cunning, while the Dolphins were more direct.

Fee gave Euryale the title of gamekeeper, but there was no role for her in the city mansion, so Fee suggested they say she had come to the city to study art. Fee arranged for a master artist to come and instruct Euryale, who spent two hours every morning with him. Within a week, she'd learned to cut stone as easily as if it were cheese and to shape red-hot bronze into beautiful liquid shapes: birds' wings, the sails of boats. She was happier than she'd ever been before. Her teacher was odd-looking, small, with a shock of yellow-white hair like a bird's crest. He frightened her; whenever she did something he didn't like, he shouted at her, and Euryale would forget that she was a ten-foot-tall monster and would feel exactly like the timid, elderly lady she now resembled. But her fright was due to her respect for her teacher. She understood that he was a hunter of truth, and she was willing to follow in his train like a hound, because she knew that he could flush the truths of art from their hiding places and set them running before her. She dismissed Poseidon entirely from her mind, and when she thought of the Minotaur, she thought only of the pleasing oddity of his shape.

There was something about the teacher that Euryale concealed from her friends. He was a passionate supporter of the Shells because he had an extreme devotion to the goddess Athene. He worshiped her because of what he called her gift of tekhne, which meant making-power. Euryale hadn't said a word about the way the same goddess had used tekhne to transform Medusa from a beautiful girl into an unhappy monster. She hadn't said anything because she, too, had taken to paying secret visits to a goddess shrine, praying for inspiration, for the power to make and transform.

Fee's old life had completely absorbed her energies, and she began happily attending symposia, complex nighttime parties that began with a dinner and ended in contests of wit or treasure hunts or philosophical disputes. Euryale saw, dimly, that, for Fee, living in this way was a kind of art, though it didn't seem to her the truest kind.

Corydon and Lamia were thrown together, and neither of them was happy. Fee had introduced them as guests, so there was nothing for either to do but sit around Murax House all day or walk about the city. Lamia, it was plain, disliked the city and was not willing to join in with Fee's pursuits, though Fee often invited her to do so, albeit languidly. Alone of the monsters, Corydon was worried about their mission; nothing in the city interested him enough to distract him. He also went on worrying about Gorgos and about the way the days were slipping through his fingers. What would happen to the Minotaur if he, Corydon, failed to keep his bargain with Poseidon? But of his lost friend—or the Bull— Corydon could learn nothing. In his many restless hours, he tried talking to the servants, but they shut as firmly as clamshells when he asked questions.

His worries, pressing as they were, faded in comparison with the terrors of the Atlantean nights. Corydon and the others learned about these on their first night at Murax House. Sthenno had just been about to go outside to verify the position of some crucial stars when the elderly manservant barred her way.

"It's after curfew, lady," he said. "They'll be coming soon. You must stay indoors." Sthenno was astonished, but she went in without asking questions. The monsters, drawing together in the Murax House living room, noticed the servants scurrying about, placing what appeared to be charms in windows and doorframes, building up fires in chimneys and hearths. Then all the servants, and Fee and her brother, Phaidros, too, stood in the front hall and began a low humming chant that seemed to fill the house with shivering energy.

Outside, a stranger noise began, as if in response.

To Corydon, who had heard the rushing, wailing shades of the dead, it was both similar and different. There were many heavy footsteps. There were low cries, and through the tiny chinks in the curtains, which had been drawn across the windows, the monsters could see a dim reddish light filling the streets. The light thickened till it was the color of old blood. The Murax chanting increased in volume; to Corydon's ear, it had a desperate ring. An elderly man detached himself from the other servants and began frantically painting symbols around the front door.

Corydon soon saw the reason for the servant's action. Amid the general noise from outside, he discerned slow, heavy footsteps approaching the front door.

Something was coming.

The footsteps halted, and then there was the sound of something clutching at the wood of the door, as if trying to pry it open. There was a hungry snuffling, and with it came a smell so dreadful that even the monsters felt faint, a smell of decay and old marshes and the cold unburied dead.

The light went suddenly black. The fires no longer gave out

heat. The door began to shiver. It was clear that it would burst open in a moment.

Sthenno ran to help the man painting the magic runes and began drawing a much larger master rune on the door itself, with hands that were clumsy but quick. As she completed it, it lit with burning silver light. The door stopped shivering and visibly grew thicker and wider, so much so that the monsters could no longer see light through the cracks in it. The terrible smell dissipated. In a few moments, they heard the heavy feet moving away.

"Are they the dead?" Sthenno and Euryale were not afraid. But the Murax House family went on chanting, ignoring all questions, until slowly the sounds drifted away down the deserted street.

"Was it . . . ?" Corydon heard Fee ask, in a tone that suggested even she was afraid.

Her brother shrugged, his face white and tired. "Probably," he said eventually.

Corydon spoke directly to Fee. "What's happening?" he asked, trying to sound curious rather than frightened.

Fee shrugged. "Corydon," she said, "I can't speak of it."

Corydon looked straight into her eyes. "Who was it that came up the steps trying to get in? You do know, Fee. I know you know."

Fee sighed. "Yes," she said. "I do. But they must never be named. Not by day nor by night. Or next time they *will* enter. I will say only one more thing, Corydon Panfoot. In Atlantis, we do not rule. We are ruled by others. You heard them. They are our masters in every way." She closed her mouth firmly, turned away from him, and began walking up the stairs. Corydon was dumbfounded and utterly baffled.

The servants were even more unhelpful, and one of them

actually hit him when he asked questions about the mysterious nightwalkers. After that night, though, the servants respected Sthenno. They called her strige and refused to touch her, but they were impressed by her power. And Sthenno spent more and more time poring over books of Atlantean lore, trying to find out what was wrong. All Corydon could learn was that they came when the moon was dark. When he heard this, he shivered, remembering his younger self crouching on a hillside, waiting to enter the realm of the dead. But he had tamed the dead then, redeemed their land. Now it seemed something new was amiss with death, or why were these hungry revenants haunting the city? He decided to glean what he could before the next dark night of the moon.

To his surprise, he found an ally in this in Fee's brother, Phaidros.

They spent much time together discussing news from the war. It was odd, Corydon thought, but here in the city, there were no signs that a war was going on not far away. People did discuss it often, but in a tone of polite regret, as one might discuss inclement weather. No one seemed frightened or upset. But Phaidros was genuinely interested, and he kept Corydon awake at night, debating tactics and building small models of the Shell and Dolphin positions. Sometimes Corydon would try to remind him that men were dying—women, too, perhaps. He never understood, but Corydon remembered only too well the deaths he himself had caused, and his heart ached.

Their friendship began with Corydon listening to Phaidros's dreams of glory; Phaidros longed so earnestly for an audience that he was prepared to overlook Corydon's low status whenever he felt he wanted to talk.

Phaidros's main hope was in katabathos, and he played for the Shell team, which was to face the Dolphins in a final, terrible match. Since Poseidon had told Gorgos that this would somehow involve the monsters—though Corydon couldn't see how—he spent some time with Phaidros trying to learn what katabathos was.

Phaidros explained that the game was played in deep tanks and that sea creatures were released into the tanks during the action. The aim was to take a round ball and to hit it into a net defended by your opponents, but scoring these goals was made more difficult by the sea creatures. Sometimes these would be harmless and merely intrusive, like large fish. At other times, they would be deadly creatures of the deep. Each player was armed, but only with a small dagger. Players had to come up for air from time to time, and that was when they often died, caught by the sea creatures. Occasionally, players had stabbed one another by accident. Drownings were frequent. And yet precisely because the game was so dangerous, it was a mark of great honor to play it. Through Phaidros's eyes, Corydon came to see that katabathos was like war. And though the real war was distant, Corydon was often shocked by how warlike Phaidros sounded. Once he said he would like to drown every Dolphin.

And yet he also said that the Dolphins had not won a game for two hundred years. He was scornful about their chances. "Of course, everyone says it's the curse, but I think it's that the goddess helps the Shells. After all, we are her team. . . ."

"What curse?" asked Corydon.

"They say there was a player called Protagoras. He fell out with the team leader and was dropped from the Dolphins' team, but he'd been chosen by Poseidon to be the greatest katabathos

187

player ever. They say that he threw himself in the harbor and, before he died, spat out a curse, and blue-haired Father Poseidon heard him." Phaidros added, "I think it's just an excuse," and shrugged. "Anyway, Poseidon doesn't have anything like the power of the Lady," he added.

Corydon decided not to tell him about all the evidence of Poseidon's power that he'd seen with his own eyes. It seemed a waste of breath. And he felt too listless to waste any breath on anything.

Phaidros was on a strict training regime, trying to ready himself for the game. He swam miles every day in the harbor. He wrestled against his training coach. He ran for miles in the green forest near Murax House, which he called a park. He ate special foods, most of which tasted horrible to Corydon, all of which were supposed to make him able to stay underwater for longer. He was big, and he was quick, but Corydon found him strangely helpless; he had no guile at all. Once, desperate for extra training, Phaidros challenged him to a wrestling bout. Corydon had never been much of a wrestler, and he was encumbered by his new disguise-body, but he managed to throw Phaidros to the floor almost at once.

After that, Corydon began to gnaw on a new worry: it seemed to him that if Phaidros entered the katabathos contest, he would be killed.

Meanwhile, where could Gorgos be?

Perhaps it was lucky that Corydon couldn't see.

Gorgos, too, had encountered the nightwalkers. Unlike Corydon, though, he had not been behind thick walls when they came. He had been out in the streets.

His first warning was when other people began to walk faster. The yellow dragons vanished from the skies, and the few hurrying humans disappeared into houses or other buildings. The streets were all at once eerily quiet.

Then the sky darkened, not with the darkness of night but with a bruised bluish darkness. The noise began so gradually that he wasn't sure when he began noticing it: a soft wailing at first, as if a very young baby were crying alone and inconsolable. Then it gathered, and moans broke out, cries of pain, sickening screams. Then the pounding footsteps sounded, heavier, heavier. The sky began to turn blood-red. There was a horrible smell of rot and decay.

And then he saw them.

At first, he took them for wounded soldiers. They were deformed: some had missing legs, others missing arms. And their faces were strange: human in shape but somehow blurred, as if a giant hand had partially erased their features. Their bodies were somehow blurry, too; they were sculptures gone wrong. As Gorgos looked at them, he saw that their skin was shiny and slippery. With a shudder, he saw that the slippery substance was the dark red of old blood.

His hand flew to his sword hilt, but before he could draw, a small figure raced out of a doorway, flung itself at him in a kind of tackle, and pulled him to the ground. He hit the ground hard and felt an explosion of pain in his right knee. "Down!" said a voice in his ear. "Down!" Gorgos lay flat. "Crawl!" said the voice imperiously. Gorgos, to his own slight surprise, obeyed. His wits told him these . . . things . . . would not be stopped with a mere sword, not even a semidivine one. So he crawled desperately and reached a hole in the pavement just as the first creature broke into a terrible, plodding run. Without further thought, Gorgos dived down the hole, still holding his rescuer by one hand.

He fell some way, perhaps two lengths of his own body, and landed in cold water. It was too dark to see, but beside him, a heavy splash told him his mysterious savior had landed, too. He heard the thudding footsteps of the creatures above his head. The footsteps went on, faded into the distance. Gorgos turned to his rescuer, only to find that he was alone.

He shouted. He called. But there was no answer.

Now Gorgos began to realize that he was in something of a mess. He was at the bottom of a hole, and he had no way of climbing back out without a rope. But perhaps up was not the only way out. . . . He began to grope sideways as his eyes grew used to the thick darkness. Soon he found a wall. Feeling along it cautiously with his right hand, he was able to walk forward, and so he discovered that he was not in a hole but in a tunnel—a tunnel with deep, smelly water, but a tunnel nonetheless.

He walked, splashing along the slimy bottom, feeling colder and colder. He kept on and on. He didn't come to anything except more darkness and cold water for a long, weary time.

But finally he began to hear something, some kind of voices ahead in the darkness. And the darkness lessened a little. On the other hand, the water grew deeper. It was up to Gorgos's waist now. His teeth would have chattered if he had been a human boy. As it was, he set his jaw and plodded on toward the faint sounds. As the sounds grew louder, and discernible as Greek voices, he slowed, hoping to approach without frightening whoever it was. But the eddying of the water betrayed him. Suddenly the voices sounded alarmed. One cried, "Look! Something comes this way! See, the water shakes!"

Now Gorgos knew he must be quick rather than stealthy. He flung himself fully into the water and with great strokes heaved himself through it at cutting speed, surfacing—to his amazement—in a well-lit cavern, long and narrow but wider than the tunnel. There was a kind of beach of dry land stretching away from him. Perched on it were twenty or so very tiny figures, each only about two feet high.

They were white all over: their hair, their staring eyes, their faces, even their lips and tongues. They looked as if they had been carved from snow. But it was plainly not so. They were gathered around a small fire, which glowed comfortingly. They did not melt in its radiance.

Gorgos leapt eagerly from the water and started toward them, holding out his hand in a gesture of friendship. They flinched, and he could see that they might run, so he spoke as kindly as he could. "I am in your debt. One of you saved my life on the streets. My life is yours, small rescuer."

He wished Corydon were here. Corydon was much better at putting people at ease.

But his words had an immediate effect. One of the small white people came hesitantly forward.

"I pulled you," it—no, she—said. "They were coming."

"What are they?" Gorgos asked. Someone more sensitive might have waited longer before putting this question, but Gorgos wanted to know the answer at once. The little girl—for that, Gorgos saw, was what she was—didn't seem to mind. "They are our opposites," she said. "They are now the creatures of She Whose Name Is Drowned Deep, the thrice-holy one who watches every crossroad. Once they were the servants of the people of Atlantis. But now they serve her."

"I don't understand," said Gorgos bluntly. "Serve who?"

Another of the small white creatures approached. This one was plainly older. "Sit down," she said, "and accept our hospitality." Gorgos sat, and they pressed a tiny cup into his hand. He took a tentative sip, and they seemed reassured.

Into this calm, the older white lady began to speak.

"Many centuries ago," she said, "the people of Atlantis lost their city thanks to the malice of a god. They decided to build a new city that would be the wonder of the world. Their cleverest man, a man named Daidalos, designed it, many-towered, astonishing. But the people were few. To build it, they needed strong backs. At first, they asked the northern giants of Albion to help, but the giants proved too clumsy. However, seeing them gave Daidalos an idea. He determined to build his own race of giants from the clay of the land itself, servants that could be controlled and managed by him alone. He was not only clever, he was also a great mage and sorcerer. He learned the secret of creating life, discovered that he must paint each clay figure with an animating rune in human blood. As long as that rune, that blood, remained there, the giant would be strong and active and obedient. But to create enough giants to build the city, Daidalos needed a lot of blood. So he slew his apprentice, who was also his nephew, a boy named Phrynos, and used the boy's blood to make the giants."

There was a silence.

Gorgos hugged his knees, horrified, but waited eagerly for the rest of the story.

"His spell worked. The giants built the city, towery as you see it today. And when the city was finished, their master sought to dismiss them. He wiped the mark from their foreheads one by one and laid their bodies in a great pit. But the blood of the murdered boy called out for vengeance. When the boy's parents came to know what Daidalos had done, they declared a blood feud that split the family. From that feud have sprung up centuries of warfare, a war so old that it no longer knows where its own beginnings lie.

"But a foolish Shell heard the story of these giants. She was an apprentice mage, and she longed to serve her people. She thought the giants would make a powerful army. She began to research the spell Daidalos had used, and eventually she found the rune that would animate the giants. But her casting went all amiss, for she did not control the forces she summoned. And when She Whose Name Is Drowned Deep was invoked, she destroyed the mageling, so men say, and raised the rotting, decomposing bodies from their tomb of clay. Since then, they search for more blood on every night when the moon is dark. We call them the Morge, for they are indeed walking dead."

Gorgos wished, again, that Corydon or Sthenno or even Lamia were beside him. They would know what to ask next, and he had no idea. He simply sat still and waited. Perhaps that worked best, for the small creature went on resolutely.

"Now I must tell you of my own people. We are the twins of the Morge, and yet their opposites. We, too, were made to be the servants of human beings. And there is a terrible story about our making. You see, young hero"—Gorgos flushed with pride—"we were made in the power of Artemis, when the moon was new and slender and white, but were also made, somehow, of babies that had died untimely. The enchantress who made us took the souls of babies and used them to ensoul us. She did not kill the babies to do it, you understand, but it was still a wrong, because it kept those babies from death, and from their proper place in things.

"We were made not for building but for art, for the arts of living. We are artists. We decorate, paint, cook. We make clothes. We make gardens, and we make them grow. But when the others, the Morge, began to haunt and plague the city, people banished us. They did not want us anymore. We were too sharp a reminder of what they feared most.

"Those of us who did not die came to live underground, in these caverns that we had hollowed out to help water escape from the city. Others of us went out into the countryside. Nourished with milk from the deer of the White Lady, they grew tall and strong, and we call them the Selene Amazons, the Daughters of the Moon. They are makers, too, makers of peace.

"Now the humans of the city have forgotten some of what we taught them in the arts of living, but the city's foods and its arts are our doing still."

Gorgos looked at the faces around him. Each was as white and polished as the new moon. Each had a swirl of frost-white hair and long, clever fingers like bent twigs. Their appearance bore out the story, however fantastical.

"Do you know any magic?" he asked abruptly.

"We have the powers of Artemis," the storyteller replied with dignity. "Powers of the moon. And in Atlantis, there are many, many kinds of magic. We know of the ones that have to do with art, though we ourselves do not practice them anymore."

"Could you make a spell so the Dolphins win the war?" Gorgos asked bluntly. The small creature frowned. All of them began to mutter disapprovingly. Even Gorgos felt he had said the wrong thing. There was an icy silence.

Then the storyteller spoke. "We are not Dolphins nor Shells.

We seek only to preserve ourselves and the works of our hands. Now, come and feast with us."

Gorgos felt a nagging doubt: he was sure he remembered stories advising against sharing food with those plainly supernatural. "No thank you," he said, trying to still his growling belly.

"Our food will not harm you," said the small white creature. "Though it might harm one fully human. For there is less human in you than in us." Putting her hand on his forehead, she was silent for a moment, then said, "You are the child of the sea god, and your mother was a monster. We have no power over you." For a moment, Gorgos heard a plangent note of regret in her voice. He wondered briefly what they had planned to do with him.

Gorgos was tired. He had heard a very long story, and he didn't feel ready for another. He rolled over beside the fire and was all but asleep in a few seconds, lulled by the light, high voices, the gurgling of nearby water. As his eyes finally closed, Gorgos heard a faint lowing, as if the small white people kept a vast animal down there somewhere. It was not enough to disturb his dreams.

SIXTEEN

Lamia had been worrying, too. She felt unhappy being in the same house as Fee, and she missed her birds. In her current form, she couldn't seem to lure the City birds or eat them, nor could she exchange her body with snakes or conjure them with her spit. She had to fight a feeling of utter helplessness and power- lessness. It was worst when she could not escape from Fee and her friends. Fee was so glowingly happy that she found it difficult to understand that shopping made Lamia even more unhappy. With misguided kindliness, she kept trying to cheer Lamia up with new fashion items. Last time, it had been a fur cape that made Lamia miserable just to look at it. Every time she did, she seemed to see the bleeding bodies of animals. Eventually she buried it in the small garden.

And she was haunted by dreams. Memory reared up inside her dreams and caught her in its glare like a cobra about to strike. It ate away at her disguise, and she longed to get away from Murax House.

Eventually her dreams showed her a way. When she had

thought through her plans carefully, she went to the library, where Sthenno was scrabbling about eagerly. Lamia waited for a moment, but Sthenno never even noticed her. So she went to the garden to find Corydon.

He was sitting in a hide he'd made at the bottom of the garden; he'd dug himself a small koumos trench and draped pine branches over it so he couldn't be seen. Lamia knew without being told that, like her, he felt horribly trapped in the wide, empty rooms of Murax House.

From the hide came the tentative sound of pipe music. Then it stopped, and Lamia heard Corydon sigh. She knew he could no more make songs than she could call her birds. Like her, he had not flowed into the shell of his disguise. Instead, he wore it like a suit of clothes that had been designed for someone else. It looked ill-fitting, heavy.

She called softly, "Corydon, are you there?"

Corydon came out at once.

He was glad of company. He had never felt so useless in his life. They sat together under the garden's only tree.

They were both silent. Corydon was thinking of the time Fee had taken him to a restaurant. There had not been snail porridge, but perhaps he would have liked that better than what she and her friends had eaten: some kind of very thick, heavy meat. Corydon couldn't bear to eat in a room so crowded with people, so noisy, so full of strange smells. He had felt, unhappily, that he was sulking. Sthenno and Euryale had managed much better: Sthenno didn't eat, but that was not unusual, and it was not obvious because Euryale had eaten both their dinners. . . . Then there had been the concert Fee had taken them to . . . music that sounded enormous and important but that Corydon had been unable to like. Again, he thought he might have liked it if he had been alone on an island hillside. . . . His anxious thoughts pattered here and there, getting nowhere. He was under a tree in the garden of Murax House. And the Bull and the Minotaur were no nearer.

Within minutes, Lamia was shivering; she could never remember to wear garments that would guard her against the Atlantean weather. Corydon offered her a sheepskin Fee had bought him; it had been a considerate attempt to make him feel at home. She wrapped it around her, thinking that it didn't smell like his old one. He knew it didn't. Now his true self was becoming an empty masquerade, and he wasn't sure who he was.

To cheer herself up, Lamia whistled to a little bird.

It ignored her. A tear trickled down her nose. Corydon's heart ached for her.

After a minute, he said, "That's the trouble with this kind of spell, isn't it? You get lost in it."

Silence fell again. Lamia spoke. "I would like to talk of something else. We have been here for days, and we have done little to find the Bull."

Corydon hunched his shoulders. "I know. But there's obviously no Bull here." They hoped Sthenno would uncover some clue in the library, but so far there was nothing.

Lamia sighed. "Of course not. So we must follow Poseidon's guidance. We must find the place where he told us to go, the Cittavecchia."

"Do you know how?" Corydon asked, his mood suddenly lifting. If only she did.

"Well," said Lamia, "I know where to start. But I do not know how we might reach it. It is not in this city, Corydon. The Cittavecchia is the Old City, the first Atlantis, abandoned centuries ago. At the temple, the girls would whisper of it, whisper of girls who were given a map to the chambers under the most ancient of all the sea god's temples. I was myself not so favored. But I know that we must start at the temple on Little Bear Mount—my temple, Corydon."

Corydon stood up. There was no time to waste. Why had she waited so long to speak of this? But he did not ask her. "Let's go," he said.

Lamia sighed. "You can't enter the temple. I have to enter it alone—and try to find the way," she said. Corydon allowed a little of his frustration to show in an angry, muttered response: "We have so little time left to find the Bull and win back the Minotaur." Suddenly it came to him in a rush that he hadn't had any dreams of the Minotaur for a long time. . . . What did it mean? Could he dream truly in this body?

"Oh, Corydon," said Lamia. "I know. I want to help. You can come and wait for me there, but only I can find the way. Let me be the one to help. You're not the only one who cares about the Minotaur."

How horrible he sounded. As he thought this, the door into the garden swung open, and Sthenno darted toward them.

"I have it," she said, triumphantly waving one of the curiously large and solid parchments. "I have found the Bull at last. Somewhere in the Old City is the doorway through which the Bull will pass. The door has been flung shut in anger; it glistens with the wrath of a discarded girl. And I have the map that shows where we can find it. Look." She held out a drawing that looked much less frayed and scrawled than her usual pieces of parchment. It was simple and elegant, with scrollwork and delicate colors. Corydon could see, too, what Sthenno meant about wrath. It showed what looked like a trackless labyrinth of meandering paths, some red and some green-blue and sparkling. In the center was a square depicting the small figure of a bull.

Corydon felt an icy tingle of excitement.

"That's it. The Bull," breathed Lamia. She turned and looked at Corydon. "We must go at once," she said. "Sthenno, will you come with us?"

Sthenno dashed to one side to think, like a bird of prey frightened from a kill. "I am troubled about Euryale. Something is not right here."

"Nothing is right here," echoed Corydon.

Both Corydon and Lamia wanted to leave at once, but Fee insisted they stay for the katabathos game. "Gorgos will surely be there. And it will be our first task—completed." She was firm. "Then I will arrange for the dragons you'll need and send you fully equipped. You will be going near the war zone, and I know you are not as . . . resourceful . . . as usual." She was almost pleading. Corydon realized that she found it hard to accept that they longed to leave Murax House as much as she, apparently, had longed to leave the Island of Monsters.

Suddenly Corydon found himself thinking of Gorgos again. Would he truly be at the katabathos game? Perhaps he had gone before them to look for the Bull; Poseidon had probably told his son things he hadn't told the other monsters. Corydon only hoped he wasn't in jail.

* * *

Gorgos had taken a regretful farewell of the tiny white Selene, promising to return, and had emerged into the streets of the city once more. Luckily, it was the hour just before dawn. so no one saw him come out, but when the streets got busier, he attracted plenty of curious stares; his torn cloak, his dark skin, and something indefinably odd about him seemed to put the Atlanteans on their guard. Besides, many saw in him a Dolphin boy, and the city was Shell-dominated. With no money for a dragon, Gorgos had to walk.

Every now and then, he would stop a passerby and ask for directions to the katabathos stadium. Most were helpful, though one woman, whose smoothness reminded him of Fee, wrinkled her nose. Gorgos began to wonder if he had picked up an unpleasant smell in the city's underground rivers.

After walking for over an hour through a crowded, busy part of the city, never catching sight of the harbor he had hoped to see again, Gorgos found himself unexpectedly crossing a bridge over an arm of the sea itself. He hadn't noticed at first because the bridge was lined by houses and shops. But there was one shop that had its door and windows open to the sea, and through it Gorgos suddenly saw the realm of ocean that felt so much *his*.

He asked the woman in that shop if the stadium was close, and she pointed to the end of the bridge. Gorgos saw the curving, shimmering walls of what must be the katabathos stadium rising from the cliffside that dropped away sheer to the harbor. He smiled briefly at the woman, then turned and ran toward it.

People were startled to see him running, but Gorgos didn't care. He felt he must get there or burst. But how to get inside? There were many doors, and all of them were shut. . . .

He stared into the water for a minute, then leapt suddenly to the top of the cliff wall. A man in the street below shouted, "No! Don't do it!" but Gorgos ignored him. He dived, a fabulous, graceful parabola, and broke water far out from the cliff wall. He waved cheerfully to the man who had shouted—Gorgos noticed that the man's mouth was open in amazement, and no wonder, for he had dived about fifty feet—and then he plunged his head under the water. There was a current, but it was only a tickle. He concentrated on feeling the entrance to the katabathos tank. His father had implanted a very strong picture of it in his mind. He could feel it like a tug in his head, in his body. He turned in the water and swam straight for it as swiftly as the great dolphin, his father's servant. Yes, there was a narrow inlet, and he could sense that it led to the big tank; he could feel the pressure of water above him. As he rose, swift and light as a bubble, he became conscious that there was more than water in the tank. There was something ancient and powerful there, a great sea animal. It was not asleep but still, with a stillness that he sensed could turn at any moment to lightning speed. It had many arms, too many to count. It had a bulging body, like a bag, with a single eye and a birdlike beak.

Gorgos knew its kind; they lived in the warm waters of the Middle Sea. He had sometimes teased and played with them, and villagers liked to eat them. But this creature was fifty times the size of those with which he had played.

Now he felt its will awaken and its cold eye watching him.

A tentacle snaked toward him, weaving elegantly through the clear water. He saw that it was covered in gripping suckers; the tentacle was thicker than his arm.

He dodged, and while he did so, he tried to greet the creature, using the sea call his father had taught him: "Water dweller, I am of the cool greenness, too! We are brothers!" But the octopus didn't respond, and Gorgos sensed that its mind was not of the kind that communicates. It was coldly settled on food. And Gorgos could see that he was the only food in town.

He decided to attack it before it could attack him. He drew his sword, the blade glinting in the sharp shafts of sunlight that pierced the water. The octopus didn't respond to his menacing gesture, didn't seem to understand it. He braced one foot against the tank's wall and pushed off hard, cutting swiftly through the water toward the great cold eye; his sword was clasped between his hands, extended before him like a battle lance. The creature swerved, but slowly, like a drifting flower. Gorgos got in a glancing blow on the side of its head, which only served to madden it. It sprang up, and he got a terrible glimpse of great swirling arms. He saw the huge beak snapping, and he sprang nimbly backward, then raised his sword again, hacking at the tentacle nearest him.

As he expected, it was too rubbery to be cut even by his exquisite blade, but with extra pressure, he managed to open a gash, and black blood swirled out, dimming the bright water. Now it was harder to see the lashing arms, and Gorgos decided to head to the surface, hoping to force the great sea beast up with him. In daylight, he would see it better than through the now-inky water. He sped up but, to his surprise, hit his head on something hard before he reached air.

The octopus had pursued him, and now it used his momentary shock to attack again; its beak almost closed on his leg. He twisted away and, as he did so, discovered that the ceiling his head had struck did not cover the whole tank; there was an area of brighter water to his left. He made for it at once and sped so fast that the octopus seemed to lose sight of him in the brilliant glare and dazzle of the surface.

Gorgos surfaced into full, brilliant sunlight. The octopus was thrashing around below him.

Gorgos dived back and blew a long stream of bubbles to attract it. It turned immediately and launched itself at him, but he sped away again to the surface; it was like a game of tag, and he laughed, baring his white teeth.

He had lured it up, and it broke the surface of the water with a ferocious whooshing noise, all its long arms extended to pull him into its mouth. Gorgos feinted, then, as the great sea beast leapt for him, turned and drove his sword into its eye.

Black blood spurted out, and the octopus's baglike body deflated as its life ran out into the water of the tank.

Gorgos smiled happily.

Then he was startled by a burst of applause.

He had been too busy with the octopus to notice, but now he saw with his customary quickness that the tank in which he had done battle was surrounded by tier after tier of spectator seats. High up, there were a few tall, strong-looking men, slightly older than he appeared, far older than he truly was.

They were clapping.

One stood up and ran lightly down the tiers of seats toward the edge of the tank. He bent forward toward Gorgos.

"Welcome!" he cried, his smile friendly. "By Blue-Haired Poseidon, you are a natural! Have you come to claim your place on the Dolphin team?"

Gorgos grinned back. "Are you the team leader?" he asked.

"I am," said the friendly man. "My name's Parmenion." He had darker skin than most in the city and very long hair swept back in a thick black braid. Narrow black eyes regarded Gorgos.

"Who are you?" he asked. Gorgos smiled again.

"My name is Gorgos, son of Poseidon," he said, extending his hand in a friendly gesture, "and I am a Dolphin. I will gladly serve you in any way I can, for it is my father's wish that I play this game and win in it."

There was a sudden silence. The team leader's eyes narrowed still more. Gorgos was used to producing this kind of silence in his listeners; it often meant he'd said the wrong thing. But the young man didn't seem angry, only—what was it? Gorgos wished he knew about how people felt. Awed.

"Gorgos, son of Poseidon," Parmenion said eventually, "men may laugh at us both, but I believe you are who you say you are. Your victory over a beast that would normally require the efforts of our whole team speaks volumes. And I believe, too, that you can breathe water—is it so?"

For answer, Gorgos dived to the bottom of the tank and sat there for twenty minutes.

When he surfaced, without so much as a single gasp, he found the whole team had assembled and were arguing about whether to go down and rescue him. He shouted to make them notice.

When they did, it was they who gasped. Then a great roaring cheer broke from them. They stripped off their outer garments and plunged into the tank with him, holding him up on their shoulders.

"Now," said Parmenion, "*now* we will be victorious!"

SEVENTEEN

O<small>N THE DAY OF THE GREAT KATABATHOS MATCH, IT</small> seemed to Corydon as if everyone in Atlantis were heading toward the stadium. Luckily, the Murax family and their servants had many tickets because Fee's brother, Phaidros, was playing for the Shells.

Corydon was concerned for Phaidros. Katabathos was known to be the most dangerous game in history, and almost every match had a body count; Phaidros himself had told tales of matches where no one on either team survived. But he knew, too, that Phaidros had longed to play, and he had been given a place on the team at the last minute when one of the Shells had sustained a bad injury training with a huge saltwater crocodile.

As they walked, Corydon felt his dread of the match recede— the thronging crowd was terrifying enough. He had never seen so many people, thick and swarming like flies.

He clung to his disguise, knowing a mob like this might tear a monster to pieces in seconds. Yet the more afraid he felt, the more worried he became that his disguise would melt; nor would the excitement of the match be helpful.

He asked Lamia about the problem as they struggled through the throng around the enormous amphitheater. Lamia pointed to the guards around the arena bearing clubs and identifiable by their thick, heavy bearskins. All were very tall men with long, golden braids.

"They are here to keep the peace," she said, her low, resonant voice oddly audible above the hubbub. "And I can repair the spell if I act quickly." Corydon was grateful for her presence.

Beside them, an enormously long and supremely glossy black dragon had just landed. On his back was a woman clad in rich purple silk from head to foot and a man in shimmering green.

"The priestess of the Lady and the chief priest of Poseidon," hissed Lamia. "They rule the city with the Council of the Great— that's made up of the heads of the twelve Great Families, including the Murax family."

The pair were shown through the crowds to the main entrance. Corydon noticed that no one was cheering their arrival. He looked at their hard, cold faces and could see why. Suddenly the priestess seemed to notice Lamia. "Hello, my dear," she said in a voice that could have cut crystal. "How pretty you are!" Lamia was tongue-tied, but Sthenno darted forward. "Thank you, Your Worshipfulness," she said, stumbling over the words. The priestess smiled scornfully and moved on.

Worming along the line of people waiting to enter the stadium, Corydon crept close to Sthenno. She and Euryale were looking about, bright and birdlike. They were not troubled by the crowds. Somehow, Sthenno had become less timid now that she was less noticeable.

"Sthenno," hissed Corydon hastily, "can you see Gorgos anywhere?"

Sthenno peered about. "No, mormoluke. I cannot."

Euryale turned to him. "Frankly, I doubt if we would see him in this crowd even if he were right on top of us. Why do you ask?"

Corydon began to remind the Gorgons of what Poseidon had said about katabathos, but Euryale interrupted him. "Yes," she said, "I, too, remember all that. But I mean something different. Why do you still seek him? He must find his own way."

Corydon felt bruised. It seemed the Gorgons were all but abandoning Gorgos. "It may be that he will find his own path," he said hotly, "but he is only a small child in his mind and heart. He needs us. He needs to be prevented from doing harm."

"He needs to fulfill his fate," said Sthenno. "But the stars, too, are different here. . . ." Her face was dreamy, remote.

Euryale spoke again. "Corydon," she said gently, "you, too, are young. You cannot carry the world."

This conversation had carried them as far as their entrance to the vast arena. The monsters found that they had been assigned seats on the top tier, which meant climbing up seven flights of steep and narrow stairs.

When they came out, they were high above the tank. Fee and her parents, on the other hand, were barely visible below and could only be picked out because they carried an awning in the colors of Murax House to shelter them from rain. They were almost jammed against the thick, transparent wall of the katabathos tank, where they would have a perfect view of the match's underwater spectacle. Corydon and the others would only be able to see what was going on when the teams broke surface to shoot at the two enormous golden nets, one at each end of the tank. Both nets were funnel-shaped, like Poseidon's triton shells. At the end of each was a big clamshell-shaped bronze plate, and Lamia explained to the monsters that, to score, a player must not only get the ball in the goal but must make the bell at the end of the goal sound its note.

They were sitting on hard wooden benches without backs, and Corydon noticed that everyone around him was a Dolphin supporter. They all bore Dolphin banners and wore clothing with pictures of dolphins on it, and they flourished ribbons in the Dolphin color, a dark greenish blue. On the other side of the stadium, Corydon saw a sea of floating pink and white and guessed that was where the Shell supporters sat.

Next to him sat an enormous man wearing Dolphin blue from head to foot; he had even painted his face and hair blue. He turned to Corydon. "Are you a Dolphin fan?" he asked suspiciously, eyeing Corydon's plain gray robe.

Corydon didn't know what to say. "I have been in the country most of my life. I have never seen a match before."

As he had hoped, this last admission distracted his big companion from asking any more about allegiance. Instead, the man began eagerly explaining what was to happen and how much better the Dolphins were. Corydon didn't like to remind him that because of the curse of Protagoras, the Dolphins hadn't won a game for two centuries. "You wait," the man said. "In just a minute, they'll sound the gongs."

As he spoke, enormous bronze gongs began booming so loudly that the air seemed to vibrate.

The crowd cheered.

As they did, bronze doors at each end of the katabathos tank opened, and the teams came out. They were on some kind of rafts and were wearing thin suits in team colors and heavy leather dagger belts.

There were twelve on each team, all men. Corydon scanned the Shell team and spotted Phaidros, who looked radiant with pride and excitement. He could see the Shells much better than the Dolphins, because they were across from him. It was not until the Dolphin team reached the center of the water that he noticed the dark figure behind the team leader.

Gorgos!

The teams paused, facing each other. Each player lifted his arm to his opponent in a salute. Then, with one voice, they cried out, "Courage of Poseidon! Cunning of Athene! Be ours! Let our blood be yours!"

Suddenly Corydon saw that katabathos was bloody for a reason: it was a kind of sacrifice to the gods.

Then, with sinuous grace, all twenty-four players dived into the water.

The rafts on which they had ridden were drawn back on ropes. Then one of the guards appeared, bearing a golden ball. He tossed it between the two teams. The gong sounded again. And the game began.

Corydon soon saw that there were few rules. A Shell player leapt almost out of the water and managed to tip the ball with the very end of his finger, pushing it in the direction of the Shell team. Immediately a Dolphin flung himself in its path, caught the ball one-handed, and thrust it toward the Dolphin goal. A Shell tore after him, but the Dolphins moved to block his way. The water was churning so much that it was hard to see, but suddenly something pulled the Dolphin with the ball right under the water. At once, several other Dolphins dived, too, and Corydon noticed that there seemed to be fewer Shells about. He realized abruptly that the Shell players had pulled the Dolphin under to stop him from scoring a goal.

Now more and more of the players disappeared under the water. Soon, only two players near the goals were left. Corydon craned, but all he could see was a melee of dark shapes moving through the water. . . .

Suddenly there was a great cheer from the Dolphin spectators as a Dolphin player burst to the surface with the ball in one hand and shot it straight at the goal. The Shell player tried to block it, but the ball flew sure and true. There was a loud clanging sound.

The Dolphins had scored. The whole Dolphin team surfaced and took the victorious goal scorer on their shoulders, holding him proudly up to the Dolphin spectators. Being at the Dolphin end, Corydon could see his face clearly.

It was Gorgos, now standing straight and proud on the team leader's shoulders, waving to the crowd. Then, with the grace of a sea-born creature, he slid down into the water again.

Now the game began anew. In just a very few minutes, the Shell team had equaled the score; three Shells managed to cling to Gorgos's legs for long enough to allow one of their number to place the ball in the goal.

Then the Dolphins formed a tight, spear-shaped press, with the ball at its apex, and drove forward to put the golden ball in the goal for a second time. The Shells were unable to impede them from under the water because anyone underwater was immediately attacked by Gorgos.

At that moment, a new sound began.

It was not the roar of the crowd or the clang of the gongs in the goals. It was a low, rich sound, and Corydon saw that it came from a man who was blowing a triton shell at the very top of the tier. The sound echoed even in the crowded stadium.

The players all looked up. Corydon noticed that the Dolphin team leader's face had grown stern, like a man going into battle.

By the edge of the water, seven men in brilliant green robes appeared. Each had a huge bag in his hands. With one gesture, they loosened the ties on their bags and flung the contents into the water, on top of the players.

Corydon heard the Dolphin leader shout, "Dive!" and at the same moment saw all the Shells also turn and plunge down.

"What is it?" he asked Lamia. It looked to him as if the men had thrown coils of blue and golden rope into the katabathos tank.

"Sea snakes," said Lamia coolly. It was plain that she rather liked them.

"But they are poisonous."

"Yes," said Lamia. "Very."

Corydon could see that the snakes were maddened by being carried about in bags of seawater and then suddenly flung out into the tank. Many were attacking one another, but there were so many that it seemed impossible for the players to avoid them.

Because he couldn't see what was going on under the water, Corydon couldn't be sure about what was happening, but when he saw dark tendrils of blood beginning to well through the clear water of the tank, he realized that the teams must have drawn their daggers to defend themselves.

Then two things happened at once.

A Shell player surfaced. His whole face was contorted in horrible agony, lips drawn back from teeth. He threw back his head and gave a scream.

Gorgos surfaced with the ball in his hand. At once, three Shells tried to thrust themselves between him and the goal while another Shell cut through the slithering snakes to keep them safe. But Gorgos simply dived down again into the melee below the water and emerged between them and the goal.

As he did so, the Shell who had plainly been bitten by a writhing snake screamed again. All three Shells turned to look.

And at that moment, Gorgos threw the ball clean and sweet into the goal. The ringing noise was not drowned out by the dying man's screams of pain.

With the goal safely scored, Gorgos swam toward the distressed Shell. The other Shells fended him off.

The water was now dark with snake blood, and the hacked bodies of snakes floated on the surface. The dying Shell gasped and drifted toward the edge of the tank, holding out imploring hands.

Another of the men in green appeared. He bore a knife in his hand.

"Your blood is for our master," he said, his voice ringing above the sudden silence of the crowd. Then he pulled the Shell's hair back so his throat was exposed and made a small cut in his neck. The man collapsed as his lifeblood poured into the water, and his body slid slowly out of sight into the deeps of the tank, weighed down by his belt.

Other men with green robes were using nets to remove the dead and living snakes. When they had been cleared away, the triton shell trumpet sounded again. Corydon's heart contracted with dread. He found that Lamia was clutching his hand.

"Oh, Corydon," she said. Her eyes were glittering with tears. She gulped. "The snakes. . . ."

For once, Corydon felt impatient. It *was* sad about the snakes, but the fate of the *man* was far more horrible.

The Dolphin and Shell teams gathered in the center, backs to each other. One of the men in green threw in the ball, and play began again, but it was clear that everyone was waiting for something else.

There was a slow creaking noise, as if ancient carriage wheels were turning. To his surprise, Corydon saw that doors had opened in the side of the tank—two doors, three, four, five, and one he could only just see, below them. The players stopped and drew their daggers.

Something huge and gray, with a sharp nose, was being pushed out into the tank. At first, Corydon thought it was a dolphin. Then he felt utterly cold as he remembered a picture Phaidros had shown him, a picture of the most feared creature in katabathos, one that always took many lives, one that sought and drank blood.

It was a great white shark. Followed by five more, slithering and tumbling into the water of the tank.

The two teams drew together, back to back. Sometimes by grouping together, men can frighten even a pack of sharks. These, however, were maddened by the blood in the water. They drew their circle tighter and tighter around the men. Now the men were pressed together, daggers outward. Those who had been foes were forced into alliance by the menace.

But the Shells had the ball. And, fatally, the Shell player who had it decided to try a shot at the goal. To do it, he had to move just a little away from his fellows, and as he rose out of the water, the biggest of the sharks lunged suddenly at him. Fresh red blood bubbled into the water as the shark closed its terrible teeth on the man's arm. He dropped the ball and screamed. Now the knot of men broke up as two Dolphins dived frantically for the sinking ball while others defended themselves desperately against the freshly blood-maddened sharks. Phaidros managed to kill one of the sharks, stabbing it again and again with his small dagger, and two others at once began eating the dead shark as it sank, trailing blood, to the bottom of the tank. But that still left three, and while two went on attacking the men on the surface, one dived, with horrible speed, to follow those chasing the ball. Corydon couldn't be sure, but he felt certain one of those was Gorgos. The white body of the pursuing nightmare was vivid even in the murky water.

The shark stopped suddenly, as if it had run into an invisible wall.

Then it turned around and struck savagely at a nearby Shell's outstretched legs. The man roared. Other Shells gathered.

And Gorgos, with the ball in his hand, sped for the surface. Now the sharks on the surface, too, stopped what they were doing. Slowly they moved between the surviving Shell team members and the goal, almost as if they were guarding Gorgos. Corydon realized, with a mixture of relief and utter horror, that Gorgos had commanded them to do exactly this.

As the sharks kept the Shells at bay, Gorgos fired the golden ball straight through the open mouth of the goal. There was a loud, ringing clang. And the triton shell blew again. The match was over, and the Dolphins had won. As the Dolphin supporters cheered, hugged, kissed, sang, leapt in the air, and celebrated, the men in green quietly slew the members of the teams whose wounds were fatal and then the sharks, too.

The enormous man next to Corydon was so happy about the Dolphins' victory that he was crying. He embraced Corydon, who began to wonder if he would prefer to face the sharks. Corydon looked dumbfounded at the human carnage. How could such pain make the crowd so happy?

Gorgos was carried three times around the arena, flushed, happy, cheered. Garland after garland was brought to him. The last was made of shark teeth, and he gave that graciously to the Dolphin team captain. Corydon could see Gorgos's shudder in the gesture, knew that he could have cried for the sharks that had been killed to make it. The crowds roared on, but as dusk started to thicken, they began leaving for the taverns and inns of the great, pulsing city.

Corydon and Lamia could not reach Gorgos, though they shouted; nor could they see Fee and her party anywhere. Luckily, Fee had given them a few drachmas. They stood outside the stadium for several minutes, whistling frantically for a dragon, and Sthenno finally managed to persuade a small yellow one to land in front of them. The dragon she had attracted, though, was strangely shabby; his scales were flaking in places, giving him a mangy appearance, and he seemed exceptionally small and thin. Also he didn't speak much Greek. "Your will?" he croaked.

Sthenno began to climb onto his back. "Murax House," she said firmly, trying to sound as the family did. The dragon scratched his head with his claw. "You know where this house is, lady?" he asked. Sthenno frowned. "I think so," she said after a while. As

Euryale, too, sat down, the dragon gave a groan. And when Lamia flung her leg across, he rebelled. "No can, lady! Too many this old dragon no come along. You whistle, 'long another dragon come. He take. See?" Lamia carefully withdrew her leg, and without further ado, the small, molting dragon took off before they could ask Sthenno to summon another. Lamia and Corydon were left standing in the dark street.

"At least it's not the dark of the moon," said Corydon at last.

"Let's try whistling again," said Lamia as calmly as she could. But however hard they tried, nothing happened.

"Maybe we'd do better farther from the stadium," Corydon said at last. "It's so busy here. And at least if we go north, we'll be headed toward Murax House." They set out, the flares of the city lamps guiding them through the narrow, dark streets.

"Do you want to go back there?" Lamia asked suddenly.

Corydon was surprised by her question but barely had to think to know the answer. He didn't want to go back to Murax House. Actually, he hated Murax House with a fervor that surprised him. But what else could they do?

"We might go and look for the Bull now, without waiting for Fee's letters and money," said Lamia softly. "If we can find a dragon."

"If we can. Let's keep walking for a while."

One of the nightmare features of the illusory body Corydon now wore was that it tired very much faster than the inner monster-body that held his true self. After they had walked two miles through dark little streets, past mean houses that seemed ready to collapse into the road, his legs ached and his feet were sore. He wondered if this was how humans felt; if so, perhaps it was envy that made them hate monsters and worship the gods.

The streets in some areas were crowded with celebrating Dolphins, drunk like villagers on festival days. Wine poured into the gutters.

In other places, much larger crowds of miserable Shells were equally drunk but also angry. One mob, holding Shell banners, was shouting, "Dolphins are cheats!" over and over again. Another group was arguing ferociously, and Corydon heard one of them say, "It's that new player. There was something not right about it. Not right. I reckon he used magic." The others roared their disappointment.

Suddenly the streets began to feel not only lonely but unsafe. He saw a fight begin in one tavern, its wide-open shutters framing Shells and Dolphins hitting each other with wooden clubs made from what a moment ago had been furniture. "They should ban the lot of 'em from the city," shouted one drunk Shell. "Get rid of 'em all! It's their fault. It's their fault, I tell you!" Outside the tallest building in the city, the slender-spired turret of the temple of Athene Nike, a huge and angry crowd had gathered. "Shells! Shells! Shells!" they shouted. "Let's get rid of the Dolphins ourselves!" cried one big man. "We all know a few. Let's get 'em!" Corydon's heart filled with dread, because beside the man he could see the bright eyes of Athene herself, telling him just what to say to set the crowd off.

With a hungry roar, the crowd was indeed off. Within seconds, the sound of more fighting, and sounds of splintering and breaking, reached the ears of Corydon and Lamia. There were distant wails, even screams. And the thick crackle of fires.

"We'd better hurry," said Corydon, taking Lamia's hand. They ran north, trying to reach the quieter suburbs by the little wood park before the raging crowd caught up with them. But it was useless. As they ran, a group of Shells broke round a corner and hastened after them, crying out, "Stop! Stop! Are you Dolphins? Or Shells?"

Corydon turned. He could see that if they kept running, they made a target. "Dolphins? No! We do not love the Sea Lord." This at least was true. The ground rumbled a little under Corydon's feet, but he decided Earthshaker must make the best of it.

"Have you seen any Dolphins pass this way?" the Shell leader demanded.

"No, no Dolphins," said Corydon. "I must take this lady to her home. She works up at Murax House. But I can't whistle up a dragon for love nor money tonight."

"That's another thing," the burly Shell said. "Dolphins always get all the best dragons."

"Well, we certainly aren't having much luck," said Corydon, trying out a comradely grin.

"And that's another thing!" the big man roared. "Blessed Dolphins! Never want anyone to have any fun!" The man clapped him on the shoulder. "You'll grow up to be a loyal Shell, won't you? Ah, I know you will. Now, friends"—here he addressed his followers, who had hung around drunkenly—"let's go and finish the job. Make sure there's not a Dolphin left alive—in Five Points here, anyroad—by first light. Safe journey home, youngster!" he called. Then they disappeared down the alleyway.

Corydon and Lamia kept walking through streets glittering with broken crystals. Just as he felt he really couldn't take another step, Corydon's forlorn whistle finally brought down a dragon without the need for any enchantment.

"Where to?" the beast asked as he landed, claws outstretched.

"You up for a bit of a round-trip?" Lamia asked. The dragon nodded. "Murax House first, then the downtown market. Then an out-of-town destination—the Little Bear Mount. We . . . er . . . want to have a picnic."

EIGHTEEN

THEY WENT INTO MURAX HOUSE WITHOUT LOOKING around, without speaking to anyone. They scribbled a note, grabbed the map, snatched up the purses of money Fee had given them the day they arrived. Neither had spent any because both of them had so much disliked going out into the city. Then their small and nimble dragon whizzed over the varied stalls of the marketplace, letting Lamia off to make a range of lightning purchases. Finally, with a large bag stuffed full of necessities, they flew off to the north, with the sun right overhead.

As they passed over Murax House, Corydon noticed something curious. The house had changed in the brief time since they had left it. Every window was draped with a black banner.

"Look!" he shouted. Lamia looked down.

"Corydon," she said, "someone is dead."

"What? Who?" Neither of them said anything for a while, both fighting their knowledge of who it must be. "It might be a servant," said Corydon. He didn't wish it was, though; the Murax House servants were kind, if slightly dull.

"No," said Lamia, a little bleakly. "They would only black two or three windows for that."

They both knew the truth. Corydon remembered Phaidros's eagerness; it was cruel for it to end this way, in black windows. Finally he said, "Should we land?"

"No. We cannot help them. And unless we can find the Bull, we cannot help the Minotaur either." Each sank back into solitary thought.

They flew west for miles, across more houses and towers than Corydon had thought there were in the whole world. Lamia directed the dragon. But after they had been in the air for about half an hour, the houses began to thin and their gardens grew larger. Then green fields and woods took over completely, with slow, lazy rivers meandering among them. The dragon's voice reached Corydon's ears.

"Have to cut around to the north," he bellowed. "Don't want to fly over the armies! Very dangerous!"

"Why?" Corydon bellowed back. He had been hoping to learn something about the way the war was going.

"We could get shot at by the archers!" the dragon cried. "Both sides have used dragons! As transport and to carry weapons and drop them on the enemy. And to breathe fire."

"Are you a Shell or a Dolphin?" Corydon asked.

"Dragons mostly don't care either way," the dragon said. "But we can be hired, see? Paid for. We all need to build up a hoard before we retire. Shells pay better, see? But if you're a dragon"— and here he smiled, showing a lot of pointed teeth—"it's important to be able to sing 'The Goddess Song' and 'Blue-Haired Lord' with equal enthusiasm. If you were Shells, now, I could give you a chorus: 'Gray Lady of brilliance, Gray Lady of might,' " he sang. His voice was hoarse and off-key. Corydon didn't like to tell him to stop. The dragon went on for several verses, then favored them with the more rousing sea chantey tune of "Blue-Haired Lord." His voice was no better, but the song suited its hoarseness.

"Look," said Lamia. "There is the army of the Dolphins."

"Better not get too close," said the dragon. Without warning, he plunged from the sky. Corydon and Lamia clung to each other desperately.

"Look," said Lamia. "There it is. Little Bear Mount."

She pointed to a tall, steep hill whose entire circumference was traced with intricate spiral lines that formed a path leading up to a big house—or rather a temple, for it was white, with a stiff porch of many gilded pillars at the front. On the roof was a huge silver crescent moon pointing to the sky. Held in the cup of the moon was a small silver statue of the goddess Artemis. But dwarfing it completely was the enormous statue of a fully robed Athene standing in front of the main building. As the dragon swooped lower, Corydon could see that Athene's robes were the dull color of old blood but trimmed with bright silver.

The dragon set them down, then flew off with most of their money as his fare. Corydon heard him chuckling about his hoard as he shot eastward, yellow as a streak of fire.

The statue frowned down at them. Something about its angry, hard face made Corydon want to run.

"Lamia," he hissed, "are you sure you want to do this?"

"We have exactly four days to find the Bull and bring him to where Poseidon will meet us," she said bleakly. "Four. Sthenno said

the gateway to the Bull is in the Old City, and I know that somehow the temple will lead us there."

"What shall I do to help?" Corydon asked worriedly.

"Try to get the lay of the land," Lamia said. "Perhaps you will
find some hint of the Old City. And every night, climb the spiral
path to the temple. I will try to meet you."

"And I can find out how the war is going," Corydon said resolutely.

"Be careful," said Lamia, and with a wave, she began to climb
the stairs to what had once been her unhappy home.

At first, Corydon felt odd on his own, but as he climbed slowly up
the next hill, a delight in being alone in the country began to creep
over him, banishing loneliness and apprehension. This wasn't his
beloved island, but this country was beginning to speak to him,
through the soles of his feet, through the air he breathed. As he
drew in deep breaths of its freshness, he knew suddenly that his
father, Pan, was with him, in the soft green grass; in the hard
sparkling gray rocks of the land; in the animals that grazed on the
far hillside, the sun gilding their fleeces. The familiar scent of
sheep mixed with unfamiliar aromas, plants he didn't know and
couldn't name.

He spotted a small village but skirted around it—he was so
relieved to be alone again, he couldn't bear to see anyone. As he
wandered, Corydon noticed a small shepherd's hut—at least, it
looked like one—far away on the opposite hillside.

Suddenly his heart was full. He would lie out there, wrapped
in his fleece. He would make a real fire. He was a little hungry, but

he would rather starve than go back into a town again now. He reached the hut just as the sun sank below the horizon and before the moon rose. It was so dark he could barely see the grass in front of him, but his acute sense of smell told him that no one was there at present. As his eyes grew used to the darkness, he found a neat stack of wood and began to build himself a fire. Then he lit it using a flint, and it blazed up high and hot. Corydon took out his pipes and began to play the tune that had once led him home from the realm of the dead. Suddenly he realized that he felt much the same as he had then: unspeakably relieved to be once more in his proper place. He had finished the tune and begun another before something about his leg gave him a sudden jolt of surprise.

It was his Pan-leg. It was back. In the rising light, he could see that he was once again Corydon Panfoot.

His first response was joy. He had hated the body he had worn in Atlantis and the person it seemed to make him—someone muffled, someone useless, someone who could not sing. But then, with a sinking feeling, he remembered that he was supposed to return to Little Bear Mount tomorrow night to meet Lamia. How could he go there in his monster-shape? But how could he let her down by failing to appear?

He had no idea what to do. But even his dilemma couldn't altogether crush his feelings of pleasure and delight. Finally he lay down in the warmth of the fire, his nostrils twitching with the rich, delicious smell of woodsmoke. Looking up at the stars, familiar and blessed, he fell asleep.

And he had a dream, a dream in which his arms were around the furry back of the Minotaur. He noticed his fingers couldn't feel the great beast's fur; the Minotaur was wearing clothes, clothes like the people of the city. Somehow that was monstrous, truly monstrous; his huge bull head was too rough for the silliness of city clothes. Suddenly Corydon realized they were both riding on a yellow dragon, floating over the towers of Atlantis, and city music swelled around them. It didn't seem real. The Minotaur didn't seem real in his smooth jacket. The dream was light as a puff of cloud, and it was not real. Something about it frightened Corydon, and he was glad to wake and feel his Pan-leg, a reassuring sign of what was true. He woke just before dawn as the birds began singing songs he did not know. Their rich tunes were mingled with a stranger, fuller, deeper sound.

After a moment's sleepy puzzlement, Corydon recognized it. It was the lowing of a bull.

His drowsy brain refused at first to realize the significance of what he'd heard.

Bulls? his mind asked, and then suddenly a rush of memory woke him completely, abrupt as a cold shower. Bulls! The Bull of Poseidon.

Could it be?

He sat up. Astonishingly, the sound now seemed softer.

He lay down again.

Yes. He could not be mistaken. The Bull was lowing deeply somewhere within the earth underneath him. It was some distance away; if Corydon's monster-body with its exceptional senses had not been restored to him, he might not have been able to hear it at all. With his knowledge of animal cries, Corydon could hear that it was a lonely, savage cry, the cry of one who had long been pent in narrow pain. As the light grew stronger and day broke, the sound faded—not as if the Bull were falling silent but as if it were moving away. Soon, it was so faint he could hardly hear it at all. But he noticed the direction in which it was moving. It was moving back beyond Little Bear Mount, where he had come from last night.

Even as he listened, Corydon was making a plan, quick kleptis planning. And kleptis action, too. He would have to slip into the village and steal a garment that would cover his legs, a robe or a cloak. And he would have to go to Little Bear Mount and hope his weak disguise would hold. Perhaps then Lamia could restore—but no. Corydon suddenly stood up and spoke aloud. "I will be false to myself no longer!" he shouted to the hills. And he felt his father heard him.

Perhaps Pan was with him, because as he crept swiftly along behind hedges toward the outskirts of the village he had seen the night before, he saw a long cloak hung on a twig to dry. There was no one in sight, so he snatched it up and wrapped it around himself. It covered his Pan-leg well, because it was a man's cloak, long and brown, home weave. Corydon knew, though, that his true face was lean and brown and all cheekbones, like a goat's, and that his thick brown hair stood up in a kind of bush—that he did not look like most fair-skinned Atlanteans. But he would have to chance any suspicions.

He also found some food in the village: a woman had left her bread on the windowsill to cool. He seized it and wrapped it in his cloak, speeding off to the hills again, where he sat and ate it. It was good, warm bread but made with a grain he didn't recognize, more golden and less grayish than the bread of his homeland. He spent the day wandering the hills, learning their shape and secret contours. He was happy, but he learned nothing, and then it was time to meet with Lamia again.

As the sky darkened, he made his way up the thin path that spiraled around the hill. He walked against the sun, in the direction of the moon. All the while, he was conscious that his steps were tracing a kind of invocation, a sign of power on the grass. Now that his true form had been restored, he felt his own power merging with the power of the earth itself, the power traced on the land by the moon. Looking up at the moon, he noticed that she was waning, well into the last quarter; soon the mysterious horrors would again be hunting on the streets of Atlantis. But the night of the dark moon was also when many doors were open that were usually shut. And sunset, too, was a time for walking between the worlds. Corydon felt sure that wherever the Bull was, the way to him would be open at the sunset of the dark of the moon. What time could have more magical portent and power?

He told Lamia all this when he spotted her at the top of the hill. They spoke in anxious whispers, each confiding but also concealing much. Corydon said nothing of his dream, and Lamia concealed her concerns, too. They agreed to meet again the following night, and beset by a sense of futility, Corydon sped away. He was used to the richness of darkness, and his monster-sense guided him effortlessly back to the hut.

Lamia felt the cool marble strike a chill on her skin as she reentered the temple buildings where she had been so miserable as a girl. Even though she was in human form, her heat-loving reptilian self was daunted. But to her surprise, she hated it all less than she remembered. There might have been many reasons why this was so: she was on a mission; she was not as sensitive or full of feeling as she had once been. But what really made a difference was that she had learned how to pretend. On her first night at the temple, in her shared bedchamber, the girl next to her said, "You know, new girl, your hair might be quite pretty if you only had it colored and restyled."

The others laughed. Lamia felt herself tense, but her tension was more a kind of alertness, like a soldier before a fight.

"Thank you," she said shyly. "I'm never sure what would look best. Yours is amazing." She had remembered that sometimes sweet submissiveness worked better than wit. And now she didn't mind saying this. She had been tempted to say, "Your hair looks like a nest of decomposing worms." But something hard and calculating inside told her that this kind of approach would not help her locate the Bull.

The Little Bear temple was a training ground for priestesses of Athene, although it also gave the upper-class daughters of Atlantis a year or two of priestess-like seclusion in dedication to a virgin goddess. Athene had swallowed up what had once been the territory of Artemis, the Earth Huntress, but though the girls now belonged to Athene, the temple and its inmates did not quite forget their past. They all had some of the Moon Lady's magical wildness. The temple hummed with a kind of energy that came from so many girls cooped up in one place. The younger girls still had the ferocity of bear cubs, tumbling loose on the mountainside. Even when they were sewing dull, neat seams for yet another festal robe for the Gray Lady, they wriggled vehemently on their chairs with a longing to be outside. The older girls wanted to be outside, too, but for a different reason. They had already found that having two armies nearby meant they need never be lonely.

Soon it became clear to Lamia that the wildness of the youngest girls was somehow connected to the painted image of the Bull that was part of her own memory of the temple; the young girls had the same sort of moony sheen of newness, freshness, unconquerability. It came from Artemis. It was sad to see the older girls losing this and collapsing dully into some soldier's embrace, exchanging their brilliance for the eclipse of love. As a solitary, Lamia disapproved. She preferred the unforgotten, boring routine—prayer, sewing, cleaning—though it absorbed her energy and dulled her mind.

Every time she had the chance, Lamia tried to bring the conversation around to bulls, but it became clear that almost no one was interested in them. Only one of the very youngest girls, a girl called Kharis, was interested.

"I've heard him lowing," she said. "At night."

"Where?" Lamia asked, trying to keep her voice casual.

Kharis dropped her own voice so low that Lamia hardly heard it. "The Old City," she said.

Lamia's heart began to thunder. The Old City! But Kharis said no more—even whispering the name had clearly filled her with dread.

The next day, Lamia was listlessly digging the vegetable garden with the other girls when one of the older ones began a long, incoherent boast about her moonlit tryst with an officer by the lake.

"Ugh," said her friend. "I wouldn't go there."

"Don't be a baby," laughed the first girl, hurling shovelfuls of earth inexpertly onto the path.

"But, Atthis . . . I was there once, and I heard a . . . well, a kind of . . . roaring sound . . . like . . ."

"Don't say ghosts!" laughed Atthis. "The only thing I saw there was something I wanted to see. Or *someone*."

Her friend was silent, her face pale despite the digging. And Atthis added hastily, "Of course, I didn't . . . you know . . . cross the lake. . . ."

Memory rushed into Lamia like oil pouring into a great metal jar. She had thought the answer lay in the temple. But now she realized it lay in herself, in her own past. She let these memories pass through her mind, feeling that they had happened to someone else, coldly combing them for clues.

Lamia had been fourteen, new to the temple. She had been plain and gawky, with a thick curtain of black hair and dead-white skin. It would not be true to say the body she was in was the only one she had ever known. Although she was not yet a monster, she had felt like one. She remembered when she had had the body of a little girl: small, slight, strong. Then changes had come, unwanted changes. Budding breasts that spoiled her hardness and smoothness. She grew her hair long and thick, not to hide these things but to hide her eyes so that she need not see them in the mirror.

But Fee had been there, and she could smell Lamia's discomfort with herself, and she drank it in like incense.

There was a new torment every day. Some days, Fee would pretend to be her best friend, taking her arm, holding her hand. Other days, Lamia would be ignored completely. On still other days, Fee would explain, sweetly, poisonously, that everything about Lamia was wrong, from her hair to her clothes. There were the nicknames, the little song: " 'Lamia' sounds like 'La-ame.' " . . . And she had to laugh until her face felt as if it would split or Fee would say that she couldn't take a joke.

Sometimes there were tricks. A half-eaten fish left under Lamia's bed and many remarks about the smell. "Is it you, Lamia darling? I'd wash a bit more if I were you." Fee said this with every appearance of friendly concern, but Lamia knew she'd put the fish there. What made it worse was that she was desperate for Fee's approval even while hating her for what she was doing. The love fed vampire-like on the hate.

Fee and the others—the memories were halting now, because Lamia had spent many years resolutely ignoring them—had played a cruel trick on her. . . . She had been ambushed, smothered in a cloak, dragged to the lakeside, fighting and kicking . . . then bundled into a boat, and they had rowed her out to the Old City. They had untied her there, hurled her from the boat, and fled. . . .

And it was then that she had herself heard the lowing. . . . Her heart had stopped, dead. Then she had run and run and run, longing only to hide from the pitiless sun, which saw her ugliness, her body exposed, daubed with hatred, as if the hatred stuck to her like clay. . . .

And soon she could run no more. Water hemmed her in on all sides.

She sat down and felt herself between earth and sky, between girl and woman. The stillness was calming. A kind of strength came from the ground itself. It was as if the Old City still contained some of the magic of its makers.

She was herself, she thought firmly, and could not be anything or anyone else.

As she thought this, she was surprised to feel something forming between her hands, forming and twisting. She looked down to see the strong, well-shaped body of a python.

It looked on her with its cold eyes. She did not flinch. Instead, she scratched its head. The python now looked up adoringly. Its worship warmed and soothed her aching heart.

And then it began to wriggle. Now Lamia's priestess training helped her; it was a soul-guide, a psychopomp. It wanted her to follow it. And she did, in a wild dance, as eddying as a watery current. Even when it led her underground. Toward a white sheeny light like that of the moon. Toward the shimmering outline of a Bull. . . .

"Remember," it breathed. Then it slid up her leg.

It led her back to the surface; it led her to a boat. Fee and the others were unpleasantly surprised to see Lamia calmly eating her evening meal in the hall after they had returned soaking wet from a rainstorm over the lake. And this was only the first in a series of very unpleasant surprises for them.

Lamia had fed the python with scraps purloined from the table. Its friendship and love were balm. It was just as beautiful as Fee, but unlike Fee, its worship was constant and unwavering.

Lamia kept it hidden for weeks. Then there had been a day when it came out, searching for her, lonely. It emerged into the sleeping quarters. Screams broke out in only a few minutes. Lamia sat still, drinking them in. Her only regret was that in the confusion, the python fled.

But she soon made new friends. Literally made them. Made them out of herself. She had discovered that she could form new serpents every time she grew angry or afraid. It was as if her feelings took form. They had begun as gentle giants, like the python. But soon she began to make cobras, adders, snakes so deadly that none knew their names—all came forth from her hands.

When she felt her own body changing, it seemed not a loss but a respite from the more terrible destruction of her girlhood. Fee teased her about her *green-tinged skin, but Lamia did not care. Freed from the body she hated, she no longer needed Fee's love to redeem it.*

Thoughtfully, she filled Fee's bed with cobras. It was worth it to see her face whiten. . . .

The new Lamia sat and reviewed those memories as if they were a village procession arranged for her benefit. A catlike smile played over her face.

It was time to meet Corydon.

NINETEEN

THE NEXT TWO DAYS HAD PASSED SLOWLY FOR CORY-
don. He had returned to the temple every night, but the second
time, no Lamia had appeared. So he tried to remain calm, a quick
kleptis raid here and there keeping him supplied with food. The
Atlanteans he saw didn't seem to notice his foot, and he wondered
if Atlanteans had a pharmakos myth at all. If not, maybe this was a
kind of paradise. . . . In his forays, he learned much about the village on which he was preying. It was a Dolphin settlement. Its people fished the streams for many kinds of purposes, seeking crayfish
but also precious metals. They were more careless and cheerful
than those of his own village on the island had ever been. He
scouted the hills for the Selene, remembering Hades' advice in his
dream, but saw no trace of them.

He thought he might pose as a boy running away to join the
Dolphin army. Corydon couldn't altogether trust Poseidon; perhaps if he could find out where the Minotaur was imprisoned, they
could still rescue him themselves if Poseidon proved false to his

word. He had fashioned himself a new slingshot, and by now he had something more to offer: he knew every inch of the land around the sheep hut, and he knew a secret pass through the rocky hills that avoided the narrow gorge on the main road that the Shells would have to pass through. So, disguised in his heavy cloak, Corydon drew a deep breath and approached the army outpost, which lay three or four miles south of the village he had been raiding.

It was manned by cheerful, slightly undisciplined soldiers who, as Corydon approached, were standing around talking and laughing.

"Ho, a boy!" said one heartily. "Come to join the Dolphin army, lad?"

Wincing a little at the loud speech, Corydon recognized the same joviality in the speaker that he recalled in the voice of the Dolphin spectator at katabathos.

"Yes," he said, trying to sound equally cheerful, and aware that he didn't. "I really want to serve the Dolphins!"

The men reacted, as people always did to Corydon, with a marked lessening of enthusiasm, a shade of loss of ease. They tried to go on sounding hearty and pleased, but it was clear that they didn't feel as pleased as they had. "That's fine, youngster," said one, the oldest, probably the one in command. "Would you like to go along and report to the leader of Delta troop?"

"Wait," said one of the younger men, eyeing Corydon suspiciously. "Are you just going to let him right into the camp like that? Wearing that cloak? Shouldn't we at least search him?"

Corydon felt a cold finger on the back of his neck. What would the men make of his Pan-leg? The older man shrugged.

"All right," he said. "Better safe than sorry. If you're a true Dolphin, boy," he said, "you'll understand the need to safeguard the army."

Corydon removed his cloak. He could see he had no choice. To refuse would make them sure of his enmity. He waited for their horrified reaction.

To his surprise, they barely seemed to notice his leg. They were much more interested in his weapon.

"That's a nice sling," said one.

Corydon waited for them to notice his leg at last. But they glanced at it as though it didn't matter to them.

"All right, youngster," said the young soldier who had demanded the search. "Off you go. And unless I'm much mistaken," he added, "you'll be seeing your first battle before too long. Scouts tell us the Shells are closing in."

Corydon felt a surge of courage and confidence. "But we have machines, don't we?" he asked.

"We do!" The soldiers' cheerful optimism was clear. "We have all kinds. The porcupine, the great tower—"

"And now you have me and my sling," said Corydon, trying to sound cheeky and cheerful, like a true Dolphin. The soldiers clapped him heartily on the shoulder and sent him down the dusty track.

He could see the main body of the army ahead of him, spread out under trees and in makeshift tents. Horses were picketed nearby, and he caught the hot, spicy scent of a whole phalanx of great silver dragons. They were talking amiably, boasting of their hoards. Soldiers moved briskly to and fro on errands. Corydon looked around and saw a man in a long green cloak who looked as if he might be a commander. He approached and caught the man's eye.

"I've come to join the army," he said.

The commander looked down at Corydon. Corydon felt he was being assessed. As usual, something about him suggested slyness or stealth. The commander said, "Good. We can use you as a spy, if you're a local lad."

Corydon began to feel that he had traveled around in a gigantic circle. He nodded his head.

"Well, we have scouts' reports of a Shell army coming up from near the City to reinforce the local Shells. Their stronghold is yonder—"

"Sir," said Corydon, "I came from there and saw no army."

"Useful information. My thanks. Which way will they come, then?"

"Through the pass, sir. Unless they have enough dragons to bear them all.

"Sir," added Corydon boldly, "I know a way around the pass. Some men could hold them at the narrow place while the rest ride around and catch them from the rear."

The commander was taken aback. "Shepherd boy, aren't you?" he said. Corydon nodded, surprised at the man's perceptiveness. "So you're saying I should take the word of a shepherd boy and expose this army by following some kind of plan in which we could easily miss the Shells entirely if you're wrong or find ourselves trapped in our turn if you are a treacherous spy for them. . . ."

Corydon looked up. His eyes met the commander's. Their gazes held for a long, long moment, then Corydon let his eyes fall. But the commander seemed oddly satisfied. "I find I trust you, lad," he said. "I can see you've told a thousand lies in your life, and probably stolen a million sheep, but that's why I trust you. Only a true shepherd boy would know the land so well. Now," he yelled, "scouts, mount up! We have a new recruit here, and he is going to show us where our next battle will be fought. Fetch my horse."

"Sir," Corydon asked as men scuttled about fetching mounts, "sir, what is your name? Whom do I have the honor of serving?" To his own surprise, he almost meant it.

"My name?" said the man with a smile. "Alexandros. Ride with me."

Corydon was not exactly overjoyed at the sight of his impossibly tall horse; he had once or twice ridden the village donkey and had found it unpleasantly bumpy. Nevertheless, they mounted and galloped toward the pass. Corydon was jolted about like a badly packed saddlebag in front of Alexandros, but he managed to shout out directions. He was too bruised and preoccupied to think any further than reaching the secret pass itself, but after an hour's hard riding, he saw its gray rocks rising above the green hills. He shouted again, and the little group of riders scrambled swiftly up the slopes, the horses slipping and sliding on the loose scree.

When they reached the top, Alexandros pointed to the road looping toward the hill on the wide plain. Everyone immediately saw the vanguard of a mighty Shell army inching toward them. Alexandros shouted to one of his men and sent him galloping back to the Dolphin camp to rouse the army to readiness while he made a plan. In the front ranks were Shell warriors on foot, wearing heavy bronze breastplates, arm and leg greaves, and thick helmets that hid everything except their glittering eyes and grim mouths. Corydon saw the dark thicket of their spears, the scales of their close-held shields. At their sides were swords.

Behind them came companies of men in chariots drawn by glossy black horses, and Corydon could see that some of the chariots were ferociously scythed, their wheels bristling with blades designed to cut down the enemy. He also saw the tall weapon towers. . . . What! Had the Minotaur been working for both sides? Then the mystery was solved as one of the Dolphins spat on the ground. "Look, Captain," he said, "they've brought out the battle towers they took from us at Adrianopolis."

Corydon had to ask it. "Who made them?" he said abruptly.

Alexandros looked surprised. "No idea. They come from Pharos. That's all I know. We had a lot of wonderful new weapons from there at the start of the campaign. Nothing lately, though."

"When was the last time you had something new?" Corydon tried to sound like a curious boy. He was aware of rising suspicion.

"Around a month or so ago," Alexandros said. "Why do you ask?"

"My father told me of the inventor of Pharos," Corydon said. "He said the machines would win us the war."

"He was wrong, then," said Alexandros. "Weapons are nothing. Ideas are what count. You need a good battle plan to make a good victory." Corydon thought the Sphinx would have agreed. "Talking of battle plans . . ." Alexandros called together his men to explain what he had in mind, and several scouts galloped off to direct the army into position. Corydon had no idea whether Alexandros's plan was bad or good; he only knew that their present position might give them surprise and deny the Shells the opportunity to use their stolen war machines. But it looked as if the

Dolphins wouldn't be able to use their machines either; it would be impossible to drag them up the precipitous rocks.

It turned out, though, that Alexandros did have a plan for using them. When the cavalry and the infantry legions panted up the steep hill, the leader told Alexandros that the ballistae and other war machines were being dragged slowly around to launch a final surprise attack. The idea was that the forces on top of the hill would drive the Shells into a gully near the main pass, where they could be pinned down by fire from the deadly weapons.

The Dolphins lay low, just over the ridge. The Shells came on.

Corydon suddenly noticed that the Shell commander was sending out cavalry scouts in all directions. One was being sent straight to the gully where the great machines of war were being placed. If he saw them . . .

He tapped Alexandros on the arm. Alexandros saw the danger at once. He sent a man around to try to intercept the scout without revealing the Dolphins' position.

Corydon pulled his sling from his belt.

He looked a question and saw Alexandros nod.

Whirling the sling fiercely, he prepared for a long throw. His first shot missed, but at the hard *pock!* of the stone on the rocky hillside, the scout looked around.

Corydon now did something without thinking: he stood up from shelter, whirling his sling. The man saw him and began to turn toward him.

Corydon fired again.

This time, the pebble hit the man hard on the temple. He slumped in the saddle, then tumbled to the ground.

Corydon flung himself flat in the dust. None of the Shells

appeared to have noticed, and the other scouts had not seen the Dolphins. Corydon breathed a sigh of relief. Alexandros clapped him on the back, then put a finger to his lips. By now, the Shells were almost immediately below the pass.

Alexandros gave a strange, high war cry, the same cry Corydon had heard in the katabathos stadium from Dolphin supporters.

Every Dolphin stood, then charged down the hill. Their feet thundered on the rocks.

The Shells looked up as their doom rushed toward them. Corydon could see the questions in their eyes, the horror in their faces. The Shell commander ordered an about-face, but the order came too late, and before it was half out of his mouth, the rout had begun. Shells turned not toward the enemy but away. They crashed back against their own ranks, knocking one another to the ground, as the first wave of Dolphin cavalry hit them with the terrible force of a curling white wave. As they ran, the Dolphin cavalry cut at them, pursuing so savagely that the entire Shell vanguard turned and ran before them, ran into the gully.

There, under the hot sun, the machines waited. Machines the Minotaur had made.

Corydon had run along the ridge for a ways to see what was happening, but his flying feet were halted by the sight of the machines. As the Shells poured into the narrow, rocky cleft, Corydon heard one of the Dolphins shout an order, and the machine in the center fired a burst of flaming tar toward them, a bubble of black fire. It hit the leading men, and Corydon heard their screams. The other machines fired, too, and the Shells recoiled as they were assailed by twelve-inch wood splinters sharper than knives, by stones, by a hail of angry fragments of hot flint that wormed under their armor.

Corydon was reminded of the battle against the heroes, but it was not quite the same here; the Shells were no more evil than the Dolphins. . . . He saw one of them burning like a torch. He was screaming and dancing. Finally flames engulfed him completely, and there was nothing left but a pile of ash. Another was looking, astonished, at his own entrails as they lay spread in the dust. A stone crushed a man's skull. Corydon thought of the man he himself had felled, a man who had only been following orders.

Enough, thought Corydon. He'd seen enough. He hurried away but could hear the clash of swords nearby. Then he remembered that what they had been fighting was only the vanguard of the Shell army. The real army must have arrived.

Then he heard a new noise above the battle tumult, a noise that sounded like children screaming. . . . He ran up to the top of a hill and looked out over the battle going on below him. He could see Shells and Dolphins attacking each other ferociously.

But now his eye was caught by a new group of warriors. They were white from head to toe, and as they opened their mouths in battle yells, Corydon saw that even their tongues and the inside of their mouths were white. Their eyes, too, were the livid, glowing white of diamonds. In their hands, they held swords shaped like the sickle moon, with hilts of some polished white metal, shaped and chased with infinite care.

Corydon looked at them in wonder. After a minute or two, he realized that they were trying to come between the two sides.

As he watched, one dazzling white girl flung herself between a hulking Dolphin warrior and his Shell opponent. She held the

Dolphin, apparently without effort, and put the tip of her sword to the neck of his *Shell* foe. She gave a high, piercing scream, teeth bared. Then she said in a high, clear voice, "Stop this battle! What is the point? You cause misery to everyone! Stop! Enough!"

Corydon gulped. It was just what he had been thinking himself.

The soldiers were stunned. They had never heard anyone oppose the war before; usually they'd been greeted by crowds eager to see them fight. They had never before heard a cry for peace. It stopped them in their tracks. They stood with their swords slack in their hands. One *Shell*, obviously the commander, stepped forward. "We must defend our goddess!" he cried. "These Dolphin infidels deny her powers."

"We do not!" a Dolphin replied. "We admit she has witch powers. But we worship the good Lord of the Ocean, Poseidon. . . . Atlantis is his!" Warriors on all sides began trying to draw their weapons and resume the fray.

"What of the innocent men and women killed in these wars?" shouted one of the white warriors.

"We do not come here to argue," added another. "We come to warn you. Look at what you have already wrought. You have brought the Morge upon the city with your desperation, your longing to win. The city cannot stand against them, and you know it. They are your doom."

"That was the Shells!" shouted a Dolphin.

"It was the war," the white woman insisted. "Just as it was the war that left the gully next to this one full of burning bodies." There was a somber silence.

"And there is another weapon yet to be unleashed," the tallest of the white women said, "a weapon that will make victory sure for one side. Even now, the emissary of a deity is working to unleash new terror. But all this can be averted if you stop now."

Corydon looked at the war machines the Minotaur had built, and the thought came to him like a jolt of lightning: Could his old friend really be the same if he had built those fiendish instruments of death? Or had he somehow been corrupted to work for Poseidon—as part of Zeus's greater plan?

"But there is still hope!" cried one of the moon-white women.

"Yes," cried a Shell, "hope that our true goddess might receive her due from these worshipers of seaweed and slime—"

"Stop!" The white women had now formed a line between the two armies. "Now," said their leader, low and dangerous, "go. Disperse. We will watch you. The only hope is peace."

As if in a dream, a few men began to walk away from the armies. Their commanders shouted at them to stay, but they were oblivious. They had seen friends die, countrymen die. They had seen that man was but a handful of dust. Now they wanted only to see their homes and families again. Soon more and more of the armies joined them. Soon huge chunks of the armies broke away, as someone might rip off a hunk of bread from a loaf. Eventually the commanders followed, their peaceableness enforced by the swords of the white women. Corydon at last heard one of them name those who had forced them to make peace.

"The Selene," the man whispered. "Votaries of the Huntress of the White Deer."

Corydon remembered that goddess, how she had deftly brought Gorgos to birth. Now, too, something had been born: a bloodstained peace. But was it too frail to survive?

Corydon knew that this peace was his opportunity, his and Lamia's. They must release the Bull. Now. Tonight. And if the Minotaur had been . . . damaged . . . then he could be healed, but only if they rescued him. Corydon set his jaw. He lit out at a run, leaping nimbly over rocks. He did not go in search of Alexandros to bid him farewell. He knew that he must hurry if he was to keep his rendezvous with Lamia.

TWENTY

As Corydon reached the temple, he saw that Lamia was waiting for him. He approached, feeling awkward; it seemed an age since they had met, and he felt he was walking toward a stranger. She, too, seemed shy, but that was not unusual. Clearing his throat, Corydon asked abruptly, "Have you found the way?"

"Yes," she said in a whisper, rubbing the toe of her sandal on the ground. "I know what to do." She seized his hand. "We must go *now*. Must. It is now."

"But how?"

"It is near. Very near. But it is a secret, forbidden."

Corydon's spine rippled with shudders. The last Atlantean secret he had encountered had been the Morge.

He followed her through a tangled wood and up a hill. And suddenly, ahead of them, he caught the gleam of water. At first, he took it for a lake, a long sickle shape of silver and green sheen that split the land like a knife blade. But as he drew closer and heard the wails of the gulls, he realized it was an arm of the sea, a lagoon. How had they missed it before? Had it been there? Just as he was thinking this, a group of hunters on horseback broke from the woods to their left. They halted and stared disapprovingly at Corydon and Lamia.

"No one must see us!" Lamia hissed. "The Old City is utterly forbidden except to a very few. No one even comes to the shore unless—" An idea seemed to strike her with sudden force.

"Quick, kiss me!" she gasped, and drew him abruptly into her arms. Before he could think, Corydon found she was pressing her lips against his.

He hadn't meant to kiss her back, but somehow he found he was. He put his hand up and touched her face softly. Under his hand, her skin seemed to change, became smoother, and he felt her snake self breaking through her disguise.

Then she let him go just as suddenly. "Now," she said, "they will only think I have a lover." She raised her hands, and Corydon caught a last flash of snake color before she submerged herself once more in her disguise. Still, the kiss was enormous in his memory. He felt oddly undone. And so he fell back on their mission.

The water was shining with gray-green and turquoise light. And at its center, there it was: the old ruined city of Atlantis. What he had hazily interpreted as submerged trees took shape as ruins. There were towers, just as lofty as the towers of the modern city, but there was something wrong with these: they leaned sideways and backward, like trees uprooted by a savage storm. Beside them were low clumps of houses.

"Is that it?" he breathed. "Is it here that we will find the Bull?" he asked carefully.

She nodded. Her face was still scarlet after their kiss. Corydon felt himself going scarlet, too.

"Old Atlantis," whispered Lamia. "The Old City. We were never allowed to go there unless summoned. It was the domain of Poseidon alone. A Dolphin city. Something happened to it; they say it was built in the salt marshes here, on the western edge of the sea, and that somehow its people angered their own god, so the sea began to take it back. They say it started slowly, with big waves washing the streets only at high tides. But then the tides began to undermine the houses at their foundations, and they gradually tipped on their timber pillars and piers, until each started to fill up with silt and effluent, so that soon no wall was straight enough to hang a mirror. At first, its people tried to keep up their lives, tried to prop up each slipping wall. But as the city shifted more and more with each wave, each tide, they saw that they could not resist the god's anger, and they fled to the harder, firmer lands to the east, to build again, with the deadly help of the Morge."

Corydon felt absolutely no impulse to visit a place so rotten with the anger of a god. But Lamia seemed certain that this was where they must go.

He said, "We must try to find a boat or someone who works on the water: a fisherman or some such. I know, I know"—he caught sight of her worried face—"but they must take people there sometimes. Occasionally."

They began combing the shore methodically for a boat. And, almost at once, a movement caught Corydon's eye. Near the opposite shore, a small figure shot from a hut and out to a boat. Oars flew as the boat jetted toward them faster than a dolphin could swim. It seemed like magic, the answer to a prayer. But if Corydon had learned one thing, it was that prayers were rarely answered in the way you hoped. *Especially* prayers pertaining to a place the gods had already cursed.

The boat came nearer.

As it did so, Corydon got a better look at the oarsman: a humble-looking fisherman in a plain blue robe.

Reassuring—except his monster-sense was tingling. Instinctively he moved away from the shore—

—just as the fisherman hurled himself out of his boat and into the water. The boat shot onward, but the water around it seemed to come to a violent boil. From it arose the huge, ferocious cara-pace of a gigantic black crab that now towered above the water, above the ruined City, so huge it almost blotted out the sun.

Corydon turned to run, but as he did so, a memory tugged at him—something Sthenno had told him once, long ago, about a fisherman who could change himself into any shape.

"Hold on to him!" he cried as he remembered. But Lamia had already run backward from the shore. With a despairing cry, Corydon flung himself at the outstretched pincer that reached for him—

—only to find himself clutching the sinuous body of a water eel, so slimy that it almost wriggled from his grasp, but as he held on with all his will, the coils changed into—

—the hoof of an old white horse that kicked viciously at his head but, when he hung on to it, became abruptly—

—an enormous striped cat whose claws raked his arm, and then, as he felt his own blood run down his hand—

—it burst into red flame, making him cry out in pain, when it abruptly—

—became an old man so gnarled and twisted and ancient that he was like a piece of driftwood from the first shipwreck.

"Proteus," said Corydon, breathing hard. "Proteus. That is your true name. By your true name and true self, I charge you to carry us to the Old City."

The old man gaped. Then he began to laugh hysterically, maniacally, as if what Corydon had asked was the most stupid request he had ever heard in his life.

From Proteus's boat, Corydon saw the Old City creeping closer. Ruined houses edged the sky, their broken walls marking its limits. Inside one crumbling house, Corydon glimpsed a painting, its colors smudged by water. A few half-collapsed ceilings still glinted with gold. Against the jagged brick and wood shards, the sea alone was smooth and cool, indifferent to the rot of what human hands had made. The water flowed in the streets of the city it had taken back. It was too strong for anyone, man or monster. It was too strong to fight.

The old man was still giggling annoyingly as they pushed past these first houses. They were in a kind of canal, and reflections of light off the water traced eerie shapes on the walls of the ruins on either side.

Proteus swung first left, then right, then around. The canals narrowed. As the journey continued, Corydon felt himself growing bewildered. Usually, his strong shepherd sense allowed him to understand a landscape, to tell which way was north, which way to go. But here, immured in water, his Panfoot separated from the ground by its eddies, he could feel nothing. A sea fog was rising, wrapping the ruins in a thick gray blanket. Broken towers humped out of it as they drifted past more once-bright houses now decorated only with the green velvet of moss. Had they passed this house before, the one with the cracked beige stucco? This one with the broken shutters?

At last, however, they came to somewhere different, a place even Corydon felt sure he hadn't seen. It was a large open space, one in which there had never been houses. It felt strange and even intimidating after the narrow water lanes; it also felt colder. A solitary tree, long dead, stood in the center, its blackened branches decayed. A short distance away was what had once been a very large building; its tall tower leaned drunkenly, but its walls were still imposing. In the center of a paved space stood some large round container, its metal lid half eaten by rust. Trails of rust ran red down its sides, as if it had once held blood. Around it stood a circle of pillars like broken teeth. Grass and moss had almost covered them.

"Right!" screamed Proteus. "Get out! Get out of my boat. You. And you. Get out." Corydon and Lamia obligingly clambered onto the slippery pavement. Proteus rowed away as if all the Olympians were on his heels. Corydon tried to ask him to wait, but it was plain that he had no intention of doing so.

As the splash of his oars died away, Corydon noticed the silence. It was absolute. Not an ant seemed to stir. And it was growing dark. There was no sunset, but the violet of the sky was deepening to purple.

"We must hurry," said Lamia. Taking his hand, she led him toward the ring of broken teeth. "I know what to do," she whispered, her face drained of color. "I know. Oh, Corydon . . ." She seemed to be asking forgiveness. Corydon felt baffled. He patted her hand, and then she sighed, raised her arms above her head, and began a slow dance, a dance that seemed to call on night and blackness. And as her feet and hands traced intricate patterns on the stone and in the air, a great darkness began to thicken at the center of the circle of pillars. It mounted and increased as Lamia danced faster and faster. Almost breathless, she beckoned to Corydon to join her. As he did so, he noticed that her feet left bloody footprints on the stone, and he thought of a tale about a siren who had loved a mortal but had been unable to walk on her feet without pain. Was it like that for Lamia? As the blood slicked the stone, the darkness they were creating began to buzz and hum like a crowd of hungry hornets.

"Now!" said Lamia. She seized his hand and pulled him into the blazing darkness they had created. Corydon's foot struck one of the broken pillars; his other foot tangled in what felt like vines; he almost fell. But Lamia pulled him on. His head rang with the ferocious humming of the dark. And suddenly it stopped, and he was left standing in a hall made of white marble set with rich red porphyry.

He didn't speak for fear of breaking the spell. It was obvious, however, that the magic dance Lamia had done was time magic, had somehow returned them to a time before the city was destroyed, a time when the Bull could be free. Perhaps it was a time when he was meant to be free; perhaps, in this time, his captivity was a mistake.

Lamia gestured ahead. Corydon realized she wanted him to follow.

The palace was as mazelike as the ancient city itself. The

twisting, turning passages of white marble were lit only with guttering torches. They ran down a tight spiral staircase, ending in a storeroom. It looked anonymous, as if they had come to the wrong place. But Corydon somehow knew—this was the center of power. Lamia led him to the room's back wall, and then he saw it: a tile with a bull as white as woodsmoke on it.

Corydon instinctively put out a hand and touched the bull's horns. He didn't know why he was doing it. Something about the tile seemed almost to compel him.

At first, nothing happened. Corydon and Lamia stood staring at the wall.

Then Lamia let out her breath in a hiss. As she did so, the tile began to grow under Corydon's hand. As it grew, it became transparent, as if it were getting thinner, like ice melting. It began to shake with a fine, hard tremor, and around it, the wall, too, was pulsing. There was a faint lowing sound, which grew stronger and stronger, and then Corydon grabbed Lamia's arm and dragged her backward, only just in time, as the entire wall caved in when the Bull pressed through it somehow—afterward Corydon could never quite think how—and ran directly at them, its immense nostrils flaming red. At the last moment, Corydon and Lamia flung themselves aside as the Bull charged fiercely at the opposite wall of the storeroom. Soon that wall, too, hung in tatters of shattered stone.

"Come on!" Lamia shouted. "We have to catch him!"

"How?" cried Corydon. "He's completely and utterly wild! We don't even have a rope!"

"But we have to get him to the god!" As she spoke, Corydon looked into her wide, dark eyes and saw his own doubts mirrored there. Had they been right to release the Bull? He had thought to somehow tame the beast, but after seeing him, it seemed hopeless, like trying to tame wind or moonlight. . . .

"What about magic?" he asked desperately.

"He's too fast," said Lamia despairingly. "Come on, Corydon! We must run with him. Perhaps something will come to us— a god . . ."

But as they burst out onto the open square, Corydon saw that the Bull wasn't running. He was standing in a patch of moonlight, as if he were somehow soaking up its rays. And as the moonlight shone on him, he grew. Already he was the height of a mighty wave. He lifted a hoof the size of a big man and pawed the ground fiercely. A wave washed Corydon knee-deep, but the land under the beast's feet lurched and grew, like the Bull himself. Now the Bull shot forward again, and wherever he stepped, the land regrew, so that a long island marked the Bull's passage as accurately as an arrow. When he reached what had been the shore, he pawed the ground again and half the hillside began to crumble.

"This is what Poseidon wants!" Lamia cried in despair as they tore after him. "Corydon, he's Earthquake! Don't you see? There'll be nothing left of Atlantis if he's turned loose in it. It'll be like the Old City." Corydon almost swallowed his thumping heart. Was that how the Old City had been destroyed? He looked back. Already the Old City had collapsed into ruins once more; whenever they had been, they were now back in the present.

As she spoke, the Bull went on burgeoning and swelling. The hill could hardly bear his terrible weight. Then he tossed his head and gave a deep bellow, so deep that men three valleys away woke and turned pale. Then he cocked his head, as if he were listening for the voice of a god. With another bellow, he moved off in the direction of the city. His legs were by now so immense they were like moving pillars.

"We've got to warn them!" Lamia cried, and set off after him. Corydon followed, running, but thinking hard. The Bull was Earthquake, yes—but the Bull was also the same white as the warrior women who had stopped the battle . . . the Selene Amazons. . . .

As the thought came to him, he knew they were the only hope. Poseidon had turned the Bull into a weapon . . . just as he had turned the Minotaur into one . . . but perhaps the Selene Amazons could restore him to peace if Corydon could get to them in time. . . .

Then a thought stopped him. What about the Minotaur? Surely he would not be released if Poseidon knew that Corydon was trying to *stop* the Bull. But perhaps Poseidon had already released him? And if the earthquake destroyed the city, could the Minotaur survive?

"Lamia," he gasped, "Lamia, I know who can help us. Stay with him, warn the city. I'll get help. The Amazons . . . I've seen them, Lamia. They'll know what to do. You must trust me." But he could not wait for her reply. He turned and ran back toward the battlefield. "And look for the Minotaur," he called over his shoulder. As he ran, he could hear the terrible slow thunder of the Bull's strides.

He couldn't run all night, but he only dropped to a walk when he couldn't go another step at full speed, and then he ran on again as soon as he could bear it.

Still, at his best speed, it was a while, perhaps half an hour, before he reached the first soldiers' camps, and he couldn't see the white women at all. He kept stumbling into Shell warriors and having to elude them, slipping off repeatedly into the darkness, using all his kleptis skills. But finally he saw a pale fire on the top of a hill on the horizon, and somehow he knew in his aching limbs that this fire had been made by the white women. It was a fire that burned with the dead glow of the moon. The light made him think of Persephone's hair, of the whiteness of the shades. Suddenly his heart was cold with fear. But he had to go on.

Before he could speak, a clear voice stopped him.

"Corydon Panfoot," it said. "You come to seek our help. You have loosed the Bull."

Another voice, colder still, spoke: "You did not heed our warning, mormoluke. Now you have unleashed Earthquake."

Corydon peered around. In the shadows, he could distinguish the outlines of three pale, pale forms.

"I had to," he burst out. "The Minotaur—"

"—has been all but destroyed," said the first voice. "It may not be possible to save him from what he himself has done."

Corydon gasped. "My dreams!" he cried.

"Were true and false—as everything," said all the voices together. "But now the Bull requires us. We will help you. We want only an end to these wars."

"Do you serve the Olympians?" Corydon asked.

"We serve the goddesses," they said in unison, their voices rising in a kind of eerie, high hymn. "Hera the mother, Demeter the earth, Artemis the moon . . ."

"What of Athene?" Corydon asked suspiciously.

The voices were silent. A silence so long, so cold, that it was a worse rebuke than any words could be. Corydon understood. Finally a voice said, "Our people were exiled because of the enchantress. They live now beneath the city, as they can. And with them went all the arts of the city, mormoluke, jewelry and baking and painting and clothing and sewing, the graciousness of life."

Corydon was puzzled. "But Euryale . . ." He thought of her art lessons.

"Yes, a little remains. Her teacher is descended from us. That is why he is still a true artist. But most of the people live among works they can no longer understand, live in terror, live in dread, because of the Morge, because of what they themselves have made. And the Morge bind them closer to the goddess, for they mistakenly think only she can protect them—when it was she who plotted with her dark half sister Hecate to resurrect them. . . ."

"What can we do now?" Corydon asked.

"We must tame the Bull. Whoever rides him will control the future, the earthquake. . . . He is the raw power to create. But what can create can also break and destroy. . . . If he falls into the wrong hands . . ."

"What about the Minotaur?" Corydon asked. "Poseidon and I had a bargain. . . ."

There was another icy silence after he had spoken the name of the sea god. Then a chilling voice said, "We make no bargains with Zeus and his allies. And if you do so, you are a fool."

"Maybe," Corydon muttered angrily. "But the Minotaur is my friend. I have seen him, seen his sufferings, in dreams. There is no one to help but his friends. And he once helped me."

The voices were silent again. Then one, the coldest, asked, "What if we told you that he is already lost?"

"I know he's not dead," Corydon said. "So I choose to hope.

He may have lost himself. Maybe you are perfect, but we monsters make mistakes. We do lose ourselves sometimes. We need our friends to find us then. And to help us remember who we truly are. It is our destiny, as it is yours to be cold and shining."

"We are not perfect," said the cold voice again. "And we see that you cannot be dissuaded. Then we must take the Bull to Poseidon and try to prevent him from annexing its power."

"Come on, then!" Corydon shouted. "The longer we leave it, the worse it will be! Another friend of mine is already trying to catch the Bull. . . ."

"Is she protected against the madness he induces?" one of the women asked sharply.

"I don't know," Corydon answered. "Perhaps. Neither of us was affected when we released it."

"But did you touch him?" the Selene asked.

"No," Corydon said slowly.

"Then we must hurry indeed. . . ." The pause now was very bleak. "Get up, mormoluke. We use our chariots when we have need of haste. Ride beside us."

A hard, dry, slender hand seized his arm and swung him into what turned out to be the flint-hard seat of a chariot. Peering into the swirling darkness, he could just make out the shape of a pale horse, which had the same smoky, moonlit quality as the Bull itself, and beside it a denser darkness—a dark horse. . . . As he tried to make out the shapes, there was a sudden jolt, and the chariot rushed forward into the night. Corydon quickly lost track of time; the stars whirled overhead, and the chariot swayed under him, jostling him. But he longed to go faster still; he could almost have screamed at the horses to hurry.

Lamia . . . madness . . . the Bull . . .

What had he done?

It seemed an age till he saw the first red lights of the city, though the Selene chariot was in reality as fast as a dragon and much more silent. The lights of Atlantis were fainter than he expected....

Then he remembered. It was the night of the moon's full dark. The Morge would be in the streets.

As he thought this, he smelled the Morge smell, heard the soft thud of their heavy clay feet. A group of them were snuffling around one of the houses on the outskirts.

The high voice of the Selene reached him.

"Cover your face!" she cried. Corydon pulled his cloak down. The chariot clattered by. The Morge did not even turn their immense heads.

When they were safely past, Corydon looked up. "Why didn't they see us?"

"Because we are not what they feed on. I cannot stop to explain all now...." They galloped past another group of Morge. Corydon could see that these had broken into a house; the door was in pieces, shards, and one Morge was holding something in its fist.... It looked like a human. It hung limp, and it wasn't screaming. Corydon turned his face away, feeling sick.

"Do not look at them!" warned the Amazon, but it was too late. The Morge had felt Corydon's glance, perhaps felt his horror and sadness, his fear. It dropped the body of its victim and sprang after the chariot.

With a long, high whistle, the Amazon called to the horses, and they ran faster and faster, but Corydon could hear the great, heavy thuds of the Morge drawing nearer, nearer.... The Amazon suddenly gave an even higher cry and this time swung the horses around in a huge, wide curve, so that the chariot pointed back at the Morge. Corydon sprang up. Battle was at hand and concealment useless.

The Morge came on, and its stink was like everything that had died in the city since it had been built.

The Amazon drew her curving sword. Runnels of white light poured from its blade. She held it high over her head. As the Morge bent to seize Corydon in its great red fist, she brought the shining sword down on its head.

The Morge gave a heavy cracking sound as the dark magic that knitted it together was shattered by the sword's power. It fell like a tree. Just in time, Corydon grabbed the side of the chariot as the horses nimbly dodged the huge earth-body. Now the driver sang to the horses once more.

To Corydon's amazement, the chariot turned onto one of the city's great, wide avenues and they found themselves accompanied by a sampling of all its inhabitants. The Morge lumbered along but ignored them; their dull red eyes were fixed on something ahead. Corydon saw more of the moon-white Selene creeping out of doorways and from buildings. There were people, too, ordinary city dwellers, steering well away from the Morge, cautiously skirting the walls of the buildings, but persisting. And their eyes were full of light, too.

Everyone was following the white moony glow of the Bull.

Amid the thick, heavy tread of the Morge, Corydon had begun to hear the crisper tattoo of the Bull's strides. The earth was quaking like a new-made cheese. Now he looked up and saw the immense white smoke-form of the Bull. As he watched, the Bull lowered his head and gave a deep, harsh bellow.

Corydon's head was swimming with the immense power of the magical god-beast. He clung to the shreds of reason. He must get the Bull away . . . he must get the Bull away . . . before it became a weapon, before someone found out how to use it to make the earth shake really badly. . . .

But he felt the Bull-madness growing in his own mind. Already, all he wanted was to follow the Bull to infinity. His eyes began to glow, too. Seeing this, one of the Amazons looked at him sharply. Then, from her neck, she drew off a necklace bearing a gem that shone with the same light as the Bull. She fastened it around Corydon's neck, and as she did so, the mist in his mind seemed to clear, and he thanked her with a nod.

"Moon-madness," the Selene said. "The whole city has it."

Corydon saw that this was true. The people following the Bull were behaving very oddly. Even the Morge were less purposeful than usual. They smiled, even, and Corydon saw one lying full-length on the ground in a side street, laughing at the sky. But most were drawn to the Bull himself. Corydon spotted Lamia alighting from a golden dragon whose eyes were white with moonmania. Like him, she was trying to fight the madness, apparently with more success.

The avenue opened out into one of the City's broad squares. This, plainly, was where the Bull had been heading all along. It was the square that contained the broken statue of Poseidon. The Bull came close to the statue and nuzzled it briefly with his immense nose. Then Corydon felt the Bull's rage begin to gather as he took in the statue's ruination.

He raked one forefoot along the ground. The ground gave a brisk shake, like a carpet that a housewife flings aloft to get rid of the dust. A lot of people fell over. But they stood again, even those

262

plainly injured, and looked up transfixed at the great white-and-golden face, the luminous eyes.

To his amazement, Corydon saw at least a dozen people run across the now-shaking ground to the Bull and attempt to vault themselves onto his back. But the Bull shook them off, like a dog shaking off droplets of water.

And now, on the south side of the square, the crowds parted, and Corydon saw what he had been hoping for and dreading. A lone figure approached the Bull, head held high. Corydon saw the sharp whip of a long cloak in the wind. An eddy of dust stirred at his feet.

Tall, poised, strong. Skin green-black like the shell of a mussel.

It was Gorgos.

"No!" cried Corydon, but in the rumpus, Gorgos had no chance of hearing him. The crowd recognized him in some fashion, and some even began to cheer. Gorgos bowed stiffly, but he never took his sea-dark eyes from the Bull's eyes. Two Morge stepped aside for Gorgos, caroming into a group of onlookers as they did so. Gorgos didn't even incline his head.

Now the Bull saw him.

Gorgos didn't hold out his hand. He simply kept walking at the same pace.

The Bull backed up slowly. And as he did so, he bent his head down, then his legs.

He crouched at Gorgos's side.

Gorgos bowed to the ruined statue of his great father of the ocean.

Then he unsheathed his sword. The white light of the Bull made it blaze like a comet. The Bull lowered his head still farther.

He's going to kill it! Corydon thought, and again cried, "No!" But the press of people and Morge and Selene was now so great that Corydon couldn't hope to reach Gorgos in time. . . . And if Gorgos killed the Bull, the Morge would be released from the moon madness and everyone would die. . . . Could the Bull be killed?

Corydon had been so preoccupied that he had not noticed what his Amazon guides were doing. They had sprung lightly down from the chariot and were waiting, lithe, strong, by its side. Now, as if at a signal, they began weaving their way through the thick crowd. People moved aside for them. Corydon leapt down, too, and tried his best to follow but found it more like squirming through mud than walking. . . . And now he could see far less . . . but, at last, he and the Selene together managed to break into the front row of the watching people.

Gorgos was still holding his sword but seemed to have no intention of using it on the Bull. Instead, he lowered and sheathed it and then cried, "In the name of Poseidon, shaker of earth!"

In one bound, he sprang for the Bull's back, graceful as a dancer.

But something, someone, interrupted his spring.

Corydon saw that something, someone, dark was holding Gorgos back. Clinging fiercely to him.

It was Lamia.

Or rather, it was the Snake-Girl, for in the truth and drama of the moment, her disguise had fallen from her.

No one but Corydon noticed at first. Then, as the Snake-Girl twined her long, glowing tail around Gorgos to hold him more firmly, there were some gasps, confused murmurs, pointing.

Gorgos, however, managed to writhe free. It was as if the blood of his mother, Medusa, came alive in him, giving him power over her snaky strength. With one swift gesture, he unwrapped her tail. She clung to his arm, but he shook her off, and she fell to the ground. Corydon could see that she was crying. Two of the Selene Amazons ran to her and enfolded her in their arms.

Meanwhile, the Bull waited, immense and shining.

And now Gorgos was ready, and once again he attempted to mount the great beast. Corydon shouted. "No!" The Selene Amazons shot forward, like arrows from a taut bow, and formed a chain around Gorgos.

"He is not moon-mad!" Corydon heard their leader cry. "It is something else!"

"It is!" Gorgos sounded confident and impatient. "I know you, Selene. I have met your people. I come to return this Bull to my father, Poseidon. I do but his bidding."

Corydon noticed that Gorgos sounded not like a hero but like a boy playing a game and pretending to be a hero. He was entirely unafraid because it was to him a game. Were all heroes like that?

"But if you mount the Bull," the tallest Selene said steadily, her flaming eyes never leaving his, "you will destroy the city. The Bull will begin the earthquake. And the ground will tremble. And the city will fall."

"If that is its destiny," said Gorgos calmly.

"And what of its people?" said another Amazon sharply. "The people spread here before you? Do they count for nothing? What of your friends, Sthenno, Euryale, Fee, the friends you have made on the katabathos team? What of the Selene who helped you? What of the Snake-Girl? And Corydon, your oldest friend, who has long striven for you? What of the woman there—yes, there—

the one holding forth her baby and hoping only that it shall live? Can you doom all these?"

"Is this," asked the tall Amazon, "is this truly the work of a hero? Is it not rather a hero's lot to save the helpless than to doom them?"

Gorgos really hesitated. In the silence, the Bull's breath whiffled his dark hair.

Then he spoke, slowly. "My friends, I will not mount him. But I will ask your help in bringing him to my father. I have sworn to do so, as has Corydon. We would not be forsworn, and we will not fail our friend the Minotaur. After that, you must contest my father's will for him, if it should fall out that his will displeases you."

"It is graciously agreed," said the tall Amazon. In her cool voice, Corydon could detect no relief.

Somehow the Amazons brought from among their garments a rope made of something blue—the hazy blue of moonlight on water. Courteously they extended it to Gorgos. He flung the rope around the Bull's neck, and the Bull stood up ponderously, heavily, as if a building decided to grow taller. Then Gorgos began to lead the Bull along the avenue, followed by a great, spreading wake of people and Morge and Selene, their eyes reflecting his glow as the sea reflects the moon.

Corydon ran straight over to the Snake-Girl . . . Lamia . . . now he wasn't sure which she was.

She was sitting crumpled in the gutter, her head between her hands. Without thinking, Corydon put his arm around her thin shoulders.

The Snake-Girl looked up at him with her eyes that had seen the asps dancing in Egypt, and his heart was filled with peace. She might be mad, but she was at least herself again.

Corydon had an idea. Undoing the necklace the Selene Amazon had given him, he carefully extended the chain it was on until he could pass it over her head, too.

She gave a final dry sob. Then suddenly she gasped.

"Oh, Corydon," she said. "Thank you." And she squeezed his hand.

He tried to joke. "I don't know what to call you now. Is it Lamia or Snake-Girl?"

"I am neither, really," she said drearily.

"What would you like to be called?"

She sat in silence for a moment, listening to the retreating thunder of the Bull. Then she said, "Call me Snake-Girl. I liked myself better then."

Corydon smiled awkwardly. "All right," he said. "We'd better go, Snake-Girl." She smiled, too. Carefully they got up, the necklace wrapping them together. Walking was rather like a three-legged race. Luckily, the Morge were slow, and they soon caught up with the crowd; they could see the great light of the Bull ahead.

"We must get to Gorgos," they said to each other. They squirmed forward, using all Corydon's adroitness, all the Snake-Girl's sinuous ability to wriggle. They reached the front row of the crowd just as Gorgos and the Bull reached the harborside.

TWENTY-ONE

GORGOS WAS ALREADY INVOKING HIS FATHER. "GREAT Poseidon!" he cried. "Father!" Corydon ran to stand beside him as the sea began to heave itself into the wavelike shape of the sea god. The Bull snorted excitedly and pawed the ground again. Evading Gorgos's restraining hand, the Bull tried to run into the sea, as if eager to embrace the sea god.

Poseidon ignored both his sons. Instead, his foam-flecked, cavernous eyes sought Corydon's.

"Panfoot," he said, "you have made yourself my servant now. You have done my work. Your love for your friends has always been your undoing."

Corydon suddenly found an eruption of fury hotter than magma in his own heart. "You wouldn't know about that," he said. "You don't have any friends. No Olympian has friends. You have sons and worshipers and grovelers and enemies. But you don't have one single friend."

Poseidon was silent for a second, a heartbeat. Then he

268

laughed with the harsh sound of a ship's hull striking a reef. But Corydon had sensed under the laughter his sudden uncertainty. However, it was only momentary. The laughter became harder and crueler.

"Well, Corydon Panfoot," he said, still laughing, "here is your friend whom you value more than the lives of the many Atlanteans standing here. I wish you joy of him. You may decide our bargain was not such a good one for you as you believed."

With that, the wave that was the sea god rolled over the pier. Everyone stepped backward, some slithering and screaming. The Bull surged forward. But the inundation was only for a second; the great green-gray wave withdrew from the pier, and Corydon saw that it had left behind a bundle wrapped in coarse fishing nets, a bundle that struggled feebly. It was the Minotaur.

The Bull looked down as if remembering that this hulking bundle was his son. He blinked, and for a second Corydon had a vision of a beautiful woman whose face was full of fear and madness, riding on the Bull's back to glory and shame . . . the Minotaur's mother . . . the Bull-madness. . . . But then the Bull blinked again and snuffled impatiently.

Corydon ran to his friend, Lamia forced to follow, and together they began slowly unraveling the Minotaur from the fishing nets. Already, Corydon could see that there was something wrong, badly wrong. The Minotaur didn't struggle, didn't seem to want to help himself, and his great eyes were dull, his fur harsh. As they worked to free him, Poseidon spoke again.

"Now, people of Atlantis," he said, "you are mine. You belong to my Bull. Shells, you have three days to convert to my ways. After that, my Bull and his servants will hunt you down like hares. You will do their bidding in all things. There will be no more goddess worship. The island is mine. As Zeus always intended."

"You speak very freely of what Zeus intended," said a sweet voice. For the first time, Corydon noticed a tall youth dressed in Shell colors. Memory nagged him; there was something terribly familiar about him.

"Who has a better right than I?" the sea god said. Corydon heard the jagged edges of killing rocks in his voice.

But the youth was not daunted. "Be careful, Sea Lord," he said. "It is possible that you do not know me. But my people will always know me, and those who know me know also that I will not surrender Atlantis to you and your heavy-footed clodharrower here. You may have bought yourself help from the monsters— shame to you—but you will learn that my people and I can command help, too, and you will not like it. Victory is not yours yet." Here his voice became lower. And somehow Corydon could see the gray eyes glinting through the mist of the disguise. "It's the Lady," he hissed. "Athene."

Her head snapped round.

"And I know you, little goat-boy. Take what remains of your friend. He has already been destroyed. And he will not be the last to perish in opposing me." Her laugh was triumphant, exultant. "Shells," she said. "Shells, you may suffer at first. But we will not be defeated. Forward to victory!"

Only a few ragged cheers answered her, because of the Bull awe still on the crowd, but she glowed from them until she was as bright as the Bull himself. Poseidon lashed at the pier with angry wavelets, but she raised her arms as if welcoming his fury and absorbing it into her person. The Bull, disturbed, began to paw and snort. Gorgos held on tightly to the Selene's rope; so did the tall Amazon.

"Victory!" The sea god's voice was a cold and lashing wave of scorn. "You will not have the victory!" He raised his arms in invocation. "Bull!" he shouted. "Bull-son! Gorgos!"

The Minotaur stirred feebly in Corydon's lap, tried to raise his great, heavy head in response to the god's commands. Gorgos responded much faster, lifted lightly as the sea picks up a boat by the will of its lord and master. He pulled at the Bull's head.

The Bull stamped his foot once, violently.

The ground rocked, as if it had become as liquid as the ocean. Corydon felt a great wave of earth pass under his feet. Buildings in the city began to totter.

And every person present wearing Shell clothing fell to the ground, their eyes bulging, screaming with the pain in their heads. It was as if the wave the Bull had conjured had somehow entered them, made them writhe as the earth was writhing.

Corydon and the Snake-Girl stood safe within the circle of the moonstone the Amazon had given them, but all around, Corydon could see thrashing pain. One woman's head was bent back in a kind of rictus of despair, her hair draped on the ground like seaweed. She gave a hard and horrible scream.

And then Corydon suddenly saw that it was Euryale.

He clapped his hand to his mouth with horror, then waited for her to turn back into a ten-foot Gorgon in the extremity of her anguish. But it didn't happen. She remained a little woman, writhing.

Then, somehow, the terrible pulsing stopped. A tower had fallen in the city. The Shells were shakily getting to their feet.

Poseidon's booming voice sounded again. "If you disobey me and deny my rule," he said, "I will make you suffer. I will level your city."

The gray-eyed Athene stared flintily at him. "I will not allow my people to suffer your tyranny for long," she proclaimed. Then she faded into gray mist and was gone. At Poseidon's command, Gorgos led the Bull away toward the City. Poseidon himself vanished into the sea he ruled.

As soon as he was gone, Corydon took the necklace off, gently moved the Minotaur's head to the Snake-Girl's shining, scaly lap, and ran over to Euryale's side. "Euryale," he gasped. "Are you all right?" What he wanted to say was, "How are you a Shell?" but he couldn't bring himself to upset her when she'd just been hurt by an Olympian.

"I am fine, little mormoluke," she said. "Fine. And I know you want to ask why I am a Shell. Do you know, I didn't know I was one until now? I didn't choose to be a Shell, Corydon. The Gray-Eyed Lady chose me. Things change, my mormoluke. Did you think change was only for the young? It is not so. Even when you have lived for centuries, with every day the same, change can catch at you and hurl you into new places, new ways of being. . . . Now I have learned that I am an artist. And that I was always one. And the hunger in me is filled."

She clung to Corydon's arm, then slowly rose, straight and dignified, if still disconcertingly tiny. Then she spotted the Snake-Girl and her heavy, inert burden. "Oh, Corydon!" she cried. "The Minotaur—you have him back. . . ."

"I did not change," said the Minotaur's heavy voice. "I lost myself in a labyrinth. Now I do not know who or what I am."

"You are the Minotaur," said Corydon, feeling foolish.

"No," said the bowed creature. "I *was* the Minotaur. I hated war. But they broke me, and they made me—" To Corydon's horror, the great beast began to weep. His shoulders shook with sobs.

"They made you build the machines," said the Snake-Girl softly. The Minotaur nodded his terrible head. His sobs had ceased. He sat up and in silence stared at his hands, as if horrified by what they had done.

"But I know you tried to resist!" said Corydon warmly. "I saw you in dreams."

"That was before they gave me the hazary," the Minotaur said bleakly.

Euryale looked alert and birdlike suddenly. "Corydon," she said, "hazary is a drug; it brings on dreams and visions, but those who use it crave more and more of it every day, until they die of it, for it is also a poison."

"Is there a cure?" Corydon asked.

"The person to ask would be Sthenno. Shall we take him back to Murax House?"

About to acquiesce, Corydon suddenly decided against it. "Euryale," he said gently, "I know you have loved it there. Perhaps it's your home now. But it was never his or mine or the Snake-Girl's. And the city isn't safe for you or for any of us with the Bull around. I have to get him away from the city. I know a place. He will heal fastest if he is alone. You know monsters need loneliness to heal."

Euryale smiled. "Little mormoluke, you needed no city to become your true self. You have always been that. I shall go back to Murax House, however," she said, cutting across their storm of protests. "It is not my home, but it is where I became an artist, and now I cannot imagine being without my art."

"But you can be an artist anywhere," said Corydon, puzzled.

"I need my paintbrushes," Euryale said seriously. "And my palette. And I am at work on a group of figures, called *Monsters of the Mist*, including a Sphinx like our friend on the island—I've been using gouache. . . ." Her face became very animated as she spoke.

"We can bring them with us," Corydon suggested.

Euryale patted his arm. "We could. But I do not wish to abandon the city that has given me such gifts. I will stay. And so will Fee, I think. But I will send you Sthenno if you can give me clear directions for her. She will know what to do to help the Minotaur." She snapped her fingers for a dragon, and Corydon snapped for another. They flew off in opposite directions.

When Euryale was nearing Murax House, though, she saw a squadron of Dolphin soldiers moving down the steps. They were carrying something in their arms.

Horrified, Euryale recognized her sculptures, her paintings.

"We're taking all art into custody, madam," said the officer in charge when Euryale confronted him furiously from the back of her dragon. He had to shout, and she urged the dragon downward. The dragon was reluctant to go closer to the soldiers.

"Why?" she shouted.

"All art has been banned as Poseidon-forsaken goddess-stuff," the man said. "And I agree, madam. If it hadn't been for those artists, we wouldn't be dealing with the Morge. Run along inside is my advice to you, madam," he said patronizingly. For a flicker of a second, Euryale's rage was Gorgon-sized. Bronze light began to gnaw at the edges of her dull tweediness.

"Give me back my things!" she cried. But the men took no more notice than they would of a crying child.

If the men had looked around, they would have seen Euryale's human disguise explode upward into winged bronze splendor, like a firework going off. Spreading her enormous wings, she shot toward them with the energy of a swooping falcon while her dragon watched openmouthed. Then the men saw her, and their faces turned gray with shock. They dropped everything and ran. The dragon fled at such speed that he left a scorch mark on the pavement.

Euryale checked her sculptures lovingly. One of them had broken in the fall, but Euryale could suddenly see the idea of a broken monster being born from its wreckage. Carefully she gathered them all into her strong arms and carried them indoors.

She barked her forehead on the lintel. She had forgotten she was ten feet tall again. Sthenno heard her curses and came running down.

"Sister!" Nothing in Sthenno's demeanor for the past month had shown that she had missed the old Euryale. But she had been nervous about the new Euryale blossoming in front of her, this new Euryale who talked for hours to other artists and thought only of art. Would this new person still want to live with her?

Sthenno had tried not to think such thoughts. She had tried not to think of the desolation of centuries alone. But then even Corydon and Lamia had left her.

To bury her dread, she had immersed herself in the library at Murax House, and in doing so, she discovered something that she had not yet told the other monsters.

Their new, human bodies were not just weaker. They were mortal.

As they grew into the disguises the Snake-Girl had shaped for them, the monsters had been tying themselves to human life and to human time. In these new bodies, they could be killed, but they would also wither and die, as humans did.

But worse, she suspected that this was what the Olympians had intended all along.

Zeus had lured them away by kidnapping the Minotaur, and Poseidon kept them weak by involving them in impossible tasks and endless quests. Poseidon had entangled Gorgos in his web of war and had ensnared Corydon and the Snake-Girl through their love of the Minotaur. Athene had enmeshed Euryale in art. And Sthenno felt sure that a day would come when no feelings, however strong, would release the monsters from their human forms.

We all become what we pretend to be, Sthenno thought. We should have been more careful about what we pretended to be.

Knowing this, Sthenno had spent long and sleepless nights wondering how to thwart Zeus's plan. Her first impulse had been to confide in the others. But Corydon and Lamia had gone, and Fee would not want to hear. And she worried that Euryale would refuse to believe it because she would not want it to be true.

But here she stood in her bronzy glory, and Sthenno could have cried hard gold tears because her loneliness was at an end.

Euryale grinned in almost the old way.

"I got very angry," she said, putting down the artworks she had salvaged. "They tried to take my art. Sthenno, I've been a fool. Why can't I be an artist like this? A ten-foot-tall bronze artist is what this city needs now. In my true form, I can defend art and artists from those barbaric Dolphins. And anyway," she added, "it will make it much easier to do a big canvas. I think my claws are dexterous enough for a brush. . . . I might try applying paint directly with them, as if they were palette knives. . . . I must try that. . . ." Dreamily she moved toward the studio.

"Watch the doorway!" yelled Sthenno. She was too late. Euryale had bashed her forehead again.

Following her into the studio, Sthenno sat down while Euryale began to assemble paints in delirious profusion. She poured out her idea about the Olympians' plan. Euryale listened, her great bronze head cocked.

Then there was a terrible silence as she registered the fact that she had been trapped by what she most loved. Her face set hard, like the face of a bronze statue. She didn't bother to deny what she could see plainly was true. But the goddess had seemed her friend . . . yes, *seemed,* that trickiest of plotters, that lady skilled in the arts of lying. . . . The one who had cursed Medusa. How could she have been such a fool?

Being Euryale, she didn't waste time blaming herself. She looked around the studio and could see that there was some truth in what she had made even in her delusion. That was all that mattered.

She was practical. She knew she would think better at work. Laying paint thickly on her canvas—delightedly finding that her claws did work just like palette knives but more dexterously—she asked, "What about the others? I know Corydon is all right—I saw him—and the Snake-Girl is not Lamia anymore. But what about Fee? And Gorgos? And you yourself?"

Sthenno darted out of the room and then reentered carrying a small book. Euryale grinned again. It was like old times. She began scratching out a rough portrait of her sister as she remembered her, into her canvas. Suddenly she saw that what she was painting were the woods around the island cave. There were the furze bushes. . . . As she looked dreamily at her memory, *Sthenno* spoke.

"I've been augmenting my spell," she said breathlessly. "This is a magical book, a grimoire, and it told me how to increase the power of the spells of others. I used it because my human identity kept slipping away from me. But I can dissolve it."

"Do it, then," said Euryale gently. "I miss your wings."

Sthenno thought for a second, then bronze light broke out all over her skin, and her human self cracked and came away from her glowing golden form as she grew. Her wings spread, like an opening flower's petals.

Sthenno bashed her head on the ceiling and uttered a cry. Both sisters gave their high, birdlike laughs. The Murax House servants ran in to see what was happening.

As they confronted two ten-foot giants with claws and golden wings, they stood in silence. Then they ran.

TWENTY-TWO

"WELL, THERE GOES THE STAFF." FEE CAME IN, TAPPING her foot. She smiled in amusement at the two Gorgons. "I hope you two are good cooks."

"Actually, I am," said Sthenno with dignity. "I can make wonderful bread."

"I remember it," said Fee, smiling. But her smile was wrapped tightly around an anger so dense it was like an extra person in the room. Suddenly Sthenno saw that Fee's anger had been the source of her hydra-headedness: she had needed many hissing faces to express her displeasure adequately.

Both the Gorgons saw at once that Fee was menaced by their metamorphosis.

"You don't have to go back," said Euryale gently, "just because we have."

"I don't want to go back," Fee said.

"Fee," said Sthenno, frowning at Euryale, "you don't understand. If you stay in that body"—she took a deep breath—"you'll die. You'll live out a human span, and then you'll die."

Fee went white. She went over to the window and looked out unseeingly at the trees surrounding the park. The noise of angry Dolphin soldiers rose up clearly.

She turned. "I can't change back," she said bleakly, but with her head held high. "This is me. It always was. It was my hydra-self that was a disguise. If I have to die, I will die in this body, in this city. In my own home." She smiled, and now her smile was free, even carefree. "In style," she added.

"But, Fee," Sthenno said eagerly, "I can change you back. In a second, I could make you immortal again. . . . And, Fee, it's my fault, because I haven't explained. . . . You're doing just what the Olympians want. This was their plan all along. . . . To trap us in these bodies. To make us mortal. . . ."

Fee spoke sharply. "Do you mean Lamia is in league with them? She created these bodies. Disguises."

All the monsters fell silent.

"No, surely not," said Euryale at last. "She is always so sweet. And she's gone back to her own true shape. . . ."

"Yes," said Fee, relentless, "but did she do it of her own will?"

Euryale paused. "I don't know," she said.

Sthenno spoke briskly. "This is pointless speculation. What we need to do is get out of the city and away from Atlantis, with the Minotaur. There will be time enough for questions when we are all safe. It is clear that the Dolphins and their god will control every-thing in a matter of days and that the power of the Bull—" Suddenly her eyes opened wide, flashing bronze beams. "But Gorgos!" she almost wailed. "Where is he?"

Fee spoke dryly. "He is now the Dolphins' leader in the City. It is he who controls the Bull that Lamia helped to release, a fact that also tells against her." Both the Gorgons began to protest, but she ignored them. "How else would she know how to release the Bull?" she asked.

"I . . . showed her," began Sthenno hesitantly. "And Poseidon—"

Fee went on speaking. 'I do not trust her. And as if this is not enough, Gorgos now does his father's will. It is he who is ordering the destruction of all art—even fashion!" she added with eyes blazing. Both Gorgons noticed that despite her rage, no hydra-shapes shadowed her slender and elegant face. "But do not think we Shells are beaten. We will act."

"I do not think we should know your plans," said Euryale quickly. Even now, she was afraid of getting entangled in a Shell plot.

"No, be innocent of it, for what we shall do is as terrible as what we face." Fee's voice was as hard as stone.

Sthenno began to scrabble for the right magic volume. "Euryale," she said, "pack up. You should be able to carry what you need. But you can't bring everything. I will cast a finding-spell to locate Corydon and Lamia."

Fee concealed her surprise at Sthenno's newfound skills, her mouth twisted into an ironic smile.

Sthenno carefully drew an immense circle on the floor. "Mind the rug!" Fee cried, and pushed it back, but it was too late. The rug was smeared with earth. Fee sighed.

"Now I need fire and water," Sthenno muttered, and Euryale ran to bring a lamp and a jug. Sthenno made new circles inside the first one, with the water first and then by pacing with the candle in her hand.

She began a high song that rose in a shriek of power.

In the air before her, a shimmering picture began to form. As it grew clearer, they could all see that it was a map of Atlantis, the whole island, so clear and so detailed that it was possible to see armies moving on the roads, stags running in the hills, a leaf falling from a tree.

The chant continued, and Euryale could hear Corydon's name, then the words "Snake-Girl" repeated in it.

A bright pinpoint of light appeared on the map.

It stood just above a rough hut set low on a hillside, with sheep all about it. Sthenno peered at the pinpoint of brilliance. Yes, she could see Corydon. And standing beside him was the Snake-Girl, shimmering—but she was accompanied by no pinprick of brilliance.

Puzzled, Sthenno tried calling her name again, but the figure of the Snake-Girl still refused to light up. She called out the Minotaur's name, and the hut took on a glow. Sthenno tried calling her Lamia and Snake-Girl and every other name she could think of, but nothing made the figure light up.

"It isn't her," she announced flatly. "It's some kind of impostor."

"I told you so," said Fee, equally flatly.

Euryale spoke sensibly. "Well, whoever it is, we've found Corydon and the Minotaur—so we must go there. We can investigate when we are with them. It may be that all this metamorphosis and change has somehow upset the spell. . . . I will not accuse anyone until I am sure." So she and Sthenno collected their things together. Then they paused.

"Fee," said Euryale, "I would like to thank you. You have given me myself. If I can help you, I will, but I cannot fight in the war."

"You will not have to," Fee replied. "I will make my own path. But I will give you a final gift." Going to a cupboard in the hall, she removed a huge key.

"Take this," she said. "But use it only when all is lost."

"What is it?" Euryale asked.

"It is a Portal key," Fee replied as they moved toward the door. "Each of the twelve Houses has one. They are a mage-art lost to us now, coming once from far in the east, but they still work. I will never use it, for I will never choose desertion. But you can use it to escape. The door is near here, the key will find it. Now go," she said with a smile, "before anybody sees you." Giving them a push, she turned away, but not before Euryale saw a single tear streak her perfectly formed cheek.

Euryale and Sthenno made for the door, jammed the doorframe, apologized to each other, and finally sprang aloft.

"It's good to fly again!" Sthenno shouted. She led the way, following her memory of the map she had seen. As they shot over the City, a few yellow dragons gave them glances of horror, then plunged, terrified, in the opposite direction.

Corydon was glad to be back at the hut, though he was worried about the Minotaur. All through the long flight, the Minotaur had been strapped to a complaining dragon, a deadweight, but a deadweight that moaned and shivered and sometimes even cried. Corydon and the Snake-Girl were helpless witnesses to his suffering.

"Should we give him some hazary?" The Snake-Girl's voice sounded tremulous. Corydon knew she was bothered by the Minotaur's pain.

"We don't have any, and I think it would be wrong."

She had fallen silent then, but the Minotaur's faint moans were audible even from several feet away.

Now he lay in the hut on an improvised bed of heather and straw, and they took it in turns to check on the great monster. Corydon and the Snake-Girl had built a fire outside, and they basked in its warmth. Corydon had caught and slaughtered a goat, had exercised some kleptis skills on some loaves of bread left to cool on a farm windowsill. The plainness and freshness of the food, the brightness of the strange stars, began to restore his spirits. But they couldn't persuade the Minotaur to eat at all, and the Snake-Girl still seemed uneasy. It was as if she didn't fit her old skin as well as she once had. Corydon remembered that she had sloughed her skin sometimes when on the island. Maybe she needed to do that again. He put a tentative arm around her shoulders.

There was a sudden thud and an explosion of shrieked curses. Corydon looked up sharply. His heart remembered that sound from happier island days.

It was the Gorgons.

Without waiting for a second, he ran to them, and they enfolded him in their great bronze wings. They hugged and hugged, then they all sat down by the fire to tell their stories.

The Snake-Girl sat still, mesmerized by the Gorgons' transformation.

"How did you regain your true shapes?" she asked finally. Sthenno and Euryale began to explain. Euryale broke off to store her art carefully in the hut. It almost crowded out the Minotaur, and he groaned. Corydon began a mild protest, but Euryale grinned. "It won't impede his recovery," she said. "It might even

help. There's some kind of magic in the monster-forms, I think."
She ignored Sthenno's skeptical mutter. "Anyway," she added
loudly, "Sthenno knows some spells that would help. Don't you,
Sthenno? She's become a sorceress while I was becoming an
artist." She cast her sister a shy look.

"That's right," Sthenno replied. It was obvious to Corydon
that something was up. The Gorgons were clumsily hiding a plan.

Sthenno began reading from a parchment—not a codex but
one of her oldest scrolls.

"Why do it out here?" Corydon asked, puzzled.

"It has to be done under the stars," Sthenno explained hastily.
She went on speaking in the unknown language.

As she did so, words of fire began to form in the air. As they
shaped themselves, thickening like smoke, Euryale moved unobtrusively to stand behind the Snake-Girl. When the letters were
almost solid and giving off heat, Sthenno gave a long, shrill cry.

And Euryale acted like a swift bird of prey: she seized the
Snake-Girl's hand and thrust it into the fiery letters.

The letters burst apart with a musical sound. Sparks flew into
the air. The Snake-Girl gave a shriek, and before the dumbfounded
Corydon could act, she began to change. Her appearance rippled like the sea when a light wind strikes it.

It was not a metamorphosis but a revelation. Corydon could
see now that her beautiful tail was enameled metalwork. He could
see the tiny metal nails that secured the mask of her gleaming,
scaled face, the shapeliness of her hair, each hair crafted, made. . . .
His mind brought him the memory of Hephaistos's servants, those
delicate metallic beings.

"Yes," she said hoarsely. "You are right about me."

Corydon stood up. His first impulse was to seize this impostor. . . . Fury almost choked him.

"Where is she?" he asked. "Where is the real Snake-Girl?"

"I don't know," said the machine. "I only know that I replaced her."

"When?" It was important to Corydon to ask this. Had none of it been real? The kiss?

"At the drugged feast at Hephaistos's forge."

"But you helped us get away. . . ."

"Part of the plan. You had to trust me so I could ensnare you with these mortal bodies." She spoke—yes, mechanically, as if she didn't care, could never care about anything.

"Ensnare us?"

"Corydon." It was Sthenno speaking. "Mormoluke. It was part of the Olympians' plan to make us mortal by catching us in mortal life. The Minotaur with drugs, Euryale with art, Gorgos with hero-power . . ."

And me with love, thought Corydon. How well they knew our needs, and how they have used them as a stick to beat us to death!

"What is she?" he asked.

"I am an eidolon," said the machine. "A copy of a person."

He longed to attack the mechanical girl that sat before them, staring defeated into the fire. But he knew his violence would be pointless.

"What did they do with the real Snake-Girl?" he asked.

"Kept her prisoner, I think. Or—they might have killed her."

Corydon, driven to desperation, could no longer withstand his own fury. This must be how Gorgos feels, he thought as he seized a heavy log and prepared to destroy her.

But when he saw her cringe, he could not bring the wood down on her. He threw it from him with a cry of despair.

She spoke again then, her words falling over one another.

"Corydon," she said, "in a way, it was real. When Hephaistos made me, he copied not only Lamia's body but her heart and mind as well. So I would do what she would do. Feel what she would feel."

"You can't know that, and neither can I," he said. "You are a machine. Her feelings might change. Yours can't."

"No," she said. "I can never change. And I was supposed to bind you closer to your human body. But I failed. Entirely. So there is no fear for you, Panfoot." As she spoke, she circled her arms suddenly in a high swirling movement. And with that, she disappeared.

Corydon and the Gorgons looked at one another. Euryale put her arm around Corydon's shoulders. "We'll find her," she said uncertainly. "The real her, I mean. . . ." She trailed off.

"I know," Corydon managed to say. But at that moment, to his horror, he didn't much care. Rushing to his friend's rescue had been a trap before—how could it not be again? And worse, what was the Snake-Girl to him now that he had been so long deceived by her copy? What was the value of a person if that person could be imitated so perfectly? Could he ever talk to the real Snake-Girl without thinking of conversations he had had with someone who didn't even exist? Who was now blurred in his head with the person he thought he had loved, the real person who had been his friend?

Adding to his cold lump of aching misery was the form in which the Minotaur had been given back to them. Corydon had not realized how much he had hoped for from the Minotaur. He was a last link with Medusa, the always-solid companion of his journey in Persephone's Realm. Now it was brutally clear that the person lying in the hut was not his old friend.

He wasn't sure if it was possible to bring the Minotaur he loved out of the shattered bulk that lay inside. He felt helpless.

But Sthenno had already darted into the hut, brandishing a parchment and a clawful of pungent-smelling herbs and flowers. Reluctantly Corydon followed her, finding himself unwilling to confront the spectacle of the prostrate Minotaur, his nostrils wide with pain.

Sthenno had brought in a pot of boiling water, and into this she now threw the herbs, chanting something softly to them in her high voice and consulting the parchment from time to time. As she did so, a thick and scented steam began to fill the hut. As her chanting went on, it grew difficult to breathe. The air thickened so much that Corydon could hardly see the gleam of Sthenno's bronzy wings.

Abruptly, the Minotaur sat up.

In the air before him, the thickened air of Sthenno's herb magic, a shape began to form. It was a man with a sword.

The Minotaur lurched to his feet.

The man-shape solidified. Now it was plainly a hero: small round shield, bright iron sword. Behind him were three hazier shapes, impossibly slender and curved beside the solid bulk of the Minotaur's head and muscled body: three gray horses, each with a long, thin horseman mounted. The horsemen bore fine, slender spears. As Corydon watched, they leveled them at the great, heavy bull-head.

Somehow the walls seemed to have expanded, melting away like the steam of Sthenno's potion.

"These are the daimons of hazary," said Euryale, who had come in behind Corydon. "He must fight them." Sthenno looked a warning, and she subsided.

The Minotaur lowered his great horns and charged the man.

The man brought his sword low, too, ready to intercept the monster's attack.

The horsemen pirouetted away from the Minotaur's charge, looking oddly comical, like clumsy dancers. As he ran, they swung around again, and all three drove their spears into his back.

Corydon took a step forward, but Euryale held him tightly.

The Minotaur began bleeding, great gouts of red blood soaking the floor. But the spears did not check his charge, and the lone hero on foot had to spring sideways to avoid the great spread horns.

Now the men on horseback were defenseless, and the Minotaur was furious. He gave a great bellow of rage and charged savagely. As he did so, the horses briefly changed forms, and Corydon saw the grinning skulls beneath their gray coats. Their teeth gaped wide as they flung back their heads. The riders, too, were exposed as slender corpses as the flesh melted from their bones.

With a heavy roar, the Minotaur flung himself at each horse in turn, tossing their bodies on his great horns. They curved extravagantly into serpent shapes in their death throes. The men were flung clear, and they lay in crumpled heaps of bone.

Now there was only the hero left. He waited cunningly for the Minotaur's charge, hoping to use the beast's own momentum to stop him. His red shield gleamed as bright as blood in the lurid thickness of the air.

The Minotaur flung himself into the attack.

The hero stood steady, his sword outstretched, waiting for the Minotaur's heart to run onto it.

At the last moment, both sidestepped, and both in the same direction.

The hero's sword caught the Minotaur in the shoulder. But the Minotaur's horn buried itself in the hero's exposed belly.

The hero's face grew ghastly, but his sword reached for the Minotaur's life even as his own poured out.

Then he was gone. The Minotaur sank to his knees. The steam and smoke of the spell began to dissipate, and a clean perfume filled the hut.

"Hello, mormoluke," said the Minotaur dully. "I think I might have a wound somewhere. . . ." And then he lurched sideways and fell into blissful unconsciousness, with no hazary dreams to trouble him.

"Well, that's done," said Sthenno, satisfied. "Let him sleep, Corydon. But help me, Sister—let us take him out to sleep under the stars. Their light will help him." Together, the two Gorgons bore the Minotaur away. Corydon felt hopeful about him, though it didn't ease the ache in his heart about the false Snake-Girl's treachery.

TWENTY-THREE

CORYDON'S SLEEP WAS TROUBLED BY TERRIBLE DREAMS, like the others joined to the visions of the Minotaur. Mostly of a face, green as death, with a gaping mouth and eyes of black fire. He couldn't see the body that went with the face, but he could sense its immensity. It was the face he had seen before in dreams. Vreckan.

It was a huge face, big enough to swallow cities, islands. It was a hungry face; its mouth gaped in longing to suck everything down into itself. It was somehow imprisoned behind bars of black flame that didn't allow the thirsty tongue one droplet of blood, but Corydon could see that the face had never forgotten the taste and that only the bars held it back. It was a face that could never feel remorse.

Worst of all, the face could see him.

Corydon saw the flame bars shake, just once. The mouth gaped wider, and a dribble of saliva ran down its chin. The long gray tongue came out and licked the saliva. As the mouth opened,

Corydon saw, to his utter horror, that there was a shape struggling inside the creature's mouth. Then the mouth closed and it vanished. He hoped he had imagined it. . . . What hell it would be to be savored by this terrible face as a long mouthful for days and weeks and years. . . .

Whatever food the creature had was not enough for its raging appetite. The eyes wanted him, too. He would not sate their hunger, though. Nothing would. And the mouth would forget him as soon as he had been swallowed. It would be as if he had never existed. The face wanted that, wanted him to be gone forever.

So this was a Titan. Not a monster like himself. Not smooth or tricky like an Olympian. It was something far older, darker. Something that hated monsters and Olympians alike. Something that could not love even itself. Something that had never felt a moment of joy in a long eternity of hunger.

Corydon felt cold sweat on his brow. Then, instead of waking, he heard his father's voice, a voice that wove together the sweet and comforting sounds of hillside and Pan-pipe.

"My son, you see before you one of the powers that ruled the world before monsters or Olympians, a power that knows nothing, not even itself. Men sometimes call them Titans, though some Titans grew into knowledge and love."

Kronos, thought Corydon. *The old man was kind in his way.* And even as he thought this, he saw a likeness between the endlessness of Kronos's search for books and knowledge and the bottomless hunger of the face he had seen.

"Yes," said Pan's voice. "You think rightly. The Titans were all born hungry. There is a little of this hunger in us, in your friend Euryale especially; it comes to her from her father, Typhon. But she has found a right use for her hunger in making. The form you saw cannot, for he is terribly flawed, broken. He has never been loved, not even for a moment. And so he does not know what love is. Or even that love is."

Corydon wondered how in that case he or Euryale or anyone else could be helped; none of them had received much love, being monsters. He began to wonder if the green face was a monster after all. Ugly and frightening—did this not make the Titan a monster? His rebellious thoughts made his father laugh his sly laugh.

"You are always too clever, my little kleptis. Yes, he is a monster, in a way. As we all are And he used to rule the sea before Poseidon took it That is why he is full of hate now. But sometimes, my little one, my son, hatred bites so deep that a monster cannot come back from its coldness into the warmth of love. It is so with him. As you will find.

"Now you must hear me If he rises, the will of Zeus will be fulfilled, and Atlantis will fall to him."

"To Zeus?" Corydon felt his heart rebel.

"No, to Vreckan. Vreckan will take back the seas outside the Middle Sea, and there will be no more land left on which a man may stand."

"But why does Zeus will the destruction of Atlantis? I thought Athene—"

"Yes, so she believes," said Pan with another sly laugh, "but her father deceives even her, his most loyal subject. He is using her and his brother Poseidon so that the Atlanteans will destroy themselves."

"But why?"

"Because if Atlantis were united—courage and cunning, art and war, sport and work—it would rival even great Olympos itself. The Atlanteans weaken themselves by battling one another. If it were not for the war, they would have begun to unseat Zeus the Mighty from his pinnacle. He cannot risk that. And there is another reason also. Zeus has plans for an Atlantean colony, a city called Troios. He will not allow them to interfere."

The song of his father continued. "Even now, someone is in the city who has the power to set Vreckan in motion. You must stop the ritual, my son. It is the last hope for Atlantis. And if you cannot stop it, then you must flee through the Portal."

Corydon felt a hazy image of a door as his father's presence began to fade from his dream; he tried desperately to stammer out his questions to the receding god, but before he could ask about the Portal, about the ritual he was supposed to prevent, about the strange colony called Troios, it was too late. His father had gone. He awoke and was instantly beset by a feeling of urgency.

"Sthenno," he called softly. "We must go back to the city. I have dreamed . . . Something is wrong."

Sthenno was crouched over the fire. She darted toward him, bird-swift. "Yes," she said at once. "I, too, feel something wrong. . . . And the stars are reeling in terror. Tonight they hide their faces from what will be done. Mormo, we must hurry. We must fly. I will wake Euryale, and she and the Minotaur can remain here in safety."

"Why?" asked the Minotaur, sitting up, his great bull-head looking impossibly heavy on his now-emaciated man's body. "I will come. I wish to help. I have done wrong, very wrong. I must at least try to make amends."

And I have done wrong, to save you, Corydon thought. It is my actions that force them to this extremity. The Bull . . He wondered whether the eidolon of the Snake-Girl had subtly influenced him, then tried to shake off the thought like an annoying fly. Aloud, he said, "It is time and more than time. We must go now, though it may already be too late."

The Gorgons, carrying Corydon and the Minotaur, took off in heavy flight, their wings beating the air.

When they landed in the square next to the broken statue of Poseidon, they could feel that something was badly wrong. Usually, the square was busy with shoppers and shopkeepers, but now all the shops were boarded up. The square was utterly empty, save for pieces of paper blown in an uneasy wind.

Yet the air felt heavy, too, as it did on nights when the Morge came.

"They'll be in the temple," said Euryale tersely. "Come. I know where it is." She led the way across the square to a delicate metal staircase squeezed between a shop that sold perfumes and a shop that sold the strangely scanty garments favored by women like Fee. Corydon began climbing the stairs ahead of Euryale but she pushed him back firmly.

"Let me go first," she said. "And then the Minotaur. Sthenno, guard the rear; we may have to escape in a hurry. And remember, all of you: the goddess is clever, and she loves tricks and games. She will try to deceive you. . . ." They climbed hastily, in silence.

All Corydon's instincts warned him that danger was beating a swift pulse at the top. He could feel the menace gathering.

The stairs ended in a black iron door, barred and bolted. But Sthenno spoke a word to the bolts, and they dissolved into ugly, brackish puddles. The monsters pushed the door open quietly. They were in a huge circular room with a floor of black obsidian.

All around its circumference were heavily hooded figures singing or chanting something. In the center was a fire that burned with a red-and-black flame. It was not unlike the room where the priests of Poseidon had tried to compel the Minotaur by magic, the one Corydon had seen in his long-ago dream, but it felt even darker, more wrong. Corydon looked up, expecting the hooded figures to be looking at him, but they weren't. The ominous chanting grew louder, darker.

The figure at the center stood up and began to move toward the fire.

Corydon heard its footsteps. They were fast, as if the person who was walking was in a hurry, but firm. The tread was light on one step and hard on the other two. Two? People don't have three feet. The robes hid everything. Perhaps it was a monster, like him. As Corydon and the Gorgons looked round, the person threw back her heavy, dark hood.

All the monsters drew in their breath. The woman-like figure—for now they could see it was no person—was divided in half.

On the left side of her face, she was stern, beautiful almost, with a firm, sad mouth. Long raven-black hair flowed round her pale face. On her right side, she was a skeleton. From the eye socket of her skull shone a living eye, darker than midnight. The other eye was closed, blinded. The contrast was terrifying, and comical. In her right hand, she carried a staff made of bone, bleached white, with three dog skulls at its top. The skulls, too, were unnaturally alive; their deep sockets glowed with red light.

"It is the Morge-mage," hissed Sthenno. "The one who called the Morge from death. She moves in the power of Hecate."

The monsters stood ready to confront her, but she saw them as soon as they began to move.

She waved her staff imperiously. As Corydon tried to leap at her, he found he couldn't budge. Not even a finger. It was the same with the other monsters. Sthenno was preparing to cast a spell, Euryale was leaping into flight, and the Minotaur was charging. They looked like sculptures.

It was like being turned to stone, Corydon thought. He had always wondered how the heroes had felt when Medusa did that to them. His mind still worked; he saw and heard and smelled. But he could do nothing. He couldn't even scream.

Seeing the intruders so helpless, the other figures threw back their hoods, revealing the heavy, thick clay faces of Morge. They were impassive, strong, like great lumps stolen from the earth itself.

The Morge-mage began singing in a different language than the other Morge and danced a strange dance with many twisting leaps. Then, with her staff, she drew a glowing green circle of power around the flame. It was the same sludgy algae-green as the face in Corydon's dream.

The Morge-mage stepped back as symbols in the same language that had been on Hades' Staff filled the circle. Corydon's eye was drawn to ten or twelve people—or were they Morge?—who hadn't thrown their hoods back. Now they did, and Corydon saw that they were humans: six men, six women.

One of the women was Fee.

Corydon wanted to cry out, to tell her this was wrong. But he couldn't.

And Fee seemed utterly indifferent to their fate. She didn't even glance at him.

The mage began uttering cries, little cries like the sound made by hungry puppies.

"We bring him and his hunger. He comes to us! To drown the Bull under, to eat the Bull, to leave not a wrack. We bring him from death, from his deep burying place! Deeper, deeper than the dead he lies! We must go down, down to the deepest places, below the realms, where there is no light and nothing moves! We must go!"

Then she began calling in the voice a huntsman might use to call his hounds.

"Come, Vreckan. Come, Vreckan. Come, Vreckan," she sang. The humans began to repeat the chant. The Morge in their heavy, low voices followed suit.

The air began to hum.

Now the Morge-mage's voice rose above the others.

"I am become Death," she shrieked, "the destroyer of worlds. He arises in might, and no one shall stand before him. The Bull shall perish and leave no trace of its rising! Come, Vreckan. Come, Vreckan. Come, Vreckan!"

Corydon wondered why nobody but himself seemed alarmed by these announcements; couldn't Fee and the others see that the Morge-mage was mad with power, serving the will of Zeus? He tried desperately to open his mouth to tell them. It was like lifting up a boulder, but he managed to part his lips. The Morge-mage was putting so much strength into her incantations that she was letting her hold on them slip.

Corydon noticed that Sthenno had begun to move enough to cast an extinguishing spell, though with agonizing slowness. The Minotaur had moved, too, trying desperately to charge; his head was just a fingerbreadth lower. Euryale had begun to shift, managing to spread out one wing. The other unfurled very slowly as Corydon managed to unlock his lips, enough for one cry.

"Now!" It sounded as if spoken underwater, but all the monsters managed to respond as Sthenno's incantation reached a slow climax.

But it was already too late.

The Morge-mage raised her arms and brought them down fiercely, as if she were plunging twin knives into the heart of Atlantis.

All the followers did the same.

And from outside there was a ferocious roar from the sea.

"I hunger!"

Everyone turned.

"Eat and be filled, Great One!" cried the Morge-mage.

"I will!" came the terrible reply. The voice alone filled the sky.

"Feast on the sons of him who usurped your throne!"

"I will! Bring them to me!"

Corydon looked toward the door, and through it he could see the harbor and the terrible face that united sea and sky in its vast, monstrous appetite. The heavens and the waters were now a vast, gaping maw.

Beside this horror, one remembered Poseidon's wrath as a sparkling wavelet that briefly caught the sunlight.

Wrenching themselves free of the last vestiges of the spell, Sthenno and Euryale unceremoniously scooped up the other monsters and fled through the door. Only an immortal could hope to live through what was to come.

They landed in the square.

"What now?" Sthenno asked.

"We have failed. Let us try to lead some of the people to safety through the Portal. That is the only hope left." Corydon's voice was as bleak as a winter sea.

"But . . ." The Minotaur hardly liked to say it. "How can we? Who would listen to us?"

"They don't need to listen," said Euryale, pointing upward. "They only need to look."

As she spoke, the monsters saw Vreckan's tongue come writhing out between his lips. Like a vast gray lizard tongue, it suddenly shot out and seized something in the city.

It was the Bull of Poseidon.

It was being lifted up toward the terrible face. Corydon saw the vast creature writhing desperately, struggling, but the tongue held, as a chameleon's tongue holds a fly and pulls it down to sate its hunger.

The great mouth was open wide. The Bull was folded into it, a meager mouthful.

There was the crunch of bones. A dribble of golden blood spilled from the vast sky lips.

The Bull was gone. The Shells cheered.

"I hunger!" cried Vreckan.

"You shall be filled!" shrieked the Morge-mage. She stood on the lowest step of the temple and thrust her terrible dog skulls at the sky. The dogs howled, too, though they had no throats.

In reply, Corydon saw a group of Shell priests wearing hooded robes and leading a group of Shell soldiers. The soldiers were dragging on a long robe a prone figure, so tightly tied with rope and chain that it was barely possible to see who it was.

Then the monsters saw the thick black hair, streaked with dust, and glimpses of green-black obsidian skin.

"Gorgos!" cried Corydon, and started forward. Evading Euryale's restraining claw, he dived for the hapless bundle that was Gorgos. A Shell soldier shoved him roughly away.

"Come not between Vrekan and his prey!" The shriek of rage came from the Morge-mage.

"What will you do," said Sthenno, speaking directly to the Morge-mage, "when it asks for more? What will you do when you have given the Titan every life in the City but your own?"

The Morge-mage smiled. "Give him my life and find the oblivion I have so long sought, the peace taken from me by the City," she said, her voice now soft, caressing.

"So you seek to destroy the world?" Sthenno was horrified and uncomprehending. "If you long so for death, why not offer yourself to the creature you have summoned now?"

"But I long still more to see others die!" said the Morge-mage with a strange little giggle. By now, everyone could see that she was mad. Even the Shell priests looked unhappy. Corydon noticed the droop of Fee's shoulders; she looked like a gambler who has risked her whole being and lost.

The priests holding Gorgos began to try to lift him onto the shattered shield of Poseidon's fallen statue. It formed a kind of makeshift altar. They had not heard the Morge-mage's words and were still eager to appease their new and powerful ally, reward him for slaying their foe, the Bull.

Sthenno spoke hastily. "Minotaur, Corydon, you must rescue Gorgos. I will fight the Morge-mage. Her powers in magic are beyond your strength. Sister, make ready to take them to the Portal, win or lose."

"I will not leave you," said Euryale stoutly. "After so many thousand years, how can you ask it? I will use the magic I have. It is Shell magic, so it may help."

Sthenno smiled. Together, they began to try to bind the Morge-mage with thick chantings. Slowly her mad movements stilled.

Corydon and the Minotaur plunged forward.

As they did so, lunging toward the altar, Corydon was amazed to see small, white-haired figures gathering. One ran up to him, light as a puff of seed.

"Take his sword to him," she cried, lifting it up. "This is the moment that was long foretold."

Corydon seized the hilt hastily and kept running, light and lithe.

As the men maneuvered Gorgos, the great mouth in the sky licked its lips. "I have hungered too long," it said. "Hurry. Cut his throat that I may drink of his warm blood." The eyes in the dreadful face were lit from within by its greed.

Corydon dived under a Shell soldier's arm as the man finally managed to hoist Gorgos onto the shield. The man reached for his knife, whether for Corydon or to use on Gorgos they never knew, for Corydon drew the sword and in one stroke slashed Gorgos's bonds.

Without a trace of cramp or stiffness, Gorgos broke the last bonds and grabbed the sword from Corydon's hand. Before the Shell soldier could even raise his knife, Gorgos's sword was buried in his belly.

The other soldiers charged into the fray, drawing their swords. Then the Minotaur lowered his head and charged at a group of soldiers. Corydon seized Gorgos by the arm and tried to draw him out of the battle, but Gorgos was immovable. He stood, legs planted, astride the fallen body of his father's statue and defied the looming menace of heavens and seas.

Vreckan looked down. Balked of his prey, he screamed at Gorgos.

"I hunger!" The terrible tongue lashed out.

"I care not!" Gorgos brought his sword down on the lizard tongue of the great Titan.

Vreckan gave a scream of rage. Black blood burst from his mouth, and where it fell, the stones of Atlantis melted. Gorgos raised his father's broken shield above his head.

"My father defeated you, you great belly! And so shall I!" He prepared to strike at the Titan's face, but it was too remote.

"Gorgons!" Gorgos commanded. "I need to borrow your wings."

Euryale landed beside him in a clatter of bronze. "Gorgos, no. You cannot fight an immortal."

"I must. There is no one else. And he will take the whole of Atlantis if I do not."

"And he will also take it if you do, with the trifling difference that you will be dead," said Corydon firmly from his other side.

Euryale spoke again, more urgently: "It is certain death."

"I cannot abandon my father and the people who trust me," said Gorgos. "I must try."

"Why don't you try thinking?" yelled Corydon. "It's as if you've got hold of some book of rules about how to be a hero. Why don't you use your fame and prestige to get people to follow you to the Portal?"

Gorgos had not taken his eyes off Vreckan.

"What Portal?" he asked, a little absently.

"The Portal that can save everyone! It leads to somewhere outside Atlantis. I don't know where."

As they argued tensely, Vreckan was recovering, and all of them could feel his wrath beginning to build. Now he spoke, his voice wet with his own blood.

"I shall destroy you all! I shall not wait!"

As he spoke, the sea began to grow denser, more solid. It leapt high into the air and took on a ferocious dull green glow, like a great marsh light. The sea began slowly to turn, heavily, like a great mill wheel.

"He summons the winds!" gasped Euryale. "Gorgos, you must act now! Lead them to safety!"

A new voice spoke from the sea. "Yes, my son, lead them to safety, or lead such as will follow you. Vreckan is my foe."

"Father!" Gorgos cried.

"He is beyond even your strength. Go. Save my people. Save them all. Leave him to me." The god of the sea shook his trident. The land began to shiver. The sea turned a little more slowly. "But none may live where two gods do battle. Go!"

His eyes running with tears, Gorgos turned to the crowd.

"Selene! Dolphins! Shells! You must follow us! Atlantis can no longer live! Follow me if you value your lives! We must find hope elsewhere!"

The milling crowd gaped at him. Then many surged up to him. But others ignored his words and fled in many directions from the gathering wrath. Gorgos called after them in vain.

"We must save those we can, Gorgos," said Sthenno. "There is little time." As she spoke there was another terrible, sweeping quake of the ground under their feet. Nearby, towers crumbled into dust as people screamed. A few huge blocks of falling masonry landed in the crowd. There were more screams. The green light grew deeper and thicker. Now the air was so thick with seawater that it was becoming hard to breathe. There was a smell of rotting seaweed.

Gorgos sighed. "Lead us," he said. "I will gather whom I can."

Corydon and the Gorgons and the Minotaur began running in the direction of Murax House.

"What—about—Fee?" Corydon gasped as they ran.

"She, too, can flee if she chooses," shouted Sthenno above the waters' steadily growing roar. They ran and ran, and a crowd streamed after them, but many others were lost. Waves were beginning to break into the streets of the City as the great god and Titan battled each other. The ground was rocking as if they stood on the deck of a ship in a storm. All around them, towers were toppling. And there were screams of pain and terror.

"We must—reach—the Portal!" Gorgos gasped. "Do—you know—where it—lies?"

"I can feel the key pulling me!" Euryale cried. "It can't be far! Hurry!"

"Can—we—fly?" Corydon asked.

Gorgos spoke sternly: "We must lead the others. All who choose to follow.

"Follow!" he cried breathlessly to the terrified people running in panic. A few seemed to join them, but most simply fled. The little light-footed Selene came, though.

"My tutor!" Euryale suddenly cried. "I must help him!"

"There is no time," said the Minotaur sternly.

"I will not leave him to die! I will fly and be with you soon—"

Sthenno grasped her sister's wing as she was poised for take-off. "Look, Sister, they would rip you out of the sky as a hawk takes a dove."

Euryale looked up. Looming over the trembling City were the enormous, voraciously hungry face of Vreckan and the storm-wave force of Poseidon. As they grappled, huge waves were hurled into the streets, which were full of spumes of lacy white foam. The sky itself was a terrible green-black. And the waters around Atlantis were churning faster and faster, a huge and ravenous whirlpool. Already the very air was being sucked into its cold heart. All the monsters had begun to feel its terrible tornado wind.

It was becoming hard to run. Hard, even, to stand. As the monsters looked up, they saw a loaded dragon snatched from the sky into the whirling mouth of the sea.

Euryale braced herself hard against the eddying currents of the spiraling winds. "Let me at least call him!" she begged.

"He will not hear you," said Sthenno as gently as she could. "I can barely hear you myself." By now, the two great sea masters were roaring bestially at each other, like furious leviathans.

Oddly audible, a light Selene voice said, "We will go." And

before anyone could stop her, the tiny, nimble creature had dropped into a tunnel and gone.

"We must hurry!" shouted Gorgos, and with their bodies braced against the terrible, almost solid air, the monsters formed a defensive wall around the people who trusted them. Thus hampered, they crept toward the Portal.

A wave swirled at Corydon's feet.

Heavy drops of rain began to fall from the overloaded sky. But it was salt rain instead of fresh. Towers fell all around them as the earth tore itself at Poseidon's command. They turned into the street that held the Portal. Now they could see what must be it, a crumbling archway containing a door still surprisingly solid.

Heads down, pushing against the rain, the monsters did not at first see the Morge-mage. Then they heard a mad cackle that rose above the wind, above the waves.

"No," said the Morge-mage. "None shall pass this way. None shall escape. You called for death, Atlanteans. And death has come. I have had to endure a terrible, wrong half-life. I want to be dead once more. And I cannot unless I am richly accompanied."

She shook her staff.

Vreckan's mouth opened, and his tongue lashed out. Though it still bore the scar of Gorgos's wound, it had healed enough to be a terrible danger.

Gorgos drew his sword once more. But before he could act, Vreckan's face contorted. Poseidon's trident had stabbed into his eye. The earth shook so ferociously that no one could stand. When Corydon lurched to his feet, he was covered in wet dust from the collapsing houses all around. Nothing was left standing in the street except the Portal. Another, larger wave flooded toward him. Vreckan's scream of pain and fury filled his ears.

"Eat!" cried the Titan. "Be full!" His tongue lashed out again. The monsters all leapt away . . . but the Morge-mage stood still, her face oddly calm.

"Yes, eat," she said dreamily. "Eat."

The scaly tongue curled around her.

As she vanished into the terrible mouth, Corydon saw her face. It wore a smile of sleepy satisfaction.

Battling against the wind, Corydon and Gorgos reached the Portal. Sthenno pulled out the key and fitted it to the iron lock. While she twisted it, there was a pause. Corydon looked at the faces of the little crowd: frantic mothers, crying children, wide-eyed Selene. And in the short silence, all the monsters looked toward the sea.

A wave was rearing up, so vast it was a whole mountain range of water, so vast that the last towers of Atlantis left standing looked like dolls' toys beside it.

Poseidon was trying to wrest the sea back from Vreckan. The wave was being pulled and deformed by the terrible winds of the whirlpool. And Vreckan was crying. "Mine, mine!" he screamed as the waters mounted and mounted and mounted.

"Now!" shouted Corydon above the roar. Sthenno wrenched the door open. The Selene and Atlanteans poured through. At the very last moment, a small boy and girl appeared from nowhere and squeezed in. The Minotaur ran inside, holding another little child in his huge arms. And up the street raced a Selene leading a small, white-haired man—Euryale's teacher. . . . They almost flew through the door.

Gorgos waited until last Then, as the tremendous wave began to break, began to roar down the street, he shoved Corydon inside, dashed through the Portal himself, and slammed the door shut behind him.

TWENTY-FOUR

As the door closed, there was no more sound from Atlantis.

It was as if the City, the battling gods, everything, had simply vanished.

"Yes, you are between the worlds now," said a voice in Corydon's ear. He thought it was Sthenno's voice. Corydon looked round, but he couldn't see the speaker. All he could see were slowly swirling blues and purples, shot with streaks of red and black, blazing through the other colors like comets.

"You can see no one but yourself in the Portal," said the voice.

Corydon felt a lurch and sensed himself moving slowly forward, as slowly and jerkily as an old tortoise. Yet it was not his limbs that moved. Somehow, the floor—or was it the air?—carried him forward, pushed him onward, as if it were a river and he a heavily laden boat. The swirling got slightly faster and the blazes slightly slower.

The voice spoke again. "Your friends are safe, Corydon

Panfoot. You must travel a different path from them with me. I will show you what you have done. What you have not done. Come."

By now, Corydon was certain that it was not Sthenno's voice he was hearing. And yet the voice was familiar. Suddenly, oddly, he remembered the bent old woman who had come to Medusa's funeral. Was it she? Why should he think of her now? He peered into the spinning lights but could see nothing. As she had said, you could not see in the Portal.

Then the spinning and the movement stopped. Corydon waited. As he stood still, overwhelmed by the thick, heavy blackness that surrounded him, light began to grow: a pale morning light, like that on a mountainside at dawn on the island. It seemed to come from nowhere; it simply gathered in the air, then began to solidify into something else.

Corydon was looking at a huge tree. It was far bigger than any tree he had ever seen. Above him, its many branches stretched up higher than he could see, cool and leafy. Below, its trunk also stretched away endlessly. The only sounds were the soft, sad cooing of doves and the rustle of leaves.

"You see the tree of the world," said the voice beside him.

Corydon turned. Beside him stood the bent old woman he had seen just once before. But living in Atlantis had given Corydon some skill in detecting false appearances. He was certain that he was not seeing this person as she truly was but only as she chose to seem. Her voice, for example: it was not the voice of an old woman, creaking with age, but a light, rich, firm voice, like a young woman on her marriage morning.

"Come, my doves," she crooned.

Three white birds flew down from the tree. Corydon blinked; now three priestesses in pure white robes stood before them. They were hooded, but he could see that one was young, one motherly, and one older than the rocks.

"Show him the cataclysm," said the old woman in black who had led Corydon.

"Must he see?" asked one of the priestesses.

"Yes, he must," said another.

"Show! Show! Show!" they all cried, their voices sounding more than ever like cooing doves. And before him, Corydon saw. Somehow, the leaves of the tree formed a picture. He was powerfully reminded of Persephone's tapestry.

Corydon was suddenly looking at the island of Atlantis from high in the air. As he watched, he saw Poseidon's trident lifted, pouring wave upon wave on Vreckan, each mightier than the last, trying to fill in the frightening, gaping hole. That hole was spinning so fast that, at first, Corydon thought it was still, but as he watched, he saw its outer edge touch the shore of Atlantis. At once, the shoreline crumbled and gave way in quakes so ferocious that gashes were torn in the earth.

The hole was Vreckan's mouth, Corydon saw. He was—literally—devouring the island.

Corydon watched what he had utterly failed to prevent. His mouth went dry with horror.

Another huge wave began to mount. This one was so vast that Corydon could see it trembling with its own weight. Heedless of the living things on the island, Poseidon allowed it to crash directly against the shoreline, taking his opponent by surprise but crushing most of the City as he did so. As the wave flooded into Vreckan, it

carried with it flotsam and jetsam and desperate people. . . .
Corydon saw it all drain into Vreckan's bottomless maw.

Now the island began to give way under the terrible pressure
of the gods. A slice of it broke off and fell into the sea; seawater
rushed into its valleys.

Poseidon gathered himself one more time.

Atlantis groaned under the pressure from Vreckan. Still more
of the land crumbled into his mouth.

And Poseidon struck. He rammed his trident down Vreckan's
throat, like an arrow striking home.

But the force of the blow struck at Atlantis, too.

At the same moment, what was left of the once-great land
snapped into pieces.

Vreckan screamed as his scaly skin began to peel away.
Beneath was a pulsing green light the color of slime. Soon only the
light remained. It shook and then grew. It grew until Corydon was
blinded with it.

Then it disappeared. All Corydon could see was the ocean
and a shaken and weary Poseidon.

But Atlantis had gone. It was nowhere in sight. Only miles of
floating flotsam—human, animal, inanimate—remained.

The vision faded. Corydon was left with a stinging emptiness
in his heart.

The old woman turned to him.

"You did not prevent it, Panfoot," she said. "Indeed, it was in
part because of your acts. . . ."

"I know," said Corydon numbly. "I know."

"You did only what you meant to do," said the woman. "You
saved your friend. And a few of the City dwellers. But that act will

stretch as far into the future as this tree does to the heavens. Atlantis will live on in the world. Its colonies will take in its exiles, and its arts and its thought will grow until they fill the world. It is not places that matter, little Corydon. It is ideas. And we Olympians cannot prevent them spreading like weeds over the face of the world. They will choke us, my Panfoot. We need awe, not thought. One day, the ideas of Atlantis will swallow us, and there will be no one even to know our names." Her head drooped. Corydon wondered whether to offer her a comforting pat but felt instinctively that it would be an unforgivable insult.

"Which ideas?" he asked tentatively. She smiled and raised her head.

"That men and women can remake themselves. Then they will not need us."

Corydon felt a cold jolt. Her words reminded him of Fee . . . Lady Nagaina. . . . He felt overwhelmed by grief. He had not done enough. . . . He gathered his thoughts and his courage.

"I don't know who you are, but would you mind telling me this? What did you do to save Atlantis yourself? For I think you hold greater might than I ever will."

There was a long silence. Then the woman threw back her hood. Corydon saw the gleaming golden hair of Hera.

The goddess laughed, mocking laughter.

"Who said I wanted it saved?" she said, and her voice was as hard as stone. "The Atlanteans never made sacrifices to me. It was always Poseidon and Athene who had their hearts. Even Hecate got something. I was left with nothing. No, nothing for Hera. And now"—her voice held satisfaction—"now there is nothing left for anyone. I wonder what Athene must feel." Her voice was spiteful.

"I thought—"

"You thought I wanted your help? Well, so I did. It was because of your presence—yours and Gorgos's—that I succeeded. And Zeus will be so pleased with me," she added. "And Gorgos is now a hero. That may be useful to me in future. But which side will he take? Mine or . . . hers?" She appeared lost in reverie.

Corydon felt a powerful urge to hit her. He knew it to be the height of unwisdom, so instead he deliberately stalked over to the tree.

From behind him, he heard her sigh, then draw in her breath as if with renewed determination.

"Mormo, farewell," came her voice. "We shall meet again very soon. Zeus has not forgotten what he owes to you." Her mocking, shrill laughter lingered after she had vanished.

Corydon wondered about what she had said. He had never thought so hard before.

She had said that eventually the Atlantean ideas would swallow the Olympians.

It sounded wonderful, but— A thought struck him. What would life be like without the Olympians? He had always imagined it as perfect, living peacefully on the island with no one to menace or control him. But if there were no Olympians, would it be so simple?

He thought of the Atlanteans. Would they have been better if the Olympians hadn't been there to corrupt them? Or would they simply have fought and struggled for power over one another? Perhaps they would never have acquired enough magic to destroy their own island, but they could have killed many in battles and wars.

And his own island? Would the villagers there accept him with no gods to drive them to hatred? Or would they still reject anything different from themselves?

Corydon had a strange and sickening feeling that it would be the same.

Because with the gods gone, men would be free to make *themselves* into gods. There would be enormous wars, conflicts to see who was the biggest, strongest. There would be races for who was more advanced, like siblings arguing for attention. The monsters and pharmakoses would be attacked as never before. Things would be just as bad.

Was it worth it, then, attempting to stop the Olympians? If they failed to destroy them, then things would be as normal. If they succeeded, the result would be virtually the same.

He bent his head in despair.

Then, slowly, a new idea came to him. In his mind, he saw his father's kind, sly face and felt his loving embrace. He saw the sweet face of the Lady of Flowers. He saw the dark face of Hades, tormented with love for his precious wife.

The trouble, he saw, was that men had learned only the love of power and cruelty from the Olympians, so that now each tried to be a little Olympian in his own sphere. Or hers. Even the Olympians learned new cruelties from one another; Hera had just destroyed a nation because she thought it would please Zeus.

What men and monsters needed was not *no* gods but kinder gods. Gods like his father, who knew what it was to be lonely and outcast. Gods like the Lady of Flowers, who understood death and grief. Gods who did not want to rule but merely to live alongside men and monsters alike. Suddenly he remembered what his father had said to him the first time they met.

"The Olympians conquered because they made men think that there was only one way to be beautiful. . . . Everything else they chased into the corners of dreams." So, too, the Atlanteans had become little Olympians, making rules for themselves that included some and left others wailing on desolate pharmakos rocks inside themselves.

But his father had also said that the old powers had not been beaten. "And it is you who will lead them to victory." Corydon knew he had done that in the Underworld and against Perseus.

But in Atlantis, he had lost his way. Perhaps even Vreckan might have been redeemed if he had only known how to do it.

And the tears came. He was shamed by the sight of the drowning Atlanteans.

Now he saw something familiar. The gates of the Realm of the Many opened before him.

He was jostled and driven forward in a crowd of shades, a crowd so thick it seemed impassable. They thronged around him more thickly than any shades ever had, even those seeking his blood. As they passed through the gate, they began to assume the shapes of their true selves.

And every single one of them began to cry.

Some lay down on the grass and wept. Others held one another, crying heartbrokenly. "Atlantis, Atlantis," they moaned. Others sighed words that sounded like, "Why did we ever have to fight each other?" Still others cried that it had been a mistake to release the Bull or lamented the summoning of the Morgemage.

Their grief seemed endless. A river sprang up from their tears and burned the grass of underearth with its salty bitterness.

Now some became angry. Corydon saw a shade that hacked furiously at the green grass, another that turned wrathfully on a nearby tree and began beating it with a stick. Many swore oaths to all gods and none. Some older shades, not from Atlantis, tried to embrace them; the angry ones shook off the caresses, but some other shades collapsed tearfully into their warm hugs.

They began drifting apart, spreading out over the grassy plain. And some, as Corydon watched, began to revive a little. One began to pick a few flowers and shyly offered them to a fellow Atlantean. Two girls—one wearing Dolphin colors, the other dressed in Shell pink—walked hand in hand; as they talked, their colors flowed together, no longer pink and blue but the soft lilac twilight of underearth. Others, especially those with white hair, began drawing or making art that expressed their grief for their towered City. Corydon began to see that the Olympians might kill only people, not ideas or arts. And since it was ideas and arts that they feared, this limited their victory.

It was then that he saw Fee.

Unlike Medusa, she had not chosen to enter eternity as her monster-self, but she had kept a trace of the Hydra about her: her hair was moon-gold, and she was wearing a silk dress as brilliantly blue as her heads had once been. She walked with her head held high. Corydon saw that her face was a mask of dried tears.

As she walked, Corydon heard her whisper, "It's my fault, it's my fault, it's my fault . . ." Her words were deadlier to her than any gas or fireball she might once have made.

"No!" he cried, forgetting she couldn't hear him. "It was my fault. Hera said so. Well, almost . . ."

Fee sat down, careless of her dress, on a small, grassy hillock.

Her tears flowed and then sprang up again as a fountain. Angrily she scratched at the ground with her long nails.

Answerable to her desires, the land behind her began to swell and heave, transforming itself into a double row, a whole street of the kind of shops and market stalls she loved. The Underworld was desperately trying to heal her grief and the griefs of all the dead of Atlantis.

Fee turned her head and saw the shops. A watery smile lit her sad face.

She stood up and remembered to brush the grass off her dress.

As she was about to enter a shop, a portrait artist leapt out from behind a tree and began sketching her. Fee turned her head and preened a little. The artist, dazzled, offered her a sketch for nothing. Fee smiled graciously and declined. Then she disappeared into one of the shops.

Corydon wasn't sure whether to laugh or cry. Beside him, he sensed a presence. It was the Lady of Flowers.

"This is a kind of heaven," he ventured.

"You made it," she said. "It is for others to make it now. What is in their imaginations becomes visible. For some, it will be flowers, and for others—shops. As you see."

Corydon saw Fee gazing delightedly at some golden dresses.

"What if what one person wants is to hurt?" he asked.

"That is not permitted," she said gravely. "Here you may do as you will, but you must not do harm. Both these things are the laws. The only laws."

Perhaps, thought Corydon, one day the world of the living will take these as its laws, too.

Still, he wondered whether he would have redeemed the

Underworld if he'd known it would help Fee go shopping. . . . "Might she get . . . tired . . . of shopping?"

"In a few centuries. Or in a few weeks. Who knows? Let her find out herself."

As these words swirled through Corydon's head, the Underworld began to fade, like color washed out of a painting by rain. Soon Corydon was back in the unworld of the Portal, going faster and faster. The colors were now a frenzied blur, with a light coming nearer and nearer. Or was he coming closer to it? Corydon wasn't sure, but before he could get things straight in his ever-questioning head, he had been flung through the burning white light and out into a burst of color and sensation.

He was in the world again.

He hit something hot and slippery with a thud. He realized he was rolling down a slope; he tried to brace himself, but he slid farther and farther down, rolling over and over. Corydon realized the slope was made of small, slithery pebbles, blinding white. From his confusing view of the world, Corydon could see that there was nothing at the bottom of the scree he was rolling down, which must mean there was . . . a cliff—

But it was too late. He was plummeting into air. With a crash that jarred every bone in his body, he landed on a small ledge sticking out from the cliff face.

Corydon looked down toward the bottom of the cliff. There below were rocks as pointed as a shark's teeth.

He could see no sign of the other monsters. But with a strange feeling that this had all happened before, he called for help.

"Gorgos! Where are you?"

But there was no reply. Somehow, Corydon was not surprised.

He sat down to wait. The sea stretched on forever, to the sky, and Corydon wondered if the battle to control them would ever end. Somehow, he felt that more battles were to come. He had seen what could happen in the visions of the tree. His heart was black with dread as he faced the future.

GLOSSARY

A note on geography and the Greek city-state

Our first book, *Corydon and the Island of Monsters*, was set entirely in the world of Greater Greece (Magna Graeca). Greater Greece is the world of Greek colonies. The Greeks themselves thought of Greece not as a place but as wherever people spoke Greek. Atlantis is also part of this world, but it is not geographically within Middle Earth, which is the literal meaning of "Mediterranean." The Greeks often fantasized about colonizing the world beyond the Pillars, but they did not imagine what it would be like. Atlantis is not Mediterranean but North Atlantic, with gray skies and green oceans and bitter cold.

We don't use the word "polis," or "city-state," in our story, but the idea is very important. It means more than the buildings; it means the people who live there and the power of their hands and voices. There are really three phases in Greek history: The Archaic period, about which all the myths are written; the age of the city-states; and the Hellenistic period, when Greek civilization was cross-fertilized by Near Eastern culture. Although all our books are *set* in the Archaic period, the age of heroes and myths, this second book *represents* the era of the polis, while the third book will represent the dilemmas of the Hellenistic world.

Amazons (*AM-a-zonz*) This is a myth the Greeks made up for themselves (though you will read pseudohistories that claim they were real). In ancient Greece, it was unheard of for women to be involved in politics or war. So the Greeks imagined what a world where women ruled and fought might be like. (The modern equivalent would be for children to rule adults.) Like Atlantis itself, they can be whatever you want them to be: sturdy hockey girls, dark witches, flower-loving hippies. Ours are none of the above; they are the artistic principle in a fighting society.

Apollo Helios (*a-POL-oh HEE-lee-os*) Apollo as the sun. There will be more about Apollo in *Corydon and the Siege of Troy*.

Ares (*AIR-eez*) The ugly face of war. Not a marching-band, bright-uniforms, and martial-tunes kind of soldier but a man covered in blood running toward you with a naked sword, his mouth open as if ready to drink your blood. He is brutal; he is a coward and a rapist and a destroyer of villages. The Greeks knew all about war, and they knew it could be ugly. Ares was not popular even with the Greeks; he had few shrines. He is one of only two children of the marriage of Zeus and Hera; the Greeks seem to have thought that power and respectability could only produce trouble as their child.

Artemis (*AR-te-mis*) Sometimes called the Maiden. Goddess of hunting, wild animals, young girls before marriage, wild nature (woods, mountains). Virgin, but also a midwife and goddess of birth. Some links with the chthonic gods.

Athene (*ah-THEE-nee*) One of the twelve Olympians. Extremely powerful goddess who represents cunning (inherited from her mother, Metis—whose name means "cunning") and warrior skills, but also weaving and other useful arts, olive trees, and the city of Athens. Zeus ate her mother and gave birth to her through his forehead. So Athene admires the brainy.

Atlantis (*at-LAN-tis*) It's named for the Atlantic Ocean or vice versa. A lot of adults are silly about Atlantis and spend money that could be better used elsewhere trying to work out where it really was. The reason this is silly is because Atlantis is a fantasy novel—like the one you've just finished reading but better—by the Greek philosopher Plato. In his story, Atlantis is a great and proud city that becomes so proud that the gods destroy it with a giant wave. Plato thought it would have seven circles divided by water canals; we think he saw a plan of the katabathos tank and drew the wrong conclusions. The

Greeks thought of it as the ultimate polis, the ultimate cosmopolis; the summit of Greekness but also unimaginably different. Everyone is a wide-eyed hayseed, rube, and hick when it comes to Atlantis. Because it is a fantasy, it can be whatever you think a great city is. When we think of a great city and northern skies and gray-green seas, a city on an island so great that it takes away your breath, a great polis beset by vice and internal strife and crowned by virtue, there can be only one name: New York. Hence the joking reference to Five Points and the less-joking reference to gang wars. We've also squeezed in the ruins of another great island city, Venice.

chthonic gods (*k-THON-ick*) The opposite of Olympians. Gods that are incarnate, low, and little. They are bound to Middle Earth for good and ill. They are powerless beyond it. Or nearly. So outside Middle Earth, Pan cannot intervene to help his son.

cosmopolis (*koz-MOP-e-lis*) Another Greek myth, but this was one the Greeks tried to bring into being. The ultimate city-state. A cosmopolis is a city that contains the whole world; "cosmos" means "the universe." So this is a huge city where every race, every creed, every kind of person can have a place and can also move chaotically about, bumping into other people and learning that people can be different from one another but still good and gentle. The cosmopolis also contains all the ideals of the Greek world and all its learning and know-how. Atlantis was once a cosmopolis, but by the time Corydon gets there, it's losing that excellence and degenerating into stasis. In history, the first Greek cosmopolis was Alexandria in Egypt.

Daidalos (*DEED-e-los*) Ah, the clever men in white coats, so keen to dominate nature. Their symbol is the labyrinth, in which the mythic inventor Daidalos caged the Minotaur. Our Daidalos also built Atlantis by exploiting power in harmful ways. He represents the way all cities draw power from the landscape but turn their back on what they exploit and the mess it makes. Like other brave scientific pioneers, he was not keen on new scientists on his turf, which is another reason why he killed his nephew Phrynos. *See also* Morge and mage.

Demeter (*DEM-et-er*) Goddess of seed brought to life as plants; without her blessing, nothing can grow. A mother first and last.

Dionysos (*die-oh-NIGH-sos*) The strangest of the Greek gods, and the god of strangeness. You know those times when people get drunk or even just carried away by a party atmosphere and say things they swore they'd never reveal? That is Dionysos and it's not just the wine, it's excess. Dionysos is everything too much. A whole package of chocolate cookies. Ripping up your clothes. Dreams, visions, ecstasy—which literally means going outside yourself. The first tragedies ever performed belonged to him. The word "tragedy" (*tragoidos*) means something like "goat sacrifice" or "goat song." Dionysos's maenads used to dance up Mount Parnassos barefoot in deep winter snow. The mountain is eight thousand feet high. Don't try this at home, boys and girls.

dragons Like the Kraken (Q.V.), the dragon is a northern European monster of which the Greeks had heard. The dragons of Atlantis are the cold-blooded fire-drakes of northern legend, but there are also Asian dragons in Atlantis; they are multiethnic. They are also an affectionate tribute to Manhattan taxi drivers, who do not always favor outsiders, and to the White Witch of Narnia, who, on arriving in London, begs for a well-trained dragon. No one ever procures one for her, but we wondered what a city that had them might be like.

Echidna (*i-KID-na*) The second monster. A vast snake-woman who was Typhon's girlfriend. The children that they had were numerous, but many of them were killed or captured by heroes and by the gods. The children are the Chimera, Cerberus, Orthrus (a two-headed dog), Geryon, Sthenno, Euryale, Argus, the Hydra that Herakles killed, and the first-ever Nemean Lion. Echidna, too, was killed, but slowly and hideously in Tartarus by being dipped in a vat of boiling blood. And not just any blood—the blood of her children and their descendants who were killed by heroes. Thus we see the justice of the Olympians.

eidolon (*EYE-doh-lon*) A double or copy of a person or creature. This sounds as if it is an anachronism, which means "a modern idea stuffed into an old story," but it isn't. It was invented by the Athenian dramatist Euripides, who wrote that Helen of Sparta did not go to Troy at all but to Egypt, where she studied magic and herbs. She was replaced by a badly behaved eidolon.

Euryale (*yoo-ree-AH-lay*) One of the two immortal Gorgons.

Geryon (*GE-ry-on*) A gentle cowherd who loves his beasts and mourns his dead dog, Orthrus, but not the brightest monster; living proof that three heads are not always better than one. He is rather like a pensioner whose retirement has been spoiled by a thug (the thug is Herakles).

Hades (*HAY-deez*) Zeus's brother, but much sadder. King of the Underworld.

Hecate (*HEK-ah-tee.*) Goddess of the dark of the moon, witchcraft, and women too old to have babies.

Hephaistos (*hef-EYE-stos*) Zeus and Hera's other legitimate son (brother to Ares), and the only monster among the Olympians. Hephaistos is lame, like Corydon, and he is a maker, also like Corydon. He is a smith god. In ancient legend, smiths were always linked with death; they were blackened with the soot of their work. But they were also magical because they could make metal obey them in shining streams and heavy folds. Both these things and his association with earth give him a partially chthonic identity. Hephaistos loves his mother, Hera, but she is ashamed of him, just as the Minotaur's mother is ashamed of her son. His marriage to the goddess of lust ends unhappily, leaving him alone once more.

Hera (*HEAR-ah*) The wife of Zeus. The ultimate desperate housewife, Hera is an angry woman whose husband constantly strays. She adores him but she also hates him. She longs for him to love her again. A mother to whom her children mean nothing, her husband everything. The opposite of Demeter, but she sometimes pretends to *be* Demeter to trick those who long for a mother of their own.

Homer The greatest storyteller and the greatest poet in history. Our inspiration. Stories say he was blind. He made up his songs in his head. He uses comedy and sadness alongside each other, which is one reason that we do, too.

Hydra (*HIGH-dra*) A beast with many heads; every time one is cut off, two more grow in its place. Lady Nagaina has plainly been in battles before, since she has five heads when the story opens.

Kraken (*KRAH-ken*) Another northern monster well known to the Greeks. The Kraken is a kind of giant squid. Ours is lost and bewildered, having swum into the Mediterranean by mistake, which is why he attacks the boat. The sailor (who recognizes the Kraken) has clearly traveled far or at least talked to others who have.

Lamia (*LAY-me-ah*) Snaky monster below the waist, beautiful woman above. Can sometimes seem human all over.

mage, Morge-mage (*rhymes with "page," MOR-ge-mage*) A mage is just a wise person—wise not in the sense of knowing a lot about life but just in the sense of being clever at doing magical things. The Three Wise Men of Christmas were mages and are also known as the Magi (which is simply the plural of "magus"). The word "magus" refers to a man, but "mage" could just as well be a female magic user.

Medusa (*me-DOO-sa*) The third Gorgon and the only

mortal woman. Medusa was transformed into a snaky-haired monster after violating Athene's temple.

Minotaur (*MY-noh-tor*) Son of Queen Pasiphae and a bull; hence a terrible embarrassment to his mother. Kept in a maze called the labyrinth like a dark secret.

Morge (*MOR-ge*) The name comes from the Greek word for "death" coupled to the word for "earth." The creatures in this story are our invention, but they are meant to recall the Hebrew legend of the Golem, a man of clay made by the rabbi of Prague to defend the Jews.

Mormoluke (*mor-mo-loo-KAY*) Mormo demon. Greek children used to play a game where one of them dabbed black ash on his face and jumped at other children the scary faces were Mormo-faces. Greek demons can often be recognized because there's something wrong with one of their legs.

Nemean Lion (*neh-MEE-an*) A monster from the Labors of Herakles. The lion's skin is so tough that it can only be pierced by one of its own claws.

Olympians (*oh-LIMP-ee-anz*) Olympos is the highest mountain in Greece, where the earth touches the sky. So "Olympians" means "sky gods." High gods. Gods who look down on everyone else.

Pan Goat-legged god of wild nature, shepherds, pipe playing, and being alone. His name is the origin of the word "panic" because he can make people very afraid (especially in lonely places). One of the chthonic deities. Usually opposed to the Olympians.

Persephone (*per-SEF-oh-nee*) Daughter of Zeus and the goddess Demeter. Abducted by her uncle Hades and taken to the Land of the Many. Before her abduction there were no seasons and flowers bloomed all year round.

Perseus (*PER-see-us*) A really famous hero. Son of Zeus and the mortal woman Danaë. When he cut off Medusa's head, both the golden man Khrysaor and Pegasos were born of her blood.

pharmakos (*FAR-ma-kos*) Means "scapegoat." People would choose the ugliest person in a village and drive him out into the desert to carry away bad luck and disease. People still use the word "scapegoat" to describe an innocent victim blamed for something many people have done wrong.

the Pillars Herakles is supposed to have put up two graceful little white pillars at the entrance to the Mediterranean. Other stories tell of fierce clashing rocks that crush ships. We think the latter sounds more like Herakles, but either is psychologically important; the Pillars mark the place where Middle Earth stops. Beyond is the unknown. For some reason, the northern one has been identified as Gibraltar.

Poseidon (*poe-SIGH-don*) A great one among the Olympians, but with some paradoxes. Poseidon is solitary. He is also attached to his domain like a chthonic god and hence not usually inclined to look down on humans and monsters from too great a height. He has some of the relentlessness of the sea, of a wave that will keep rolling shoreward.

Protagoras, Phaidros, Alexandros (*pro-TAG-or-us, FED-ros, al-ex-AN-dros*) *Protagoras* is the name of a Platonic dialogue. So is *Phaidros*. Alexandros is the real name of Alexander the Great. Even our minor characters have real Greek names!

Selene (*se-LEE-nee*) Goddess of the full moon. (Artemis is the waxing moon, and Hecate is the waning and dark moon.) Pan lures Selene's frail light into the darkness of his forests. Their love partly explains why the Selene Amazons are drawn to Corydon.

sirens (*SIGH-renz*) In our mythology, predators who live in the sea and sing songs that draw men to them so that they can be devoured. Not unlike mermaids; if so, a third northern legend the Greeks knew.

Sphinx (*SFINKS, rhymes with "stinks"*) The Sphinx is originally Egyptian; there's a huge carving of her by the Great Pyramids. She's part woman, part lion, and part bird, which means she combines the desert's fierce wildness with the bird's soul magic. The Greek Sphinx asks riddles, including one addressed to the hero Oidipous about the nature of man.

stasis (*STAY-sis*) Not stillness, as people think, but the murderous fight between two factions that makes it impossible for government to act and renders it paralyzed. It was dreaded and hated in all Greece. The Shells and the Dolphins are in stasis.

Sthenno (*STHEN-oh*) Sounds impossible to say, but it's quite easy if you try. One of the two immortal Gorgons.

Titans (*TIE-tenz*) A race of giants who combined earth

and sky in their bodies; they were the children of Ouranos (heaven) and Gaia (earth). They ruled earth before they gave birth to the gods who became the Olympians. Their other children were buried in the earth and became the parents of the chthonic gods and the monsters.

Typhon (*TIE-fon*) The first monster. He is huge, made of hissing snakes and fire, and has an enormous, dragonish skull. When the Olympians saw him coming, they all ran away to Egypt and put on animal heads—except for Zeus. He fought Typhon and lost, and his immortal tendons were ripped out. Immortal tendons are the muscles to which most ambrosia goes (there will be more on ambrosia in *Corydon and the Siege of Troy*). The tendons were carefully guarded by Typhon's girlfriend, Echidna, and a female dragon who was her friend. But Hera stole the tendons back again and gave them to Zeus. Typhon and Zeus began fighting again, throwing mountains at each other. Eventually a huge mountain named Etna landed on top of Typhon and became Sicily. Some say he still is under Etna, and every time it erupts, he's trying to escape. Maybe one day he will succeed.

Vreckan (*VREH-ken*) Named from Corryvreckan, a naturally occurring whirlpool near Scapa Flow. You can see it beautifully dramatized in a film called *I Know Where I'm Going!* In our myth, Vreckan is the Titan of the North Atlantic, an incarnation of its terrifying power, darkness, and cold.

Zeus Herkodon (*ZOOS HERK-e-don*) Literally, Zeus with his tongue between his teeth. The Zeus who hears and binds oaths.

Zeuxis (*ZOOK-sis*) The greatest painter of the ancient world. The Greeks invented art as we know it. Euryale is part of that, but her art is based on that of Matisse, the leading fauve artist of the twentieth century. "Fauve" means "wild beast," so we thought they might be monster-artists.

RESOURCES

·

The cities of New York and Venice.

Plato, *Timaeus* and *Critias*.

Andrew Dalby, *Bacchus*.

Italo Calvino, *Invisible Cities*.

Ernest Hemingway, *Death in the Afternoon*.

Homeric Hymn to Dionysos.

Euripides, *Bacchae*.

The Perfect Storm, book by Sebastian Junger and film by Wolfgang Petersen.

Pablo Picasso, Vollard Suite (sketches of the Minotaur).

Hilary Spurling, *Matisse the Master: A Life of Henri Matisse, the Conquest of Colour, 1909–1954*.

Cynthia Eller, *The Myth of Matriarchal Prehistory*.

E. R. Dodds, *The Greeks and the Irrational*.

I Know Where I'm Going! film by Michael Powell and Emeric Pressburger.

Age of Mythology: The Titans Expansion (PC game).

Victor Hugo, *Les Misérables.*

Richard Wagner, *Siegfried* and *Götterdämmerung.*

Jean-Pierre Vernant, *Myth and Tragedy in Ancient Greece.*

Francesco Colonna, *Hypnerotomachia Poliphili,* 1499, printed in Venice.

J. Robert Oppenheimer, inventor of the atomic bomb, quoting from the Bhagavad Gita: "I am become Death, the destroyer of worlds."

ABOUT THE AUTHORS

Tobias Druitt is a pen name for the mother-and-son writing team of Diane Purkiss and Michael Dowling.

Their first book together was *Corydon and the Island of Monsters,* praised by *Kirkus Reviews* as "a captivating trilogy opener. Reading this witty, profoundly sapient take on the old tales will leave readers impatient for the sequels."

Diane Purkiss earned a Doctor of Philosophy degree from Merton College, Oxford University, and is currently on the faculty of Keble College at Oxford. Her key academic interests are classical literature and women in literature.

Michael Dowling attends the prestigious Dragon School, where he is studying ancient Greek, among many other subjects.